Friends Forever
Hickory Hills: Book 1

Sue Stewart Ade

To Pat

Sue Stewart Ade

2017

1

Published by
Satin Romance
An Imprint of Melange Books, LLC
White Bear Lake, MN 55110
www.satinromance.com

ISBN: 978-1-68046-337-8

Cover Design by Lynsee Lauritsen

My book is dedicated to my family for all their support and love—my husband, Larry; my children, Nelson and Missy; and my grandchildren, Hali, Hayden, Payton, and Madison.

My thanks to my critique group, Write Stuff, for all those question marks, commas, and insightful suggestions - Marilyn Gardiner, Sue Hemp, Debby Miseles, Angela Myers, Elaine Orr, and JD Webb.

And to my writing partner, LJ Hippler, for his advice and honesty.

Chapter One

He slid the key into the door. *Click.* The massive wooden door swung open. He stepped into the dark foyer of his house. Behind him, a gust of March wind swept the door closed.

He held his breath. *Tick. Tick. Tick.*

The grandfather clock in the foyer struck one. He started. Christine wasn't expecting him home tonight. She thought her husband had flown to a medical conference in Las Vegas. She had no way of knowing he'd gotten a call.

Tick. Tick. Tick.

A soft glow from the neighbor's security light spilled through the living room window, illuminating the staircase in front of him. He slipped off his brown wing-tipped shoes and crept up the carpeted stairs. One, two, three. Each step brought him closer.

When he reached the top, he gripped the newel post and looked toward Christine's bedroom. His pulse quickened. A shaft of light from the open doorway pooled onto the plush carpet. Was Christine awake? Had she heard him sneak into the house?

He took a deep breath, rounded the corner, and stepped into the bedroom. His heart slammed against his chest. In the middle of the sleigh bed was Christine. In her hand was a small caliber gun—pointed directly at him.

Winston swallowed. He'd underestimated her. She wasn't the weak gosling he'd thought. He hadn't expected her to have a gun, just as he hadn't expected her to ask for a divorce. He kept his voice low, not wanting to disturb their daughter, Phoebe, in the bedroom at the end of

1

the hall. "Put the gun down, Christine. I'm not an intruder."

She didn't flinch, but her voice trembled. "I'm leaving, Winston. You can't stop me."

He stepped forward. "Put the gun down and we'll talk."

Her hand shook, and the gun wavered. "Don't come any closer. We've already talked. I told you our marriage was a mistake."

"A mistake?" He gave a derisive snort. A mistake was what you made when your bank account didn't balance. A mistake was what you made when you dialed a wrong number. Marriage was not a mistake. "You vowed until death us do part."

"So you've reminded me. That's why I have a gun. I'm taking Phoebe and leaving."

"No." He gritted his teeth to keep from shouting. "Phoebe stays with me."

Christine's voice rose. "She's my daughter."

He shook his head. "She's my daughter, too."

"Not for long. Leave before I count to ten."

Winston crossed his arms and stood at the corner of the bed.

Christine began counting.

She wouldn't shoot him. He was certain of that. But on six, his eyes began to blink. On seven, his throat tightened. She was serious. On eight, he dropped to the floor and rolled along the side of the bed. He reached for the cord on the nightstand lamp and yanked it toward him. The ceramic lamp slid across the table and tumbled over the edge. The ruffled shade flew off and the exposed light bulb struck the floor. Winston turned his eyes toward Christine.

Pop. The bulb shattered. A burst of light. Christine blinked against the blinding glare.

Winston pounced. He grabbed the gun, aimed, and pulled the trigger. "Ten."

Craaack.

He jerked back, stunned by the sound of the gunshot. Enough light filtered through the sheer curtains for him to see Christine's head twitch and hit the headboard. Her mouth froze in a silent scream. Red blood streamed from her matted hair, spreading onto her white nightgown.

Winston's body went slack. He dropped the gun and collapsed onto the floor. It wasn't his fault. She'd bought the gun. She'd threatened to kill him. She'd made him do it.

What if he went to jail? Oh God, who would take care of his precious Phoebe? A burglary. He'd make Christine's death look like a robbery gone bad.

Was Phoebe still sleeping or had the gunshot awakened her? She was only four years old, and skittish around him. But that would change. Now he was her only parent. Just him.

He rose and shielded his face with his hands to avoid Christine's accusing eyes. Padding down the hall, he passed the guest bedroom and continued to Phoebe's room. He opened the door, expecting to see his daughter snuggled beneath the covers.

He stared at the white canopy bed. Empty. Where was Phoebe?

Chapter Two

Laney Elam scurried up the steps to the lawyer's office, pulling the child behind. Her heart pounded as she glanced over her shoulder, first left, then right. The quiet downtown street, a block from the courthouse square, was deserted. No one was watching. No one was wondering about a stranger clutching the mittened hand of the little girl beside her. She let out a worried breath and relaxed her grip.

The courthouse clock *bonged* six times. Shivering, she pulled her long wool coat tightly around her thin body and tried to settle her jumpy nerves. *Everything was going to be all right,* she assured herself. But when she turned back to the lawyer's office, the sign next to the door on the yellow brick building read "Monday-Friday, 8-5." It was closed. Now what was she to do?

The plan had been simple. Drive to southern Illinois, go to the lawyer's office, and claim her grandmother's estate. Laney hadn't counted on how many times she would have to stop for a potty break, for a snack, for whatever else was needed to keep a child happy.

The little girl tugged on Laney's coat. "I'm hungry."

Laney stared down at the four-year-old. With her boyish haircut, red baseball cap, and blue parka, no one would suspect she was a girl. But today was Friday, and all the money she had in the purse was $3.47. Was it all going to come unraveled?

Unsure of what to do next, she turned away from the lawyer's office. Across the street was a white clapboard church with colorful stained glassed windows. Tightening her grip on Phoebe's hand, she descended the stairs and checked for traffic. Turning the corner and driving toward them was a black-and-white police cruiser.

She froze. What if the policeman saw the Michigan license? What if he ran the numbers? Would they be looking for the car? She rushed forward, pulling Phoebe with her, and stood in front of the rear license on the small gray Ford Fusion.

The squad car drove past, disappearing down the block. He hadn't even glanced at them. Laney tried to calm her racing heart as she walked across the street and into the church office.

The plump woman in the print dress folding the Sunday bulletin looked like the typical church lady except instead of featuring a judgmental glare, she warmed Laney's heart with a wide smile. In fact, the woman was so helpful with information about the location of the food pantry and its hours that when she asked, Laney almost blurted out her real name.

Now, with her high-heeled shoes clicking against the concrete, she headed toward the pantry and practiced their new names. They were no longer Melana Elam and Phoebe Prescott. They were Quincy Matthews and her daughter, Taylor. She repeated the names. *Quincy Matthews. Quincy Matthews. Quincy Matthews and my daughter, Taylor.*

The wind picked up a discarded paper cup, swirling it along the deserted street. She shivered from the March wind and her need to protect Phoebe—no, Taylor. And she was Quincy.

The child tugged on her hand. "Are we there yet?"

"Just a little farther."

Hunger gnawed in Quincy's stomach. Two days ago, they'd fled Detroit. She'd been too nervous to eat. All she could think about was getting away. They'd spent the night at a cheap hotel where she'd cut their hair. The rest of her money had been spent on fast food for…Taylor.

Quincy stopped in front of a two-story, corner building. "Loaves and Fishes Food Pantry" was painted on the red bricks. A large plate-glass window next to the door reflected the image a tall woman and a child. The woman's straight black hair was cut even with her jaw. Long bangs covered her forehead and skimmed the tops of brown-framed glasses. Laney was surprised when she realized she was staring at her own reflection.

No one in Hickory Hills would recognize her, not after all these years. Even her voice was different—low and sultry from the surgery to remove some cysts from her throat. The voice might not fool one person, but he was married and living in Chicago. Besides, she'd been sixteen the last time they'd been together. Now she was twenty-nine.

"I'm hungry," said Taylor. "Are we going in?"

Quincy's face reddened, not from the biting wind, but from the thought of opening the door and asking for a handout. Oh, why wasn't Chrissy here? She would know what to do. Quincy didn't understand the first thing about raising a child.

She'd worked hard to earn her college degree and become a teacher. She was proud of her independence. So what if the first whispers about the new woman in town were that she couldn't afford to feed her child. She would not be made to feel less, and she would not let Taylor go hungry just because of what a few gossips might say. Still, she remembered the sting of her childhood when she'd been on the wrong side of the glass. Just like now.

She checked up and down the sidewalk, making sure no one was following. Then she leaned over and touched the brim of Taylor's Cardinals baseball cap. "Remember," she whispered, "we have to play our little game."

The girl gazed up at her with big blue trusting eyes and nodded. Quincy tried not to think about the day when Taylor would realize that this wasn't a game. Shifting her bulky shoulder bag, Quincy gripped Taylor's hand and pushed open the door. A short woman with tightly permed gray curls stood behind the counter. Quincy was relieved that no one else seemed to be around. The woman filled the empty room with friendly chatter and placed two grocery sacks on the counter, one with canned goods, the other with packages of frozen meat.

Quincy picked up the sacks and thanked the woman. As she headed toward the door, she glanced back to make sure Taylor was following. She stepped forward and collided with a man who had opened the door and was carrying a crateful of bread. The loaves of bread went flying into the air. The sacks of groceries split open, spilling cans and packages of frozen hot dogs and hamburger meat onto the floor. She stumbled backward and caught her heel on the welcome mat.

6

As she started to fall, the man in the leather jacket reached out and grabbed her shoulders. His hands were large and strong, steadying her. "Are you all right?"

She gazed up and was startled by his intense blue eyes. They enveloped her, just as they always had. The scent of the leather jacket and the man himself permeated through her senses. He was broad shouldered, and his once sinewy arms were now muscular. His dark hair was longer, and the five o'clock shadow gave his face a rugged handsomeness that he hadn't possessed as a boy.

Joy shot through her, followed by a force stronger than the hunger gnawing in her stomach. Fear. He must not recognize her—for the child's sake and his own.

He was still holding onto her, gazing into her face. She held her breath, hoping her new look would deceive him. Besides her short straight hair, she wore amber-tinted glasses and contacts that changed her natural eye color to a dark walnut brown. Even the small gap between her two front teeth had been corrected.

He cocked his head. "Laney?"

She backed up, easing away until his hands slid off her shoulders. "I'm afraid you have me confused with someone else."

He blinked. "You look like a girl I used to know." He raised his hand as if to touch her hair, but stopped. "The color's wrong, and voice is different. But…"

Her heart thudded. She couldn't let him know who she was. She dropped to her knees and scrambled around on the floor, gathering the cans and packages of meat.

Ace knelt and retrieved the scattered loaves of bread. When he finished stacking the bread into the gray crate, he squatted next to her, handing her two new brown grocery sacks. "I'm A.C. Edleston. Everyone calls me Ace."

She averted his gaze as she took the sacks. "Quincy Matthews," she said, and began stacking the canned goods into a sack.

"Quincy? Do people call you Quinn?"

Quinn. She liked that. "Yes, Quinn."

"Who's your helper?" he asked.

Quinn lifted the sacks and stood. Taylor was at the edge of the counter, cowering. Quinn slid the sacks onto the counter and hurried over to her. Slipping an arm around the girl's shoulders, she pulled her close, hoping to give her a feeling of safety. "This is…Taylor."

Ace rose and leaned his hip against the counter. "Hi, Taylor."

The child scurried behind Quinn, clinging to her coat.

"I know children aren't supposed to talk to strangers." He lowered himself to her level and stuck out his hand. "I'm Ace. Now we're not strangers."

Taylor peeked out from behind her shield, but didn't shake his hand.

He tried another tactic. "I bet I can guess how old you are. Let's see. You must be eight."

Taylor frowned.

"No. How 'bout six?"

The child's blue eyes widened and he almost received a smile.

"I've got a boy about your size. He's seven and likes to play ball. I bet you do, too, son."

The smile turned into a scowl. "I'm not a boy." The child ripped off the cap, revealing a crop of short auburn hair. "I'm a girl!" Then she held up four fingers. "I'm this many."

Ace peered closer. If her hair hadn't been buzzed and her scowl was replaced with a smile, this boyish waif might look like a girl. "Girls play baseball, too, don't they?"

She stuck out her lower lip. "I never played baseball."

"Really?" Ace straightened and raised one eyebrow as he surveyed the mother again. She was a few inches shorter than his six-foot frame, and she might be pretty, too, if she ditched those hideous brown glasses and brushed all that hair away from her face. He grinned, hoping to pull a smile from her. "Guess I struck out."

Instead of smiling, she plopped the Cardinals cap back on her daughter's head.

Ace noticed her long, slender fingers and the gold wedding band. A wave of disappointment rippled through him. He frowned. Why was he disappointed? He wasn't interested in women. He hadn't dated for over a year and planned to keep it that way. His marriage had ended badly, and he'd vowed to steer clear of women. He'd had enough of conniving women who batted their eyelashes and came to his door with homemade casseroles. This woman, however, almost seemed to be avoiding him. Yet from the moment he'd touched her, something had shot through him, and he'd been drawn to her in some inexplicable way.

"You and your daughter must be new in town. Where are you staying?"

Without answering, she turned and picked up the sacks of groceries from the counter. "We'd better be going."

So she didn't like questions. Well, he would respect her privacy, although she wasn't likely to get much. Hickory Hills was a small town, less than four thousand, and people made it their business to get to know each other. He didn't think of them as nosey, but as people who genuinely cared about their neighbors. Within a few days, he was sure he would learn everything there was to know about Mrs. Quincy Matthews and her daughter, Taylor.

She turned toward the door, but he reached it first. "I'll carry those to your car."

Behind the glasses, a flicker of indecision flashed in those dark eyes. Not waiting for an answer, he scooped the sacks out of her arms. She hesitated and then gripped the child's hand.

By the time they reached the car parked in front of the lawyer's office, Ace felt oddly unsettled. He'd tried to engage Quinn in conversation, but she'd given him crisp 'yes' and 'no' answers. He wanted to learn more about her and her child with the sad eyes. But once she got into the car and drove away, he wouldn't know when—or if—he'd ever see her again.

"I'm hungry," said Taylor, tugging on Quinn's coat.

"Well, that makes two of us," said Ace. "I was just heading over to eat at the Blue Moon. Why don't you join me?" He swung his eyes to Quinn. "My treat, of course."

Quinn remembered eating at the Blue Moon. Grandma had loved to cook, but Sunday was her day of rest. When Grampa didn't feel like fixing supper, they piled into his old pickup truck and headed for the diner.

She and Taylor were hungry, but spending time with Ace wasn't a good idea. "Thanks, but we're in a hurry." She dropped Taylor's hand and opened the door. "Just put them in here."

Ace slid the sacks of groceries into the back, and Quinn reached for Taylor.

The girl backed away. "I want to go eat." She crossed her arms and stomped her foot.

Quinn's cheeks flushed. Now what was she supposed to do? She didn't want Ace to think she couldn't control her own child.

Ace grinned. "Looks like you're outnumbered."

Quinn had learned from teaching that she needed to be firm or the next time would be harder. She wrapped her arms around Taylor's waist and hoisted her up. The docile child began kicking and fighting. Her hands clawed at Quinn. They caught the strap of her purse and ripped the leather bag off her shoulder.

It thudded onto the brick pavement. Spilling out on the ground were a tube of red lipstick, a pink hairbrush, and a .38 Smith and Wesson.

Chapter Three

Quinn drove her car up the bumpy gravel lane lined with overgrown elms and oaks. The weathered trees were bent and twisted together to form a leafless canopy. The evening sun filtered through the limbs, casting shadows onto the ground in front of the car. On the last turn the trees cleared, and a rustic, slate-gray barn appeared. The white trim was peeling and on the cupola, a weathered rooster twirled in the wind. The familiar sight was a balm to Quinn's weary mind and body.

She pushed away thoughts about the incident with the gun and tried to sound cheerful. "We're here."

Taylor squirmed in her car seat in the back. "I don't see a house."

"That's because we're going to live in a barn."

"A barn? Animals live in barns."

"This is a special barn." Quinn had always loved the loft with the garage below. She pulled up in front of the double doors secured with a padlock. "The bottom is the garage, and we'll live upstairs."

"Really?"

A pain shot through Quinn. How much did Taylor actually understand about her new life? Yesterday, they'd left Detroit and everyone Taylor knew. After a while, she would realize this wasn't a game, and she wouldn't be going home. What would happen then?

Shaking off the troubling thoughts, Quinn checked the small turtle at the foot of the landing. When she saw two keys hidden in the shell, she was overwhelmed with gratitude. At least they wouldn't be sleeping in the car until Monday.

She used one of keys to unlock the barn door and parked the car

11

inside. She helped Taylor out and unloaded the three suitcases in the trunk. As they climbed the outside stairs, she looked back toward the lane to make sure they hadn't been followed. Then she slipped the key into the lock and pushed the door open.

She reached inside and flipped the light switch. Nothing happened. She hadn't called the power company. No heat. No electricity. Just add those to the long list of things they didn't have.

Still, as soon as she stepped across the threshold, a sense of relief swept over her. She was home. When she was growing up, her grandparents and this place had been the only constants in her life.

Light from the sun setting over the lake spilled into the room from the dirt-streaked windows along the back. Quinn put the suitcases down and led Taylor to the window. "Look." She rested her hand on Taylor's shoulder, and they stood together, spellbound by the show of colors as the sun dipped toward the horizon.

"Wow. The sky looks pink. I didn't know it would be a different color here."

Quinn was too tired to explain. "Yes, everything will be different here."

Not just for Taylor, but for her, too. She'd never planned on having children until she was financially secure, until she could give them a solid home. But life didn't always turn out the way you expected.

Quinn walked away from the window and set her purse on the round oak table. She was relieved to see starter bricks and logs next to the woodstove. As she worked on building a fire, she looked around at the loft with the high-beamed rafters and the wall of exposed barn planks. So much had stayed the same. At the front door was a denim rag rug. Quinn had watched Grandma crochet strips of denim from old jeans as she sat in the rocking chair next to the wood stove. The brown couch, which had been new when Laney was a teenager, was now threadbare and sagged in the middle.

As she inhaled the familiar scent of the burning wood, memories flooded back. Grampa fishing on the lake and gathering hickory nuts in the woods. Grandma picking wildflowers and tending to the garden. Sunny days with picnics and rainy days with card games. She could almost imagine Grandma at the other end of the great room, turning from the cook stove and wiping her flour-covered hands on her print apron. Her weathered face would light up with a welcoming smile and a "my, my, look how you've grown" every time. Then she'd throw her arms around Laney and fill her with love.

Grampa would be stretched out in his leather recliner next to the large bookcase, reading, but he always had time to listen to her chatter or answer her questions. She was glad the books had been left as always, stacked and tucked in all directions. Grampa's westerns and Grandma's gardening books lined the upper shelves. Her books on the lower shelf were still there, almost as if they'd been awaiting her return.

A tear trickled down her cheek. She hadn't anticipated how alone she would feel without her grandparents. More than anything she needed their loving guidance. But she was Quinn now, not Laney. Quinn, who didn't have a past here. She needed to remember that. She brushed her hand over her damp face and then picked up the suitcases. "Let's go see your room."

Taylor followed Quinn through the kitchen and into a short hallway with a bedroom on each side. At the end of the hallway was an alcove with a large octagon window and a padded chest. Laney had loved sitting there, reading or playing with her dolls. And her best friend, Chrissy, had loved it too, the one summer she stayed at Hickory Hills.

Taylor raced to the end of the hall and twirled around in a beam of light streaming through the window. "Can I play here?"

It was the first spark of excitement Quinn had seen from Taylor, so she resisted the urge to correct the 'can' to 'may', as she would have with her students in Japan. "I think it was made especially for a little girl like you. Maybe you should open the window seat."

Taylor lifted the lid. Her eyes widened. "Barbies and clothes and furniture and everything. Can I play with them?"

"For a little while. It'll be dark soon. I'll put our suitcases in the bedrooms and then find some matches to light the oil lamp."

In the kitchen, Quinn opened the pantry door and was grateful to see the first two shelves were lined with pints and quarts containing Grandma's green beans, tomatoes, and pickles. The third shelf contained mason jars of strawberry jam and blackberry preserves. At least she wouldn't have to worry about canned goods for a while.

13

She cringed as she remembered how Ace's eyebrow's had raised as he handed her the gun. "I suppose you have a permit."

"Of course," she'd lied, and hastily stuffed it back into her purse. But Taylor had won, and Quinn didn't protest as he took her arm and guided her and Taylor down the street to the Blue Moon.

Little had changed in the years since Quinn had been gone. Red-and-white checked oil cloths covered the tables, gray Naugahyde booths lined the side, and a blackboard near the door listed the daily specials.

Quinn loved the fluffy blueberry pancakes and was delighted to see them still on the menu.

"What can I have?" Taylor asked, as she stared at the menu.

"Anything you want," Ace said.

Taylor's eyes widened. "Anything? I can really have anything?"

Quinn nodded and wondered about Taylor's surprise. Then she realized Taylor couldn't read. "What about some chocolate chip pancakes?"

"I've never had them."

"They were...."

"What can I get you?" asked a pretty, red-ponytailed teenager with a sprinkling of freckles across her nose.

Quinn swallowed, glad the waitress had interrupted before she'd blurted out that chocolate chip pancakes had been her mother's favorite.

Ace gave the waitress his order and an easy smile that made her face turn as red as her hair.

When the food arrived, Quinn didn't make polite conversation, but attacked the plate-sized pancakes. Ever since Detroit, her stomach had been queasy, but the pancakes stayed down and tasted as good as she remembered. When she finished the last syrupy bite, she pushed back her plate and looked up.

Ace was studying her. "I like a woman with an appetite."

Staring at her plate, Quinn blushed. "I guess mine was pretty big."

Taylor tugged on Quinn's sleeve and whispered, "I have to go."

Quinn pushed back her chair to rise.

"I can go by myself," said Taylor. "I'm not a baby."

Quinn quickly sat down, but kept her eyes on Taylor until she disappeared behind the door marked "Women."

Then she turned and met Ace's gaze. "Thank you." She smiled at him, hoping to convey all the feeling her words couldn't.

He leaned forward, reaching across the table and covering her hand with his. It was big and strong, and the palm was calloused. He had used his hands for a living, yet his touch was surprisingly gentle. After all these years, she had not expected an immediate connection, but the feel of his rough skin against her bare hand sent a familiar spark shooting through her.

Reluctantly, she slipped her hand away and folded it in her lap. She knew he'd probably noticed the gold wedding band, but she didn't want him to ask about her husband. She wasn't married and couldn't bring herself to lie, not now, not after the kindness he had shown her and Taylor.

Ace settled back in his chair. "So what brings you and Taylor to Hickory Hills?"

"I didn't think the city was the best place to raise a child." At least that was true.

"So you're staying?"

"Maybe." She hoped they could stay. She hoped no one would find them. Then she and Taylor could fade into oblivion and start their new life together.

"Did you and Taylor come here alone?"

She nodded.

He leaned forward again, but kept his hands wrapped around his half-filled coffee cup. "I'm a good listener...if you need to talk."

She couldn't meet his gaze. "I'll remember that." She wanted to pour it all out. Tell him who she was and the danger they were in. But she couldn't let him get involved. What if he insisted she go to the police? What if he told his wife who told her best friend who told...? No, Quinn couldn't risk telling him the truth.

She noticed there was no ring on his finger, but maybe he just didn't wear his wedding band. He'd talked about his son, and she knew he'd married. She'd read about his wedding in the society pages of the *Chicago Tribune*.

She wondered what kind of woman Ace had chosen. She hoped he had a good marriage and was happy, although she felt a stab of jealousy.

15

They had played together in the summers when she stayed with her grandparents. But that last summer, when she was sixteen and he was eighteen, they were both surprised when he teasingly grabbed her and skimmed his lips across hers. After the initial shock, his eyes lost their amusement, and he drew her closer. She didn't resist, but enjoyed the warmth of his lips that sent a pleasure pulsing through her that she'd never experienced. He'd explored her mouth and she'd reveled in his taste.

"Well, well," Ace had said, when he finally pulled away. "This kind of changes things."

He had kept his arm draped protectively over her shoulder as they had strolled down to the dock, slipped off their shoes, and listened to the night music.

She had never met another person who understood her and touched her heart as much as Ace. Sitting across from him at the restaurant today, she knew that hadn't changed.

Quinn chided herself for getting lost in foolish memories. The light filtering into the kitchen pantry from the window over the sink was almost gone. She reached up to the top shelf for a box of matches. She hoped the hurricane lamp on the table was filled with oil.

Within minutes, she wet the wick, lit the lamp, and adjusted the flame. As she carried the kerosene lamp with its familiar scent down the hall, shadows danced along the wall.

"Time for bed." She set the lamp on the window sill and bent to help Taylor put away the dolls.

When they finished, she led Taylor into the bedroom that had once been hers. The room was small, but had an adjoining bathroom. Bunk beds were in the middle of the far wall. A white desk was on one side and a painted dresser with an oval mirror above was on the other.

She was glad the mirror was too high for Taylor to see her reflection. Quinn had almost wept when she'd cut off Taylor's thick auburn curls, leaving her with a cap of hair less than an inch long. Even so, the child looked like a charming little urchin.

After Taylor changed into a night gown, she knelt by the side of the bed to pray. Quinn knelt with her and prayed for God to help her keep Taylor safe. After Taylor crawled into bed, Quinn bent over and pulled up the covers.

Taylor stuck out her lower lip. "I always sleep with Lovey."

In the front of the suitcase, Quinn found the black-and-white stuffed cow. She handed it to Taylor and brushed a kiss across her soft cheek.

"Will we see Mommy tomorrow?"

The longing in Taylor's big blue eyes tore at Quinn's heart. She shook her head.

Taylor's eyes filled with tears. She rolled away from Quinn and curled up with Lovey. "I miss Mommy."

"I know." Sitting on the bed, Quinn reached over and pulled Taylor into lap. "I miss her, too." She wrapped her arms around Taylor and rocked her back and forth until she fell asleep.

After Quinn tucked Taylor into bed, she paused in the doorway and gazed back into the room. Moonlight streamed in through the window, illuminating Taylor's innocent face. Quinn slumped against the door jam. How was she ever going to find the right words to tell this precious little girl she would never see her mommy again?

Chapter Four

The crack of a gunshot...Chrissy slumped against the bed—the life draining from her eyes. A man stood with his back to the hallway. A gun at his side. Hide. She sprinted down the hall and slipped into the guest bedroom. A closet.

She felt along the wall until she found a door. Her palms were sweaty. She turned the knob.

Squeak. The door opened.

Fear rose in her throat. Crouching down, she crawled toward the back. A long gossamer gown grazed her cheek. She brushed it aside and scurried behind. She huddled in the corner, trembling.

Footsteps. He was coming. Her entire body shook. He was closer. Any minute, he would rush into the room and open the door.

The footsteps continued, down the hall to the bedroom where she'd been sleeping. He was going to Phoebe's room. Well, he wouldn't find her.

Like a crazed beast, he ransacked the house. He raced from room to room, shattering glass and crashing furniture as he searched for Phoebe. Then she heard his footsteps as he entered the guest room where she was hidden. The closet door opened.

Quinn blinked against the light. Her heart raced. Where was she? A sliver of moonlight drifted in through the window. Relief washed over her. She was at Grandma Elam's, curled up in the rocker.

She rose, steadying herself. She'd put Taylor to bed and gone outside to pump a bucket of water from the well. When she'd returned, she'd sat down in Grandma's rocker and dozed off. That's when the nightmare had returned.

A week ago she'd been Melana Elam, an English teacher, living in Japan. Then her best friend Chrissy had sent an e-mail.

Friends forever, come together.

Those were the words she and Chrissy had chanted on a hot August afternoon when they were twelve years old. They'd knelt under the branches of the hardwood tree and pricked their fingers. Swirling their blood together, they'd become sisters.

The pact was a bond and a promise. If either was in trouble, all she had to do was contact the other with that message. Her friend would come no questions asked.

Laney had used the pact numerous times, but for the first time, Chrissy had needed her. So at the end of March, Laney had left Japan and heeded the last words of the e-mail: *Tell no one.*

Quinn drew the afghan around her shoulders and walked through the darkness to the row of windows. Her eyes searched the leafless trees until she spotted the massive trunk by the lake's edge. The tree had grown and matured, just as she and Chrissy had. Its budding branches silhouetted against the water looked like slender fingers waving in the wind. Behind the bare branches, the full moon flitted in and out of the clouds, casting shadows on the surface of the lake. Somewhere in the distance, a lone coyote howled. Quinn shivered and drew the afghan tighter.

Intent on the moonlit water, she almost didn't notice the light. A small beam flickered through the trees. She held her breath. Was it her imagination or was the light moving closer?

The moon slid beneath the clouds, plunging the view into darkness. The tiny beam of light shone brighter. Something or someone was definitely in the hickory grove. Standing in front of the window, she felt exposed. She crouched down and peeked over the window sill. The moon slipped out of the clouds, outlining a figure hunched forward and creeping steadily toward the barn.

Her heart pounded. How had he found her so quickly? He couldn't have. Unless he had known about the plan and followed them or had attached a tracking device onto the car.

She knew he would come after Phoebe. He had a legal right to her.

But he mustn't have her. A surge of motherly protectiveness shot through her.

The door. Was it locked? She threw off the afghan and raced across the room. The door was bolted. The lock was old and wouldn't keep out anyone determined to break in. She dragged a wooden chair from the kitchen and propped it under the door.

Then she hurried back to the window. The light was gone. Maybe she'd imagined the crouching figure. She'd been dozing; her mind was fogged with sleep. She rubbed her eyes and looked again. No one.

If someone had been there, he was gone—or had moved closer. Right now, he could be climbing the steps, ready to hurl himself against the door.

The gun. She sprinted to the table and reached into her purse. Her hand shook as she cautiously lifted the .38 Smith and Wesson. At least she'd been smart enough to unload it. She fished in the zipper pocket, found the three remaining bullets, and slid them into the cylinder.

Rushing to the rocking chair, she sat and pointed the gun toward the door. Her heart raced as her finger rested on the trigger. Until a few days ago, she didn't know if she was capable of killing. Now she knew. If someone broke in, she would shoot.

A noise. Not from the front door. The sound came from the bottom of the barn.

After she'd parked the car, she must have forgotten to padlock the doors. *The trap door.* Grandpa called it their fire escape. It led from the barn to the loft. Was the door still there?

Quinn slid out of the chair. With the gun awkwardly in front of her, she crawled across the floor. She pushed away the rug and felt for the door. She found the opening and pressed her ear against it. A scraping sound. Shoes climbing up the ladder.

He was coming. Her heart hammered against her chest. Could he hear her? Smell her fear? She inched backward and lay on her stomach. Propping herself up with her elbows, she aimed the gun a few feet above the trap door.

She cocked the trigger and waited. The moon disappeared behind the clouds. The room went pitch black.

Whoosh.

The trap door opened.

Thud.

It hit the floor. She held her breath and steadied the gun. *Wait. Wait.* Make sure he was through the opening. Silently, she began counting to ten. *Five, six, seven.*

This time when she heard the sound of a gunshot, it wouldn't be a dream.

Chapter Five

His eyes dilated as he shined the flashlight into the loft. A small handgun was pointed straight at him. Holding the gun was Quincy Matthews. He shifted to the left.

Pop. He felt the bullet hit his arm. *Ping.* Another ricocheted behind him. He dropped the flashlight, plunging the room into darkness.

"Don't shoot! It's me, Ace."

He heaved his body up the ladder and into the room. Light from the moon glinted onto the barrel. He lunged forward, grabbing for the gun. It flew across the floor. She pounced on him, landing on his back, flattening him to the floor. Her fists punched wildly, pummeling his ribs and head.

He bucked, knocking her off, and rolling on top of her. Her glasses fell off, crunching beneath them. He grabbed her wrists. "Stop fighting, Quinn. It's me. Ace."

Moonlight flooded into the room. Her eyes were wild and filled with fear. He shook her. "Quinn, it's Ace. Ace!"

She blinked. Her eyes focused and then widened in recognition. "Ace? Oh my God, Ace. It's you. It's really you."

All the fight went out of her, and she collapsed onto the floor. He relaxed his grip and leaned back on his heels. Pain throbbed through his arm.

Unexpectedly, Quinn rose and threw herself against him. She wrapped her arms around his neck and clung to him, practically toppling him over.

"Ace, I'm so sorry. So sorry." Her voice shook as much as her body.

"Are you all right? Did I hurt you?"

Earlier that day, Quinn had barely looked at him. Now she had her arms around him, and her husky voice was thick with concern. Her face nuzzled his shoulder, and her warm breath caressed his neck. She smelled so sweet and fitted against his body, making him forget the pain.

Her cotton nightgown was thin. He moved his hands, encircling her small waist, and pressed her closer. Her body was firm and her breasts soft. Surprised, he felt an overwhelming need to protect her. He looked down at her moist cheeks and put a finger under her chin, lifting her face to his. Her long lashes were wet with tears. He thought again of her resemblance to Laney. But there was no gap between her front teeth, and her voice was different. He swiped his thumb across her cheek. "What's this?"

She pushed his hand away and struggled to choke back the tears. Instead, they broke loose. Not restrained tears, but a torrent that wracked her body from head to toe.

He could hear the pain and tried to comfort her. He held her tighter and moved his hand up and down, whispering, "It's okay. It's okay."

He felt her fighting for control. "No, no. You—you don't understand. Ace, you could have been killed. *I* could have killed you. You could be dead just like—"

"I'm not going to die. It's only a small wound."

Quinn's head jerked up. Her eyes widened. "You're hurt? Where?"

"My arm."

Her hands moved down his shoulders. When her fingers touched his wound, he winced.

"I actually hit you?" He heard her surprise.

"Lucky shot." He grimaced, fighting the pain that had returned as soon as she'd moved away.

She helped him over to a chair. "I don't have any electricity yet." She lit the kerosene lamp and moved it to the end of the table.

In the halo of the light, her eyes squinted at his wound. "We need to stop the bleeding. Take off your shirt."

His fingers fumbled with the buttons on the chambray shirt. Impatiently, she pushed them away and unbuttoned it. Carefully, she eased his arm out of the sleeve. "I hope this isn't a good shirt." She didn't wait for his reply before she ripped it into strips.

"Not anymore."

She tied one strip around his arm above the wound, making a tourniquet to staunch the flow of blood. "I don't have any water, except a bucket from the well." With another strip she dabbed the blood around the wound. "It's not deep. I'll get some gauze and bandage it."

She returned with a small first-aid kit. He gritted and bit back an oath as she swabbed the wound with antiseptic and wrapped it with gauze. "The bullet only grazed the surface, but you should see a doctor."

"Great. Now people will know I was shot by a woman."

"I'm sorry your manly pride was hurt, but it's your own fault. You shouldn't have been sneaking into my house."

His dark brows knitted together. "Your house?"

Ace knew Grandma Elam had willed the property to her granddaughter, Melana Elam. In the dim lamplight, he peered at Quinn. If her hair were golden brown and curly. If her eyes were green. If her front teeth had a slight space. No, it wasn't possible. This couldn't be Laney. Not with that low, breathy voice.

"Who are you?" His question hung in the air between them.

She turned away and walked to the bucket, plunging her bloody hands into the icy water. When she stepped back, the frail, needy woman he had held in his arms was gone. The softness he had felt was replaced with an outer shell of fierceness.

Her words took on the same impersonal tone as earlier. "You never told me why you barged through the trap door."

Ace fought back his anger. At her, at himself. She had touched him, made him feel something he hadn't felt in a long time—tenderness for a woman—and now she'd pulled away. "Don't do that. Don't use that tone of voice with me as if we were strangers."

"We *are* strangers. I only met you today. You don't know anything about me."

"Then tell me something."

"All right." She stiffened her shoulders. "This isn't my place. I'm renting it."

"From whom?"

"Melana Elam."

"You know Laney? Where is she?"

"Japan."

He felt as if she'd thrown the bucket of icy water over him. Until now, he hadn't realized how much he'd counted on Laney returning.

"We were both in Japan, teaching English. She knew I was returning to the States, so she offered to rent me this place."

"How is she? Is Laney—"

Quinn cut him off. "I answered your question. Now answer mine. What were you doing breaking in?"

"Breaking in?" He didn't curb his temper. "I have money. I can buy whatever I want."

She lifted her chin. "Like I can't."

"Don't put words into my mouth, Quinn. If I'd meant that, I would have said it." He hadn't been thinking about her getting a handout from the food pantry. He didn't fault her for trying to feed her daughter. But he realized she wasn't as tough as she pretended, and, intentional or not, his words had penetrated her armor, revealing a pain he hadn't expected. He reached out and took her hand. "Quinn, I—"

She pulled her hand away and stepped back. "Don't—don't touch me. I—I was distraught. Unnerved by the accident. I don't usually throw myself into the arms of a stranger."

"I wasn't complaining."

She folded her arms over her thin nightgown. "I may have given you the wrong impression."

"And what impression should I have?"

"I'm just a mother protecting her daughter from an intruder."

"I'm not an intruder. I was outside helping my dog birth a litter of puppies. When I saw smoke coming from the chimney, I came to check."

"Most people would have used the front door."

"Last week, I caught some kids trespassing. I gave them a break and didn't report it. I thought maybe they'd sneaked back. This isn't New York or Chicago. You don't need a gun. Around here, we take care of each other."

She bent over and picked up the gun from the floor. "I can take care of myself."

He placed his hand on his wound. "You've made that clear."

25

A sound caused him to turn toward the hall. Taylor stood in the doorway, dressed in a nightgown, clutching a black-and-white stuffed cow. Her eyes were heavy with sleep. When she saw the gun in Quinn's hand, her eyes popped open.

"Is he a bad man, too?"

Chapter Six

On Saturday, Winston walked out of the Detroit airport and slid into the back seat of a waiting limousine. He gave the driver his home address. He opened his briefcase and pretended to read the notes from the medical conference in Las Vegas, but he was too jittery to concentrate. In less than an hour, he'd be home and have an answer to the question that had haunted him for the past four days. *Where was Phoebe?*

That night, when he hadn't found her in the house, he'd assumed she was at a sleepover, something Christine allowed, even though Winston thought Phoebe was too young. But why hadn't someone brought her home? Maybe Phoebe was with Christine's family, something else Winston didn't like. Christine's mom and sisters spoiled Phoebe, allowed her to eat anything she pleased. Well, now that Christine was gone, those family visits would stop. But if Phoebe had been with relatives, why hadn't they found Christine's body when they brought Phoebe home?

The night of the accident, Winston had called his twin sister, Dr. Wendy Prescott, a pediatrician. Wendy didn't blame him or scold him about the accident, only asked how she could help. Together they devised a plan. Wendy bought a ticket on a red-eye flight from O'Hare to Las Vegas in her husband's name. She drove Winston to Chicago and handed him her husband's driver's license. "I slipped it out of his wallet while he was sleeping. Buy me a medical book and express mail the book and license to my office."

Winston didn't look like Wendy's husband Richard, but they were similar enough in size and age to pass the inspection of a blurry-eyed agent.

After landing in Vegas, Winston had called home on his cell to establish a phone record of his whereabouts. He checked into the American Podiatric Medical Association Conference and, that morning, assisted in a hands-on cadaveric workshop on external fixation and plastic surgery, used primarily on diabetic feet. Wearing green surgical scrubs, he stood center stage in front of a crowded classroom of colleagues. On the table was a female cadaver. Most of her body was draped. Only the bottom portion of her legs and feet were exposed. Every time he looked down, he imagined Christine's feet. Cold, stiff, and purple.

Winston forced himself to finish the surgical demonstration, but as soon as the procedure was completed, he rushed back to his room and regurgitated.

Throughout the day, he continued to leave messages on their home answering machine and on Christine's cell. Each message revealed his escalating concern. *Christine, where are you? Why haven't you returned my calls?* The panic in his voice was real. Not for Christine, but for Phoebe.

By Friday, his nerves were raw. He paced the hotel and phoned home several more times. On Saturday, before he used his original ticket and boarded the plane back to Detroit, he'd called a neighbor to check on his wife. Still, after he landed, no one had contacted him about Christine's death. The last thing he wanted was to come home and find a four-day-old bloated body.

The driver turned onto the quiet street, lined with affluent houses. A police car and several other vehicles were parked in front of his two-story Colonial. When the limo stopped, Winston shoved open the door and raced up the sidewalk. A detective stopped him at the front door.

"I'm Dr. Prescott. This is my house." Winston fumbled with his wallet and took out his identification. "Where is my daughter? Is she all right?" Then he realized he needed to show concern for Christine. "What about my wife?"

The detective led him into the house. The stench overpowered him. He didn't have to pretend to be upset when the officer told him about his wife's death. He *was* upset—over Phoebe. No one knew where she was.

The detective tried to reassure him. "Don't worry, we'll find your daughter."

But by the end of the day, Winston had come unhinged. The police told him Phoebe had gone to preschool on Wednesday, the day before spring break, and Christine had picked her up. After that, no one had seen her.

They checked with neighbors, friends, and family. Phoebe had vanished. She'd simply vanished.

Chapter Seven

Ace finished checking on his golden retriever, Nugget, and her litter of puppies. When he walked out of the machine shed and slid the large metal door closed, pain shot through his arm.

Earlier, he'd driven into town to see Doc Morgan. Doc, younger than Ace but with already-graying dark hair, had eyed him suspiciously. "If I didn't know you better, I'd say someone caught you cheating at cards."

Ace scowled. "Something like that."

Doc and Ace were regulars at a nickel-and-dime poker game held each month at the community center.

"You know, if this were from a gunshot, I'd have to report it."

"Barbed wire."

Doc wrote out a prescription for pain pills and handed it to him. "Be careful around those sharp barbs."

Ace cleared his throat. "I'd appreciate you not spreading this around—especially to the guys."

"What about the women? I could make it sound real bad. You'd have a line of private nurses fixing you food for a month."

"Keep the women on your doorstep. I definitely don't need them."

Doc reveled in bachelorhood. Ace, however, had strengthened his resolve to steer clear of women, especially after last night. When he'd held Quinn in his arms, she'd sparked feelings he'd thought were buried. The moment had been fleeting, but when she drew away, he'd felt empty. He didn't want that kind of pain, especially not from a woman like Quinn. He had known her for less than twenty-four hours, and

30

already she was wreaking havoc on his life. The less he saw of Quincy Matthews, the better.

Now, as Ace walked toward the house, he heard a flock of honking geese flying over the lake. He turned and watched them skitter across the water, splashing and playing. He smiled and inhaled the crisp morning air. Gone were the stone-gray skies of winter, replaced by a brilliant blue. The grass was spring-green and the trees were filled with buds.

The simple pleasures of nature and love of the land had drawn him back to Hickory Hills. But when was the last time he'd actually experienced the joy of a new day? Maybe being shot made him appreciate being alive. Since his divorce two years ago, he'd plodded forward, one day to the next. He'd stopped loving his wife long before she packed up and returned to Chicago. She hadn't broken his heart, but losing his son had.

From the first moment he'd held Jason in his arms, Ace had been filled with awe. Being a father was one of life's greatest surprises. He loved Jason with a fierceness he hadn't expected. Ace had been the one who'd stumbled out of bed in the middle of the night to warm a bottle, and Ace had been the one Jason had run to for hugs and kisses.

A month before Jason's fifth birthday, Stephanie had packed up and left. The divorce was messy. Ace had filed for custody, but Stephanie had enrolled Jason in some prestigious academy in Chicago, so the judge awarded her custodial rights. Ace was granted visitation in the summer and alternate holidays.

He hated part-time parenting. The first summer, Ace hired an extra field hand, so he could spend more time with his son. But last summer, Stephanie had signed Jason up for a month of baseball camp. When Ace protested, she convinced him he was being selfish. "Do you want me to tell Jason he can't go to camp with his friends because you miss him?"

Ace had squelched his own needs, and Jason hadn't come until after the Fourth of July.

At Christmas, Ace had expected Jason for the entire school break, but Stephanie said Christmas wasn't a two-week holiday. She agreed to Christmas Eve and Christmas Day. Ace and Jason spent the two days in a hotel room in Chicago. No Christmas tree to decorate, no candlelight church service, no home-cooked meal. On Christmas Day, they ordered room service. Ace had pretended it was special, but it was easy to see Jason wasn't happy. He'd just played games on his phone, and when that wasn't in his hand, he acted bored. They'd gone to the latest Disney movie, but overall, the trip was flat and had left Ace frustrated.

With each passing day, Ace could feel his son slipping away. If Jason wanted to play ball this summer, Ace would sign him up for Little League here. He was not giving up one single day.

As Ace walked onto the deck behind the house, he glanced through the small grove of hickories to the Elam place. No smoke was coming from the chimney. How did that fool woman plan to take care of herself and a child without heat or electricity? She'd built a fire in the woodstove last night, so at least she knew enough to do that, and plenty of wood was split and stacked behind the garden shed. Maybe he should make a neighborly visit, see if she needed anything. Of course, this time he'd use the door. No, best just to leave it be. Quinn had made it clear she didn't need his help, and he didn't need the complication.

Turning away, he slid open the door, stepped into the house, and hung his coat on a kitchen hook. Warm sunshine flooded into the kitchen through the floor-to-ceiling windows he'd recently installed. On each side of the cast iron sink were light oak cabinets, and around the stainless steel stove was a brick hearth. He'd put on work jeans and a T-shirt because he'd planned to finish laying the red-brick floor tile today. But he'd need to use the wet saw set up in the middle of the kitchen to cut the tile and his arm was already hurting. Maybe if he took some pain pills, his arm would quit throbbing.

As Ace made a pot of coffee, he thought about last night. Quinn hadn't been as crazy as he'd originally thought. She was alone in a strange place. Someone was breaking in. It took sheer grit to use the gun to protect herself and her daughter. He admired that.

Quinn's daughter tugged at his heart. With her head practically shaved and her arms and legs no bigger than sticks, she looked like a little orphan. Maybe she'd been ill. Cancer? Some incurable disease?

He didn't think so. He pictured her rosy cheeks and big blue eyes. Besides, if she had health problems, they wouldn't move to a Hickory Hills, a one-doctor town with a small hospital.

No, Taylor's words were the clue. "Is he a bad man, too?"

Ace could guess who the bad man was. Quinn's husband. She'd probably jerked Taylor out of his life just like Stephanie had jerked Jason away from him.

Ace washed down two pain pills with a glass of water just as the doorbell rang. He hoped Doc had kept his promise and hadn't sent some well-meaning woman over to nurse his arm.

He jerked the door open. Quinn and Taylor were standing on the front porch. Quinn was wearing jeans and a tan Carhartt coat that he recognized as Grandma Elam's. Taylor had on her red baseball cap and blue parka. He crossed his arms and leaned against the door jam, surprised to discover how pleased he was to see them.

The morning light shone on Quinn's face. She wasn't wearing those big glasses, and he could see her brown eyes—not green like Laney's. Now why had he thought of Laney again? He shifted, uncomfortable with the way those needy eyes peered up at him. They were unbalancing him, making him feel protective. Not good. He rubbed his arm, reminding himself that Quincy Matthews certainly didn't need protecting.

She twisted a long strand of hair near her face. "I came over to check on you."

He frowned. The woman who had shot him, then thrown herself into his arms, now seemed shy. He placed his hand over the bandaged arm. "Doc says I'll live. But he advised me to quit cheating at cards."

A small smile tugged at her lips. She whispered something to Taylor and nudged her with an elbow. The little girl's hand shot out from behind her back. She was clutching a fistful of red-and-yellow tulips. "We picked these…for you."

Ace's heart melted. He bent down and reached for the tulips. "Thank you, Miss Taylor. It's been a long time since a pretty girl brought me flowers. They're almost as pretty as you."

She gave him a shy smile that matched her mother's, but her big blue eyes didn't sparkle.

He straightened. "Coffee's done. You might as well come in and have a cup while I find a vase."

Taylor gave him a serious look. "I'm not allowed to drink coffee."

Ace chuckled. "How about hot chocolate?"

Taylor looked at her mom. Quinn's eyes flickered with indecision.

Ace raised his hand as if taking an oath. "I swear not to lace it with arsenic."

Her shy smile widened into a real one, changing her whole appearance. Not exactly beautiful. The bangs were still too long, but those eyes surrounded by dark lashes were definitely appealing, and he remembered how good she'd felt in his arms.

Quinn tilted her head questioningly, and Ace realized he was staring. He straightened and stepped back, gesturing with his hand for them to enter.

He led them into the marble foyer, through the living room, and finally brought them to the kitchen. "You'll have to excuse the mess. I'm doing some remodeling."

Quinn's eyes lit up when she saw the row of windows on each side of the sliding glass doors. "The view of the lake is spectacular. And the willows along the bank are perfect."

Ace rocked back on his heels, pleased with her reaction.

She glanced around the kitchen. "I told Taylor maybe she could play with your son. Is he up?"

His smile faded. "I'm divorced."

She turned to him. "Oh Ace, I'm so sorry." The depth of caring in her voice and the understanding in her soft brown eyes unnerved him.

"So your little boy lives with his mother?"

Ace jammed his hands into his back pockets and nodded.

"That must be hard."

He didn't deny it. "Jason'll be here for the summer."

"Good. A boy needs to spend time with his father. A dad can teach him things a mother doesn't always know."

Her words surprised him. Not what he'd expected from a woman who had moved here with her daughter and, so far, hadn't mentioned a husband or father.

He glanced at Taylor and again noticed how thin she was. "Want some breakfast with that hot chocolate?"

Now why had he done that? He'd told himself the less time he spent with Quinn the better. But as Taylor and Quinn both nodded, he was glad he'd invited them.

He rummaged through the cupboards, found a vase, and placed the tulips on the table. "They brighten the room, just like you—and your mother."

Quinn looked uncomfortable with the compliment and didn't meet his gaze, so he turned toward Taylor. "My son has some toys in his room if you want to go up and play with them. And if you clean your plate, I'll take you to down to see the new puppies."

"Puppies?" Taylor's eyes widened. "I'll eat everything."

Good, she needed some meat on those spindly bones.

Ace led Quinn and Taylor upstairs to Jason's room. When Taylor saw a set of Lincoln logs, she plopped down and started building. "I'm making a puppy house."

He chuckled and walked downstairs, pleased that Quinn followed. She took off the oversized coat to reveal a pale blue sweater and designer jeans that clung to her long slender legs.

"I can help with breakfast."

He pulled his eyes away from her and reached into the cupboard. "You can fix the toast while I cook the eggs. Scrambled all right?"

"Sounds better than the stale box of cereal we found in the cupboard."

Ace handed her a loaf of bread and reached into the refrigerator for the butter and a carton of eggs.

"So you're remodeling the kitchen. Are you a carpenter?"

"A farmer. But during the winter, I do some carpentry. I still have to put up the backsplash, paint the walls, and install a dishwasher. I would have been finished except for Grandma Elam...she lived in the place you're renting."

Quinn dropped two slices of bread into the toaster. "Laney told me about her grandma."

"She was a special woman. Her biggest regret was not finding her granddaughter."

Ace thought he saw sadness in Quinn's brown eyes, but when she blinked, it disappeared.

"When Laney received a letter about her grandma's death, she was shocked. Laney's mother had told her Grandma Elam had already died."

The brown egg in Ace's hand cracked and fell into the bowl. "That

35

explains why, when Laney left after she turned sixteen, she never came back here." Ace cracked another egg, and another.

"Are you serving shells and eggs?"

"What?" He looked down and saw he had dropped the last three eggs into the bowl without removing their shells. "Guess Nugget gets these." He grabbed another bowl and started again.

"Did Laney's grandma know why her granddaughter never returned?" Quinn asked.

"She thought it had something to do with the custody. After Laney's dad died, the Elams tried to get custody. Laney's mom was an alcoholic and didn't pay much attention to her daughter, but the judge only granted the Elams summer visits. When Laney was sixteen, Grandma Elam filed for custody again. She knew Laney would choose to live with her, but Laney's mother kept moving them around."

The toast popped up and Quinn buttered it. "If Laney's mother didn't care about her, why did she want custody?"

Ace whisked the eggs. "Probably for the monthly government check."

"So Grandma Elam died alone."

"No, I was with her." Ace poured the eggs into the skillet. "Cancer. She was gone in three months."

"She sounds important to you."

"She was." His voice cracked. The two words didn't begin to describe the love he felt for the Elams. His parents had wanted one child. Ace was their second son. His mother said she wasn't giving up anything to raise another child—and she didn't.

She went to her bridge parties, golf games, and charity events. His father was busy building his fortune, and any fathering he did was for their first born. Craig was seven years older and the chosen one. Ace had been left with a string of nannies. He was the extra child no one had wanted...except the Elams.

Grampa Elam farmed the Edleston land. By the time Ace started school, the nannies had been replaced by the Elams. He wasn't sure what kind of deal his parents worked out, but they built a new machine shed and gave the Elams the old barn, plus the three acres surrounding it.

Ace had been eight when Grampa converted the barn to a house.

He'd handed Ace a hammer and taught him how to drive a nail into a board. When Ace could pound a dozen nails straight into a board, Grampa took him down to the hardware store and bought him a hammer.

Ace's eyes strayed to his tool belt hanging in the mud room off the kitchen. Now he mostly used a nail gun, but he still had that hammer, even though the handle had been replaced twice.

"I think your eggs are done."

"What?" Ace looked down at the skillet, seeing that the edges had already browned. "Guess you can tell I'm not much of a cook." While he dished up the over-cooked eggs, Quinn went upstairs and returned with Taylor.

He set a mug of hot chocolate in front of Taylor. "This is Grandma Elam's recipe. She used to live where you do."

"I think I'll try some hot chocolate, too," Quinn said.

As Ace fixed another cup, Quinn and Taylor bowed their heads and said a foreign word he didn't understand. They had done the same thing at the restaurant. He handed Quinn her hot chocolate and started to ask what it meant when the phone rang. He frowned, not happy about the interruption, especially when he saw on the display it was his ex.

Ace didn't intend to let his breakfast get cold. Stephanie had ruined enough things in his life. He answered and said, "I'll call you back."

"That's what you said last time."

He glanced at Quinn and Taylor, waiting, and gestured for them to eat. "Okay. Make it quick."

"We need to talk about this summer."

"What about it?" He couldn't keep the annoyance out of his voice.

"You haven't changed, have you, Ace?"

"What's that supposed to mean?"

Ace picked up a pencil as Stephanie recited a list of what she considered Ace's worst traits. Then she started talking about new plans for the summer. The pencil snapped. Ace placed his hand over the receiver. "I'm going to take this in the other room."

Chapter Eight

From the kitchen, Quinn couldn't hear Ace's side of the phone conversation, only his low, angry voice. As she nibbled on her toast, Quinn chided herself. She needed to be more cautious around Ace. Last night she'd been so distraught over shooting him, she forgotten she was Quinn Matthews, a stranger to him. And again, this morning, when Ace told her Jason lived with his mother, she had reacted as Laney, not Quinn. But she was not Melana Elam anymore. She was Quincy Matthews. Her safety and Taylor's depended on Ace and others believing their new identities.

After she finished her breakfast, she carried her plate to the sink. As she turned on the faucet, Ace stomped into the kitchen and strode across the room. He bumped against the worktable. A sack of nails flew into the air and scattered onto the floor. Mumbling, he jerked the patio door open and marched onto the deck.

Quinn shut off the water. The phone call had definitely upset him. "Stay here, Taylor, and finish eating. I'll be right outside."

Quinn followed Ace onto the deck and slid the door closed. He didn't seem to notice her as he walked back and forth across the empty deck.

"What's wrong?"

He didn't answer, only fisted his hands and kept pacing.

She walked over, tentatively touching his arm. "Something has upset you. What?"

His body tensed. "Go back inside, Quinn."

She couldn't leave him. He needed someone. "Tell me what's

38

wrong."

He clenched his teeth. "I can't talk right now."

Behind the anger, she sensed the pain. "Maybe I can help."

"It's not your concern. Go finish your breakfast."

"Why don't we both go inside? Your eggs are getting cold."

"I've lost my appetite." He combed his fingers through his hair. "Maybe you should take your daughter and go."

"I'm not leaving you like this."

He fished his keys out of his front pocket. "Fine. Stay as long as you like." He bounded down the stairs and strode toward his truck parked near the house.

She couldn't let him drive. He was too angry. She leaped off the deck and raced across the lawn. Reaching the truck first, she planted herself in front of the driver's door.

Surprised, Ace pulled up short. "What're you doing?"

"Keeping you from getting behind the wheel."

"This is none of your business."

She reached out and snatched his keys.

Ace growled. "Give me those keys."

Quinn stuffed them into the front pocket of her jeans and lifted her head defiantly.

Ace glared at her. He was angry at Stephanie because she'd decided to take Jason to Europe for the summer. The call reminded him why he shouldn't get involved with another woman. "I can just imagine what would happen if I went after my keys. You'd say I attacked you, and I'd be hauled off to jail." He muttered an oath. "Women. You're all alike. You just bat your eyes and pretend to be helpless. Then take whatever you want. You don't care about your husband or your kids."

"You don't know anything about me."

His eyes raked over her. "I know what I see. Strutting around in your designer jeans while your daughter is half-starved and—" He stopped in mid-sentence. She looked as if he'd slapped her. What had possessed him to talk to this woman like that? "Quinn, I—"

She fumbled in her pocket for the keys. "If you want to wrap yourself around a tree, go ahead." She started to toss the keys in his face. She must have realized that's what he wanted because her arm stopped midway. "Well, no matter how mad you make me, I won't let you get behind the wheel."

He grabbed her wrist. "Give me those keys."

"Think about your son. Getting into the truck and killing yourself isn't going to help him."

"Tell me. How many times has Taylor seen her father lately?"

"That has nothing to do with you."

"You're right. And my life has nothing to do with you."

The patio door slid open. Ace turned and saw Taylor. "Can I see the puppies now?"

Quinn's eyes widened. "Let go of me. I don't want to upset Taylor."

He dropped her arm. "That's the first thing you've said that I agree with." He gritted his teeth. "I'll take your daughter to see the puppies. While we're there, get your things and clear out of my house."

Quinn nodded and dropped the keys into his open palm before hurrying across the lawn. "Ace said he'd show you the puppies. Let's get your coat."

They went inside, and she bundled Taylor up in her parka. Ace's leather jacket was on the hook next to the door. She grabbed it and walked outside. Ace stood in the yard, waiting. His brows were still furrowed, but his eyes had lost their dark rage.

He pointed to the machine shed. "The puppies are down there."

Taylor hesitated, and then after a nudge from Quinn walked toward him. "Can I pet them?"

"Probably not. They were just born yesterday. Nugget's the mother, and she doesn't know you." He tilted his head and glared at Quinn. "Some mothers want to protect their young."

Quinn threw the jacket at him. He made no effort to catch it, but let it fall to the ground. Taylor picked it up and held it out to him. He bent down and took it, then said something that made her giggle. Quinn let out a sigh of relief. That was the Ace she knew, the one who would never hurt a child.

Quinn returned to the kitchen, picked up the nails scattered on the floor, and finished the dishes. More than ten minutes had passed, so she grabbed her coat and walked toward the machine shed. Maybe she could peek at the puppies. The wide double doors were open. She stopped short of the entrance.

Ace and Taylor had their backs to her. Ace was on one knee with his arm around Taylor's waist. They were watching the beautiful golden-haired retriever and the five puppies with their eyes still closed squirming around the straw-littered floor.

Taylor squinted up at Ace. "Can I have a puppy?"

"Maybe. When they're old enough. But you'd have to ask your mom—or dad."

Quinn held her breath. What would Taylor say? She shouldn't have left her alone with Ace. Quinn hadn't coached Taylor about her dad. She had to warn her. *Phoebe* rose in her throat.

Quinn choked the name down just as Taylor answered. "I can't ask Daddy."

"Why not?" asked Ace.

Taylor pointed up. "He's in heaven."

Quinn sagged against the door. Thank goodness, Taylor had simply told Ace the truth.

Chapter Nine

On Monday, Quinn met with the lawyer. He seemed satisfied with the notarized power of attorney giving Quinn the legal authority to handle Melana Elam's affairs while she was in Japan. He didn't object to wiring the money to Melana's account in Japan. "It will be transferred today."

Quinn was shocked that Grandma had left her fifteen thousand dollars. The money was more than she expected. For her grandparents to have saved that kind of money must have been a tremendous sacrifice. Quinn thought about the threadbare couch, the chipped porcelain sink, and the mason jars of canned vegetables. Grandma had taught her to sew on the old Singer still in the bedroom and Grandpa had showed her how to crack hickory nuts, pick blackberries, and fish.

With her own savings of twenty thousand, Quinn could be a full-time parent to Taylor—at least for the first year. Quinn understood the loss of a parent and how difficult it was for a child. Her own father died when she was seven. She vowed to do everything possible to help Taylor through the grief.

As Quinn stood to leave the lawyer's office, she spotted an envelope on the desk with Melana's name on it. She recognized her grandma's handwriting. She pointed to the letter. "I can mail that to Melana."

The lawyer picked it up. "Mrs. Elam requested I give it to her granddaughter, personally."

"Melana won't be returning any time soon."

"Well, it's not important." He dropped the envelope onto his desk.

Quinn tried not to sound eager. "I'm sure Melana would appreciate reading it. I'm sending the rent this week. I could include the letter."

Hesitating, the lawyer straightened his bow tie, and then picked up the envelope and handed it to Quinn.

Next, she and Taylor went to the post office and the electric company. At each place, when Quinn filled out the form, she reminded herself she was Quincy Matthews and carefully wrote out her new name and address.

Later that afternoon, she took Taylor outside behind the barn. They picked bouquets of purple lilacs from a bush near the shed. She arranged the sweet-smelling blossoms into three mason jars and took them to the cemetery next to the country church she'd attended as a girl. She placed the first two bouquets in front of the gray marble stone with the name "Elam" etched across the front. Quinn wanted to let her grandparents know how thankful she was for their love. Even now, after they were gone, they were helping her. Bending down, she placed the third jar on a smaller stone, her dad's grave.

When she rose, she took Taylor's hand. "This is your grampa," Quinn said. Then, remembering to keep up with the charade, she quickly added, "Well, he would be your grampa if I were your mommy."

With all the innocence of a child, Taylor said, "But you're not my mommy."

The words sent a hot flame searing through Quinn. What had she expected? That Taylor would just forget Chrissy, who'd raised her for four years, and embrace Quinn? That they would somehow naturally bond?

That night, after she'd tucked Taylor into bed, Quinn pulled the letter out of her purse and sat down in the rocker. Seeing Grandma's scrawled handwriting on the flowery stationary brought tears to Quinn's eyes.

> *Dear Laney,*
> *The barn was always alive with you here. I hope it will be a part of your life again. When you have your own family, bring them to enjoy the nature. It has a way of restoring the soul.*
> *I understand why your mother kept you away. If I had*

a daughter like you I would have done anything to hold onto her. I'm sure she knew we wanted you and by necessity moved around to keep us from finding you.

She sent me pictures of you from time to time. One from high school graduation, another from college, and one of your engagement. You still have that wide smile and those golden dancing curls. I'm sorry I never got to know the beautiful young woman you've become. At least it is a comfort to me to know you're happy.

You won't believe it, but Ace grew into a fine young man, and we loved him like the grandson we never had. I guess it was just an old woman's foolish dream that you two would eventually find each other. Neither of you fought more fiercely or laughed more often than when you were together.

Don't look back. I have no regrets except for missing you. I lived a good life and have wonderful memories.

All my love, Grandma

Quinn dropped the letter into her lap and wiped at the tears streaming down her cheeks. *Oh Grandma, if you only knew what you've given me. A place to keep Taylor safe. Even now, I can feel your and Grampa's love, just like always.*

Quinn was glad Grandma thought she was happy and didn't know the mess she'd made of her life. In the aftermath, she'd fled to Japan and stayed almost five long years.

Ace's life didn't seem much better. Grandma had called him a fine young man. Quinn would be eternally grateful that he'd helped Grandma when she needed it. Ace had been kind to Taylor and her, buying them a meal, but the man she saw the next day had been cruel. Who or what had hurt him, made him so bitter that he'd lashed out at her?

Of course, he didn't know she was Laney. But his words had cut deep. She'd hoped they might have a second chance, but too much had happened. They were not the same idealistic kids who'd once vowed to love each other.

Still, she was glad she'd returned to Hickory Hills and planned to stay. If someone didn't discover she was Melana Elam, if someone didn't recognize Taylor, if someone didn't connect them with Chrissy... *If, if, if...*Quinn pushed away all the scenarios and slipped the letter inside the book she had been reading. Stephen King's *The Stand* was a fitting title for her determination.

In the following days, Quinn stayed away from Ace. Whenever Taylor begged to see the puppies, Quinn made up an excuse. If she started to weaken, she remembered the way his eyes had slid up and down her, disgustedly. He'd made it clear what kind of woman he thought she was, and he wanted nothing to do with her.

Grandma's letter made her remember how she and Ace had fought. The only time Grampa ever laid a hand on either one of them was when he found them rolling on the ground, pounding each other with their fists.

He'd jerked them up by their shirt collars. "Fists never solved anything. Ace, if you want to be a decent man, you'll never hit a girl, and Laney, if you want a boy to treat you with respect, you'd better act like you deserve it."

Ace's cruel words still echoed in her head. *Look at you. Strutting around in your designer jeans while your daughter is half-starved.* He had inflicted more pain with those words than his fists ever could have. Quinn wasn't sure she was strong enough to withstand that kind of hurt. Especially from Ace.

The first week they established a routine. In the morning, Quinn did housework: dusting, washing windows, cleaning cupboards, or doing laundry. Some days Taylor helped, and others she played in the alcove with her Barbies or stretched out on the floor, watching her favorite DVDs from the library. At least Quinn didn't have to worry about the news since she hadn't had the cable TV hooked up.

In the afternoon, they were together, getting to know each other, sitting cross-legged on one of Grandma's soft denim rugs, playing card games like Go Fish and Old Maid, or coloring pictures. They also played school. Quinn taught Taylor how to print her new name and address and was amazed how quickly she learned.

In the evening, she sat in Grandpa's big leather recliner with Taylor curled up on her lap as Quinn read to her. Dr. Seuss was Taylor's favorite.

But the nights were long. That's when Taylor would look up at her with those tearful blue eyes and ask, "When's Mommy coming? Why doesn't she call?"

Quinn would hug Taylor reassuringly. "Your mommy loves you very much. She'd be here if she could."

Each night after she checked and rechecked the doors and windows, making sure they were locked, she and Taylor knelt by the bed and said their prayers. She always thanked God for Taylor and prayed for Him to keep them safe. Sometimes Taylor wanted to sleep with her. So she'd crawl into Quinn's big brass bed and snuggle close, their arms and legs wrapped together as they drifted off to sleep. On those nights, the nightmares never came.

The second week, on a rainy day, Quinn found Taylor sitting on the window seat with her nose pressed against the rain-streaked glass. She was staring out at the muddy lane.

Quinn sat next to her, wondering what was going through Taylor's mind. She slipped her arm around Taylor's thin trembling shoulders.

"Hey, Lady Bug." Taylor didn't smile even when Quinn used her pet name. "What's wrong?"

"I miss Mommy."

She squeezed her shoulder. "I know."

Taylor's lip trembled. "She's not coming, is she?"

Quinn gazed out the window and wished things had turned out differently. She wished with all her heart she didn't have to tell Taylor the truth. "No, honey, she's not."

"Is she in heaven with Daddy?"

Quinn nodded.

Taylor buried her face against Quinn's chest and burst into tears. Quinn broke down, too. They cried together. Quinn for her best friend, and Taylor for the only mommy she'd ever known.

Chapter Ten

Dr. Winston Prescott slumped in the chair in front of his wife's home computer. Where was Phoebe? Why hadn't the police found her?

He knew the first forty-eight hours after a child went missing were the most crucial. Phoebe had been gone for two weeks. He couldn't eat, couldn't sleep, couldn't work. All he could do was think about Phoebe.

At Christine's funeral, her mother had stood by the closed casket and pointed her finger at him. "You killed my daughter, and you're hiding my granddaughter."

Sympathies changed. People no longer viewed him as a grieving widower and father. He was a suspect. His confirmed alibi of the medical conference did not deter the police. They simply switched their investigation to a murder-for-hire and continued to harass him.

Today was April first. He wanted to believe it was all a cruel April fool's joke. Tomorrow he'd wake up, and Phoebe would be in her bed. He'd have his old life back.

He reached over to the bookcase next to the desk and pulled out his favorite picture album. Reverently, he ran his hand over the red cover decorated with candy-striped letters spelling out *Florida Vacation*. Below the title was an oval picture with three smiling faces in the center. His family. *His first family. His perfect family.* They were dressed casually in shorts, souvenir T-shirts, and hats as they stood on the white sandy beach in front of a cloudless blue sky.

Winston was in the middle of the picture. An average thirty-five-year-old father with reddish hair, green eyes, and a scattering of freckles. Nothing special, except how happy he looked with one arm wrapped around his wife, Georgeanna, and his other hand resting on his five-year-old daughter's beautiful auburn curls.

Their last vacation had been perfect. The beach, the theme park, the water slides, the fun. His perfect life, a once-upon-a-time kingdom.

In med school, he'd found his passion: podiatry. Others students passed up that specialty, joking about boring feet. They couldn't see beyond toenails, fungus, bunions, and calluses. To him, the foot was fascinating.

He'd met Georgeanna the first year he'd opened his practice. She laughed when he said he fell in love with her—feet first. But it was true. They were "sole mates." The rest of her was an added bonus. Georgeanna was as beautiful as her old-fashioned name. She was petite, full of energy, and totally devoted to him. He wasn't particularly pleased when, after three years of marriage, Georgeanna became pregnant. They had discussed the possibility of a child, and he thought he might like one, someday, but he wasn't ready to share his Georgeanna. Not even with a baby.

What he knew of babies was mostly from his twin sister's pediatric practice. Wendy always talked about colic, runny noses, and childhood illnesses, like measles, mumps, and chicken pox. Why would he want to subject his kingdom to those problems?

At six weeks, Georgeanna had already looked very pregnant. At seven months, her belly protruded so much, people asked if she was carrying twins. She wasn't. He didn't mind her mood swings or her cravings for greasy fast-food hamburgers and Cheetos. He allowed her those little indulgences. What he minded was what pregnancy had done to her feet. She didn't walk gracefully. With each step, the baby shifted from side to side, making Georgeanna waddle like a top-heavy goose. The beautiful feet he worshipped were so bloated she could barely wear shoes.

He used to enjoy the sight of her naked feet with her perfectly pedicured candy-apple red toenails. But when she was pregnant, he could hardly stand to look at her swollen ankles and bloated toes.

Then he became interested in reflexology. He studied the ancient Chinese practice and learned the zones in the foot that affected parts of the body. Finger-tip pressure and manipulation to these zones could eliminate stress and return the body to a natural homeostasis.

While Georgeanna was pregnant, he practiced reflexology on her feet to increase the circulation. The swelling went down. When she hadn't given birth by the morning of her due date, he massaged the area between her ankle and heel. Within minutes Georgeanna felt her first contraction. Right on schedule, their daughter, Fiona, was born.

When the nurse placed the bundled baby girl in Winston's arms, he stared down at her wrinkled face, curly hair, and blue eyes. He wasn't sure why Georgeanna's cheeks were glowing with such happiness. He thought the baby was mildly interesting. Then he unwrapped the pink blanket and saw Fiona's feet. He rubbed his fingers over the baby-soft skin and fell toes-over-heels in love with her.

Like a typical new father, he showed off pictures of his baby girl. The difference was that most of his pictures were of his daughter's feet. He even hung a sixteen-by-twenty picture of Fiona's feet on his office wall.

His patients seemed to enjoy the picture, so when Fee turned one, he added another of her pink feet. He continued his gallery, a series of six pictures, arranged chronologically, birth through age five, all of Fiona's feet. They hung on his office wall, right beneath his framed medical degree.

Then the pictures stopped, leaving the right side of the wall empty— just as his life had become empty after that cold December night, five days before Christmas.

The three of them–Georgeanna, Fiona, and he—were going into the city to see *The Nutcracker*. For the past two years, Fiona had been enrolled in dance classes, and *The Nutcracker* was her favorite ballet. She was excited about the live performance, but earlier in the day, snow had started to fall, and the roads were slippery.

"Maybe we should cancel," he'd said, as the snow piled up.

"We have to go. P-l-e-a-s-e, Daddy. P-l-e-a-s-e."

Why hadn't he said *no*?

He hadn't wanted Fiona to take ballet lessons. He'd treated ballerinas' feet and seen the results. But Fiona loved ballet, and Georgeanna had explained, "All little girls dream about being ballerinas."

Still, Winston had talked to the instructor and made sure Fiona wouldn't be on point at this young age.

But on that December night, he didn't want to disappoint Fiona, so they'd gone into Detroit. Downtown was magical. The green-and-red lights gave the city a Christmas glow. The ballet with the beautiful, dancing princess was perfect.

On the way back to the suburbs, the car was warm and full of holiday cheer. Outside, heavy snow fell so fast, the windshield wipers couldn't keep up, but inside, it only added to the cozy atmosphere of the car.

The song "*I Saw Mommy Kissing Santa Claus*" began to play. Georgeanna slid across the front seat of the Cadillac and wrapped her arms around his neck. She sang along, ending with "Oh, what a laugh it would have been, if Daddy had only seen Mommy kissing Santa Claus last night."

He glanced in the rearview mirror, just for a second, to make sure Fiona was asleep in her car seat. She looked so angelic, her auburn curls falling onto the white fur collar of her red wool coat. "I wonder how many more years she'll believe in—"

"Winston!" screamed Georgeanna.

His eyes jerked back to the snowy road. Two beams of light were straight ahead. He must have crossed the centerline. He saw himself in slow motion, braking and turning the steering wheel away from the lights. The road was slick. The wheels adjusted too quickly. They skidded, and he lost control. The car flew off the snow-packed pavement. They were airborne, the car flying into the darkness, swirling through the giant snowflakes.

Screams. Georgeanna's and Fiona's high-pitched screams echoed as they rolled over and over.

Their gold Cadillac did not collide with the oncoming car. Those five people were safe. Their lives went on. They sang carols, opened presents, and celebrated Christmas.

His world ended.

He was the only survivor.

Everyone said it was a miracle. He thought it was a cruel twist of fate. He'd wanted to die, and probably would have, if it hadn't been for his sister, nursing him back to health.

But his sister couldn't do anything about his overwhelming grief—and guilt. For two years, the guilt had eaten at him. The wreck had been his fault. *His fault.* Even a string of psychiatrists hadn't erased the guilt.

Then a miracle. On the third anniversary of the wreck, Wendy insisted he dine with her and her husband. Winston hadn't wanted to sit in some fancy restaurant decked out with holiday glitter and pretend to be happy. He'd wanted to stay home and watch the movies of Fiona's dance recitals. His favorite was her ballet performance as a fairy, dressed in a blue-and-green tutu and satin leotard with gossamer wings. He was mesmerized as she twirled across the stage in her pink ballet slippers. But Winston knew his sister was worried about him, so he'd agreed.

When he arrived at the medical clinic to pick up Wendy, the waiting room was empty except for a woman reading a magazine, and a small girl with her back to him. The little girl was sitting on the floor, pretending to have a tea party. The light caught the girl's auburn dancing curls. Fiona.

"Fee." The name erupted like a strangled cry.

The girl turned. She wasn't Fiona. His daughter and wife were dead. He knew that, but like other times, just for a minute, something would catch his attention. The scent of gardenias that was Georgeanna's favorite perfume, or laughter that sounded like Fiona's. How many times in the past three years had he thought he'd seen his daughter or wife, only to be disappointed?

But this time was different. The child staring at him with questioning blue eyes and shining auburn hair actually looked like Fiona. As he stepped toward the girl, the woman in the corner lowered her magazine and eyed him suspiciously. Changing direction, he strode across the room and sat next to her. "Your daughter is beautiful. What's her name?"

The woman's wary expression vanished. "Phoebe."

For the first time in three years, he felt a spark of life.

Winston closed the album with the pictures of Georgeanna and Fiona and pulled out another album. His second family. Not so perfect. At first, Christine was subservient to his wishes. She was still grieving for her first husband and was willing to let Winston make the decisions.

Their shared grief over the loss of their spouses and their love for Phoebe had given them a special bond. He commemorated the day he'd adopted Phoebe by hanging a picture of her feet on his office wall, right under a picture of Fiona's feet at age four.

What a joy. Phoebe's feet were exquisite, even though she'd inherited Morton's toe, making the second digit longer than the first.

Winston booted up Christine's computer. If the police couldn't find Phoebe, he would. He'd check the history, find out where Christine had been surfing on the Internet.

He wouldn't lose another daughter, not when Phoebe was starting to become almost as perfect as Fiona.

Chapter Eleven

The next few days, Taylor wasn't interested in anything. Her mother's death had left Taylor with an overwhelming sadness, and the few pounds she'd gained quickly disappeared. She pushed her food around her plate, didn't play with her Barbies, color, or watch DVDs. She looked so sad, Quinn felt her own heart breaking.

She didn't know what to do. *Oh Chrissy, she misses you so much. I hope you're watching over her. She needs a special angel right now.*

Quinn understood about the loss of a parent. When she was seven, her dad had died. He was a teacher and drove a semi in the summer. One morning they were eating Frosted Flakes and he was roaring like Tony the Tiger, the next he was dead, his truck hit head-on by another semi.

For more than a year, Quinn had been depressed, barely able to get out of bed each day. The following summer was the first time she stayed at Hickory Hills. Her grandparents had talked about their son and showed her pictures of him as a boy. When she'd cried, they didn't call her a baby, but wrapped their arms around her, giving her the comfort she needed. They let her pick wildflowers to place on his grave. They helped her accept the loss and somehow made her feel as if her dad would always be with her, just in a different way.

That's what she wanted to do for Taylor, if she only knew how.

"Let's take a walk," Quinn said one afternoon, when Taylor was lying listlessly on the couch.

They walked behind the barn, past the garden shed and down the hill toward the lake. The April day was breezy, with enough chill in the air for sweaters. A dapple of sunlight shone through tall elms and onto the path of wooden logs terraced into the bank for steps. Along the sides of the logs, the ground was covered with patches of chartreuse moss and clumps of delicate ferns. The air was scented with the sweet viburnum blossoming like tiny white trumpets.

Taylor didn't seem to notice any of the beauty, and kept her head down. Quinn stopped near the lake where the trunk of the hardwood tree bent and its gnarly branches leaned over the water. This was where she and Chrissy had made their pact.

"Let's sit under the shade of the tree." Sunlight laced through the leaves, spotting the ground. Taylor sat cross-legged with her chin propped up. Quinn dropped down beside her. Being under this tree made her feel close to Chrissy.

How could Quinn help? What could she say? What had Taylor and Chrissy done together that Taylor missed?

She stared out at the lake and watched the light dancing across the water. The rhythmic music of the lapping waves washed over her. A gust of wind rustled the leaves.

Ask her.

Quinn's head snapped up. Chrissy's voice. She had heard Chrissy's voice. Quinn glanced at Taylor, still looking lost and lonely. She didn't seem to have heard anything, but Quinn knew she had not imagined it.

She closed her eyes. The birds were chirping and the water rippling, but Chrissy's words echoed in her head. *Ask her.*

"I have an idea. Why don't you tell me what you liked to do with your mommy?"

Taylor gazed at her with puffy red eyes. "Sometimes we baked things."

"Like what?"

They sat under the tree, talking about Chrissy, and then Quinn led Taylor up the slope to the house. Quinn pulled down Grandma's big crock and slipped on one of her aprons. She tied another apron around Taylor, laughing when it hung to the floor. Together, they made cupcakes. "Chocolate. They have to be chocolate. They're mommy's favorites."

The next day Taylor said her mommy painted her fingernails and toenails. So they played spa and lined up the Barbies as customers.

"I don't want pretend polish," said Taylor, spreading out her fingers. "Mommy let me have real polish, even on my toes."

So Quinn polished Taylor's finger and toe nails princess pink, and then Taylor polished Quinn's.

At the library, Quinn checked out *Harry Potter and the Sorcerer's Stone*. At night, she read the book to Taylor. Quinn thought the concepts might be a bit advanced for Taylor, but she delighted in the magical world and connected to Harry's loneliness and loss of his parents.

The next week, a seed catalog arrived in the mail. "I think we should plant a memorial garden. A place you can go and feel close to your mommy and daddy." That night they poured over pictures of flowers to plant when the weather was warmer. Quinn also asked Taylor what she would like to order for a vegetable garden.

"We had a water garden at school with tomato plants." Her bottom lip stuck out. "I miss school."

Quinn tried to cheer her up. "Next year, you can start school here."

"I was in pre-school, and Mommy took me to Sunday School."

Yes, Chrissy would have given Taylor a firm moral foundation. In the summers, her grandparents had taken Quinn to Hopewell Hickory Church, the old country church next to the cemetery, on top of a hill that overlooked the town. The congregation had been small, less than one hundred. Would attending church be safe?

At the library, at the grocery store, at the gas station, she'd kept her head down and hadn't chatted with the friendly people, afraid someone might recognize her as little Laney Elam. She'd glanced around, driven a different route home each time making sure no one was following her, ready to snatch Taylor away.

But she couldn't keep Taylor locked up, away from other children. She wanted her to have a normal childhood, the kind she had wanted. So church seemed the right place to start.

Chapter Twelve

On Sunday, Quinn wore her black dress with pearls, and Taylor, who now insisted on picking out her own clothes, wore a pink dress with a white-eyelet collar and ruffled skirt. Her hair was hidden under a white bonnet Quinn had crocheted. The brim, decorated with a pink ribbon, flopped into Taylor's face and covered most of her eyes. Perfect.

Taylor had been excited about church, but when they walked into the Pre-K Sunday School room, she clutched Quinn's hand. "Don't leave me."

"I won't." Quinn bent down and whispered, "But remember, we have to play our game."

Taylor nodded.

The teacher was a woman named Summer with honey-blonde hair and a fresh, girl-next-door look. She appeared to be about Quinn's age, but Quinn didn't recognize her.

Quinn introduced herself and Taylor, then added, "I'd be glad to stay and help."

Summer gave Quinn an appreciative smile as she gestured to the six youngsters scrambling around the room. "I definitely need it."

Once Summer corralled the children around the table and Quinn passed out papers, the class stayed under control. The last fifteen minutes was playtime. Taylor bravely slid out of her chair and ventured to a child-size kitchen where another girl was playing.

When the class was over, she skipped back to Quinn, who was on the floor picking up the scattered toys. "I have a new bestest friend. Just like you and Mommy."

Quinn dropped the piece of plastic pizza. Had someone heard? Would they know she wasn't Taylor's mother? She glanced around. The other children were playing, and Summer was still at the table gathering up papers. She sighed in relief.

Taylor pointed across the room to a girl with a blonde ponytail who was wearing an animal-print jumper. "Her name is Katlyn, but she likes to be called Kat."

Summer walked over to Quinn. "Seems like our daughters have become friends."

"According to Taylor, 'bestest friends'."

Kat ran over to Summer. "I want my new friend to sit by me in church."

"That's a good idea." Summer looked at Quinn. "Why don't you join us for church? My husband's gone for the weekend, so it's just Kat and me, plus my son, Levi."

Quinn hadn't planned on attending church, sitting in the congregation, worrying if someone might recognize her. But Summer, as warm and friendly as her name, coaxed Quinn to stay. She introduced Quinn and Taylor to several people before they walked into the sanctuary and sat down. The familiar wooden cross behind the pulpit and the beautiful stained glass windows depicting stories from the Bible gave Quinn a comforting sense of peace—until she saw Ace.

He was walking down the center aisle. Holding onto his arm was a frail, elderly woman, Miss May, the town librarian and Grandma's dearest friend. Miss May's gray hair was coiled into the usual bun, but her jaunty steps had slowed. Quinn felt a flush of warmth for the woman and Ace's kindness.

Then she panicked. She couldn't let Ace see her. Even if he didn't say anything derogatory about her in front of Summer, she couldn't handle his cold eyes judging her. She buried her head in the hymnal. When she looked up, they were seated in front of her.

During the prayer, Quinn asked God to continue to keep her and Taylor safe. After the prayer, the minister announced children's church.

Kat tugged on Taylor's hand. "Come on."

Taylor glanced at Quinn.

"I'll go, too." She wasn't comfortable with Taylor out of her sight, and she didn't want Ace to see them.

Summer followed Quinn. "My sister's the teacher. I'll introduce you."

Belle had spiked honey-brown hair and looked more athletic than Summer, but was just as friendly. After church, Quinn helped Belle clean up.

"I'm stopping for pizzas on my way home," Summer said. "Why don't you and Taylor join us? Belle's two boys are coming. Kat would be thrilled to have another girl. Then you and I can get acquainted."

So just like that, Quinn found herself sitting in Summer's kitchen, munching on a pepperoni pizza, drinking sweet tea, and talking with Summer as if they had been friends forever. Summer's kitchen was bright and airy. The white cupboards had glass fronts, and the cobalt blue sink matched the twinkling glass bottles on the counter.

Summer showed Quinn the house, and they stopped in a hallway decorated with a gallery of framed children's pictures. "I'm a photographer. I specialize in kids."

Quinn could see why. They weren't the usual studio portraits, but showed children at play. On swing sets, riding horses, climbing trees. Somehow Summer had captured the personality of each child.

"I'd like to take Taylor's picture—free, of course."

"Thanks." But Quinn knew she couldn't chance it.

Summer was fun and didn't ask a lot of questions, but eventually Quinn would have to say something about her past. When they fled Detroit, all she'd thought about was staying alive. But in the past two weeks, she'd come up with what she hoped was a convincing cover story. Taylor had given her the idea when she told Ace her daddy was in heaven.

So when Summer asked, Quinn took a deep breath. "Taylor's dad died."

"Oh, Quinn, how awful." Summer leaned over and hugged her.

Quinn told the truth. "Taylor was not quite three when Max died. He was a web page designer and had started his own company. One Sunday afternoon, he was playing basketball with his friends and collapsed in the gym. The autopsy revealed an enlarged heart. He was always so athletic: played basketball in high school and college. It's hard to believe he's gone."

"How did you ever manage?"

"I didn't—at least not well." Quinn lowered her head, unable to meet Summer's eyes as she fabricated her story. "I hope you won't tell anyone. I'm not proud of what I did. After Max died, I couldn't stand to be in our house or go to the places we'd been. The memories were too painful."

"What did you do?"

"I took a teaching job in Japan."

"You and Taylor have been living in Japan?"

Quinn glanced up. "Not Taylor. Just me."

Surprise flickered in Summer's blue eyes, but not judgment.

"I couldn't take care of Taylor, alone and in a foreign country. I left her with my mother. It was supposed to be for a short time, but it was almost two years."

Quinn hoped the story would explain why she didn't know details about Taylor's life.

"My mom was diagnosed with cancer," Quinn said. "She died two weeks after I returned. By that time, Taylor thought of her as a mother, more than me. So if she says she misses her mommy, she's talking about my mom."

Summer rose and refilled Quinn's tea. "Poor Taylor."

Quinn took a big gulp to steady her nerves and prepare her lies. "When Mom had chemotherapy and lost her hair, Taylor wanted her head shaved."

Summer refilled her own glass and sat down. "I wondered about her hair. She looks like a cute little pixie, but now I know why her eyes are so sad."

"I guess I shouldn't have allowed Taylor to get her hair buzzed. I'm new at being a single parent. When you asked me what Taylor liked on her pizza, I didn't even know. It helps to have a friend to talk to about Taylor. She's grieving for my mother, and I—I'm not sure what to do."

"Give her time and love."

"I have plenty of both."

"Be patient. A loss like that never completely goes away." Summer rose and walked over to the sink. Her back was to Quinn as she gazed out the window. "I had a child between Kat and Levi. A little boy." Her voice shook, and she steadied herself by gripping the sink. "He lived for one day. I still think about him and wonder what he would have been like."

Quinn hurried over to Summer and put a comforting arm around her shoulders, but didn't say anything. Quinn knew about the loss of a child. She knew no words were big enough for that kind of loss.

Chapter Thirteen

The following Sunday at church, Summer told Quinn about the kindergarten screening.

"Already?" Quinn's throat tightened. "It's only the beginning of April. What will Taylor need?"

"A birth certificate and shot records, plus her physical and dental exams."

That night, Quinn slid Chrissy's suitcase out of the bedroom closet and laid it on the bed. When she unzipped it, she opened a flood of bittersweet memories of their last day together. Chrissy and Laney, friends forever.

They'd picked up Phoebe from pre-school. It was the first time Laney had seen Phoebe since she'd been born, and Laney had been disappointed when she learned Chrissy had arranged for Phoebe to sleep over with a friend. "We need to discuss our plans," Chrissy explained, "and it'll be easier if Phoebe isn't around."

That night they huddled at the dining room table, drinking cups of black coffee while Chrissy laid everything out. Fake and real birth certificates, Social Security numbers, drivers' licenses, prepaid cell phones, and a gun.

Laney had read the forged documents all with the name "Matthews" on them.

"Now we'll really be sisters," Chrissy said. "But Phoebe will be marked as your daughter so even if they find me, she'll stay safe with you."

Laney had eyed the .38 and nervously bit her lip. She'd tried to convince herself this was just an adventure. "Where's the getaway car?"

Chrissy smiled and removed a key from a gold chain around her neck. "In a storage unit a block from Phoebe's school. It's a used Ford. A new car would be too flashy. I hope you like your clothes. I couldn't resist buying you some designer brands."

"Where are we going?"

"I'm not sure." Suddenly Chrissy's eyes brightened. "Remember the summer I spent with you and your grandparents? What about that town?"

"Wouldn't your husband look for us there?"

"He knows I have a friend in Japan, but I've never mentioned your name—or our secret. Do you think we could stay with your Grandma?"

Laney had fought back tears. "Grandma died a few months ago, but she left me her place. Finding jobs there might be hard."

"Don't worry. We have plenty of money."

"Carrying cash is dangerous."

"It's well hidden." Chrissy gave her a smug smile. "And it's something better than cash."

Chrissy had been right. It was well hidden, and so far Quinn hadn't found it. When she dug through the suitcase for Phoebe's medical records, she found the forged birth certificate and Social Security card for Taylor Matthews, a prescription box with a shot inside that she assumed was Chrissy's, and a sealed envelope with Phoebe's name on the outside. Quinn didn't find any medical records or anything better than cash.

On Friday, Quinn held Taylor's hand as they followed Summer and Kat into the school gym for the kindergarten screening. As they waited in line, Quinn shifted her feet nervously and glanced at the woman behind her. The pregnant woman looked uncomfortable as she rested her hand on the top of her round belly. Quinn felt a stab of understanding and motioned the woman to go ahead of her.

As the woman and her daughter moved in front of them, Quinn asked, "Boy or girl?"

The mother's face radiated with a pink, luminous glow. "Another girl." She shrugged and glanced down at her daughter with golden blonde hair and blue ribbons that matched her eyes. "But I don't mind. Daughters are special."

Quinn smiled down at Taylor, who was wearing her pink Sunday dress and crocheted bonnet. A stab of motherly pride jolted Quinn. "I agree. Daughters are special."

When it was their turn, Quinn stepped up to the registration table.

A woman with reading glasses perched on her nose peered at her. "Name?"

Quinn's knees wobbled as she said Taylor's name and handed the woman Taylor's forged birth certificate.

The woman barely glanced at the document. "Where are the rest of your papers?"

Quinn wiped her sweaty hand against her jeans. "What else does my daughter need?"

The woman gave an exasperated sigh. "A physical, lead screening, eye and dental exams, plus proof of immunizations."

Quinn felt like she was back in third grade, being drilled by Mrs. Gregory, asking why she always came to class unprepared. Mrs. Gregory didn't have any way to know that Quinn hadn't eaten breakfast or that there was no heat or lights in the apartment. She didn't know her mom was passed out on the floor, drunk. Quinn endured the other students staring at her unkempt hair and laughing at her second-hand clothes because school offered food that warmed her belly and books that fed her mind.

Now Quinn straightened her shoulders. She refused to let anyone make her feel unworthy again, and she never wanted Taylor to feel that shame. "I'll schedule them."

"The state requires all the proper documentation before your child enters school."

"But she can be screened today, right?"

The woman gave a dismissive *humph*. "But you can't stay."

Quinn hadn't anticipated this. She thought she'd stay right next to Taylor. She glanced around the gym. Mothers with their children and a few fathers. Nothing sinister, she assured herself. She took a deep breath and let go of Taylor's hand. "I'll be right outside the gym. Okay?"

Taylor's lower lip quivered, but she nodded.

Quinn wrapped her arms around Taylor, drawing her spindly body close. Then she rose and forced herself across the gym floor. At the door she looked back. Taylor was standing next to Kat holding her hand.

Summer was in the hallway, waiting. "Let's go get some coffee?"

Quinn stared at the closed gym door. "I told Taylor I'd wait here."

Summer waved dismissively. "She'll be fine."

Quinn wasn't convinced. If someone was searching for Phoebe, the school would be the logical choice.

"You go ahead."

Summer tilted her head. "Are you okay? You look—scared."

"Just tired. I—I had another nightmare last night."

"Was it in color or black and white?"

Quinn saw the bright red blood trickling onto Chrissy's nightgown and bolted into the women's restroom. Grabbing the front of the sink, she waited for the wave of nausea to pass. When she looked up, she saw her pale face reflected in the mirror. Dark circles hung beneath her eyes. She had to stop reliving that night. The ending wasn't going to change. She couldn't bring Chrissy back.

Quinn straightened her neck the way the Zen instructor taught her and inhaled deeply. When she'd arrived in Japan, she'd been physically and emotionally drained. The year after her college graduation, she became engaged to Truman Regal III. His wealth and privilege had opened up a new world to her, and she was no longer on the outside. Now she realized that all that glitz had blinded her.

She'd believed Truman when he said he loved her and had proposed. She'd wanted a simple wedding in a small chapel.

Truman, however, had different ideas. "My family expects a lavish wedding."

Foolishly, Quinn had agreed to everything: the rehearsal dinner, the big wedding, and the reception at the country club. She had too much pride to admit she couldn't afford it, although Truman and his family must have known. She didn't want to start her marriage feeling obligated to them, so she took out a loan.

Right from the beginning, Truman had tried to improve her. He insisted she wear braces to correct the gap between her front teeth. He told her where to shop and who her friends should be. He kept trying to fix her. But all the changes didn't satisfy him.

The day of the wedding, she'd been jittery and threw up. Chrissy was the matron-of-honor and tried to calm her. "All brides are nervous."

But an hour before the wedding, the best man knocked on the door and handed Chrissy a note. Truman wasn't coming. He hadn't been man enough to face her, just sent a hastily scribbled message. Quinn swallowed her pride and phoned him, begging him to marry her. He didn't change his mind.

Disgraced, hurt, and in debt, she answered a small newspaper ad offering top dollar for teachers abroad. It had seemed like the perfect answer. She thought it would be a relief to leave all her problems behind and start over in Japan. She could earn money, pay off her debts, and start a new life. But running was a horrible mistake.

After a few months in Japan, her voice was so weak she could barely be heard. She thought her hoarseness was from the emotional strain, but a doctor discovered cysts on her throat. They'd required surgery and afterward her voice sounded low and raspy. But she couldn't get sick now. Taylor needed her.

How long had it been since she'd slept through the night? Not just because of the nightmares. Her body was tuned to Taylor's every movement. At the mere sound of her tossing or turning, Quinn sprinted across the hall. When she saw Taylor curled up, sleeping, Quinn would collapse in relief. Sometimes she tucked the covers around Taylor and other times Quinn stood in the doorway, just watching over her.

The days were even more stressful than the nights. She worried about someone recognizing her. What if the police discovered who she was? What if they took Taylor away? What if Chrissy's husband found them? What if he was given custody of Taylor? But that wouldn't happen. By now the police must know he'd murdered Chrissy. She remembered the O.J. Simpson's case. He'd been awarded custody of his children.

Wearily, she leaned against the sink. She was exhausted. How was she ever going to live like this—always looking over her shoulder, worrying that someone would find them and take Taylor away. She'd thought with time it would be easier. So far it was harder.

When Quinn came out of the bathroom, Summer was waiting, looking concerned. "You don't seem much better."

"I'm just worried about Taylor."

"All mothers worry about their children," Summer said.

"But I'm already dreading next fall."

"Think of school as another milestone. Kind of like when she took her first step. Only then she was walking to you—now she's walking away."

Quinn hadn't been there for any of Taylor's milestones. And she didn't want the first one to be her walking away.

* * * *

By the time Taylor and Kat walked out of the gym, still holding hands, Quinn desperately needed coffee. Summer drove them to a gray stone house with a turret in the middle and gables on each side.

"A castle!" Taylor exclaimed. "Do the king and queen of the town live here?"

Summer laughed. "No, just my sister Belle and her husband." Summer led them up the brick steps to the main portico that arched above the front porch. "It's a bed and breakfast with a tea room. The baked goods are fantastic. Of course, I might be prejudiced because both my sisters work here."

Quinn paused at the top of the steps beneath a large coat of arms with a massive lion's head. Then her breath caught. A black Dakota pickup was parked along the side street. She checked the license plate. Ace's truck. What was he doing at a tea room? She almost gasped as Ace walked out the side door and strolled across the lawn. His back was to her as he juggled a box filled with white bakery sacks. Whatever had been troubling him seemed to be gone.

She watched as he slid into the truck and drove away. She felt a stab of longing. Was it always going to be like this? Sneaking around, trying to stay clear of the one person she wanted to be near?

"Are you coming?" Summer asked, as she held the door open.

Quinn sighed and stepped inside the castle. The entryway had cathedral ceilings with dark wooden beams and a massive oak staircase. In front of each newel post was a six-foot suit of silvery armor. To the right of the stairs was a small gift shop, The Queen's Jewels. On the left was a large dining room filled with tables and chattering Red Hat ladies.

A woman with straight black hair tumbling to her thick waist walked toward them. She wore a gypsy-style skirt that swayed from side to side and a peasant blouse with a scooped neck that showed off a fiery green pendant.

Kat ran to the woman and patted her pregnant belly.

Summer hugged her. "This is my sister." She pointed to the woman's stomach. "And my soon-to-be niece or nephew."

Quinn saw the resemblance to Summer—similar turned-up noses, bow-shaped mouths, and almost identical almond eyes, except Raven's were brown, not blue.

"Raven helps in the kitchen and runs the gift shop where she sells her jewelry."

Quinn admired Raven's pendant. "That stone is beautiful."

Raven held up the oblong green stone. "It's an Australian opal. I have more gems in my shop, but each piece is an original design."

Raven led them through the crowded dining room to a small alcove with a single table covered with a white cloth and set with china. "Today's special is blueberry muffins and apricot tea."

Quinn and Summer ordered the special for themselves and hot chocolate for the girls.

As Raven hurried through the swinging doors to the kitchen, Quinn inhaled the rich bakery scents. "Seems like a family business. Belle owns the bed and breakfast. Raven runs the gift shop. What do you do, Summer?"

"Besides eat here, you mean?" She pointed to a stack of brochures in the center of the table, advertising local tours. "I took the photographs and designed the brochure of the day trips." Summer gestured to the walls. "And these pictures are mine."

Quinn was drawn to the framed picture hanging over the fireplace. Two fawns in a wooded grove were caught in flight, jumping across a gully. Summer had captured the action the way she had with the children's photos. "You're really talented."

Summer's cheeks turned pink with pleasure.

Quinn picked up a pamphlet and saw the Old Slave House on the front. She gasped.

"Have you been there?" asked Summer.

Quinn remembered the summer she and Ace had ridden their bikes out to the Crenshaw Mansion. They'd never climbed the steps to the third floor where the slaves had been imprisoned. Rumors about their spirits had suddenly seemed all too real.

Before she could answer, Raven returned, carrying a tray with a china teapot and cups of hot chocolate for the girls. She poured the fragrant apricot tea, and Quinn took a sip. "This is delicious."

Summer sprinkled sugar into her tea and stirred. "I imagine you drank lots of tea while you were in Japan."

Quinn nodded. "Soba was my favorite."

"Do you miss Japan?"

Quinn shrugged. That life seemed so far away—sleeping on *tatami* mats, bicycling to school, shopping for tofu, and then coming home to the emptiness that never went away. She steered the conversation from herself. "So are there just three in your family? Belle, Raven, and you?"

"No, we have a brother. He's a lawyer in Chicago."

Quinn thought about growing up as an only child. "Having a big family must have been fun."

"Wild and crazy. We'll all be together next week to celebrate Kat's fifth birthday. When's Taylor's birthday?"

Before Quinn could answer, Taylor said, "July fourth." Thank goodness the forged birth certificate hadn't changed the actual date.

Summer smiled. "In my family, Taylor would have ended up with a name like Liberty."

"So you're named Summer because you were born in the summer?"

"The very day, June 21. When do you think Belle was born?"

"On Christmas?"

"Almost. December 19."

"Let me guess Raven's birthday." Quinn closed her eyes and concentrated. "October?"

"You catch on fast."

"What's your brother's name?"

"Pleasant Rupert, but everyone calls him P.R."

"Pleasant." Quinn scrunched up her face. "That's harder. Maybe your parents' anniversary?"

Summer gave an easy laugh. "Good guess, but after three girls, my parents said a boy was a pleasant surprise. P.R.'s the youngest, and I'm afraid he's spoiled."

The tea and Summer's conversation eased the earlier tensions, and Quinn relaxed until she noticed Summer staring at her.

Quinn frowned. "Why are you looking at me like that?"

"I was just wondering if P.R. is your type."

"My type?" Ace's soft blue eyes flashed before her.

"You're blushing. Do you already have a boyfriend?"

She shook her head.

"Why don't you and Taylor come to Kat's party next weekend?"

Quinn twisted her napkin, reluctant to go anywhere they might be recognized. "Who'll be there?"

"Just family."

"I want to go," said Taylor.

Kat's friendship seemed to help Taylor, and Quinn enjoyed Summer. A family party sounded fun, and she wouldn't have to worry about strangers—or Ace. "Thanks. That would be nice."

Nice. What an ineffective word. Summer had invited them to share a special day with her family—a real family with aunts, uncles, and cousins. It was just what she'd always wanted for Taylor and herself.

Chapter Fourteen

On Saturday, the spring sunshine was warm, and even though Quinn wore her usual jeans and a T-shirt, being outside without a coat felt liberating. She had driven past the yellow-brick house, making sure no one was following them, before she parked the car and led Taylor toward the charcoal scents drifting from the backyard.

Summer greeted them with a smile and pointed to a grassy area near the grape arbor where Belle was supervising a game of lawn darts. "Kat and the boys are down there."

Quinn watched as Taylor, dressed in a denim jumper and her hat, skipped away without even a backward glance.

Summer linked her arm through Quinn's. "I want you to meet my hubby."

They strolled toward a huge stainless steel grill where a good-looking man in khakis was cooking hamburgers and hot dogs and listening to a baseball game on a portable radio. On the front of his apron was "hot daddy." The words definitely described him.

"Craig, this is Quincy Matthews."

Craig wiped his hands on the apron, and then stuck one out to greet Quinn. "Welcome to Hickory Hills."

As they shook, Quinn had an uneasy feeling. Something about Craig's strong chin and smile seemed familiar. She tried to imagine a younger Craig without the streaks of gray in his shortly trimmed brown hair. She slipped on her sunglasses. If Craig was someone who had known her, she didn't want him to recognize her. But Craig's eyes shifted to Summer and stayed there. Quinn sighed. She wouldn't mind

70

someone looking at her with that much love, although she doubted that was going to happen any time soon.

As they talked, a tall man with blonde hair and blue eyes crept up behind Summer and kissed her cheek. She turned and threw her arms around his neck. "P.R."

Quinn saw the resemblance between Summer and her younger brother. Same blonde hair, blue eyes, and easy grin. The small mustache kept his face from appearing too boyish.

Summer introduced Quinn to P.R. He gave her an appreciative look, taking in everything from her black hair down to the cherry red toenails in her sandals. Then he gallantly lifted her hand and brushed his lips across it. "Is my sis trying to fix us up?"

Quinn shot Summer a puzzled look. "I don't think so."

"Too bad." His voice was a rich baritone, and his blue eyes held a mischievous gleam. He released her hand and pointed to the children. "Is that cute kid in the floppy hat yours?"

Quinn beamed with pride. "Yes. That's Taylor."

Pleasant was a fitting name, and Quinn was won over by his boyish charm.

"Where's your brother?" P.R. asked Craig. "I want to rub it in that the Cubbies are beating the Cards."

"He won't be over until after supper. They're forecasting rain, and he wants to work in the field as long as possible."

As Craig stacked a plate with grilled hamburgers, the radio announcer shouted, "Git up. Git up. It's outta here. A home run." The crowd went wild.

Summer threw her hands into the air and danced a jig. "Too bad, boys, the Cards just tied it up." She narrowed her eyes at Quinn. "Cubs or Cardinals?"

Quinn grinned. "Cardinals."

Summer gave her a high five. "I knew there was a reason I liked you." She linked arms with Quinn and led her away. "My husband and brother are both Cubs fans. P.R. lives in Chicago, and Craig works there as a commodity trader. He commutes to the office a few times a month. He can access his accounts online. When we moved to Hickory Hills, we were surrounded by Cardinals fans. I joined them. My husband and brother are holdouts. Maybe if P.R. found a good woman who was a Cardinals fan, he might come to his senses."

Quinn frowned. "He asked me if you were matchmaking. That's not why you invited me, is it?"

"No, but what do you think of my baby brother?"

"He's cute—in a boyish kind of way, but I'm not looking for a guy," Quinn said, but a picture of Ace flashed through her mind.

"Speaking of mothers, let's check on Raven."

They walked over to the shaded patio where Raven was stretched out in a chaise lounge. Her swollen ankles were propped up on a pillow.

"Need anything? More tea? A book?"

Raven lowered the baby magazine she was reading. "Are you pampering me so I'll forget how miserable I am?"

"That's the idea. I want lots of nieces and nephews. Besides, your husband never seems to be around." Quinn was surprised at the hint of disapproval in Summer's voice.

"I told you, he's at an important convention in Dallas." The iPhone lying on the lounge vibrated. "See, that's Carter, texting me."

Quinn turned to Summer. "What can I do to help?"

"The guys have the food covered. Belle's got the kids corralled. Let's set the tables."

Summer covered the tables with plastic while Quinn carried out the paper plates, cups, and plastic silverware. Then Summer called for everyone to wash up and fix their plates.

Belle's twelve-year-old son, Dakota, was first in line. He picked up a paper plate, tossing it into the air like a Frisbee. It spun across the yard, twirling and twisting, before it dropped on the ground near the grape arbor.

"Beat that," Dakota bragged.

His younger brother, Levi, grabbed a plate and sailed it across the lawn. By the time Craig reached the children, Levi, Kat, and even Taylor were tossing plates. Instead of being angry as Quinn had expected, Craig grabbed a paper plate and let it rip. Then P.R. threw one. Both of their plates sailed by Dakota's, and they whooped triumphantly.

Summer stood with her hands on her hips, shaking her head in mock disapproval. "When will you boys grow up?" But she was smiling and seemed to enjoy their shenanigans. After the Frisbee game, the kids lined up again—with new plates.

The five minutes of fun outweighed a scolding. She could definitely learn some parenting tips from this family.

Quinn filled her plate with a hot dog, potato salad, and chips and slid into an empty space at the picnic table between Summer and Raven. As she ate, she listened to the playful banter aimed at Raven.

Belle pointed to Raven's plate piled with food. "I see you're eating for two today."

"Yep. The hamburger is for me. The hot dog is for Baby."

"When are you going to name that kid?" asked P.R.

"Carter and I can't agree."

Summer rolled her eyes. "That's nothing new."

Belle jabbed Summer with her elbow. "Be nice."

Everyone suggested baby names until Levi stood up. "The law's here."

A sheriff dressed in a blue uniform and flat, round-brimmed hat strode across the lawn. Quinn jerked. Her elbow knocked over a paper cup and splashed iced tea onto her jeans.

She jumped up and hurried into the house. Her hands shook as she wiped off her jeans. What if he'd come to arrest her? What if he took Taylor away?

She pushed back the curtains over the sink and peeked outside. The sheriff had removed his hat and was giving Belle a kiss on the cheek. Quinn's body went slack. He was Belle's husband. Still, when she returned to the patio and Summer introduced her to Ben, Quinn kept her sunglasses on.

As Quinn ate, a sense of belonging swept over her. Summer and her sisters had made her feel welcome. She hoped she and Taylor would be sharing other holidays with them. This was the kind of family Taylor needed—and the kind Quinn had wished for all her life.

Kat begged her mom to open the presents. Summer put up a hand and said, "Soon. Let me clear off the tables."

Quinn rose. "I'll do it."

"I'll help," said Belle.

Summer smiled gladly at them and was dragged away by her excited daughter to wait by the extra chips.

Quinn and Belle gathered the empty plates and then decorated one of the picnic tables with a birthday banner and a balloon bouquet. As they carried gift bags and wrapped packages from the house, the family gathered around the table—the kids sat on the ground in front and the adults stood behind.

Each time Kat opened a present, she exclaimed, "This is just what I wanted."

When Kat picked up the package wrapped in red and yellow birthday paper, Taylor stood up. "That's mine."

Kat opened the present and held up a pink crocheted hat. She plopped the hat on her head and stood next to Taylor. "Now we're twins!"

Summer pointed her camera at them. "Smile."

Quinn stepped forward to protest, but the words stuck in her throat as she saw Ace strolling across the lawn, carrying a cardboard box. He set the box on the gift table. "Happy Birthday, Kitty Kat."

Kat ran over and threw her arms around his leg. "Uncle Ace! Uncle Ace! You came!"

Uncle? Kat was Ace's niece?

Quinn stepped back into the shadows of the patio. That's why Craig looked familiar. He was Ace's older brother. Craig was eighteen her first summer at Hickory Hills and was enrolled at the University of Illinois. He rarely returned home, and Quinn had seldom seen him.

She had to leave before Ace saw her. Quinn gestured to Taylor, but she was standing next to Kat, who squealed in delight when she pulled a wiggling puppy out of the cardboard box. Taylor shyly stepped forward and petted the puppy.

Quinn's heart skipped a beat. She knew the moment Ace recognized Taylor. His head jerked up. His eyes searched the back yard. When he spotted her, she froze. She tried to look away. But his eyes locked onto hers, willing her to meet his gaze. The laughter that had been there moments earlier was gone.

She waited for those blue eyes to turn dark, but they didn't. Of course he wouldn't make a scene at Kat's party, not in front of his family.

His family.

Summer, Kat, and everyone else here were the people he loved. A lump stuck in her throat. All her hopes of future holidays and shared fun with this family vanished.

Backing away, she slipped through the patio door and into the house. She hurried down the hall to get her purse. She'd tell Summer she wasn't feeling well and leave.

Her heart raced as she slid the purse off the coat rack and onto her shoulder. The instant Ace stepped into the hallway, she felt the air still. His boots pounded against the hardwood floor as he walked toward her.

His words were slow and controlled "What do you think you're doing?"

She clutched her purse, holding it against her chest as a shield. Then she turned and faced him. "I'm leaving."

He lifted a brow. "Because...?"

She tightened her grip on the purse and raised her chin. "I had no idea Summer was your sister-in-law. I'm not trying to make your life difficult."

"It's a little too late for that. You already have."

"I said I was leaving."

He stepped closer. Her heart pounded. This was a different Ace than the first time she'd bumped into him at the food pantry. That spark had been for the boy she remembered. What she felt now was for the man standing in front of her. She found it almost impossible to breathe.

"Quinn, I want to tell you—"

"You told me enough the last time. I don't need to hear what you think of me again."

"Maybe you do."

She reached into her purse.

He stepped back and raised his hands as if in surrender. "Is this where you take out your gun?"

The blood drained from her face. "Do you think I'd bring a gun here?"

She didn't wait for a reply. She pulled out her car keys and pushed past him.

He caught her wrist and held onto it. "Quinn, I was joking."

"Sorry, I missed the punch line." She tried to twist free, but his hand tightened.

"You're not going anywhere until you've heard what I have to say." His other hand snatched the keys and stuffed them into his front pocket.

Her mouth dropped open. "What-what're you doing?"

"Something I learned from a stubborn woman."

Her face reddened. "Ace, I'm not mad. You had every right to say those things."

She held out her hand, palm up. "Give me the keys."

He let go of her wrist, but folded his arms over his chest. He stared at her, not with the anger she'd expected, but with a warmth that jumbled her mind. He was unnerving her. She had to get out of here. "I'm capable of driving myself home."

"I'm sure you are."

"Then give me the keys. You deserved to have your keys taken away. You weren't in any condition to drive."

"I know."

"You were too angry to drive."

"You're absolutely right."

"I didn't want you to end up twisted around a tree. I tried to talk you out of it, but you—"

He placed his hands on her shoulders and looked her squarely in the eye. "Are you listening? I said, 'I know.'"

"You know?" Her body tensed. Did he know she was Laney? Did he know about Taylor? "What are you talking about?"

"You were right. I shouldn't have been driving. I was angry. I had also taken some pain pills."

Relief swept over her. "You said your shoulder didn't hurt."

"I was pretending to be tough."

"It was a pretty convincing act."

"After I calmed down, I realized most of what you said made sense."

Ace lifted his hand from her shoulder and raked his fingers through his hair. "I owe you an apology."

He didn't like to apologize. But she hadn't deserved his rude treatment.

76

"I should have come over and told you, but I was such a jerk. I didn't think you'd want to see me."

He'd convinced himself that was the reason, but now he realized he'd stayed away because of the feelings she churned up in him, like she was doing now. Feelings he didn't want to have toward this woman.

"I thought about what you said. How can Jason know I want him with me, if I let him live with Stephanie? I've decided to go back to court."

She looked up. "I'm glad you're going to fight for your son."

"That day on the phone Stephanie told me she was taking Jason to England for the summer. I was angry, and I took it out on you. I know it doesn't excuse what I said."

"It's all right."

"No. No, it isn't. I shouldn't have lashed out at you. I was angry at Stephanie, not at you. What you said was true. A boy needs his father. Jason might be impressed with Buckingham Palace and the Tower of London, but that's not what he needs right now.

"He needs to play baseball, go fishing, help on the farm. He needs to learn the things a father can teach a son—and I need him."

Now why had he added that? How could Quinn look at him and make him reveal feelings he usually kept private?

"I hope you get that chance."

"P.R.'s my lawyer. He said Stephanie can't keep Jason away from me this summer, and when we go to court, he's adding a clause prohibiting Stephanie from taking Jason out of the country without my permission. If she moves to Europe, I might have a shot at full custody."

"Jason's lucky to have a father like you. It's obvious how much you care."

"I shouldn't have been so hard on you. I had no right to judge you. All I could think about was Stephanie had taken Jason away from me, and I thought you were doing the same, taking Taylor from her dad."

Reaching over, he slid her sunglasses up to her head and stared into her eyes. He'd expected green eyes, like Laney, because they looked so much like Laney's, but Quinn's were brown and so needy. "Why didn't you tell me?"

She blinked up at him. "Tell you what?"

"That you're a widow."

He searched her eyes, wondering how he could erase the sadness.

"Because I didn't want you looking at me the way you are right now."

He tilted his head. "What way?"

"All protective. Like I'm some damsel in distress who can't take care of herself."

He rubbed his shoulder, and sheepishly grinned. "I definitely know you can take care of yourself."

"Oh, your shoulder. Does it hurt?"

"If I lied, would you take pity on me?"

She almost grinned.

His smile broadened. "Can we start over and be friends?"

"Friends?" She stared at him and then nodded. "I'd like that."

He stuck out his hand for a friendly handshake, but the minute her hand slid into his, he couldn't let go. He pulled her toward him and brushed his fingers through her hair, pushing it away from her face. Then he leaned forward and touched his lips to her cheek.

He tried to keep the kiss light and friendly, like a soft whisper. But something changed and he needed to feel her lips, to taste the sweetness he could smell whenever she was near him.

For the past three weeks, he'd told himself he wanted nothing to do with Quincy Matthews. He'd forced himself to stay away. But now, with her so close, he couldn't deny the attraction. He said he wanted to be friends, but he wanted more. Much more.

She had him pegged right. He felt protective toward her, although he had no idea why. All of her actions were those of a strong, independent woman. Yet under that hard exterior, he sensed something vulnerable—and fragile. He drew her closer and moved his lips across the side of her cheek until he found her mouth. His lips touched hers. The explosion sent him reeling.

If she'd slapped him or stepped back, he would have been prepared. But instead, her lips welcomed him, clung to his in a familiar way.

"Ace, I..." Summer gasped. "Quinn! Ace!"

Their heads jerked up, and they stepped apart. Summer stood at the end of the hallway, staring at them, her mouth agape. She looked from

Quinn to Ace.

"I see you two have met." She raised her eyebrows at Quinn as if to say we'll-talk-later. "They're ready to sing *Happy Birthday* to Kat."

"Can't miss out on singing to my favorite niece." Ace reached into his pocket and pulled out Quinn's keys. He pressed them into her hand and closed her fingers around them. "Please, stay." His eyes pleaded with her and he added, "Taylor looked like she was having fun."

That simple request changed everything. She felt almost giddy as she opened her purse and dropped the keys inside. Ace wasn't mad at her. His kiss had caught her by surprise, and she'd let her guard down. She wasn't sure how much he'd sensed about her true feelings. Thank goodness Summer had interrupted. Poor Summer. She looked so surprised.

Ace reached out and took her hand, intertwining his fingers with hers as they followed Summer through the house. Summer kept glancing over her shoulder as if she couldn't believe what she was seeing.

In the kitchen, Ace stopped and pointed to a pile of newspapers on the counter. "I brought these back from Chicago. The puppy's not weaned, so you might need some extra papers."

Quinn glanced down at the stack of newspapers. Her hand flew to her mouth and stifled a gasp. On the front page of the *Chicago Tribune* was a sidebar with the caption "Still Missing." Beneath it was a small photo of Taylor. She was wearing a red-checked jumper and white blouse with a Peter Pan collar. Thank heavens, Taylor didn't look like that now. Her hair was short and her face was fuller.

But in the photo, tucked under Taylor's arm was the black-and-white spotted cow, the one Ace had seen Taylor holding the night Quinn shot him.

Chapter Fifteen

"Still Missing." Dr. Winston Prescott sat at the dining room table, staring at the front-page photo of Phoebe clutching the black-and-white stuffed cow. The drapes were drawn, and he was alone, surrounded by stacks of newspapers. Not just the *Detroit Press,* but papers from around the country. Most of the articles were similar to the one from the *Chicago Tribune.*

No new leads in the disappearance of Phoebe Prescott, age 4, who has been missing since March 17. Phoebe's mother, Christine Prescott, age 29, was found murdered in her home, apparently the victim of a gunshot wound. Mrs. Prescott was the wife of Dr. Winston Prescott, a prominent podiatrist, who was attending a medical convention in Las Vegas.

Several items of value were missing from the residence, which leads police to believe...

Frustrated, Winston tossed the paper onto the table and picked up his cup. He downed the coffee and trudged into the kitchen. Turning on the faucet, he washed out the cup three times. Nothing he did seemed to purge the strange smell permeating the house. The odor originated from Christine's bedroom and oozed into everything. The carpet, the furniture, the dishes. Him. He put his hands under the nearly scalding water and scrubbed.

When he finished, he climbed the stairs and hurried down the hall, pinching his nose as he rushed past Christine's bedroom. After the police left, the house had been fumigated from the attic to the basement—except Phoebe's bedroom. No one had been allowed into her room.

When he pulled open Phoebe's door, a soothing scent of peppermint washed over him. He walked to her white canopy bed and picked up her pillow, rubbing the satin pillowcase against his cheek. A slight sweetness lingered.

Turning to the closet, he opened the door and knelt beside the row of Phoebe's shoes. He picked up a patent leather Mary Jane, lifted the tiny shoe to his nose, and inhaled. The faint scent of the peppermint oil he'd rubbed into Phoebe's feet each night still lingered.

On the other side of the closet hung Fiona's ballet costumes and pageant dresses. Phoebe looked so cute in them, just like Fiona. His first argument with Christine had been over those clothes.

Christine didn't want Fiona's clothes in Phoebe's closet. "She's not a replacement for your daughter."

At first Christine seemed grateful to him for loving Phoebe like his own daughter. But after they married, Christine had changed. She didn't like the way he monitored Phoebe's food and the way he dressed Phoebe in Fiona's clothes. He'd placated Christine by boxing up some of the clothes. The rest were still here.

Winston forced himself to leave Phoebe's room. Being surrounded by her things no longer soothed him, but heightened his agitation. Phoebe had been missing for almost a month. Each day, Winston became more agitated.

As he walked out of the room, the odor in the hallway seeped into him again. He reached into his pocket and pulled out a peppermint. Unwrapping the red-and-white-striped mint, he slipped it into his mouth and sucked in the flavor. By the time he reached his den and took out the phone book, he was calm enough to leaf through it.

The police no longer considered Winston a prime suspect. One of Christine's friends from her scrapbooking club had come forward with new information. Two weeks after Phoebe had disappeared, Janeen had phoned to offer condolences. During spring break, Janeen and her husband had been gone on a mission trip to Haiti. Their daughter, the same age as Phoebe, had stayed with her grandparents in Florida. No one had seen the news.

Winston had listened impatiently as Janeen rambled on about how sorry she was. "You know, Phoebe stayed with us that Wednesday night."

Winston gripped the receiver tighter. "She did? Where is she? Is Phoebe with you?"

"No. She left Thursday morning."

"Who picked her up?"

"I don't know. The woman was with your wife when she dropped Phoebe off after school on Wednesday."

Who was this mysterious woman? Why had she taken Phoebe? Winston had spent the last few weeks obsessing over the possibilities.

Leafing through the phone book, he found the listing for private investigators. The police were incompetent. He'd hire someone to find Phoebe. His fingers stopped. Of course, he wouldn't want a P.I. discovering Winston hadn't used his original ticket to fly to Vegas.

He'd been at the Detroit Metro Airport around midnight, ready to fly, when his sister phoned. Wendy had finished with an emergency at the hospital and had stopped by the clinic. As she was leaving her office, she'd spotted a medical file on top of the receptionist's desk. Attached to the manila folder was a yellow sticky note. *To be picked up by Christine Prescott.* The file was Phoebe's.

"Why does Christine need Phoebe's medical records?" Wendy asked.

Winston didn't know. After their little "discussion," he'd thought Christine had given up her ridiculous idea of divorcing him. Recently she'd been docile, agreeing to whatever he wanted. She'd even allowed him a few small indulgences, like kissing Phoebe's toes before he left for work. Previously, Christine had called his actions perverse. Phee hadn't minded. She just giggled and said it tickled.

After Wendy's call, Winston had handed his ticket to a scruffy-haired teenager who'd been trying to fly standby. Outside the terminal, Winston hadn't called his usual driver, but hopped into a waiting cab and rushed home.

Winston grimaced. An investigator might find the kid or the taxi driver. In fact, a P.I. might turn up any number of small details linking him to Christine's unfortunate death. Winston closed the phonebook. He'd handle this on his own.

All he had to do was find out two things. First, who was the woman who had picked up Phoebe? Christine didn't have a wide circle of friends. He'd insisted she devote all her time to him and Phoebe. Janeen had given the police a vague description—tall, blonde hair, about the same age as Chrissy.

Although they weren't tall, Christine's two sisters were blonde. They were also outspoken about their dislike of him. Maybe they were hiding Phoebe. He'd show Janeen a photo of them.

Second was the question about the gun. He'd wiped off his fingerprints and left it on the bedroom floor. But the police said they hadn't found the weapon. So where was the gun?

Chapter Sixteen

A few days after the party, Ace was in the field, plowing. He swung the John Deere around, set the plow in the ground, and started down another row. The steady purr of the tractor engine didn't soothe his churning emotions. He knew the cause. Quinn. What he didn't know was what to do about it.

Ever since he'd seen her again at Kat's party, she'd invaded his thoughts. He'd tried to convince himself he was finished with women and all the ways they could complicate a guy's life. And Quinn was definitely a complication. But he couldn't deny the attraction.

He thought she felt it, too. But after they cut the birthday cake, Ace went inside with Craig for a few minutes. When he returned, Quinn and Taylor were gone.

Ace finished plowing the hundred acres and should have moved on to the sixty. Instead, he steered the tractor toward home. Staying away from Quinn hadn't kept him from thinking about her. Maybe asking her out would solve the problem. His attraction might be because she reminded him of Laney. Maybe after a few dates, he would see how different they were and, like usual, lose interest.

An hour later, Ace ambled through the hickory grove separating their houses. He stopped at the edge of the clearing when he spotted Quinn and Taylor in the back yard. Quinn had a spade in her hand, trying to dig a hole in the ground. Taylor was on her knees beside her.

He recognized the straw hat on Quinn's head as Grandma Elam's, and the plaid blouse tied at her waist was so big, it was probably Grandma's too. He should have laughed at the ridiculous outfit, but even in those old clothes she looked fetching. *Fetching?* Grandma Elam would have chuckled at Quinn wearing her clothes and at him using such an old-fashioned word.

He watched as Quinn stopped shoveling and leaned on the handle of the spade. Pressing her hand against the small of her back, she stretched. Oh yeah, he was definitely attracted.

With her back still toward him, she bent down and started digging again. He slowly walked toward her and reached for the shovel.

She whirled on him. Her eyes swirled with fear as she jabbed the spade into his stomach.

He stepped back. "Ouch!"

"Ace!" Quinn dropped the spade. "I don't like being surprised."

"I should have remembered." He rubbed his arm. "I thought maybe you could use some help."

Sweat glistened on her face, but her tone was cold. "I'm perfectly capable of doing it myself."

Ace frowned. "I didn't say you weren't." He didn't like the way she'd paled when he'd startled her. Whatever she was worried about certainly had her spooked. And now her back was ram-rod stiff, and those golden-brown eyes hard. Was it always going to be like this, working to peel away the layers she built?

Taylor jumped up and brushed off her jeans. She was wearing an oversized straw hat and a T-shirt that hung to her knees. She pointed to the rose bushes and day lilies propped up against the garden shed. "We're planting a special garden."

He was pleased to see her cheeks had a healthy glow. "A special garden for a special girl?"

"Not for me. It's a...I forgot the word." She angled her head toward Quinn. "What's it called?"

When Quinn didn't answer, Taylor tugged on her arm.

Sighing, Quinn took off her hat. "A memorial garden."

"For Daddy and Mommy," Taylor said.

Quinn's hat slipped to the ground. "She doesn't quite understand what *memorial* means."

Taylor put her hands on her hips. "Yes, I do. It's for people in heaven. But we can enjoy the flowers, too."

Quinn bent down and whispered something in Taylor's ear. Her big blue eyes looked up at Ace suspiciously. He smiled reassuringly, but Taylor lowered her head and kicked her canvas sneakers in the clods of dirt. Quinn plopped her hat on and picked up the spade. She circled the ground, marking the diameter of the hole. The ground was hard, and after three attempts she'd only scratched the surface.

Asking Quinn out would be a mistake. The timing was off. He should leave. He wasn't interested in helping with a memorial for her dead husband, but he could see Quinn's determination.

He cleared his throat. "I'll understand if this is something you need to do yourself." He added quickly, "And I know you can. But since I'm here, I could dig the holes while you do the planting."

Quinn stopped and peered at him from under her bonnet. She could see he wasn't easily discouraged. She must be a sight in Grandma Elam's clothes. Nothing that would appeal to a man like Ace. She thought he would go away as soon as he knew what they were doing. Instead, he gently took the spade and started digging. Well, if he wanted to get hot and sweaty, she'd let him, but he'd get little encouragement from her.

Seeing Taylor's picture in the Chicago paper had made Quinn face reality. As much as she wanted to be around Ace, she couldn't pull him into something that could destroy his life.

For the next hour, Ace dug holes, and she planted while Taylor ran back and forth with buckets of well water. As Quinn worked, her shoulders loosened, and the muscles in her back stopped aching. Planting pushed away her problems and gave her a sense of pride. It almost made her believe it was possible for her and Taylor to have a permanent place here, too.

When they finished planting, she leaned back on her heels and smiled as she envisioned the blooming yellow flowers. She had been hesitant to spend precious money on the garden, but she'd felt such an emptiness and longing for Chrissy and Grandma Elam. She also hoped it would help Taylor.

She remembered each summer how Grandma had worked with her on 4-H projects, growing flowers and planting vegetables in the garden. She wanted Taylor to experience tending flowers and watching them blossom.

She crooked her head up at Ace, who was leaning on the spade. "I didn't realize digging in the dirt would be so cleansing."

He sat beside her and lifted one of her muddy hands. "Doesn't look too clean to me."

She glanced at her dirty hand. "I guess that doesn't make sense, but I like the feel of dirt on my fingers. Somehow, it clears my mind."

He didn't let go of her hand. Most women he knew would have looked down at their chipped nails and worried about their manicure, but Quinn had a rare way of saying something that mattered. Something that made him think. "I know what you mean."

She wrinkled her nose. "You do?"

He tried to put his feelings into words. "I guess you could call it cleansing. In the spring when I'm on the tractor, I like the fresh beginning…the connection with the earth. It's a comfort to see something green take hold and come alive out of the black soil."

She smiled, and he'd almost expected to see that gap in her front teeth like Laney's.

"I didn't realize how much I missed being around nature." She slipped her hand from his and scratched her nose. "This is a small garden. I can't imagine what it must feel like to plant acres and acres of farmland."

"Just about the way you described it."

Even though she'd moved her hand away, the connection remained. He noticed a smudge of dirt on her nose. He reached over and playfully slid his finger down to the tip and wiped it away. Her brown eyes widened. Something was happening between them, something more than a physical attraction. He could feel the physical and understood it. What he was experiencing was deeper. Something he didn't understand. Something that no longer had anything to do with the memory of Laney. He wasn't sure he liked it.

After he married Stephanie, he realized how different their values were. At night, she wanted to party. He wanted to relax at home with his family. When they divorced, he vowed if he ever became serious again, he'd know everything about the woman. So far, he knew little about Quinn—except how much he liked being with her.

She rose. "You must be thirsty. I'll get us some tea." As she hurried inside, he wondered if she was troubled by the same feelings.

He glanced over at Taylor, who was using a stick to print the letters of alphabet in the dirt. He picked up a stick and scratched the letters of his name in the dirt. Pointing to the *A,* then *C,* and *E,* he asked, "Can you read these?"

Taylor nodded and said each correctly.

He smiled. "It spells Ace. That's my name and initials. Do you know what initials are?"

She shook her head. "The initial for your first name is *T.* That's the letter Taylor begins with. *M* is the initial for your last name." He drew them in the dirt, leaving a space between. "Do you have a middle initial?"

She nodded seriously and drew a capital *P.*

"I bet that stands for Princess."

She shook her head.

"Maybe your middle name is Polly?...Prudence?...Prunella?"

With each guess, Taylor giggled louder.

"I give. You'll have to tell me."

"Tell you what?" Quinn asked as she returned, carrying a tray with glasses of iced tea.

Ace stood. "Taylor's middle name."

Quinn glanced down at the letters in the dirt. The tray tilted. Ace reached out, caught it, and slid it from her hands.

She didn't protest, but pointed to a nearby maple. "Let's sit in the shade."

Taylor skipped over to the tree and Ace followed. He glanced back and saw Quinn dragging her foot across the dirt, erasing the letters. He frowned, wondering why she'd done that.

They drank tea and soaked in the cool breeze underneath the shade tree. He liked sitting here with them. Even the silence was soothing.

Taylor slowly inched toward him. "Can we go see the puppies?"

Ace crooked his head toward Quinn, who nodded. He stood. "I think the puppies would love visitors."

Even though Taylor was excited, around the puppies, she was calm and picked them up the way Ace showed her. The puppies seemed to

88

make her lose her shyness, and she began asking Ace questions. What did they eat? How many times did he have to feed them? When would they be ready to leave their mother? Did they have to take a bath every night like she did?

He chuckled at all the questions, but patiently answered them. Except for Kat, he didn't have much experience with little girls. He was surprised at how much he enjoyed Taylor. When she giggled or smiled, she was as delightful as her mother. He walked them back to the barn, but when he returned to his own house, he felt the heavy silence and an ache of loneliness. Spending time with Quinn had made him determined to find out why she was so scared. In the meantime, he wanted to do what he could do to keep them both smiling.

Chapter Seventeen

Ace smiled as he awoke to rain pattering on the skylight above his bed. For the last three days, he'd driven the tractor and thought about Quinn. Spending time with her hadn't quieted his feelings, but had made them stronger. The fields needed the rain and now he'd have time to mosey over and talk to Quinn about an idea he had for Taylor.

As he walked in the drizzling rain, he jammed his hands into his pockets. He felt like the nervous teenager he'd once been, calling on Laney. There was something special about that first love. With Laney it was unfinished business, like a kernel of corn that had been planted and sprouted, but never matured. He ended up comparing every girl he dated to Laney, searching for what he'd experienced with her. He hadn't even dated Quinn, and already he'd made the comparison.

The ways she reminded him of Laney were uncanny. The way she'd stood up to him when he'd been ready to hop in the truck was typical Laney. Even some of Quinn's mannerisms reminded him of Laney. The way she lifted her chin when she was trying to hold onto her pride or nibbled on her bottom lip when she was nervous.

Laney, however, had not built barriers—at least not from him. She was quick to anger, and easy to love. Her green eyes churned, and stirred something deep inside him.

Quinn had the same kind of eyes. Big, brown, beautiful eyes. No matter how much she tried, sometimes she couldn't hide those inner layers. Her wariness might be because of Taylor. When children were involved in a relationship, the whole dynamics changed. You couldn't drag someone into their lives and then a few months later rip that person away. He'd be patient, take it slow, prove to Quinn and Taylor he could be trusted.

When Ace knocked on Quinn's door, he heard the lock click and the door opened a few inches. When Quinn saw him, she didn't frown, but smiled and undid the chain. Maybe he was making progress.

She was wearing a yellow sweater and those designer jeans that hugged her legs, perfectly. He decided they were worth every penny.

"I'm glad you used the door." She reached out and pulled him inside.

He liked the warmth of her hand on his wet arm and was sorry when she lifted it and took his hat. As she hung it on the coat rack, he gazed around. She hadn't done much to the place, but it looked fresh and clean. The old couch was covered with a blue-and-yellow checkered throw. New curtains hung at the kitchen window, and on the table was a vase of daffodils. Those touches and the aroma coming from the kitchen made the loft feel homey.

"I like how you've fixed up the place."

Quinn bit her bottom lip and seemed uncomfortable with his praise. Maybe she hadn't received much of it. He'd have to work on that. "Where's Taylor?"

"Playing in the alcove. I'll call her."

"No, wait." He started to reach for her arm, but stopped when he remembered how skittish she was. "Taylor asked if she could have a puppy, and I want to clear it with you first."

"She'd love one." Quinn brushed a stray lock of hair away from her face and bit her lip, again. "I'm not sure about the cost."

"Don't worry about that. I just want your permission."

Her brown eyes snapped. "It's not okay if you're planning to give her one. Those are valuable dogs, and you've already done too much."

Her pride again. He'd anticipated as much.

"I'm not going to give it to her. I need someone to look after the pups. Now that they're weaned, I can't be coming in from the field to feed and water them three times a day. If she can give them fresh water and feed at noon and in the evening, then I think she'll have earned one."

"You'd let Taylor do that?"

"I think it might be good for her. You'd probably need to help a little, but I'd make it clear, it's her job."

Quinn's eyes brightened and her face flushed. "I'll let you tell her." She called to Taylor.

Taylor didn't come into the room, but stood in the hallway with a Barbie doll in her arms, the same way she had with the stuffed cow the night he'd been shot. Only now she wasn't wearing a nightgown, but a navy dress with bright sunflowers and a yellow satin ribbon at the waist. Her hair was longer and formed a bright cap of curls around her face.

As she studied him, her blue eyes no longer seemed scared, only sad. "Mommy said you might come, so we baked giggle cookies."

Ace raised a brow at Quinn.

She blushed. "Snickerdoodles."

It pleased him that Quinn had been thinking of him. "Did she tell you I was going to offer you a job?"

Taylor shook her head.

After he explained he needed her to feed and water Nugget's litter, Taylor ran to the window, pleading for the rain to stop so she could start immediately. "This is the bestest day ever. I'm going to get a new puppy, and Mommy's going to teach me to use chopsticks."

"Well, your puppy won't be able to live with you for a while. You can choose the one you want after Jason picks his."

"Ace, would you like to stay for lunch?" Quinn's lips turned up in a teasing smile. "I could give you a lesson on chopsticks, too."

His face must have shown his wariness because she quickly added, "You can use silverware if you want. I owe you a couple of meals."

"I never turn down a home-cooked meal."

"Good. The curry is simmering. I have to put the rice in the cooker and cut up a salad."

Taylor tugged on Ace's hand. "Will you play Old Maid?"

Ace gave Quinn a pleading look. "Old Maid?"

"Taylor can teach you." Quinn's amused laugh trailed after her into the kitchen.

"You're a little young to be an Old Maid, aren't you?" Ace asked as he sat on the floor and helped Taylor deal the cards.

She gave him a devilish grin. "I'm not going to be the Old Maid. You are."

"We'll see about that." He picked up his cards.

But she was right. When the game ended, he held the last card, the Old Maid, and Taylor was delighted.

"I've been thinking about your middle initial. I wonder if you're a flower. Is your middle name Pansy?"

She shook her head.

"What about Peony or Petunia?"

This time a giggle slipped out. The sound was beautiful.

Quinn heard the laughter and looked in. "Sounds like you two are having fun."

Taylor pointed to Ace. "He's the Old Maid."

"Really?" Quinn put her hands on her hips and pretended to study Ace. "I can't quite picture you as an old maid. Maybe a grumpy old bachelor."

"Grumpy?" He lowered his brows and glowered at her, good-naturedly. "Why don't you join us?"

His words sounded like a challenge, so Quinn plopped onto the floor across from him.

Taylor was the first to match all her pairs and win. Ace and Quinn were left to finish the game. Ace held a single card and Quinn two; one was the Old Maid. She arranged the cards in her hand and held them for Ace to draw.

He glanced at the cards then lifted his eyes to hers. "Where is the Old Maid?"

She felt like his question had little to do with the game. His gaze was magnetic. Disconcerting. Those blue eyes were making it impossible to think. They were delving into her, asking, "Who are you, Quincy Matthews?"

Her mouth went dry and her hands trembled, betraying any pretense that she was unaffected by the way his powerful blues stirred her up. She couldn't think, couldn't reason, only stare back.

"Choose one," Taylor said to Ace.

His eyes flitted to Taylor long enough for Quinn to catch her breath and slow her racing heart. When he looked back, he grinned, obviously pleased with the effect he'd had on her.

Well, two could play his game. "Ace, are you a grumpy old

bachelor?" She stared into his eyes, searching beyond the sapphire blue, silently asking him what he wanted from her. She caught him off guard, found the same confusion mirrored in him. Only he recovered faster, drew a card from her hand, and left her holding the Old Maid.

She blinked. "How did you know?"

"Your eyes." He lightly brushed his fingers across her eyelids. "They give you away." Then in a sotto whisper to Taylor, "Don't worry, your mama's too pretty to be an old maid."

Quinn blushed. Had she really been that transparent? She needed to put some distance between her and those smoldering blue eyes. She rose. "The rice is done. Let's eat."

Quinn poured the drinks, and Taylor set the table. "I can count in Japanese." Setting down each plate, she counted to three. "*Ichi, ni, san.*" Then she explained. "*Ichi* is like you're itching." Taylor scratched her arm. "*Ni.*" She pointed to her knee. "And *san.*" She pointed up. "Like the sun." She turned to Ace. "Now you try."

Ace scratched his arm, scratched his knee, and scratched his head.

Taylor rolled her eyes.

When they were seated, Quinn put her hands together, palm to palm as if praying. "In Japan before a meal, it's customary to bow your head and say *itagakimasu.* The literal translation is *I humbly receive.* My friend, Tomoe, explained you're thanking the farmer for growing the food and the cook for preparing it and the food itself."

"Why do you thank the food?" asked Taylor.

"We thank the animals and plants for giving up their lives for us."

Ace stared at Quinn. "One word means all that?"

She smiled. "I never thought of it that way, but yes."

They put their hands together, bowed their heads, and said, "*Itagakimasu.*"

Quinn scooped out the rice and ladled the steaming brown curry on top. Then she picked up her chopsticks and demonstrated. She worked with Taylor and then turned to Ace, who was still struggling. She showed him several more times, before rising and returning with silverware.

Ace smiled with relief. "Thanks."

"You're a good sport, but I don't want you to starve."

When they finished, Quinn cleared the table. "Why don't you relax while Taylor and I clean up?"

"I've had plenty of practice doing dishes."

"All the more reason for you not to do them today." She gestured toward the living room. "I don't have cable, but help yourself to a book on the shelf."

Ace would have preferred to stay in the kitchen, but she shooed him away. He wandered to the bookcase, wondering what kind of books Quinn liked—romance, suspense, mystery?

Scanning the titles, he was pleased to see some romances. Then he spotted a Stephen King thriller and pulled it from the shelf. He opened the book, and it flipped to a page marked with a white business envelope. The return address was from the local lawyer's office. The name, written in Grandma Elam's familiar handwriting, was "Melana Elam."

Frowning, Ace picked up the letter and glanced toward the kitchen. Quinn was washing dishes, and Taylor was standing on a chair drying. Both had their backs to him. He slid the letter out of the envelope. As he skimmed the contents, a loving warmth spread over him as he read Grandma's words of praise for the man he'd become.

After he finished the letter, Ace stroked his chin. What was Quinn doing with Laney's letter? And why had she opened it?

He was attracted to Quinn and charmed by her daughter, but he wasn't about to dismiss the letter. Quinn having it didn't sit well with him. He slid the envelope back into the book.

Maybe he shouldn't be in a hurry to be more than friends with Quinn. Jason was coming, and his relationship with his son was too important. Besides, other things didn't add up. If Quinn and Taylor had lived in Japan why didn't Taylor know how to use chopsticks?

Quinn was hiding something. Before he became completely lost in those soft brown eyes, he needed to find out what was behind them. He needed to know more about Quincy Matthews, and he knew just the person who could help.

Summer's brother P.R. had been his lawyer for the divorce. He ought to be able to tell Ace everything he needed to know about Quincy Matthews.

Chapter Eighteen

"I'm glad you'll be teaching Vacation Bible School in June," Summer said as she sat across from Quinn at her round oak table, drinking lemonade. "The theme is 'Cooking for Christ.' You and Raven are in charge of the kitchen center, but I'm not sure how much help she'll be by then."

"I thought the baby was due in August."

Summer smiled. "Babies. My sister might be having twins."

"Twins! I'm having enough trouble with one child."

"Oh-uh. What stage is Taylor going through?"

"She wants to do everything herself. I've heard of the terrible two's, but what's the stubborn stage called?"

"I think it's independence, and Taylor probably won't outgrow it."

Quinn pressed her hand to her forehead. "How can a child bring you so much joy one minute and so much agony the next?"

"I don't know, but it's true. After Levi, I thought I knew all about parenting. Then Kat came along. She's completely different, so you'll just have to figure out what works with Taylor."

"I know she needs routine."

"Well, Taylor's had a lot to adjust to—moving here and living with you again. Routine probably makes her feel secure."

Quinn was glad she'd confided in Summer about leaving Taylor when she went to Japan, although she'd said it was with her mother and for only two years. It was a relief to talk honestly to another mother. "Yesterday, Taylor had a dentist appointment for kindergarten. I practically dragged her into the office." Quinn flushed with embarrassment. "As soon as Taylor saw the dentist, she ran out of the office and locked herself in the car. Nothing I said or did could convince her to go back. We drove home, and I haven't been able to reschedule."

"The dental exam is optional."

Quinn sighed. "But she has to have the physical and eye exam. What if she refuses?"

"Do you know why she was upset?"

"She said she didn't like doctors and shots."

Quinn knew so little about Taylor. Had she always disliked doctors and shots or was Quinn doing something wrong? Chrissy would have known what to do. She would have been able to take Taylor to the dentist.

"I feel like a failure," Quinn admitted. "I can't give in every time Taylor throws a fit."

"You aren't a failure. Taylor looks so much healthier. Her hair is curly, and she's put on weight."

Quinn stared down the hallway to where the girls were playing with their Barbies. She felt a rush of motherly pride. Then she turned back to Summer. "It helps to have a friend."

"So, friend, why haven't you confided in me about Ace?"

Quinn's smile faded. "Because there's nothing to tell."

"Come on, Quinn. I know I walked in on something at Kat's party."

Quinn rose to get the pitcher of lemonade. Summer had definitely walked in on something. Quinn remembered how Ace had drawn her close and how his kiss had felt. The day he stayed for lunch, he'd seemed to enjoy himself and was even good natured about using chopsticks. But she hadn't seen him since. So how could she explain their relationship to Summer when Quinn didn't understand it herself?

She refilled their glasses and sat down. "That day in the hallway Ace asked if we could be friends."

"Friends?" Summer raised her eyebrows. "That's not what my brother told me."

"What did P.R. say?"

"I asked him what he thought of you."

"Summer! I told you I wasn't interested."

"I was just curious."

97

Quinn couldn't help being curious, too. "Okay, what did P.R. say?"

"He said Ace made it clear you were off-limits."

Quinn gulped her lemonade. If circumstances were different, she'd be thrilled to know Ace was interested. "Ace and I agreed to be friends."

"If that's true, you need to make that clear to him."

Quinn didn't think she had to worry because Ace hadn't made any attempt to see her again. Whenever they walked over to feed the puppies, Ace was always gone. Quinn thought he would check with Taylor about the puppies, but he left her stickers, like *good job* and *nice work.*

"Ace and his brother are a lot alike," Summer said.

"Really?" Quinn knew Ace and Craig hadn't been close growing up.

"Craig and Ace don't see it. But I do. They're building a brotherly relationship, but it'll take time. They didn't have loving parents. Craig felt like he had to live up to his parents' expectations. According to him, they expected everything from him and nothing from Ace."

As a boy, Ace had said almost the same thing. But from his point of view, Craig was the favored son who'd received all their parents' attention while Ace was practically ignored.

"Where are Ace and Craig's parents now?"

"They're divorced. Their dad's in a nursing home. Alzheimer's. Their mom moved to Florida and is on her third husband. She sends gifts at Christmas, but is too busy to fly up. My mom is the only grandparent involved in my children's lives."

"Where does she live?"

"Chicago. That's where I grew up."

"You were a city girl?" Quinn was surprised. Summer seemed like such an easy-natured, country girl.

"Craig brought me here, and I fell in love with Hickory Hills. I missed my sisters, so Craig helped Ben get on with the local police so Belle could live here with us, and then Raven followed." Summer smiled like a teenager still in love. "When Craig loves, it's with his whole heart."

"Sounds romantic."

"It is. I've never seen Ace that way. He's crazy about his son, but rarely gives women a second glance."

"What about his ex-wife?"

"Stephanie and Ace were never a good match. He married her because she was pregnant. He never blamed her, although later I learned she lied about being on birth control. She's a party girl—not a mother. Ace is a family man.

"Once Jason was born, Ace didn't want to live in the city, so they moved here. Stephanie hated Hickory Hills, called it Hickory Sticks. When she took Jason away, Ace closed up. I don't want to see him get hurt again." Quinn heard the warning in Summer's voice. "He deserves someone who cares about him. Someone who will make him happy."

Summer was right. Ace did deserve someone who would make him happy. Quinn knew Ace would do anything for the people he cared about. Would it be possible to tell Ace the truth? Would he help her keep Taylor even though she was legally another man's daughter? No, that wasn't the real question. The real question was would it be fair to even ask him?

Chapter Nineteen

Quinn put down the hairbrush and frowned into the oval mirror above her dresser. Blonde roots were showing in her black hair. She'd have to wear a hat today when she took Taylor for her physical.

"Time to go," she called, and walked across the hall. Taylor wasn't in her bedroom and the plaid jumper she'd picked out was still lying on the bottom bunk bed. Quinn knocked on the bathroom door. "Taylor, hurry up."

No answer.

"Taylor?" Quinn opened the door. The bathroom was empty. She stared back at the bedroom. "Taylor, where are you?"

No answer.

At breakfast, Taylor had just pushed the pancake around on her plate. Quinn had tried to reassure her. "The exam won't hurt, and I'll stay with you."

Taylor's serious blue eyes gazed up at her, and she'd asked the oddest question. "Will they check my feet?"

Quinn chuckled. "Maybe. Just like your pretty little nose and ears and all your other cute body parts."

Now Quinn's stomach knotted. Was Taylor hiding so she wouldn't have to go to the doctor? Quinn bent down and looked under the bed. She spotted one of Taylor's flip flops. Maybe Taylor was in the closet. She pulled it out, walked to closet, and opened the door. She dropped the shoe. Taylor wasn't in the closet either.

Quinn took several calming breaths. *Why not pretend it's a game— like the Frisbees at Kat's party?*

"So you want to play hide-n-seek. Okay, ready or not, here I come." Quinn walked into the hallway. "I wonder where Taylor is hiding. Is she in the window seat?"

Quinn lifted the lid and looked inside. Barbie dolls, dishes, and Lego's, but no Taylor. Maybe she'd slipped into Quinn's bedroom while she was washing the dishes. She searched under her bed and in the closet. No luck.

Could she have sneaked into the great room? "Where's Taylor?" she called, as she walked to the middle of the room and glanced around.

She checked behind the couch, and then tiptoed into the kitchen and opened the pantry door. Doubling back, Quinn circled the loft and searched again. Taylor wasn't in any of her usual hiding places.

Baffled, Quinn stood in the great room and cupped her hands to her mouth as she called, "Come out, come out, wherever you are!"

She waited for Taylor to jump up and surprise her. Nothing happened.

Quinn put her hands on her hips. "Okay, Taylor, we don't have time to play hide-and-seek. Come out right now."

No answer.

Quinn's anger rose. "Young lady, I'm counting to ten, and you'd better be in your bedroom getting dressed."

Quinn counted slowly. "*8...9...10.*"

Taylor didn't appear.

Quinn tensed. She didn't want to go through another experience like at the dentist's. She was the parent. "Taylor. I'm not playing anymore."

Quinn marched into Taylor's bedroom and searched again, then went from room to room, checking every closet and cranny. Convinced she had searched the loft thoroughly, she returned to the great room.

Where could Taylor be?

Maybe she wasn't in the loft. Maybe she'd gone outside to the garden shed or to check on the puppies?

Quinn glanced toward the front door and spotted Taylor's tennis shoes on the rug. Taylor might sneak outside in her nightgown, but she hated going barefoot.

No, Taylor wouldn't go outside unless...

Quinn froze. Her heart slammed against her chest.

...unless someone forced her.

Winston! He'd found them. He'd sneaked in and snatched Taylor. An image of her limp little body, chloroformed and slung over his shoulder, flashed through Quinn's mind.

She gasped for air, forcing herself to breathe. How did he get in? The window. She dashed into Taylor's bedroom and jerked back the curtains. The window was still locked. Besides, he would need a ladder to reach the second floor.

The door. She raced back to the great room. The chain was hooked and looped across the front door.

The trap. She whirled toward the kitchen and stared under the table at the large denim rug. Would she be able to tell if it had been moved? Maybe Winston was inside, ready to pounce?

The gun. She had one bullet left. She rushed into the pantry. Her hands shook as she grabbed for the red three-pound coffee can where she kept the gun. It slipped from her hands and clattered to the floor. Quinn dropped to her knees and picked up the gun. She ran her hand across the floor, feeling for the bullet.

Not finding it, she shoved the trash bin aside. Cowering in the corner was Taylor. Her unruly curls sprang in all directions, and her eyes were wary, flitting around like those of a trapped animal.

"Oh Taylor." All the fright and anger seeped away. Taylor was safe. Quinn reached out and pulled Taylor into her arms. She was trembling. "Don't ever hide from me again."

Taylor wiggled, trying to break free.

Maybe the gun was frightening her. Quinn released Taylor and put the gun back in the can. Taylor jumped up and bolted from the pantry. Quinn ran after her, catching her in the hallway. She scooped Taylor into her arms and carried her to the rocking chair, settling her on her lap.

She rubbed Taylor's back, trying to comfort her. "Don't be afraid. No one's going to hurt you." Quinn softly murmured over and over, "Sh-sh. It's okay. It's okay."

She waited for Taylor to stop shaking and her breath to even out. Then Quinn pulled Taylor away and looked directly at her. "You had Mommy so worried."

Taylor glared at her. "You're not my mommy."

The words pierced her heart. "I know you don't want to go to the doctor, but you need to be a big girl. Only big girls can go to school."

"I'm not a big girl. I'm little."

Taylor struggled to get free, but Quinn tightened her hold.

"I want Lovey." Taylor stuck out her bottom lip.

After seeing the picture in the paper of Taylor holding the black-and-white cow, Quinn had hidden it, telling Taylor, "You're too big to carry around a stuffed animal."

Taylor had sulked for days, but eventually she'd quit asking for it.

"If I give you Lovey, will you go for your physical?"

"No! I want my mommy."

"I miss her, too." She kissed Taylor's pale cheek. "She loved you very much, and so do I."

"I don't love you. You're a bad mommy."

A lump formed in Quinn's throat. *Oh, Chrissy. I need you. You'd be able to get Taylor to go to the doctor or eat her spinach or get ready for bed without another snack.*

Taylor wiped off the kiss. "Bad Mommy."

They were the words of a frightened child, but Taylor was right. She was a bad mother. Why had Quinn ever believed she would be able to do this? She didn't know anything about raising a child.

She scooted Taylor off her lap. "I'll get Lovey." Quinn went to her bedroom closet and returned with the stuffed cow. Taylor snatched it and glowered, but didn't protest as Quinn picked her up and put her on her lap again. "You don't have to go to the doctor today."

As Quinn rocked Taylor, she smelled her apple-scented hair and her baby-powdered skin. Quinn's heart fisted with love, a kind of love she'd never experienced before, ferocious and binding. A tigress protecting her cub.

Eventually, Taylor's body relaxed, and she drifted off to sleep, snuggling against Quinn.

Seeing Taylor huddled in the pantry brought back memories of Quinn's own childhood.

Laney hated it when her mother drank and the voices came. Once, when Laney was four, she'd spent the whole day locked in the closet.

"I don't want the demons to get you," her mother said. "You'll be safe in here."

Laney had willingly gone into the dark closet. She hadn't learned to distrust her mom and believed the demons were real.

But Mama didn't come back. Laney was hungry and needed to go to the bathroom. Mama would be mad if she peed her pants. Only babies did things like that. Next year she would start school. She was a big girl now.

By the time Mama unlocked the closet, Laney had seen the demons, too. Mama fed her ice cubes and chicken noodle soup. She held her in her arms and rocked her. Mama smelled of stale cigarette smoke and whiskey, but Laney cuddled closer. She would have gladly gone back into the closet just to be held like this again.

Quinn stared down at Taylor asleep in her arms.

Oh, no! She'd repeated the same words to Taylor. "You're a big girl now."

Quinn swore she'd never be like her mother or do the things her mother had done. But so far, Quinn was following the same pattern. She had taken Taylor away from her home and everyone she knew. If anyone became suspicious, they would move—again and again—just like in her own childhood.

Laney would walk home from school and the car would be packed. That night they'd sneak away, and the following week she would enroll in another school. She hated being the new kid. "The next place will be better," her mother would say, but it never was.

What kind of life was she giving Taylor? She had taken away her name, her family, her friends. They wouldn't be in this mess if Quinn had faced her own problems instead of running away to Japan.

Taylor was right. Quinn was a bad mommy. But it wasn't because she didn't love Taylor. From the minute Quinn felt that first stirring of life inside her, she had loved her baby.

In the beginning, being pregnant had depressed her, especially since Truman had left her at the altar. When she'd told him about the baby, he gave her money for an abortion—which she never had. As the baby developed, each flutter was a new thrill. The baby gave her life purpose, a reason to get out of bed each day.

Then she remembered her childhood—being raised by a single

mother, the struggle to survive without food or heat in the house. The Christian school where Laney taught had not renewed her contract. The principal had dismissed her. "An unmarried pregnant teacher is not a good role model."

She had no job, no family to help her, and a mountain of debts from her school loans and wedding. She wanted her daughter to have a better childhood than she'd experienced. So she pushed away her own longings and agreed to Chrissy's idea for her and Max to adopt the baby.

Quinn hadn't expected the gut-retching pain of being separated from her child. She'd left the country, but the pain had followed. Every day she'd regretted giving up her baby. Now she had a second chance. But how could she be the mother Taylor needed?

Quinn leaned over and kissed Taylor's forehead. "I love you so much."

Love was what had made Quinn give Taylor up. But would Taylor understand? Would she forgive her? And would Quinn ever forgive herself?

Chapter Twenty

Later that day, Quinn sat at the table with her hands wrapped around her coffee mug. Taylor's hurtful words echoed in her head. *Bad Mommy, bad Mommy, bad Mommy.* Guilt overwhelmed her. Quinn had lived with Taylor for only a month, and already she was a failure. Other women worked, kept house, and raised children. Quinn couldn't even get Taylor to the doctor.

That morning, after Taylor woke, she'd wiggled out of Quinn's lap and stomped off. Quinn found Taylor stretched out on her bedroom floor, coloring. When Quinn asked to see the picture, Taylor threw her body over it and told her to go away. At lunch, Taylor pushed around the corn and left the chicken leg on the plate. When they went to Ace's, she showed none of her usual joy, even when the puppies yipped at her feet.

In the afternoon when Taylor lay down for her nap, Quinn re-dyed her hair. It didn't improve her mood. Taylor's rejection made Quinn's own childhood surface. She tried to focus on the good memories of when her dad was alive, but the images of her mother's disapproving face pushed through.

Her mother usually held a job at some fast-food chain until she showed up drunk once too often. By eight years old, Quinn had learned to wash and iron, shop, and cook the meals. But still, her mom complained. The clothes smelled of greasy French fries, and the collars of her shirts were never ironed to a crisp point. The hot dogs were flavorless, the macaroni and cheese mushy.

Nothing Quinn did was good enough. Quinn knew it was because she wasn't good enough.

All the people who had loved her were gone. Her dad, her grandparents, Chrissy. She needed to know she mattered to someone. She needed to see Ace.

Quinn stalled Taylor until early evening before they walked over to feed and water the puppies. When Taylor finished, Ace still wasn't home.

"Let's take the puppies up to the house and give them some exercise," Quinn suggested.

She helped Taylor carry the puppies up to the yard and sat on the deck, watching Taylor and the puppies scamper around the lawn. The puppies seemed to be good for Taylor. Color had returned to her pale cheeks, and she didn't look scared. Just another thing for which Quinn had to thank Ace.

When his truck drove up the gravel lane, Nugget ran to greet him. Quinn and Taylor stayed on the steps, petting the puppies. Quinn watched as Ace climbed from the truck and bent to ruffle Nugget's fur. He trudged toward them, his face covered with black dust, and his T-shirt and jeans dirty. Maybe he hadn't been avoiding her. Maybe he'd just been busy in the fields.

As he came closer, she pasted on a welcoming smile. Ace merely nodded and turned his attention to Taylor. "Hey, Pumpkin."

Quinn lowered her head, afraid he'd see the hurt.

"That's not my name."

"Well, Pumpkin's my name for you tonight."

Quinn glanced over at them.

"I don't look like a pumpkin."

Ace winked at Taylor. "When you smile, you look like a friendly jack-o-lantern."

Taylor kept her mouth closed.

"You're doing a good job with the puppies. Isn't she, Nugget?" The dog, lying at Ace's feet, thumped her tail as if in agreement.

Quinn's chest tightened as she longed for Ace to turn to her with a friendly word or smile. When he didn't, she squeezed her eyes shut, willing back the tears that had been threatening all day. She told herself it didn't matter. So what if he didn't care about her? He was obviously helping Taylor. Maybe just being near Ace and seeing the way he made

Taylor brighten would ease her pain.

She inhaled deeply and mustered every last bit of courage to sound jovial. "Doesn't look like you left much dirt in the field."

Ace stood and stared down at his sweat-stained shirt and jeans. "I wasn't expecting company." He moved past them and stepped onto the deck. "I need to clean up."

Pain squeezed her heart. Company? Was that all she was to him? How foolish she'd been to think she was special. His reception made it clear. She had not been invited, and he wasn't happy to see her.

She couldn't withstand any more rejection—first Taylor, and now Ace. She rose and kept her back to him. "Come on, Taylor. I'll help you return the puppies so we can go home."

"No!" Taylor stomped her foot. "I want to stay here."

"Ace is tired and has to get up early tomorrow."

Behind her, the glass door slid open. Quinn turned and looked at Ace standing in the open doorway, silhouetted against the kitchen light. His head was tilted to the side, and he seemed to be studying her.

She shoved her hands in her pockets. Why couldn't she make her feet work? Why couldn't she walk away?

The puppies barked, and somewhere in the distance birds chirped, but all Quinn heard was the yearning in her heart.

"I finished the floor. Do you want to come in and see it?"

She hesitated. He walked into the kitchen, but left the door open. Did he really want her to come in, or was he just being polite?

Either way, she needed him. She turned to Taylor. "Do you want to go in?"

Taylor shook her head.

"Okay. I'll be right inside."

Quinn walked into the kitchen, and Ace slid the door closed behind her. He smelled of work and sweat and turned earth. The scent reminded her of her grandfather when he'd come home from the fields. Her knees weakened, and she wanted to throw herself into his arms and confess everything, Instead, she forced herself to step away and look around.

The wet saw was gone, and the kitchen looked larger. The brick-tiled floor was grouted with perfectly straight lines, and the wooden baseboards, sanded and stained oak. She imagined the room alive with the warm chatter of family. "It's…lovely."

"Summer helped me pick out the paint. Something called sunshine."

Sunshine, just the right shade and feeling. She kept her back to him and leaned on the counter. "You must enjoy cooking here."

"I'm not much of a cook."

She noticed the trash can overflowing with empty take-out cartons and paper plates.

An uncomfortable silence hung in the room. Finally, Ace cleared his throat. "I guess I need to get this dirt off me."

His boots echoed on the tile as he walked into the mudroom. Then the water in the shower started running. Quinn thought of what it would be like if it could be different between them. He'd come home from the field, and she and Taylor would be waiting. He'd sit down at the table, and she'd rub his shoulders, stiff from his day of work, and they'd eat together and tell each other about their days.

She chided herself. His cold reception told her what he was too polite to say. He didn't want her in his life.

Chapter Twenty-One

Five minutes later, Ace had changed into faded Wranglers and a plaid shirt. He didn't take time to shave his stubble, but hurried back to the kitchen, hoping Quinn would still be there.

He breathed a sigh of relief when he saw her staring out the window. The light glistened on her hair. She turned, and her eyes met his. He was surprised by how vulnerable she looked. Those brown eyes were filled with such heavy sadness—and need. He was completely unprepared for how unsettled she made him feel. Something about the way she looked at him told Ace she thought he was the one who could fill that need. He wanted to cross the room, take her in his arms and comfort her. But she looked so fragile, he hesitated, afraid if he touched her, she might shatter.

Still he had to do something, say something. He stepped forward, and she shifted toward the door as if she might flee.

"Stay." His voice was low and soft.

She looked toward Taylor, as if deciding.

"Please," he added.

She turned back and nervously twisted a lock of hair near her ear. "If you're hungry, I could fix you something to eat."

"A home-cooked meal sounds good."

She walked to the refrigerator and found some hamburger and bacon. "Which do you want?"

"Doesn't matter…as long as I'm not cooking."

"How about a hamburger steak and some fried potatoes? If you have potatoes."

"Sounds good. Just don't make me eat with chop sticks." He said it as a joke and expected her to smile, but she didn't.

Ace showed her the cupboard with the pans and potatoes, then moved to the table. He sat and watched her in his kitchen, making hamburger patties, peeling and slicing potatoes. He was surprised at how much he liked having her here. All his logical reasons for staying away from her vanished.

When he'd gone to Chicago to file custody papers for Jason, he'd asked P.R. to investigate Quinn.

P.R. stared across the desk at him. "Do you usually check out your girlfriends?"

"No, but when I Googled her on the Internet, nothing seemed to fit."

"Ben is the county sheriff. He has more resources, and it'd be quicker."

"I don't want the police involved. If something turns up, say a warrant, Ben would be obligated to pursue it."

P. R. frowned. "Do you expect something criminal?"

"I don't know. She has a gun and isn't afraid to use it."

"She and her daughter are living in the country alone. I think she's being smart, and you're being too cautious because of your ex."

"Maybe. But I'd feel better if you checked her out."

"Okay. It'll take a while. Right now I'm involved in a complicated lawsuit."

"No problem. As long as I have the information before Jason comes for the summer."

Ace told P.R. what little he knew about Quinn, and then added, "I don't want anyone else knowing. Not my brother and especially not Summer or her sisters."

Whatever P.R. turned up would probably be minor. In the meantime, why should he deprive himself of Quinn's company? When he'd left the field tonight and driven home, he'd been bone weary. Then he'd seen her and Taylor sitting on the deck. A surge of adrenaline had shot through him. Taylor was like a rare jewel, and he had to be careful not to crush her. And tonight, Quinn seemed as fragile as her daughter.

Quinn set a plate with a steaming hamburger steak and fried potatoes in front of him.

"What was the Japanese word you said before we ate?"

111

She slid into the chair across from him. "*Itagakimasu?*"

"Yeah, that's it. And what does it mean again?"

"Thanks for the farmer who grows the food and the person who prepares it."

He reached over and laid his hand over hers, reveling in its softness. "Thanks for fixing the food."

"Thanks for growing it."

Their eyes locked, until Quinn slowly slid her hand away. "I'll see if Taylor wants to eat." She went outside and returned alone.

"And the cook's not eating because…?"

Quinn only shook her head, so he picked up his fork and began. When he finished, he pushed back his plate. "Thanks, that was good."

She was staring out at Taylor again.

"Do you want to talk now?"

"How did you know?"

"Just a hunch." He wasn't usually good at figuring out women. But he was starting to understand Quinn—a little.

"It's Taylor. She needs a physical for school, but she refuses to go to the doctor. She made a horrible scene when I took her to the dentist. And today she hid, so I called Doc Morgan and cancelled."

Ace glanced toward the deck where Taylor was playing with the puppies. "Would you like me to talk to her?"

Her face brightened. "Would you?" She rose and took his empty plate. "I'll clean up and then come out."

Ace walked out onto the deck and helped Taylor carry the puppies back to the shed. Then they settled on the steps, talking until Quinn came out and sat on the other side of Taylor.

"Taylor and I have been discussing what happens when she takes her puppy home."

"I do all the work myself. Mommy just walks over with me."

"And you've been doing a good job." He patted Taylor's head. "But before any of the puppies can go to their new homes, I'll have to take them to the doctor."

Taylor scrunched up her nose. "Dogs don't go to the doctor."

"Yes, they go to an animal doctor called a veterinarian, vet for short. The vet checks dogs and other animals to make sure they're healthy, and she also gives them their shots."

Taylor's eyes widened. "Dogs get shots?"

Ace explained in what he hoped was simple enough language for Taylor to understand. Then he added, "I might have a problem taking five puppies to the vet. Do you think you could help me?"

Taylor was quiet for a long time. "They might not be as scared if I was there."

"That's right." Ace put an arm around Taylor's shoulders. "You're a very smart young lady."

The three of them continued to sit on the steps. Behind them, the kitchen light pooled onto the deck. The air cooled, and the sun lowered itself slowly behind the lake. Streaks of gold stretched across the horizon and reflected onto the water, giving off a shimmering glow. Wind whispered through the spring leaves, and the lapping water accompanied the symphony of night sounds.

He felt Quinn's hand on his arm. "Thank you," she mouthed.

The warmth of her touch made his heart swell. He lifted her hand and interlocked his fingers with hers, giving her an answering squeeze.

"Look." Taylor pointed to a bird, strutting across the lawn toward a clump of trees.

Ace stared at the robin-sized bird with a long bill and mottled russet feathers. "That's a woodcock. Some people call it a timberdoodle."

As they watched, the bird spread its wings, spiraled upward about two hundred feet, and then disappeared.

"It's gone," said Taylor, resting her chin on the palms of her hands.

"He'll be back."

As Ace predicted, the woodcock reappeared, speeding toward them with its wings musically twittering. The flight was wild and exotic. The bird dived and rotated, spinning above the trees.

Finally, it lit on its slender legs and strutted across the lawn again, making a strange *peent* sound followed by a softer *toku*.

"What's it doing?" Quinn asked.

"He's staking out his territory," said Ace.

"How do you know it's a male?"

"The female doesn't sing. The male is the song bird, and he only sings in April."

"He sounds funny," Taylor said.

Ace threw back his head and laughed. "Let's hope the female he's trying to impress doesn't think so."

With a rustle of wings, the woodcock took flight, disappearing into the shadowy night then reappearing and diving toward the ground again.

Quinn stared at the sky. "He's doing the same thing."

"It's his mating dance." Ace tightened his grip on her hand. "He's showing off for his woman."

Tonight Ace felt the same urge. Quinn had awakened feelings in him he couldn't ignore or control.

He let go of her hand and moved his knuckles to the side of her face, skimming them down her cheek and along her chin. He felt her quiver, and her eyes met his. "Are you cold?"

She shook her head. The sadness in her eyes was gone, replaced by what seemed to be unabashed admiration.

Tonight, she didn't look as if she were thinking about Taylor's father. Tonight, her eyes were on him.

His insides gyrated and twisted like the woodcock. He felt like strutting around the yard, singing the song thrumming in his head. Her eyes continued to stare at him, and he realized a man would do almost anything to have a woman keep looking at him like that.

Chapter Twenty-Two

When Quinn fled to Hickory Hills, the days had been chilly and the land clothed in muted winter garb. She'd been here five weeks, and now, in late April, the woods were alive with chattering birds and colorful wildflowers.

Nature seemed to be having a healing effect on Taylor. She was delighted by the wildflowers springing up overnight and dotting the woods, particularly the Jack-in-the-pulpits, blue bells, and Dutchman's breeches, which truly resembled britches hung out to dry. She loved the purple Sweet Williams and the lemony-yellow sumac. She laughed at the playful antics of the squirrels scampering up the shag bark hickories and was fascinated by the red-headed woodpecker and its persistent peck-peck-pecking against the trees.

Each day, Taylor reveled in some new sight. From the moment she awoke, she wanted to be outdoors. The warm sunshine tinged her cheeks pink, and fresh air doubled her appetite. She grew taller, and her moods of sadness, anger, and even stubbornness came less often. Some days she cried and grieved, but at night when Quinn tucked her in bed, she kissed her, hoping she felt safe and loved.

At the end of April, Quinn explained to Taylor about Golden Days, a week of holidays celebrated in Japan that ended with Children's Day.

"Do kids get presents?" Taylor asked.

"No, they eat special foods, fly wind socks, and display samurai dolls."

"I want an American Girl doll."

Taylor didn't ask for much, but those dolls were expensive. Quinn had earned some money when she'd filled in for Raven as a tour guide for the art deco movie theater and the Carnegie library. If she saved her money from the tours, maybe she'd be able to buy Taylor an American Girl doll for Christmas.

She wondered if they'd still be in Hickory Hills at Christmas. Hiding out and ignoring her problems weren't going to make them go away. When she was a girl, she'd never thought much beyond the struggles of a single day. Getting food, having clean clothes, trying to keep her mother away from the booze. Those daily problems were big enough. She'd been afraid to tackle the larger ones. When she was pregnant, she handled her life the same way. She never focused on after the delivery and didn't know how empty she'd feel inside. She'd pushed away those mothering feelings until it was too late.

"The only way I can handle letting you adopt my baby is a clean break," she said to Chrissy and Max. "No pictures. No e-mail. No contact."

Even an ocean away, Quinn thought about her baby every day. She wondered what she looked like. How old was she when she rolled over, sat up, took her first step?

She had missed almost five years of Taylor's life and had five years of regrets. Chrissy and Max had wanted a baby, and they'd loved Phoebe, yet after Max died, Chrissy had let another man into her life, one capable of murder. And she'd allowed him to adopt Phoebe.

Quinn couldn't blame Chrissy. Quinn understood all too well how easily someone could be duped. Hadn't she fallen for Truman's smooth words, only to learn later what he was really like?

If Quinn found out what the authorities knew about Chrissy's murder, she'd be better prepared to protect Taylor. Maybe Chrissy's husband was in custody and had been charged with murder. Then they'd be safe. Quinn could hire a lawyer and legally reclaim her daughter.

The last week of April, Quinn asked Summer to watch Taylor while she went to St. Louis to do some shopping. The real purpose, though, was to find out information. Using the computers at the local library wouldn't be safe. Too many people knew her. Someone might stroll by to chat or a curious worker might search the computer's history. St. Louis would be safer.

Quinn bought hair dye for herself and a cute little sundress embroidered with sunflowers for Taylor before she went to the library. The first website Quinn checked was *The Detroit News*. She started with the current issue and then scanned the archives. A sidebar in last week's newspaper caught her attention.

"Still no identification of the woman in the police sketch who may have information about the disappearance of Phoebe Prescott."

Police sketch. Oh God, did the police know what she looked like?

She searched every section of that day's paper, but found no picture. She checked back several issues until she saw a black-and-white drawing of a woman's face with the caption, "Person of interest wanted in connection with the murder of Christine Prescott and the possible abduction of her daughter."

Murder?

The blood drained from her face. Did the police think she murdered Chrissy? Quinn couldn't breathe. She bent over, forcing air in and out, in and out.

Quinn knew she might be charged with kidnapping. She'd taken Taylor, but Taylor was her biological daughter, and she was protecting her. Once the authorities knew she was Taylor's mother, she hoped the kidnapping charges would be dropped, or if she was charged, the judge would be lenient. She never imagined the police would think she murdered Chrissy.

What motive would she have? She and Chrissy had been best friends. She'd never kill Chrissy.

Oh, God. What if the police thought she'd changed her mind about the adoption? What if they thought she returned to take Phoebe away from Chrissy? Quinn rushed to the bathroom and heaved. She stood in the stall, her teeth chattering and her body shaking. Chrissy had arranged everything: the new IDs and the gun, but Quinn couldn't prove that. The car was registered in Quinn's name. The gun probably wasn't registered, but it was in her possession. Everything would seem as if she planned it. Premeditated murder.

117

What evidence did she have that would link Winston to the murder? Chrissy hadn't been specific about why she needed to get away from her husband. He hadn't violated them physically, Chrissy had been clear about that. She said something about Winston trying to replace his own daughter with Phoebe.

Quinn splashed cold water on her face and stared into the mirror.

Her face.

Quinn hurried back to the computer and studied the drawing. The police sketch didn't look like her face. The mouth was too small and the nose too big. Her face was rounder and her light hair was curly. They were tiny details, but the composite made her appearance entirely different. No one would be able to identify her from that sketch. But she knew there was another problem. Her fingerprints.

They were on file with the Indiana State Police, one of the requirements for her teaching position. That meant they'd probably be in the federal identification program. The night of the murder, after Winston left, she'd gone through the house and wiped off her fingerprints, but she wasn't sure she'd managed to get rid of all of them.

If the police discovered Melana Elam's fingerprints in the house, they'd come looking for her. But everyone who knew Laney thought she was still in Japan—even her mother. Everyone in Hickory Hills had accepted her as Quincy Matthews. So, if her fingerprints turned up, they would be Melana Elam's fingerprints. She was Quincy Matthews, and the police wouldn't have any reason to suspect her of murder.

But the thought of Winston being free made her angry. She couldn't let him get away with killing Chrissy. The least she could do was make sure Chrissy's killer was punished.

An anonymous tip to the police might get lost in bureaucracy. Besides, Chrissy's family must be frantic about Phoebe. Chrissy's mom had always been so loving, allowing Laney to stay with them. Once, when her mother's boyfriend moved in, Laney stayed with Chrissy for over three months. An extra plate was always at the table, and a basket of hand-me-downs in the closet.

Quinn left the library and found a pay phone. Chrissy's mom wouldn't recognize her voice, not after the surgery. She'd tell her that Winston killed her daughter and explain that Phoebe was safe.

If Quinn was careful, she would be able to give Taylor a stable life. Instead of being jerked from place to place, they could stay in Hickory Hills. And maybe Quinn could have the life she'd dreamed about since she was sixteen years old. A life that included Ace.

Chapter Twenty-Three

"I'm sorry to disturb you, Dr. Prescott."

Winston glanced up from his patient's plump pink toes to see his receptionist standing in the hall outside the examination room.

"Two detectives are here to see you."

Winston's hand slipped from his patient's foot. "My secretary will schedule your surgery."

"Surgery? But—"

Winston didn't stop to explain or console the woman as he would have. Instead he rushed to his office, closed the door, and collapsed against the back of it.

Perspiration popped out on his forehead. The police had interrogated him at his house and at the precinct, but they'd never come to his office. What did that mean? Were they here to arrest him?

No, if they had any evidence against him, they'd barge in and drag him away. The detective in charge of the investigation had made it clear he thought Winston was guilty.

Winston walked over to his desk. As he reached into the candy dish for a peppermint, his hand shook. He unwrapped the mint and popped it into his mouth. As soon as the soothing mint touched his tongue, he began to calm.

Maybe the detectives had new information. Winston remembered wiping off the gun and leaving it next to Christine's bed. When the police said no weapon had been found, he'd almost blurted out where he'd laid the gun. After the police finished collecting evidence and he was allowed back inside his house, he'd hunted everywhere for the gun.

For days he'd thought about who might have taken the .38 Smith and Wesson and why. He ruled out the investigation team. He couldn't find a motive. A more logical answer was someone had entered the house before the police found Christine's body. The most likely person was a man. Someone Christine had been seeing behind his back. Each day, he feared the police would find the gun planted in his car, his yard, his office—any place that would incriminate him. But the gun had not shown up.

Another theory was the gun had been taken by the woman who'd picked up Phoebe from the sleepover. Maybe she'd brought Phoebe back to the house, discovered Christine, and for some reason grabbed the gun.

The scent of peppermint reminded him of Phoebe. The police might not be here about Christine's death. They might be here about Phoebe. Maybe they'd found her. Maybe she was in his waiting room right now. Any minute the door might fly open, and Phoebe would rush across the room and throw herself into his open arms.

Winston slipped off his white coat and hung it on the tree stand behind his desk. Phoebe didn't like the white lab jacket and refused to come near him when he was wearing it.

The door swung open. Detective Beveridge, followed by his partner, Detective Rollo, walked into the office. His vision of Phoebe rushing in vanished. Winston gestured toward the leather chairs in front of his desk. He waited until they were seated before he sat down and steepled his fingers on the desk to keep them steady.

Detective Beveridge, a short, squat man with the tenacity of a bulldog, was in charge of the case. His flat nose, flabby jowls, and wide shoulders made him look like a bulldog. The detective had sunk his teeth into one idea. Winston was guilty.

Beveridge had even cornered Winston and jabbed his index finger against Winston's chest. "I know you're guilty, and I'm going to prove it."

Winston didn't want some mutt-faced man messing with his life, so he tried to avoid Beveridge. Winston preferred to deal with Detective Rollo, a straight-laced, military-style guy. He was a rookie, who still believed the law was black and white. Winston had seen the world that way, before the accident had sent his car skidding off the snow-covered road. Then his world became a mass of gray, brightened only by Phoebe's auburn curls and sapphire blue eyes.

Winston focused his attention on Beveridge, who had, with some difficulty, crossed his leg over his knee and pulled a notebook out of his shirt pocket. "We have some questions about the fingerprints found at your house."

Winston's hands flew open. "Fingerprints? Whose? Do you know who has Phoebe?"

"We're working with the FBI, but so far no leads on your daughter," Rollo said.

"FBI? Does that mean Phoebe was spotted outside of Michigan?" Winston had assumed one of Christine's relatives was hiding Phoebe. What if someone else had Phoebe? Oh God, what if she was never found?

Rollo gave him a sympathetic smile. "If a child is younger than twelve, the FBI often is called without evidence of interstate travel."

Beveridge made a low menacing growl that Winston assumed was a reprimand to Rollo for giving him any information. But Rollo had a son and seemed to understand a father's pain. Whenever Winston called to check on the investigation, which was several times a week, he always asked for Rollo.

"As I was saying, we have some questions about the fingerprints. Most of the identified fingerprints were yours." Beveridge's nose flared, and his eyes bore into Winston. "It seems strange, however, that no fingerprints were found in the master bedroom. It's almost as if someone wiped the room clean."

Winston knew Beveridge was baiting him, setting a trap. He met the man's cold stare and remained silent. So what if they didn't find his fingerprints in Christine's bedroom?

Rollo turned to Beveridge. "Didn't you also say no fingerprints were found in the guest room?"

Winston could not disguise his surprise. "No fingerprints in the guest room?"

Beveridge sounded disgruntled. "No fingerprints were found in any of the bedrooms."

Winston stiffened. His mouth went dry. He gripped the arms of the chair to keep his hands from shaking. His fingerprints should have been all over the guest bedroom. For the past several months he'd slept there—but he wasn't about to divulge that information. If no fingerprints were found, it meant someone else had erased them—someone who didn't want anyone to know that he or she had been in the house.

Winston gulped. But when had that person been in the house? The next morning? That night? What if someone had heard the argument and witnessed the accident? If Christine had a lover, he would have been in her bedroom. If someone was in the guest room, Winston thought it might be the same woman who picked up Phoebe. What if she hadn't come back to the house? What if she'd been at the house and left the next morning with Phoebe? He loosened his collar.

Beveridge was staring at him.

Winston cleared his throat. "Whose fingerprints have you found?"

Beveridge checked his notebook again. "Neighbors, relatives—"

"Relatives? Christine's sisters?" Winston's hopes soared. He'd forbidden her sisters to visit after one of their brats had broken Fiona's favorite doll. Phoebe was always careful with Fiona's toys and clothes.

Beveridge answered, "Not just Christine's sisters. We also found your sister's fingerprints."

"My sister visits often." Winston didn't want them sniffing around Wendy.

"Would you say your sister and wife were good friends?"

"Yes. I met Christine at my sister's clinic. Phoebe was a patient of hers." In the beginning, Christine and Wendy were friends. That was before Christine confided in Wendy her concern that Winston's attention to Phoebe might be unhealthy. She complained about innocent things, such as his dressing Phoebe in Fiona's clothes and taking pictures of her feet. After that, Winston only took pictures of Phoebe when she was dropped off at his office after her ballet lessons.

"Does your sister have an alibi for the night your wife was murdered?"

Winston leaped to his feet. He smacked his palms against the desk and leaned forward. "My sister had nothing to do with my wife's death. She isn't a murderer."

"Just exploring the possibilities, Doc." Beveridge grinned, baring his sharp teeth. "Isn't that what you asked us to do?"

Winston sat down, but his blood pressure continued to rise. He sucked on the peppermint and tried to appear calm.

"We have two partial prints that are questionable. One is from a Mexican, Ramos Rodriquez. Do you know him?"

Winston waved his hand dismissively. "He did some yard work for me."

"We checked with his employer, ABC Landscaping. The company has no record of services to your address."

"Ramos is one of my patients. He needed surgery because his hallux was severely deformed and twisted into his second digit."

Beveridge frowned. "Hallux?"

"The big toe." Winston suppressed a grin. The detective wasn't as smart as he thought he was. "Ramos couldn't afford to pay, so I asked him to trim some bushes in exchange for my fee. If his prints were found in my house, he probably came in for a drink or to leave a bill. The man has seven kids. I don't think he needs another."

"Do you often waive your fee in exchange for services?" Rollo asked.

"It's not unusual, especially if the patient's feet are in bad shape."

Winston noticed the detective didn't write anything in his notebook. "The other print might belong to a Melana Elam. Do you know her?"

"Melana Elam. The name sounds familiar. Where were her prints found?"

"A partial print was found on a coffee mug in the dishwasher," Rollo said.

"Maybe she's one of the housecleaners. We used Tidy Maids. Or she could be one of my patients. Sometimes they come to my house. I don't remember the names of all of my patients. Check with my receptionist."

"We haven't located Miss Elam, but we contacted her mother in Indiana. She said her daughter is out of the country."

Winston's eyebrows rose. "Then she couldn't have been drinking coffee in my house."

But Winston wasn't as sure as he sounded. What if Melana Elam had been in the guest room? What if she was the one who picked up

Phoebe? What if she had taken Phoebe out of the country?

His head started to throb.

The detectives and his partner stood.

"What about the reward I offered?" Winston asked. "Has that turned up anything?"

Beveridge grunted. "As you recall, we advised you not to offer twenty thousand dollars. A hefty reward only brings out more unreliable witnesses and hampers the investigation." The detective flashed a toothy grin. "Of course, that might be what you wanted."

Winston pointed his perfectly manicured finger at the detective. "What I want," he said, his voice shaking from trying to keep from shouting, "is for you to do your job. Find my daughter and bring her home."

Beveridge scowled and slapped his notebook shut. "Don't forget the little matter of your wife's murder." He turned and walked out the door.

Rollo, however, paused in the doorway. "I know you want to find your daughter. Believe me, we're trying. If you need anything, just call." He slipped his personal card out of his pocket and handed it to Winston.

As soon as they left, Winston picked up the phone and dialed his sister. He wanted to warn her that the police might be questioning her about an alibi for the night of Chrissy's accident. When he hung up, he went over the information again. Someone had taken the gun. Someone had erased the fingerprints from the bedrooms. What was the name of the woman the detective had asked about? Melana Elam. He was sure he had heard or seen that name. But where? Was she the mystery woman who picked up Phoebe? Had she been in his house that night?

If she'd witnessed Christine's death, he had to find her before the police did. He had to make sure she wouldn't tell anyone.

He swiveled the chair to his computer, clicked on the Internet, and typed in the name. Melana Elam.

Chapter Twenty-Four

Jason would be coming the week before Memorial Day, and Ace expected the time to drag. But he was busy in the fields with the spring planting, and checking on Miss May.

Last week, he'd driven Miss May to the lawyer's office. "I don't want anyone knowing I've written my nephew out of the will. He's got himself a new girlfriend, and she's too citified to come down here even for a visit. Mark my words, she'll go through his money and jilt him for a richer man."

Ace witnessed the new will, bequeathing her estate to the town to build a library. The current library was a two-story house in need of repairs.

"I worked in that building for nearly sixty years and complained about it every day. Why, I almost wish I could live another sixty years just to see all the enjoyment the town will get from the library."

"Why don't you donate the money now?" Ace suggested. "You'd be able to watch it being built and even use it."

"Nope. I don't want anyone snooping into my business, especially that nephew." Ace saw the set of her jaw and knew her mind was made up.

Ace also knew she had a good heart, but she didn't show it often and to most of the town she was a crotchety old maid.

He'd won Miss May over with patience. Hopefully, he'd be able to do the same with Quinn. As often as he could, he went over to see her and Taylor. They had become a part of his life. He couldn't go through the day without thinking about them and walking over to chat.

The next time it rained and he couldn't get in the field, he asked Taylor and Quinn to go with him to the animal hospital. Taylor soothed the puppies, talking to them softly while the vet gave them their shots. When Taylor was next scheduled for her eye exam, she went, although Quinn said Taylor had clung to Quinn's hand the whole time.

A few days later, Ace was sitting on a stool in the machine shed, repairing his chain saw when Taylor and Quinn walked in. "Guess who?" Taylor said, running over to him.

Ace looked up from the saw and did an exaggerated double take at Taylor wearing glasses. "Well, it sounds like Taylor, but this pretty girl with spectacles can't be Taylor."

Taylor put her hand over her mouth and giggled. "I told you he wouldn't recognize me, Mommy."

When Taylor skipped off to play with the puppies, Ace shot Quinn a quizzical glance. "You didn't tell me Taylor needed glasses." Ace expected Quinn to be upset about Taylor's eye sight, but she was grinning.

The next week, Ace took Quinn and Taylor to the annual Hickory Hills Community Sale. He enjoyed watching Quinn's excitement over her five-dollar winning bid on a bicycle for Taylor. Quinn and Ace began teaching Taylor to ride. She learned to balance better than she learned to brake. The second day on the bike, she rode into a tree.

Ace hurried over and scooped her up. She wrapped her arms tightly around his neck and sobbed. When she stopped crying, she wiped her tear-stained cheeks and tried to smile. One tooth was gone, and the other was so loose, Quinn pulled it. Taylor's brave, toothless smile captured his heart.

After more than two months, she wasn't the skittish little waif he'd met at the food pantry. She was different. Not just the glasses, missing teeth, and curly hair, but fuller cheeks and a healthy glow. And the eyes behind her glasses didn't look as sad, but often twinkled—sometimes with mischief.

Before they'd moved here, he'd just been making it through the day, but Quinn and Taylor had brought him a new joy and he felt alive again. He thought about the summer ahead, the four of them fishing, swimming in the lake, and going to ball games. And he hoped there would be time for him to be alone with Quinn. He had wooed her cautiously, afraid to pressure her. He'd felt like a teenager, holding hands and kissing goodnight at the door. He wanted so much more, like confidence into her life.

The night before Ace was to leave for Chicago to pick up Jason, he walked over to Quinn's for supper. She had promised to cook up the mess of blue gill they'd caught in the lake, and he wanted to hear about Taylor's visit with Doc Morgan.

"So how was the physical?" Ace asked as he looked at Taylor lying on the couch.

Taylor pointed to her arm, which sported a smiley-face bandage. "I got my shots."

"Shots? How many did you get?"

Taylor held up five fingers.

Ace patted her curly hair. "Good girl."

"I cried–just a little."

He wondered how Jason had done two years ago with his shots and felt that familiar stab of longing. "I didn't realize they gave all five shots at once. I'm proud of you."

With one finger, Taylor pushed up her glasses and gave him a toothless grin.

Ace walked into the kitchen, and Quinn handed him a glass of sweet tea. Leaning against the counter, he took a sip and watched the efficient way she worked. Her hands practically danced as she chopped up the cabbage with a Ginsu knife. She coated the fish by shaking them in a plastic bag with cornmeal and quickly whisked up a batch of hush puppies. The fish fillets were light and crispy, just the way he liked them, and the spicy hush puppies and tangy cole slaw were delicious.

A man could get used to cooking like this. But it was more than the tasty food. All the bright, stainless steel appliances and expensive fixtures he'd installed in his own house were shadowed by the warmth of this outdated kitchen with its chipped cast iron sink and old gas cook stove. Quinn was the warmth and light. Each time he returned to his own empty house he felt a new loneliness.

After supper, he lingered longer than usual, staying until Taylor was asleep. Quinn walked him to the door, and they stood outside on the landing, listening to the music of the tree frogs. A small slant of light from the open door fell on Quinn, highlighting her soft beauty.

"I'll miss you," she said, leaning back against the door jam.

He took her hand. "I'll only be gone four days." Already he was missing her. "I'm staying with P.R. He wants to go over some legal stuff about the custody. I'm not looking forward to meeting with Stephanie."

"Maybe it won't be pleasant, but Jason needs to be with you."

"And I need him." The emotion of finally being able to be with his son made the words catch in his throat.

Quinn squeezed his hand. "I know."

He brought her hand to his lips and kissed it. "Quinn, I don't think I would have made it through all those days without you."

"You're a good father, Ace. You've been wonderful with Taylor."

"I need to talk to you about something." He dropped her hand. "Jason and I'll have a lot of catching up to do."

"I know Jason comes first."

"It's not about being first. I have to rebuild our relationship." He paused as if struggling to find the right words. "I-I might not be able to spend as much time with you and Taylor as I'd like."

She looked down, but not before he saw her smile fade. "We'll be fine."

He put his finger under her chin and lifted it. "Quinn, I'm not saying good-bye." He didn't want to leave without letting Quinn know how he felt, but he wasn't good with words. So he put his hands on her trim waist and drew her to him. She slipped her arms around his neck. Standing there together felt so right.

When he looked into her brown eyes, he wondered if she felt the connection. He moved his hands slowly up her back and felt it tense. He made small soothing circles with his fingers, pressing firmly, working across her shoulders. "Better?"

"M-m-m." She relaxed in his arms.

He lowered his head and moved his mouth to her ear. "Quinn." He whispered her name and threaded his fingers through her silky hair.

Her fingers slid up the nape of his neck, sending shivers down his back. He brushed his lips across her face and playfully nibbled around her mouth. When he felt her warm breath, he touched her lips in a slow, gentle caress, the way he usually kissed her goodnight. But this time his lips wouldn't stop. He was drawn in by her scent and the warmth of her body pressed against his. He wanted to claim her, make sure she knew how he felt. Make sure she knew he would always be there for her and Taylor.

The kiss became urgent, and Quinn didn't pull away. She was lost in the safety of his strong arms and the feel of his mouth on hers. She relaxed, letting the barriers she'd built between them slip away. She remembered another time when she and Ace had parted. He was leaving for college, and she was returning home. They had both promised that it wouldn't be good-bye. But it had been.

Ace said this wasn't good-bye. He was just leaving for a few days. But when he lifted his lips from hers, it felt like good-bye.

"Ace?" She said his name with such longing that he leaned in and kissed her again. His lips found new pleasure in hers—not the sweetness that he usually felt, but a yearning that made his entire body want to respond.

She was a part of him. Without her, his heart wasn't whole. Tomorrow, he would talk to P.R. But right now he didn't care about anything except the woman in his arms. Nothing else mattered.

He'd waited since he was eighteen to feel this way about a woman again. No matter what P. R. found out, nothing was going to keep him away from her.

Nothing.

Chapter Twenty-Five

Saturday morning, Quinn lay in bed, smiling. The four days without Ace had been long and lonely, but today he was coming home. *Orreshii, I'm happy.* She stretched out languidly, and her cheeks flushed as she remembered the feel of his lips and the possessive way he'd held her. It was like turning back time and believing in love again.

The birds outside her window were chirping, matching the song in her heart. She was in love and hoped Ace felt the same. She had missed him so much. During the day, she'd stayed busy—weeding the garden, working at the food pantry, and leading another tour for Raven. Then she'd found some used cans of paint in the barn to spruce up Taylor's room. Taylor chose a different color for each wall—pink, blue, purple, and white. Quinn wasn't sure about the results until she looked over and saw Taylor's nose smudged with paint and a wide grin on her face. Then Quinn knew the walls were perfect.

Quinn had filled the days, but the nights were empty. Ace hadn't said he would call, but she'd expected it. The first night she snuggled under the sheets with her cell. When it didn't ring, she fell into a fitful sleep and was awakened by the recurring nightmares of Chrissy's death. Each night was the same, and when she woke, she was depressed and edgy.

Quinn was frightened by how easily she'd given her heart to Ace. After Truman left her at the altar, she promised herself she'd never let another man hurt her like that again. But Ace wasn't Truman. Ace wouldn't walk away and leave her.

Taylor woke early, excited to get her puppy and meet Jason. After breakfast they made giggle cookies, but the morning dragged into the afternoon. When Ace didn't call, Quinn worked herself into a frenzy. What if he'd wrecked his truck? What if Ace and Stephanie had reconciled? What if he'd found out she was Laney? What if he knew she'd kidnapped Taylor? What if...? A hundred scenarios played out in her mind.

Finally, at three, the phone rang.

She heard Ace's voice and blurted out her fears. "Are you okay? Is Jason with you? Did something happen?"

A long silence dragged on before Ace answered, "We're fine."

Relieved, Quinn collapsed into a kitchen chair. "I was so worried. When I didn't hear from you..." She'd promised herself she wouldn't tell him that she'd expected him to call. "Well, you're back. How's Jason? When can I meet him?"

Another long pause.

"Ace?"

"Now that Jason's here, like I said, I'll be spending time with him."

She frowned. Was Ace saying he wouldn't have *any* time for her and Taylor? His voice sounded distant and cold.

Taylor was standing next to her. "Let me talk to Ace. Please, please, I want my puppy today."

"All right." Quinn handed Taylor the phone.

Quinn's mind reeled. She listened to Taylor, but she mostly nodded, and Quinn couldn't piece together the conversation. When Taylor returned the phone, Ace had hung up.

Taylor was beaming. "Ace said I could come over and get my puppy now." She raced toward the door.

"Slow down. I have to comb my hair."

"Oh! He said you don't have to come. He's taking me and Jason out for pizza."

Quinn frowned. "Are you sure he said I shouldn't come?"

"He asked if I was big enough to pick out the puppy myself. And I am. So he told me to come over—alone—and we'd go for pizza."

So Quinn hadn't imagined his coldness. Something was wrong.

She walked Taylor to the edge of the hickory trees and waited until she disappeared into Ace's house. Then Quinn turned and stumbled to the loft. She couldn't hold back the tears.

Ace must have found out she was Laney. Did he feel like she had tricked him? Is that why he didn't want to see her? Maybe he hadn't found out. He'd called her Quinn. Oh, why had she been so naïve? How could she have believed Ace cared about her? He hadn't even asked her out on a date. But he'd spent time with her, kissed her. She hadn't imagined his passion.

Something had happened in Chicago, but what? Had Stephanie triggered his reaction? If he and Stephanie had argued, maybe Ace was transferring his resentment to Quinn. He'd done that before.

Quinn just needed to show Ace he was important to her and that she wasn't like Stephanie. Taylor said Ace would bring her home. She could talk to him, face to face, and straighten everything out.

* * * *

It was after six when Quinn spotted Taylor walking out of the hickory grove. She was carrying her puppy. Ace and Jason trailed behind.

Quinn sprinted down the stairs and waited at the bottom of the steps.

When Taylor saw Quinn, she tried to run. "Look, Mommy." The golden retriever wiggling in Taylor's arms was almost too big for her to carry. "I got my puppy, just the one I wanted."

Quinn knew the shy little runt was Taylor's favorite. Pushing away her fears, Quinn bent down and ran her fingers through the puppy's feathery, blond hair. "Have you picked a name?" Taylor had changed the name daily.

"Gogo."

The name fit. *Go* was Japanese for the number five, and the puppy was the fifth born. Plus she was always on the go. "Well, Gogo, welcome to your new home."

The puppy licked Quinn's hand. She laughed and then shifted her attention to Jason. He looked so much like Ace as a boy—same wiry arms and legs, same dark hair, except Jason's was straight, not wavy. But most of all it was his eyes, blue and serious.

Quinn glanced from Jason to Ace. He didn't meet her gaze.

Taylor tugged on Quinn's arm. "Can I show Jason my room and the doggy bed we made?"

"If it's all right with his dad."

Jason stared up at Ace for approval. Quinn knew how much Ace needed his son. Now she saw the longing in Jason, too.

When Ace nodded, Taylor and Jason scampered up the stairs. As the door banged behind them, Quinn turned to Ace and searched his face. The silence between them thickened. She forced herself to step closer. He smelled earthy, and she felt safe with him near.

She reached over and wrapped her arms around his neck. "I missed you."

His body stiffened, and he stepped back. "Don't." He unclasped her fingers.

She blinked up at him, trying to hide her hurt. "Don't what?"

"Don't bat those long lashes at me and think everything will be fine. I'm not a fool."

"What is it? What's wrong?"

His blue eyes bore into her. "Do you have anything you want to tell me?"

Did he know? Was he going to confront her? She remained silent.

"Then I guess we don't have anything to say to each other."

"Ace?" She reached over and touched his arm. "Don't shut me out without telling me why."

He stared at her hand on his arm. A strange expression flicked over his face. "Okay. Answer one question."

"All right."

"Tell me your name. Your *real* name."

Her hand slid off his arm, and she lowered her head. Oh God, he knew. Somehow he'd found out she wasn't Quincy Matthews.

"Did she put you up to this?" Ace asked.

"Who?"

"Stephanie. Did she convince you to move here, find out things to use against me in court?"

Quinn's head jerked up. "What are you talking about?"

His face reddened with anger. "Someone told Stephanie about the night you shot me." Ace's hand instinctively moved to his shoulder. "She'll use anything to hold onto Jason."

How could he believe she'd betray him? Couldn't he see how much she cared about him? "You're making a mistake. I wouldn't help anyone take your son from you."

"Oh, I've made plenty of mistakes. I let you into my life and cared about you. I have myself to blame for that."

Quinn only heard the words *he cared about her*. "We can work this out, Ace. Whatever you think I've done, I can explain."

"Aren't you listening? There is no *we.*"

"But you said…"

"I said I made a mistake. I won't do it again."

She saw the hard, set of his jaw and heard the barely controlled anger. This wasn't a little misunderstanding. "Maybe if we talked, we can figure this out."

"So you can tell more lies." He raked his hands through his hair. "You probably think you're clever. But a few things didn't ring true, so I had you checked out."

Her heart thudded. "You what?"

"I wanted to find out what you're hiding."

Her whole body went rigid. "You had no right to do that."

"Don't use that indignant tone with me. You're the one who breezed into town using a phony name."

Quinn was frantic. "Who else knows? The sheriff? Did you have Ben check me out?"

"I'm not answering your questions until you answer mine."

She lunged at him, pounding her fist against his hard chest. "Ace, I'm not playing games. Tell me. Who else knows?"

He grabbed her wrists and held them. "That's the difference between you and me, Lady. I've never been playing games."

Quinn wrestled to get free, but Ace held on. He didn't care how angry he made her. He deserved answers, and he was going to get them. But then he looked into her eyes and saw fear. Real fear. She looked terrified. Trapped, like a helpless doe.

135

"Ace, please, you have to tell me. If you ever cared about me, about Taylor, you have to tell me who knows. Did you have the police do a background check?"

He shook his head, trying to figure out why, after all the lies, he still wanted to believe her. When P.R. handed him the report, he felt betrayed. He convinced himself he wanted nothing to do with her. Then this morning when he stumbled into the kitchen to make coffee, he remembered her being there, how she'd warmed his house with her presence. He didn't want to go back to an empty life. Even now as she pounded on his chest, all he wanted to do was take her in his arms.

She was almost hysterical. "Ace, I'll do anything. Just tell me, who else knows?"

"P.R. He checked you out. He's the only one who knows."

She sagged against him, and he gave in, wrapping his arms around her. His voice softened. "This can stay between us. Just tell me who you are and why you're hiding."

She lifted her head from his chest. "Please Ace, leave it alone. I can't tell you."

He remembered the fear in Taylor's eyes when she first came here. "You can trust me. Is someone trying to hurt you or Taylor?"

He hadn't wanted to believe P.R. when he suggested that Quinn might be working for Stephanie, but why wouldn't she tell him who she was? "You don't need to handle this alone."

"I can't let you get involved."

His frustration built. "Can't or won't?"

She reached up and let her hand graze his cheek. "It's better if you don't know."

He took her hand. "I'll help you."

"I know." She slipped her hand from his. "But I can't let you. You have no idea what you've already done. The danger you've put us in."

"You're not in the witness protection program. I asked P.R. He said the government would never supply such a sloppy cover story. If you were supposed to be a teacher in Japan, you'd have a passport and teaching certificate. Just tell me your name."

"Why does it matter? I'm the same person I was last week."

"And who was that? Which part of you was real and which part was an act?"

When she didn't answer, he released her. "Stephanie lied to me. I won't go through that again. Trust me. Tell me the truth."

She placed her hand over her heart as if she were swearing an oath. "I do trust you. And the way I feel about you isn't a lie. I'm not like Stephanie. I would never take your son away from you."

"Prove it. Tell me who you are."

She opened her mouth. If the police found her and knew Ace had helped, he would be an accomplice. Quinn understood what it was to lose a child. She couldn't do that to Ace.

"I'm doing this for you. Telling you might endanger your custody case."

Was that true or another lie? "How could your trouble affect my custody of Jason?"

"What I'm involved in is more than a few unpaid parking tickets."

"I can't believe you embezzled money or robbed a bank or killed someone."

She raised her chin. "What if I did?"

He stared at her in disbelief. Her eyes strayed from his. He couldn't believe she was capable of committing any of those crimes. But she had pulled him in again and made him care. He needed to walk away while he still could. "Since you won't be truthful with me, I can't let Jason come over here again. Taylor is welcome at our house."

"Ace, that isn't fair."

"Fair? I'm not even sure you know the meaning of the word."

"Don't do this. Please, Ace."

He put his foot on the bottom step and paused. He looked over his shoulder at her. "You know how to stop me."

She stared at him, pleading.

He waited.

When she remained silent, he turned and vaulted up the stairs, two at a time, opened the door, and called, "Jason, time to go."

Jason came out and scampered down the stairs. "Bye," he said, waving to Quinn.

Quinn didn't trust her voice. She lifted her hand and waved back.

But Ace didn't pause. He just kept walking, down the stairs and away from her. She watched him and Jason, staring at their backs, as they disappeared into the trees. Quinn knew she'd lost him.

She folded her arms across herself to keep from coming undone. One thought kept her from unraveling. She had lost Ace, but she would not be the reason Ace lost his son.

Chapter Twenty-Six

Winston tapped his manicured fingernails on the round, wooden table in the seedy bar. Sitting across from him was Melana Elam's mother, Bonnie, who was pouring out her life story. The only other customer was bellied up to the bar, coddling his can of beer and bragging to the bartender about winning the lottery. The place had been turned into a private club so patrons could still smoke. Even in the afternoon, the air was hazy and smelled of greasy burgers and stale beer. Music drifted from the corner where a black musician sat in a chair propped up against the cracked plastered wall. His large hands held a harmonica that seemed to float effortlessly across his wide mouth as he warbled out the blues. The melancholy music was the perfect background for Bonnie Elam to whine about her sorry life.

The trip from Detroit to this Indianapolis joint called the Slippery-something had been a wash. After Detectives Beveridge and Rollo came to his office about the fingerprints, Winston had tried to find information about Melana Elam and why her name sounded familiar.

Then he remembered the detectives said they'd contacted her mother, so Winston phoned Detective Rollo and asked where Melana's mother lived. At first, Rollo was reluctant to give out any information, but as Winston talked about missing his daughter, they connected as fathers and Rollo told him Bonnie Elam lived in Indianapolis. The Internet had provided the contact information.

Winston popped another peppermint into his mouth and listened as Bonnie droned on about how unfair life had been and how much she'd sacrificed to raise a daughter alone. But she had not answered Winston's questions. He wanted to know if the partial fingerprint found in his house could be her daughter's. And if so, why would Melana have been in his house in Detroit?

"Like I told the cops, Laney's not a murderer. I raised her right. Made sure she went to church, studied hard, and made something of her life. She never was in trouble with the law. Her and Chrissy were just like that." She crossed her fingers and held them up.

So Christine knew Melana Elam. They had been friends.

Most of Bonnie's red lipstick had rubbed off on the Menthol Kools overflowing in the ashtray. Winston guessed Bonnie was in her fifties. Alcohol and hard living had sapped most of her luster. Dark bronze hair spiked from her head and made her face look sharp. Her eyebrows had been completely shaved off, replaced by penciled-in brown arches. Watching them move up and down was disconcerting, so he focused on the soft cleavage spilling out of her low-cut dress. Too bad he couldn't see her feet, but he had only glimpsed her glittery red stilettos hidden beneath the table.

"When was the last time you saw your daughter?" Winston asked.

"A few years. Like I told the other guys, she's in Japan."

Bonnie was not a casual drinker. Hard-core would be his guess, by the way she tossed back the Canadian Club he kept buying. Her brown eyes were no longer as clear as the whiskey, but he didn't mind paying for the alcohol if it loosened her tongue and made her more truthful.

"Do you have an address or phone number for your daughter?"

"Do I look like I can afford to visit Japan or pick up the phone and call? Laney contacts me a few times a year." She waved the smoke from the cigarette away from her face and into his. "The last time was Christmas Day. She didn't mention returning. No reason for her to come back. Not after the way she blew her engagement to that rich boyfriend."

Bonnie lifted her red vinyl bag onto the table and rummaged through it. Winston assumed she was looking for another package of cigarettes. Instead, she pulled out a rumpled newspaper clipping, put it on the table, and smoothed it out with her fingers.

"Laney's a looker. Takes after me." Bonnie wet her lips and gave him what she probably thought was a photogenic smile. "Here's her picture. See for yourself."

Winston almost spit out the mineral water he'd been sipping. "Picture?"

Bonnie must not have been as drunk as he thought because as soon as she noticed his reaction, she stuffed the picture back into her purse. "I'm sure you're not interested in seeing that old thing."

Winston straightened his shoulders. "Yes. Yes I am."

Bonnie lit another Kool, tilted her head back, and inhaled. She blew out a series of smoke rings, and as she watched them float away, her arm stretched across the table, and her palm turned up. "I might be persuaded to show it to you."

Money? Was she asking him for money?

Winston wasn't sure and didn't want to insult her. He reached into his gray sports coat and pulled out his wallet. He flipped through the tens and twenties and slipped out a fifty. When he placed the bill in her hand, it quickly disappeared into her purse. She was slower removing the picture and sliding it across the table.

The wrinkled newspaper clipping was more than five years old, and in the dimly lit bar, the faces were difficult to see. It was an engagement announcement of Melana Elam to Truman Regal III. The woman in the paper had thick curly hair and a stiff smile. Winston didn't think her face resembled the police sketch of the woman who picked up Phoebe. "Mind if I make a copy and send this back to you?"

"I don't want to lose it. It's the only picture I have of my daughter."

The engagement announcement would be archived in the *Indianapolis Star*, but Winston didn't want to waste time. He plucked a hundred out of his wallet, and her penciled eyebrows shot up.

"Don't know why I need that old picture. I know what my baby looks like. 'Course the last time I saw her, she was knocked up. Came waddling in, round as a barrel, and about eight months pregnant. She'd lost her job, been evicted from her apartment, and needed a place to stay. Just like always, she came begging to me. Only this time she expected me to provide for her *and* a squalling baby."

Winston put his finger on the picture and pointed to the man. "What about this Truman?"

Bonnie took a drag on her cigarette. "True man. That's a laugh. He never married her. Why should he? He'd already sampled the goods, if you know what I mean."

Winston nodded, wondering if the former fiancé would have additional information about Melana.

"I was dried out back then. Hadn't had a drink in more than ten months. The year before, I'd been down on my luck and asked Laney for a loan. That was when she had a good job and a rich boyfriend. I figured she owed me for all those years I'd put food on the table and clothes on her back.

"But my own kid wouldn't give me a dime. She checked me into rehab. Real nice place, not one of those charity dumps. She could've saved herself a bundle if she'd given me half the money she spent. I'd been in rehab before, back when Laney was about five. That time I stayed sober almost two years. Then the accident happened. Life was too hard without my husband. He was the only person I ever loved."

"But you still had your daughter?"

She seemed to consider the question, but didn't answer. "When I found out Laney was pregnant, I told her the best thing she could do was give up the baby. Lots of people willing to pay a hefty price for a baby. More than ten thousand dollars a pound for a white infant. Hers was a girl, so the money might have been less."

Bonnie downed the last of her whiskey.

"I tried being a surrogate once. Pays good. Lounge around for nine months, pop a kid, and get a golden egg. Just my luck though, I couldn't get pregnant again."

The musician stopped playing the harmonica, and a different kind of emptiness floated through the bar. Bonnie's brown eyes blurred. Then she held up her empty glass and raised her eyebrows. Winston waggled his finger at the bartender to bring another whiskey and water. He was willing to buy the whole bottle if she kept talking about her daughter. "So did Laney give up the baby?"

Her palm opened again. Winston didn't hesitate. He slipped her another hundred. Bonnie's eyes widened, and the money disappeared into her purse.

She didn't answer until after the bartender delivered her whiskey. Then she took a long drink before she answered. "Don't know. I told her she couldn't stay with me. I never saw her kid. Back then, I had a loft in the city, a steady job, and a boyfriend. I wasn't letting Laney move in and mess all that up."

This time Winston stretched his hand out, palm up. "Seems like money can't buy what it used to."

She reached over and ran her sharp fingernail in a slow circle over the palm of his hand with just the right amount of pressure to make him wonder what her feet looked like.

"My guess is, she kept the baby. Laney never listened to me. Even as a kid, she had this stubborn streak. Wanted to do everything herself. Got that from her grandma—on her daddy's side. That old bat was always trying to take Laney away from me. Said I wasn't mother material."

Winston leaned back in his chair, but kept his hand on the table. "You think she might have gone to this grandma for help?"

Bonnie smirked. "No way. After Laney spent the summers with her, she'd come back all snippy, and I'd have to straighten her out, if you know what I mean."

Winston removed his hand and nodded.

"I got tired of her sassy ways. When she was sixteen, she started talking about living with her grandma, so I told her the witch had died. Do you believe it? Laney cried for weeks." Bonnie took another drink. "After that, we moved around a lot, and I made sure the old crow never knew where we were."

"Where did this grandma live?"

Bonnie's palm went out again then slid back before he pulled out another bill. "You've been real kind, if you know what I mean." Bonnie crushed the butt of her Kool into the ashtray with the other filters. "She lived in some hick town in southern Illinois. I don't remember the name. I tried to forget everything about it."

Winston reached into his jacket and pulled out a business card. "If you happen to remember the town, I'll make it worth your while. Call—collect, of course."

"Won't do no good. The woman's dead. Passed away last winter. Some lawyer fellow came looking for Laney. I still had her Christmas card, so I gave him that address."

"What did the lawyer want?"

"Said Laney was beneficiary in the old lady's will. What a joke. Those folks were poorer than sharecroppers. They lived in a barn and tore up their overalls and braided them into rugs. Probably couldn't scrape together enough money for the burial." Bonnie picked up his business card and squinted at it. "Says here you're a podiatrist. Isn't that one of them foot doctors?"

Winston nodded and checked his wrist watch. If he started home now, he'd be in Detroit tonight. He pushed back his chair and rose. Bonnie kicked off one of her stilettos and propped her leg on an empty chair. "A guy once told me I had beautiful feet." She rolled her knee-high nylon down her leg and slid it off. "You see a lot of feet. What do you think?"

He was no longer surprised when people took off their shoes to show him their feet. It happened at grocery stores, restaurants, and even on the street. He always gave their feet a perfunctory glance and told them to call his office and make an appointment. But when Bonnie raised her leg onto the table and wiggled her toes, Winston's mouth dropped open, and he fell back into his chair.

The shape of her foot was familiar. The longest toe was not the hallux, but the second digit, a genetic trait, sometimes called Morton's toe.

He experienced an uncontrollable urge to touch her foot and moved his hand across the table. "May I?"

She didn't protest when he slid his hand under her foot and lifted it to examine. He almost gasped. The foot in his hand was longer and wider, but the shape was the same as Phoebe's. He cupped his palm under her heel while his other hand caressed her toes. "Beautiful," he said.

He stared down at her toes and remembered why Melana Elam's name seemed familiar. When his lawyer had drawn up the adoption paper to make Phoebe legally his daughter, Chrissy had shown him a copy of the previous adoption. The signature relinquishing parental rights was Melana Grace Elam.

Like cherries in a slot machine, all the pieces *cha-chinged* into a row. Jackpot. Melana was Phoebe's biological mother.

Oh my god. What if Melana had returned to the U.S. to collect her inheritance and had stopped to see her daughter? Could she have been in the house the night Chrissy died? Or did Melana come the following day and discover Chrissy's body?

Perspiration popped onto his forehead. "This grandma, do you remember her name?"

Bonnie leaned back and closed her eyes. "Don't stop. That feels...divine."

"I can give you a foot massage you'll never forget."

She practically purred as she peered at him through heavy-lidded eyes.

"Try to remember the name of the grandma." He pulled a monogrammed handkerchief from his sports coat and dabbed his forehead.

"Grandma Elam. That's what everyone called her. If you really want to know, I might be able to find my husband's death certificate." She batted her long lashes and gave him a sultry look. "Of course, you'd have to come back to my place."

Winston folded the handkerchief. The invitation was perfect, especially if Bonnie were to have a few more drinks and pass out. Then he could search her apartment and have time to enjoy every single facet of her feet.

He lifted his finger to the bartender. "Bring me the tab and a bottle to go."

Chapter Twenty-Seven

The days following Ace's return from Chicago, Quinn didn't feel like weeding or cooking or reading. She didn't want to leave Hickory Hills, but the idea flitted through her mind. How could she bear to live this close to Ace and not be part of his life?

She wondered how much he'd told his family. When Summer phoned in the middle of the week and asked what food she was taking to Ace's cookout on Memorial Day, Quinn realized he hadn't said anything.

She took a deep breath. "I'm not going."

Summer sounded surprised. "Why not?"

"Ace and I aren't...seeing each other." Saying it aloud made fresh tears sprang to Quinn's eyes.

"That explains last night. Ace and Jason were here for supper. Ace barely said two civil words." Quinn heard an edge in Summer's voice. "He's waited all year to spend time with his son. He doesn't need relationship issues now. Whatever's going on, Quinn, fix it."

"I can't."

Before Summer hung up, Quinn asked for P.R.'s phone number. "For a legal problem," she hastily added. She certainly didn't want Summer to think she was interested in her brother.

Summer gave her the number. "You can talk to him when he comes down this weekend for Memorial Day."

Quinn couldn't wait. She phoned P.R. the next day. He wasn't anxious to be her lawyer. "Ace is my client and almost family."

"How much is your retainer?"

146

The amount he quoted was a big chunk of her savings, but P.R. already knew too much. What if he told Summer or Belle, and then Ben found out. He was the county sheriff. "I'll wire you the money."

"I can refer you to someone else."

"P.R., you've already started investigating me."

"All I know is that a Quincy Matthews age twenty-nine doesn't exist. We can discuss it this weekend."

"It can't wait. Besides, I don't want to jeopardize Ace's custody case."

P.R. no longer sounded patronizing. "How does this affect Ace?"

"If Stephanie's lawyers dig into his personal life, they might find out about me. I don't want you to be blindsided in court."

P.R. finally agreed to accept the retainer.

* * * *

Friday, Quinn left Taylor with Summer and drove to Centralia to pick up P.R. from the train station. During the drive to Hickory Hills, Quinn related everything. How she'd flown back from Japan. How Chrissy was afraid of her husband. How they'd planned to start new lives.

P.R. scribbled notes onto his yellow legal pad as Quinn continued telling him about seeing Winston shoot Chrissy, hiding in the closet, and the possibility the police might think she killed Chrissy.

When she finished, P.R. read his notes back to make sure the details were accurate. "First, we need to find out if you've been charged with anything. But either way, I don't think this will affect Ace's custody."

"You're my lawyer, so you can't repeat what I'm about to tell you, right?"

"Client confidentiality," he assured her.

Quinn took a deep breath. "Taylor's not legally my daughter."

"What?" P.R.'s pen dropped to the floor of the car. He ducked under the dash, distracting her. "Whose daughter is she?"

Quinn's heart raced. She couldn't concentrate on driving. She steered to the side of the road and threw the car into park. Turning, she faced P.R. "Taylor's real name is Phoebe Prescott. Legally, she was Chrissy's daughter."

P.R.'s head jerked up. "You kidnapped Taylor?"

"Winston Prescott is Chrissy's second husband. Her first husband, Max, died two years ago. When Chrissy married Winston, he adopted Taylor." Her hands balled into fists. "Winston is a murderer. He can't be allowed to have custody."

"I know you don't want the man who killed Chrissy to have her daughter, but the authorities should handle this. They'll protect Taylor."

Quinn stiffened her back. "I'll protect Taylor." She had kept the secret for so long, she could barely force out the truth. "Taylor's my child. I'm her biological mother."

P.R. stopped writing. "Could you repeat that?"

The second time, Quinn's voice was stronger, and P.R. seemed prepared. "If you signed away your maternal rights, in the eyes of the law, you're not her mother."

"I know. But in my heart I am."

"Quinn, the law is strict about parents without custodial rights abducting their children."

"But you can help, can't you?"

"I'll try." P. R. flipped his phone open. "Who else knows?"

"No one. Even Taylor doesn't know she's adopted."

"What about Ace?"

"I haven't told him."

"Good. Keep it that way."

Quinn leaned back against the seat. "Could you at least tell Ace you've advised me not to confide in him?"

"Are you kidding? If Ace knew I had information about you, he wouldn't give a whit about client confidentiality."

* * * *

Since Quinn wasn't going to Ace's Memorial Day party, Raven asked her to lead the tour of the Old Slave House. In return, she would take Taylor to the cookout. At the time, the switch sounded like a good idea. Taylor could go to the party, and Quinn would have a reason to stay away. But now, as Quinn stood on the sidewalk and stared up at the Old Slave House, a three-story Greek Revival on top of the grassy hill, she shuddered.

Telling herself she was being childish, she gripped her clipboard of notes and walked through the white-washed picket fence leading to the front yard. The afternoon sun was warm, and her gauzy blouse and broomcorn skirt clung to her arms and legs. She stopped next to a replica of the Liberty Bell on top of a tall post. Chained to the base were leg shackles. The thick forged iron rings sent a cold chill through her.

Quinn had conducted tours of the art-deco theater and the Carnegie library, but today was her first time to lead a group through the Old Slave House. The people on the other tours had been chatty. The thirteen people here, milling around the house, were subdued, almost like mourners at a wake.

Quinn climbed the porch stairs and stepped onto a wide veranda supported by twelve Grecian columns. Staring down at the clipboard in her hand, she took a few minutes to review the facts before she began. "I'm Quincy Matthews, and I'll be your tour guide. The house in front of you, sometimes called the Old Slave House, was built from 1834-1838 by Mr. Crenshaw, who owned 300,000 acres. Slavery was not legal in the state, but the Illinois Constitution allowed slaves to be leased as laborers. So in 1830, Crenshaw leased 746 slaves from Kentucky to work in his salt mines."

Quinn stepped aside so people could take pictures of the red clapboard white-trimmed house.

"Mr. Crenshaw called the house Hickory Hills Plantation. He, his wife, and five children lived on the first two floors. On the third floor behind the peaked dormer was where the slaves were kept."

Quinn led the group to the back of the house and pointed out where wagons had brought in captured slaves. "Twice, Mr. Crenshaw was tried for kidnapping blacks and selling them into slavery. Both times, he was acquitted."

They circled the house and entered through the front door. The six rooms on the first floor were decorated with period pieces. Wire grills prevented access but allowed viewing. In the parlor, red velvet drapes hung at the long windows. In front of a white fireplace sat two Victorian chairs upholstered in plush velvet, and over the mantel was a framed picture of the house.

The second floor resembled a museum exhibit. Newspaper clippings were tacked on the wall, and two wooden cases covered with glass displayed artifacts. Quinn pointed out the more unusual items: a cigar box opener, a pea podder, and an ice shaver. The group glanced at the antiques and scanned the newspaper clipping, but their anxious eyes strayed toward the attic stairs.

Quinn stalled as long as possible. The day Raven had brought Quinn here, Raven had been too tired to climb to the attic, but she'd advised Quinn to take her time on the third floor. "That's what people pay to see." Raven handed Quinn some snapshots. "If you look carefully, you'll see the ghosts."

"You're kidding, right? Just hype for the tour?" But as Quinn studied the photos, she'd spotted a strange shadow in one picture and in another, an arm that seemed transparent.

Now, as she gripped the worn banister and climbed the scarred wooden steps, her legs felt heavy, as if they were in bound in shackles. She shuddered as she thought about the fear a young slave girl must have felt as she was dragged up these stairs.

Quinn stepped onto the wooden floor and stared down the long hallway. She had seen the pictures, but they had not prepared her for the sight. The attic hadn't been changed since the 1800's. Twelve wooden cells, used to imprison and breed slaves, lined the sides. The wood was defaced with graffiti, and the sunlight coming through the dusty glass on the dormer window made the wood appear red and stained with blood.

As Quinn walked toward the first cell, the floor creaked. She thought she heard whispering ahead, but the group was behind her.

Most of the makeshift doors on the windowless cells were wooden slats. When the doors were locked, light and ventilation were almost cut off. Quinn opened the nearest door. A wooden bed, six foot by three foot, was built against the wall. A cacophony of anguished voices cried out. Startled, Quinn stepped back and slammed the door. The others looked at her in surprise.

Trying to regain her composure, she moved to the next cell and opened it. Iron rings, used to chain slaves, were embedded in the floors. She stepped across the hall to the end one under the eaves. It was supposed to hold up to ten women and children. Raven had suggested Quinn demonstrate its cramped quarters by walking under the eave.

Quinn opened the door and entered the tiny space, not much bigger than a bathroom. The slanted roof made it impossible for her to stand upright.

She inched forward. Coldness surrounded her. She couldn't breathe. Hands reached out pulling at her from all directions. Fingernails clawed at her skin. Her head pounded with what sounded like anguished screams of mothers as their babies were ripped from their arms.

Quinn flailed, struggling to get away from their cries. Their voices followed her into the hall. Somehow she managed to continue down the hall, opening the doors to the coffin-like cells only large enough for two wooden beds. At the far end, she rattled off the rest of the information about Uncle Bob, a slave used as a stud to father over three hundred children. She told about an incident when the female slaves had been beaten so badly, the male slaves had risen up and hacked off Crenshaw's leg.

Her voice shook. "That concludes the tour. Please go down the stairs and exit through the front door."

Quinn followed behind. When she passed the women's cell, the voices grew louder, trying to lure her in. She fought to get away. Gripping the railing, she staggered down two flights of steps and out the front door. On the porch, she doubled over, gasping for air.

An elderly couple with white hair moved toward her. Quinn waved them away. "Indigestion," she said, trying to ease the worried looks on their wrinkled brows.

After the last car disappeared down the lane, Quinn hurried to the safety of her Ford. Once inside, she thought the voices would go away. Instead they became louder, blending together to chant one single word. *Danger.*

Her hands shook as she stuck the key into the ignition. She sped down the graveled lane, the tires spitting out rocks behind her. Distance, however, didn't silence the voices. The volume grew stronger and clearer. *Danger, danger.* Above the cadence she heard another word.

Daughter.

Quinn gripped the steering wheel tighter. Taylor was fine. She was at Ace's surrounded by friends. Quinn knew she was being irrational, but suddenly she had to see Taylor, had to make sure she was all right.

151

Chapter Twenty-Eight

When Quinn pulled into Ace's lane, she was frantic. Cars already lined both sides of the drive, so she parked on the front lawn and was in too much of a hurry to even take the keys out of the ignition.

She raced toward the back yard, which was filled with people she didn't recognize. Some were chatting in lawn chairs, while others were at picnic tables or on the deck. Quinn scanned the crowd, looking for Taylor, Raven, or Summer. She spotted Ace standing at the grill with his back to her.

Her heart pounded as she ran across the yard. By the time she reached him, she could barely speak. "Where's Taylor?"

Ace turned and must have noticed her agitation. "What's wrong?"

She could get out only one word. "Taylor."

He frowned, but seemed to understand as he waved the long-handed spatula toward the machine shed. "She's playing with the other kids."

Quinn looked in the direction Ace had pointed. Kat and Taylor ran from behind the machine shed, followed by a group of boys, throwing water balloons. The girls dodged them. Then one struck Taylor in the back, breaking open and soaking her.

She screamed and turned to face the boys. She began pelting them with her own water balloons. One hit Jason in the chest.

Ace chuckled. "Doesn't look like you have to worry about Taylor."

Quinn's knees weakened. Taylor was safe. She turned to Ace and saw he was staring at her. She tried to sound calm. "I just wanted to check on Taylor...see if she's ready to go home."

"She's having fun. Let her stay." Ace's eyes didn't leave hers.

She bit her lip nervously. Why was he staring at her like that? Was he upset she was here? "I should go."

He held out a paper plate. "You might as well eat."

"I didn't plan to come, I just…" What could she say? That she'd heard voices? That she'd been sure Taylor was in danger? She didn't want him to think she was crazy.

Ace waited, holding out the plate while his eyes continued to search hers.

Her heart thudded in her throat. What could she say to close this chasm between them? She reached for the plate.

Then she heard Jason yell, "Dad! Dad!"

The panic in his voice made Ace drop the plate and sprint toward Jason, who was running to him. They met near the door of the machine shed. Jason gestured with his hands and said something that Quinn couldn't hear.

Ace looked over his shoulder and shouted, "Quinn!"

Their eyes locked. The blood rushed from her head. Taylor. Something was wrong with Taylor.

Time stopped. In slow motion she watched herself running. Her arms and legs pumped through the air. The cotton skirt swished against her legs. People turned to stare, but their voices were garbled and far away.

Taylor. She had to get to Taylor. Why was it taking so long?

Finally, she rounded the corner of the machine shed. Ace was kneeling on the ground. Quinn looked down and gasped, "Taylor!"

Her face was puffy. Her lips were swollen. Her eyes were no bigger than slits. Quinn dropped onto her knees and grasped Taylor's hand. "What's wrong? Tell me what's wrong?"

Taylor opened her mouth and clutched at her throat. As she struggled to breathe, her eyes rolled back in her head.

"Jason!" yelled Ace. "Run up and tell Doc Morgan to get his medical bag." Ace scooped Taylor into his arms and rushed toward the house.

Quinn scuttled along beside as he shouted out questions. "Does she have asthma? Does she use an inhaler? Has she ever done this before?"

All she could choke out was, "I don't know. I don't know."

Ace reached Doc Morgan, who was ready with his bag. He swept the remaining paper plates off picnic table. "Put her here."

Ace laid Taylor down. She was gasping for air. Doc reached into his bag and pulled out a shot. He stuck it into Taylor's leg right above her knee.

It seemed like minutes before she stopped struggling and started to breathe normally.

Doc looked at Quinn. "You need to take Taylor to the hospital quickly. Possible anaphylactic shock."

Quinn turned to Ace. "Can you…?"

He was already lifting Taylor into his arms. "My truck's blocked. Where's your car?"

She pointed toward the front yard.

Ace glanced over his shoulder at Doc. "You coming?"

"Go ahead." He took out his cell. "I'll call the hospital and tell them we're on the way."

Chapter Twenty-Nine

Ace paced across the lounge outside the emergency room. He ignored the antiseptic smells of the hospital and the TV droning out the news. Right now the only news he wanted to hear was about Taylor. What was wrong with her? Why didn't someone tell them what was happening? He checked the big round clock above the magazine rack.

"Come sit down," Summer said from across the room. Summer, who'd ridden in with Doc Morgan, flipped through a magazine as she waited.

Ace shook his head and continued to pace. He felt so helpless. Since he wasn't a relative, the receptionist refused to give him any information. Ace glanced at the clock again. "Do you think they know anything yet?"

Summer looked up from her magazine. "Doc will tell us when he finds something."

Ace didn't know what he'd do if anything happened to that precious little girl. And what about Quinn? She must be frantic. On the way to the hospital, she'd been way too calm. She'd sat there, chillingly silent, her arms locked around Taylor.

Ace thought about the past week spent without Quinn. He had been miserable. All the logical reasons not to become involved with her had not eased the ache in his heart. His feelings weren't rational. He didn't even know who she really was. Yet he couldn't stop thinking about her. Right now all he wanted to do was wrap his arms around her and Taylor and keep them safe.

Please, God. Protect Taylor. She's so small and frail.

As if his prayer was answered, the emergency room door swung open and Doc Morgan walked out. "Taylor's going to be all right."

Ace's legs weakened. "Thank God."

"She's probably not ready to outrun the boys, but her breathing's back to normal."

Ace dropped into the chair next to Summer. "What happened?"

"Taylor had an allergic reaction."

"What's she allergic to?" Summer asked.

"We don't know." Doc sat down next to her. "I phoned Ben to find out what Taylor was doing right before she collapsed. The kids said they'd stashed a plate of treats down by the dock. Jason gave Taylor a chocolate chip cookie. Belle thinks the cookies were the ones you made, Summer."

Summer frowned. "Why would my cookies make Taylor sick? She's eaten them before."

"Did you do anything differently? Use another brand of chocolate chips? Add an extra ingredient?"

"Let's see." Summer twisted her mouth, as if remembering. "I did run out of chocolate chips, so I tossed in a handful of peanut butter chips."

"That's it." Doc rose and rushed into the emergency room.

Twenty minutes later, he strolled back out. "We think Taylor's allergic to peanuts. She'll need to be checked by an allergist."

Summer's eyed widened. "Eating a few peanut butter chips made her that sick?"

"Peanuts can be as dangerous as bee stings. In some people, they trigger an attack and cause the body's immune system to overreact."

Ace swiped his hand over his brow. "People die from bee stings. Are you saying Taylor could have died?"

"Her throat swelled, cutting off her oxygen. Eating peanut butter chips, anything fried in peanut oil, or food processed in a plant with peanuts is as dangerous as eating peanuts. From now on, Quinn will have to watch everything Taylor eats."

Ace tried not to panic. "She could have another attack?"

Doc nodded. "Taylor will need to wear a medical alert bracelet and carry epinephrine with her."

"But she's all right, isn't she?" Ace asked. "No permanent

damage?"

"Taylor's fine. In fact, she's doing better than her mother."

"Quinn?" Ace shot out of his chair. "What's wrong with Quinn?"

"Nothing physical, but emotionally…"

Ace charged toward the emergency room.

"Hold on." Doc rushed after Ace and put a firm hand on his arm. "We're getting a room ready. Then you can see them."

"A room? You said Taylor was all right."

"Just a precaution. Once the adrenalin wears off, sometimes the body has another reaction. Besides, Quinn's exhausted. I'd rather have them both spend the night here."

Ace slapped him on the back. "Thanks, Doc. I owe you."

Doc chuckled. "I'll collect at our next poker game."

After he left, Ace walked over to Summer. "Why didn't Quinn tell us Taylor was allergic to peanuts?"

"Maybe she didn't know."

Ace frowned. "That doesn't make sense. She'll be five July fourth. Surely someone's offered Taylor a peanut butter sandwich or a Snickers."

Summer opened her mouth, then quickly shut it, and picked up the magazine again.

Ace thought Summer looked as if she knew more than she was saying. "Summer, if you know something, tell me."

"All right. Maybe you should know." Summer closed the magazine. "Taylor hasn't always lived with Quinn."

Ace dropped into the chair next to Summer.

"Quinn left Taylor with her mother for the two years she was in Japan. They've only been together for the last few months."

Ace nodded. "That explains some things. Why didn't Quinn tell me?"

Summer shrugged. "You'll have to ask her."

"I've tried." Ace's voice rose in frustration. "She won't tell me anything about her past."

"Maybe she thinks you wouldn't understand."

"Is that what she told you?"

"No. When I asked what happened between you, she took all the blame. Said it was her fault. But do you really want it to be over?"

Ace's jaw tightened. "I can't think about that right now."

"If Quinn won't tell you about her past, she must have a reason."

Ace stood and started pacing again. "Stephanie's beauty blinded me to what she was like inside. I won't make that mistake again."

"Quinn isn't Stephanie."

"I know, but she is hiding something."

"I don't know about her past, but I believe she has a good heart." Summer got up and walked over to the coffee pot. She dumped the grounds into the wastebasket and began making a fresh pot. "When I first met Quinn, her eyes held this terrible sadness. But it's almost gone now. I think you're part of the reason, Ace."

He remembered those sad eyes and how they'd haunted him.

Summer waited for the coffee to perk, then poured two cups and carried one to Ace. "Quinn is good for you. Until last week you seemed happier than I've ever seen you."

Ace blew on the coffee and took a drink. "It's over, Summer."

"I saw how you acted when Doc said Quinn was in bad shape. You're lying to yourself if you think it's over."

"I cared about the person I thought Quinn was. I don't even know her…" Ace stopped before he blurted out what P.R. had told him.

"Quinn's a good mother and friend," Summer said. "She'd help anyone in need, but she has trouble accepting help."

"You've got that right."

"I'm a good judge of character. That's why Quinn is my friend."

"Maybe all those good qualities are what she wants you to see?"

"Ace, is that what you really think?"

"I don't know what to think. Whenever I'm with Quinn, I get all tangled up."

Summer smiled and patted his arm. "Oh, you've got it bad."

"Well, it doesn't matter. I don't trust Quinn, and she doesn't trust me. So that's the end of it—for both of us."

"Quinn trusted you with Taylor's life."

Ace took another drink of coffee. "Doc saved Taylor, not me."

"Your quick thinking got her medical help. And when Taylor needed to go to the hospital, Quinn turned to you."

Ace gestured with the back of his hand. "She knows I'd do anything to protect Taylor."

"Maybe that's all Quinn's doing: protecting Taylor."

The phone on the desk rang. The receptionist answered it and turned to Ace and Summer. "Taylor's in Room 220."

Summer picked up her purse and took out her cell. "Go on, Ace. I'll make some calls and let everyone know Taylor's all right before I come up."

Chapter Thirty

Ace paused in the doorway of Taylor's room. Quinn was sitting on the edge of the bed, her back to him. Remembering how jumpy she was when startled, he cleared his throat before stepping into the room.

Then he walked to the side of the bed across from Quinn and gazed down at Taylor. Her eyes were closed, and her face was as white as the sheet tucked up to her chin. But the swelling was gone, and her face looked like—well, it looked like Taylor again.

As if she sensed him standing over her, her eyes fluttered opened. He slid his finger down the bridge of her nose. "Hey, Peanut."

She gave him a weak smile.

"I guess we know for sure Peanut isn't your name."

He looked across at Quinn. "How're you doing?"

She glanced up. "Okay."

The dark rings under her eyes and her pasty cheeks showed she was far from being okay.

"I left my puppy at your house."

At the sound of Taylor's sweet, innocent voice, Ace turned his attention her. "Jason'll take care of Gogo."

Taylor's bottom lip trembled. "She might think I don't want her."

Ace scratched his chin and pretended to ponder this. "Dogs are a lot of work. Did you feed her?"

"I mixed the food like you showed me."

"Did you play with her?"

"I taught her to fetch. Gogo's real smart."

"Did you walk her?"

"Lots of times, but not down by the lake. Mommy says we can't go there."

"Did she sleep in the bed you made?"

Taylor glanced at her mom and then crooked a finger at Ace. He bent down, and she whispered, "Don't tell, but she slept in bed with me."

Quinn's eyes lit up. It was the first spark he'd seen from her. "Well, Taylor, since you took such good care of Gogo, I'm pretty sure she knows you like her."

"I don't like her. I *love* her."

Ace swiped his hand over Taylor's forehead and brushed a curl away. Then he leaned over and kissed her. "Gogo's a lucky dog." Taylor was so easy to love. He wondered if Quinn had ever been like that as a child. If so, what had happened? What had made her so closed and guarded?

Ace dragged one of the chairs over to the bed and sat down. "Nugget will be glad to have Gogo back for the night. All the other puppies are gone—except yours and Jason's."

Ace described the people who taken the last two puppies. When he finished, Summer walked in; she immediately went to Quinn and hugged her.

Ace stood. He'd planned to make sure Taylor and Quinn were okay and then leave. But Quinn looked as if she was barely holding it together. "I'm going to the cafeteria. Need anything?"

Summer nudged Quinn. "Why don't you go with Ace? I'll watch Taylor."

Quinn shook her head. "I'm not hungry."

"When was the last time you ate?" Ace asked.

Quinn shrugged. "I can't leave Taylor."

Ace knew it was pointless to argue, so he left. Ten minutes later he returned carrying a cup of coffee and a sandwich. He held them out to Quinn.

Her hands shook as she took the coffee and sandwich. "Thanks."

Summer picked up her purse. "Ace, don't worry about the party. I'll clean up and take Jason home with me." At the door, she turned and smiled. "Stay as long as you need."

After she left, Ace settled back into the chair and watched Quinn on the edge of the bed. When Taylor gave in to sleep, Quinn took a few bites of the sandwich. Ace waited for her to relax. When she didn't, he stood and walked over to her. "Why don't you go out to the hall and stretch your legs? You'll still be able to see Taylor."

He took the coffee and sandwich, placing them on the nightstand. She didn't protest as he pulled her off the bed and slid a steadying arm around her.

Once they were in the hallway, Quinn leaned against the wall, keeping Taylor in sight.

Ace stood next to her. "What can I do for you?"

"You've already done enough. You saved Taylor."

Ace jammed his fists into his pockets. "Doc says she's going to be fine."

"I know." She wrung her hands together. "But I was so scared. I thought I might lose her again."

"Again?"

Quinn blinked over at Ace.

"You said, you thought you might lose Taylor again."

Quinn crossed her arms in front of her. "Did I?" She shifted her eyes away. Had she really said *again?* She tried to come up with a logical answer and then stopped. "Look, Ace, there are things about me that I can't tell you."

His blue eyes softened. "I'm glad you didn't lie."

"I can't do that to you anymore."

"Summer already told me."

Quinn's eyes widened. "Told you what?"

"That Taylor lived with your mother while you were in Japan."

"Oh." She lowered her head, looking relieved. "I haven't been honest with you or your family, and I'm sorry. You deserve better. But I want you to know, everything I've said or done was because I love Taylor."

"I know you love Taylor." He gently placed his palm on her cheek. "I love her, too."

"Oh, Ace." If he'd said anything else, it might not have undone her. But he loved Taylor. This wonderful, good man, the one she'd loved all her life, loved her daughter. She reached up and covered his hand with hers.

Tears welled in her eyes. She'd been strong in the emergency room. So many papers to fill out, questions to answer. Taylor needed her. Quinn was all she had.

Ace's fingers brushed a tear from her wet cheek. His tender touch made a shiver run through her. Was it possible he still cared? All she could think about was how much she wanted him to hold her. How much she needed him.

She turned away and swiped at her cheeks with the back of her hand. "It's silly to cry now that it's all over."

He put his hands on her shoulders and turned her to face him. His blue eyes flooded her with warmth. "You don't have to be so strong, Quinn. If you need a shoulder to cry on, mine's empty."

He opened his arms. Quinn hesitated. She wanted—needed—his strength so much. Maybe she could just lean on him a little. She stepped forward and laid her head on his shoulder. He wrapped his arms around her, and she felt herself let go. The tears she'd held back gushed out. She didn't think about tomorrow or the next day. She thought about now. Ace had been there when Taylor needed him, and he was here now for her.

His arms tightened, and he drew her closer. Quinn closed her eyes, drawing in his strength. He smelled like charcoal and sweat and safety. She let her worries slip away. She knew it couldn't last. But for now, she wasn't alone.

Chapter Thirty-One

Quinn sat on the steps hugging her knees as she and Taylor waited for Ace and Jason to return with Gogo. Now that the crisis was over and Taylor was home, Quinn had no idea where she stood with Ace.

At the hospital, he'd been a rock-solid foundation. When the intercom announced visiting hours were over, Ace didn't budge from his chair.

"Taylor's sleeping, so you don't need to stay," she told him.

He stretched his arm across the back of her chair. "I'm not staying for Taylor. I'm staying for you."

Until then, Quinn had been too frightened to rest, but with Ace next to her, she'd relaxed and drifted off to sleep. She remembered stirring during the night and thought she'd felt Ace's strong arm around her and heard him whispering soothing words. But in the morning when she woke, the chair beside hers was empty.

She'd felt safe in his arms, and it was impossible now to hide how much she cared for him. More than ever she wanted to tell Ace the truth. She owed him that. But P.R. was adamant. "Don't get him tangled up in your legal problems."

When Taylor saw Ace and Jason with Gogo, she jumped up and ran toward them. Gogo barked and wagged her tail, wiggling all over. Taylor threw her arms around the puppy, burying her face in the fluffy golden fur.

Quinn walked over to Ace and smiled hesitantly. "Thanks for returning Gogo. That's all Taylor's talked about since she woke this morning."

Ace took her arm and pulled her aside. "Jason needed to see Taylor, make sure she's okay." He lowered his voice. "He feels guilty for giving her that chocolate chip cookie."

Quinn glanced at Jason, who was hanging back. She moved over to him and slid an arm around his shoulders. "Jason, because of you, we know Taylor has the peanut allergy. I'm grateful for that. Think of what could have happened if Taylor had eaten peanuts when no one was around."

Jason shifted his feet back and forth. "Then you aren't mad at me?"

Quinn squeezed his shoulders. "I'm not mad."

He looked up at her with those serious blue eyes that reminded her so much of Ace. "And Taylor's really okay?"

"Doc says she's healthy." Quinn pointed to Taylor, running across the yard with Gogo nipping at her heels. "Why don't you go play with her?"

Quinn saw the relief in Jason's eyes before he sprinted across the lawn to Taylor.

"That was a nice thing you did," Ace said, as he came up to stand next to her.

Quinn turned. "Jason shouldn't feel guilty. It wasn't his fault."

"Maybe you should take some of your own advice. You don't look like you rested much last night."

Quinn's whole body ached. "Hospital chairs are pretty uncomfortable. What time did you leave?"

"I'm not sure." Ace didn't admit he'd stayed in the chair beside her until early morning.

Since yesterday afternoon, he'd been running on adrenaline and coffee. Now that Taylor was home, he needed to examine his feelings. His head told him to walk away from Quinn. Yesterday hadn't changed anything. He still didn't know who she was or what she was hiding.

But his heart wasn't listening. At the hospital, she'd let her defenses down. He'd seen how much she needed him. And the honest and heartfelt way she'd eased Jason's mind touched him. Maybe Summer was right. Knowing Quinn's past wasn't as important as knowing what was in her heart.

He didn't want to live through another week like the one before

Memorial Day. He'd told himself his foul mood was because he'd been duped by Quinn's lies. That was partly true. The other part was simply that he'd missed her. Without talking to her, hearing her laugh, or seeing her smile, his days had seemed empty.

Now, as they stood together and watched their children tumbling around the yard, a sense of peace washed over him.

"Would you like some coffee?" Quinn asked. "I can put some on."

After surviving on what the hospital called coffee, the last thing he wanted was another cup. But he knew accepting meant more than sitting down and sharing a cup of java.

He glanced over at her. Their eyes met. She must have sensed his hesitation because her chin lifted and her shoulders straightened as if steeling herself for rejection. But those brown eyes couldn't hide how much she wanted him to stay.

"I'd like that."

She smiled, lighting up her face and brightening her eyes. Ace decided he'd drink the whole pot if she kept smiling at him like that.

* * * *

In the afternoon, Quinn pulled Chrissy's suitcase from the top shelf of her bedroom closet. She unzipped it and searched inside. Under the clothes, she found a prescription box. The name typed on the label was Phoebe Prescott. Inside was an EpiPen.

Quinn sank onto the bed. When she'd first searched the suitcase, she'd assumed the prescription was for Chrissy. Guilt flooded through her. She could have lost Taylor. What kind of mother was she?

Quinn never thought she'd be any good as a mother. That was one of the reasons she'd agreed to the adoption. She loved her daughter, but love wasn't enough. Quinn had been responsible for her less than three months, and already Taylor been rushed to the ER.

A lump formed in her throat. *Oh, Chrissy, I wish you were here. I could tell you anything, and you always supported me. Friends Forever. Why was forever so short?*

She checked the rest of the suitcase and pulled out an envelope addressed to Phoebe. Opening it, she saw the familiar flowery handwriting. She read Chrissy's letter. When she finished, tears streaked down her cheeks. It was as if once again Chrissy was here, supporting Quinn when she needed it the most.

Drying her tears, she tucked the suitcase back into the closet and walked across the hall to Taylor's room. Taylor was lying on the floor, giggling. On top of her was Gogo, licking her face.

Quinn lowered herself onto the bottom bunk. "Looks like Gogo missed you, too." Quinn patted the bed next to her. "Come sit. We need to talk."

Taylor stopped laughing and rolled away from Gogo. Quinn was struck by how much Taylor looked like her. She'd inherited Quinn's height, her smile, and her feet. The auburn-colored hair and the tilt of her nose were the only obvious traits from Truman.

As Taylor sat, Quinn slipped a reassuring arm around her. "I want to ask you some questions, and it's important to tell me the truth. Do you understand?"

Taylor nodded and hung her head.

"You're not going to get in trouble, and I won't be angry. Just tell the truth." Quinn took a deep breath. "Did you know you were allergic to peanuts?"

Taylor kept her head down and nodded again.

Guilt flooded through Quinn. "Why didn't you tell me?"

Taylor shrugged. "You said everything was different here. I—I thought maybe I wasn't allergic anymore."

Quinn ran a hand through Taylor's hair, caressing her springy curls. "Doc said you'll probably always be allergic to peanuts."

"It's okay."

"Yes, if we're careful, it will be." Quinn reached over to the dresser and picked up the EpiPen she'd put there. "Do you know how to use this?"

"No, Mommy always kept it."

"Well, this EpiPen is for you. I have one, too." The pharmacist had instructed Quinn how to use the shot. She demonstrated for Taylor. When she finished, Quinn asked Taylor if she had any questions.

Her eyes were wide. "Will it hurt?"

"Just a little."

"Are you going to check my food like Daddy Win? He wouldn't let me eat anything."

Outrage surged through Quinn. She remembered the first time she had given Taylor a bath and how her ribs had poked out of her thin body. Quinn vowed Winston would never get near Taylor again.

"There are plenty of foods you can eat. Once you learn to read, I'll show you how to check the labels. Then you'll know the safe foods."

"I was real careful here. I always asked what was in my food, just like Mommy taught me."

Of course Chrissy would have taught her to be cautious. Quinn remembered how picky Taylor had been at restaurants and the potlucks. Just another clue that Quinn had missed. "Any other allergies?"

"Daddy Win said I couldn't eat fish. But I ate fish here."

"You ate fish from the lake. Maybe you're allergic to shellfish." Quinn needed to have Taylor tested for other allergies, too. "Anything else?"

She shuffled her bare feet.

"This is important, Taylor. If there's something else, you have to tell me."

Her words gushed out. "Daddy Win said I couldn't have a dog because I'm allergic to dogs. But Gogo doesn't make me sick. P-l-e-a-s-e, please, don't make me give her back."

Quinn bent over and lifted the wiggly puppy onto Taylor's lap. "You've been taking care of the puppies for weeks and you're not sick. You must have outgrown that allergy."

"So I can keep Gogo?"

Quinn smiled. "Forever and ever."

Taylor threw her arms around Quinn, surprising her as they fell back onto the bed. Taylor showered Quinn with kisses. Gogo nuzzled in, licking their faces. Joy flooded through Quinn. The stress of the last few days slipped away. Replacing it was happiness—the pure happiness of a mother enjoying her daughter's love.

Chapter Thirty-Two

The first week of June was hectic. In the mornings, Summer drove Quinn, Taylor, and Jason to Bible School. In the afternoons, the kids swam in the lake, and they ate together in the evenings.

"I'll cook supper on Monday," Summer said. "Quinn, you cook on Tuesday, Ace can buy pizza on Wednesday, Belle can cook on Thursday, and Raven on Friday."

Cooking for thirteen was hectic, but each night they gathered around the supper table seemed like a party. Quinn tried to relax and not watch every forkful of food that Taylor ate.

At Bible School, she'd distributed notes requesting parents not to send snacks with peanuts. And on Ace's computer, she looked up information about the peanut allergy.

She copied lists of questionable foods and read blogs from other parents. One mother refused to allow her child to go to any theme park because she was afraid of peanut residue on the rides. Another parent wouldn't allow her child to use the school playground.

Quinn read an account of teenager who died after kissing her boyfriend who had used a knife that had cut a peanut butter sandwich.

The reality of trying to protect Taylor terrified Quinn. "Ace, how will I ever be able to watch everything Taylor does?"

He took her by the shoulders and sat her at the kitchen table. "Don't get paranoid about this. Taylor will pick up on your fear. Making her afraid of living would be worse than the allergy."

"But she could die!"

"Now that everyone knows about her allergy, you won't be the only one protecting Taylor. We'll all be looking out for her."

Relief flooded through Quinn. "You're right. Of course, you're right. Taylor needs a normal childhood." Once again, she was thankful to Ace for keeping her grounded.

They were rarely alone, and he hadn't kissed her since his return from Chicago. Well, she had her independence. Isn't that what she'd always wanted? Never having to rely on anyone. She didn't need a man to make her decisions or support her. So why did she yearn to slip into Ace's arms and lean on his wide shoulders?

* * * *

During the second week of June, Quinn's life began to unravel. It started with a phone call from Ace's ex-wife.

The four of them were in the back yard, teaching Taylor how to hit a baseball. When Ace's cell rang, he looked at the screen and frowned. After a clipped greeting, he held it out to Jason. "Your mom wants to talk to you."

Jason wound up and threw another pitch to Taylor. "I'll call her later."

"Jason!" Ace's sharp tone made Jason drop his glove and take the phone. He didn't look happy as he stomped away.

While he was gone, Ace pitched to Taylor, who hit two balls in a row.

Jason returned and handed Ace the phone. "Now Mom wants to talk to you."

As Ace took the phone, he didn't seem to notice Jason's sullen face, but stalked over to the deck.

"I had two hits," bragged Taylor to Jason.

He pulled down the brim of his ball cap. "Big deal." He picked up the baseball and zinged it toward Taylor.

Taylor ducked to keep from being hit and plopped on her behind. "Hey!"

Jason threw down his glove and raced toward the tree house. He scrambled up the slats nailed to the trunk of the sturdy oak and disappeared into the clubhouse Ace and he had built.

Taylor stuck out her bottom lip. "Now who's going to pitch to me?"

"Let's take a break," Quinn suggested, as she wondered what Stephanie had said to upset Jason.

Quinn and Taylor walked to the machine shed and drank the bottled water from the fridge. They returned carrying two more. "Taylor, why don't you take some water to Jason?"

"He's mad at me."

"No, he's mad about the phone call. He needs a friend. Maybe he'll talk to you."

Quinn boosted Taylor up to the tree house and then walked over to Ace on the deck. He wasn't on the phone and his back was to her. His breathing was heavy, and his hands gripped the railing so tightly his knuckles were white.

She stepped closer and touched his arm. "I brought…"

He whirled around.

Startled, Quinn dropped the bottle and lost her balance. Ace reached for her, catching her around the waist. "You okay?"

She nodded and gulped, trying to appear unruffled as his strong hands continued to steady her. "But you don't look okay. Someone recently told me if I needed a shoulder, his was empty. Mine's empty, too."

Ace pulled her to him, his arms almost crushing her. She hadn't been prepared for his powerful grip or hard body. He'd never held her like this—this wasn't with passion or desire, but a powerful yearning. Her ribs felt as if they might crack, but she stayed in his arms, trying to give him what he needed.

When his breathing slowed and his arms relaxed their hold, she laced her fingers through his and led him to a nearby chair. When he sat, she moved behind him and began to massage his tense shoulders.

Ace groaned with pleasure. "I could get used to this."

"You're all knotted up. What did Stephanie say?"

"I don't want to talk about it."

"Ace, I know you're upset. So is Jason. He went running off to the tree house." Quinn walked around and knelt in front of Ace. "You need to show Jason how to deal with his problems without storming off or punching someone or whatever else macho men think they have to do."

"Don't worry. I'm not hopping into my truck or punching anyone out."

She rested her hand on his knee. "You look like you want to."

Ace stared at her soft hand and remembered the comfort he'd felt when he'd held her. He'd never found much comfort in the arms of a woman. As a man, he'd offered comfort, but he'd never sought it in return. He hadn't even known he needed it until Quinn had opened her arms to him. With her pressed against him, seeming to give every part of herself to him, something inside him released. The tightness that had almost swallowed him eased. The blackness faded, and he'd been able to breathe again.

He raised his eyes from her hand and saw how much she cared. He felt an overwhelming yearning that he didn't like. Admitting to his feelings for her was unsettling, even if he didn't voice it. Stephanie's phone call reminded him of all the problems caused by getting tangled up with a woman he didn't know and acting on feelings alone.

"I'm fine, Quinn," he said, although he knew it wasn't true.

"What did Stephanie say to upset you and Jason?"

"Why should I tell you? You don't share your problems with me."

As soon as he said the words, he saw the hurt in her brown eyes and was sorry.

She stood. Without saying anything, she turned and climbed down the steps.

He watched her walking across the yard. Just let her go, he told himself. Then panic tightened his chest. What if she packed up and left? What if he never saw her again? He didn't even know her name. He wouldn't be able to find her. He shot up and raced after her.

He caught her and gently put his hand on her arm. "Quinn, don't go."

"Ace, I don't want to fight with you." She was trembling and seemed to be struggling not to cry. "You yell at me, and I yell at you, but we don't deal with the real problems. I don't want to do that anymore."

"I'm sorry. It's just that Stephanie gets me all riled up, and then I look at you and it makes me crazy wondering what you're hiding."

"I want to tell you. Don't you think it would be easier for me to accept your help?"

He gripped her arm tighter. "Then let me help you."

172

"Not all problems can be fixed. I guess we're one of those that can't."

His dark eyebrows drew together, and he frowned. "What's that supposed to mean?"

"It's my fault. I accept that." She stepped away from him. "I guess I thought—hoped—you could get by my past. I can see that you can't."

"You can't expect me to just forget that I don't know anything about you."

She was literally shaking now. "I've tried to show you who I am." Her voice thickened. "But since you won't tell me about Stephanie's call, you must still believe I'm working with her to take Jason away from you." She took another step back. "If I told you my name, it wouldn't matter because you don't really know me at all."

Surely Quinn knew how important she was to him. When she was close, like now, all he could think about was her. Not the lies. Not her past. Only her. He couldn't deny his feelings. They were too strong. "I know you're not helping Stephanie."

She blinked up at him. "You do?"

"At the last poker game, Doc Morgan confessed he'd run into Stephanie in Chicago. They went out for drinks, and he told her about the gun incident."

Ace reached out and tucked a hair behind her ear. "I never really believed you were working with Stephanie. P.R. put that thought into my head." He took her hand. "I know you're hiding from someone or something. You'd be pretty foolish to use your real name. Besides, I've gotten used to you as Quinn."

He still wanted to know about her past, but pushing for details might make her walk away. Maybe if he opened up to her, she'd eventually do the same. "Stephanie's getting married."

"Oh." Understanding flashed in her eyes.

"She insists that Jason come to the wedding...in London." He led Quinn back to the deck, and they sat on the steps.

"And you don't like the man?" Quinn asked.

"I don't know him." Ace glanced over at the tree house. "I don't want some guy I've never met raising my son. He'll be checking his homework, cheering at his games, tucking him in at night. I'm his father.

173

Do you have any idea how that makes me feel?"

Quinn whispered, "A little."

The hurt in her voice made him remember she'd been separated from Taylor. "Yeah, I guess you do."

"Ace, you need to reassure Jason."

"I have to talk to P.R. and find out what I can legally do."

"Jason doesn't need specifics. Just let him know you love him."

"He knows that."

"Does he? Have you ever told him you're trying to get custody?"

"I don't want to make promises and disappoint him if it doesn't happen."

"Don't you know he'll be more disappointed if he thinks you're willing to settle for a few weeks in the summer and on holidays?"

Ace dropped her hand and began rubbing the knees of his jeans. "Stephanie's sending me an airline ticket for Jason. She wants me to put him on a plane and let him fly to London." He clenched his hands. "I can't do that. He's not a piece of luggage. But maybe it's that I just don't want him to go. I want to keep him here, with me, where I know he'll be safe."

"Even if you could stop Jason, are you sure that's wise? Stephanie will resent you for not letting him come to her wedding."

"I don't care how Stephanie feels."

"But you care about Jason, and you don't want him in the middle."

He stood and stared at her in disbelief. "What are you saying? Do you think I should just send him to London—alone?"

"No, I'm saying you should go with him."

"Me? Why would I want to go to Stephanie's wedding?"

Quinn rose and put her hands on his face. "The wedding will be less than an hour and you'll get to meet Stephanie's husband. Then you and Jason can vacation together. Besides, if Stephanie gets Jason out of the country, she might not send him back."

He took her hands and leaned in, brushing his lips across hers. "No wonder Taylor's such a great kid. She has you for a mother."

Chapter Thirty-Three

The next morning, Quinn was in the garden, hoeing the weeds around the tomato plants. Taylor sat nearby in the yard swing, playing school with Gogo and her stuffed animals. The air smelled of rain, and a rumble of thunder made Quinn glance up at the dark clouds. She dismissed them and began humming as she hoed the weeds. After last night, even the threat of rain couldn't dampen her spirits.

Ace had seemed willing to accept her as Quincy Matthews. He'd even brushed his lips across hers, almost as a promise. Maybe, just maybe, she could have the life she always dreamed of with Ace.

She finished the last row of tomatoes and called to Taylor, "Go into the garden shed and bring me the wire cages. They're stacked in the back corner."

Taylor slid out of the swing and raced into the shed. Gogo scampered with her into the garden shed.

Quinn leaned on the handle of her hoe and turned toward the hickory grove. She was surprised to see Ace emerge and walk toward her. She peered at him from under the brim of her sunbonnet and smiled. As he moved closer his hands were clenched, and when he stopped in front of her, he didn't smile but met her gaze with his cold cobalt blue eyes.

Quinn's heart quickened. Tendrils of fear spiked through her. "Ace, what's wrong?"

He looked around the yard. "Where's Taylor?"

Quinn frowned. "Taylor?" Why was he asking about Taylor?

He pointed to the swing with her stuffed animals. "Where is she?"

Quinn glanced toward the garden shed just as Taylor ran out the door. When she spotted Ace, she dropped the cages and sprinted to him, wrapping her arms around his leg and hugging him with all her might.

Ace smiled and scooped her up, twirling her around, making her giggle. "Hey, Pest, want to go with me?" he asked, as he planted her feet back on the ground.

Quinn frowned. "Go? Where do you want to take Taylor?"

"The boys are playing baseball at Belle's, and Kat wants another girl to play with her."

Taylor beamed. "Maybe Kat and I can play baseball, too."

Quinn looked up at Ace. His eyes avoided hers. Something was wrong. She removed the straw hat and ran her fingers through her damp hair. "Did you talk to P.R.?"

"I don't have time to go into that now. Summer's at the house, waiting for Taylor. May we go?"

Crisp, polite, and angry. Quinn couldn't wrap her head around it. She turned to Taylor. "You need to take the stuffed animals to your room first."

Taylor stuck out her lower lip. "Do I have to?"

"You know the rules." Maybe with Taylor gone, Quinn could find out what was wrong.

Taylor shuffled toward the swing, but Ace's words stopped her. "Can't she do that later?"

Quinn pointed to the threatening clouds. "It's going to rain."

Ace's tone was sharp. "Summer's waiting."

They stared at each other. The air between them was charged and ready to spark.

Taylor, sensing the tension, scurried away from Ace and hid behind Quinn. She didn't want Taylor to be afraid of Ace. She knew he would never hurt her. "It's okay, Lady Bug." She leaned down and gave Taylor a reassuring hug. "Go with Ace."

Taylor kissed Quinn's cheek and pointed her finger at Gogo, "Stay." The puppy whined, but sat next to Quinn.

Then Taylor slipped her tiny hand into Ace's. Without a word, Ace gave Quinn a curt nod, turned, and led Taylor away.

Gogo stayed next to Quinn and whined as Taylor and Ace disappeared into the trees. Quinn reached down and patted the puppy's head. She felt exactly the same.

Overhead the thunder rumbled, reminding her of the stuffed animals. "Come on, girl. We need to get you and these other animals inside."

Quinn gathered the toys into her arms and carried them up the steps and into Taylor's room, all the while mulling over Ace's behavior. Had P.R. told him something?

Last week P.R. had phoned her, saying, "The police have a picture of you, Quinn."

"I saw the sketch. It doesn't look like me."

"This isn't a drawing. It's a photograph. The description says blonde hair, blue eyes, but it looks enough like you for someone to notice. You need to turn yourself in."

Her answer was the same. "I can't."

Quinn left Gogo in the house and returned to the garden. She set the tomato cages and started weeding the green beans. As she worked, Quinn couldn't shake her fear. When she reached the end of the row, she glanced up. Ace was striding toward her—alone.

She straightened and tried to prepare herself.

When he reached the end of the garden, he stopped. "All right, Quinn. I want the whole story. Who are you, and what are you hiding from?"

Quinn? At least Ace didn't know she was Laney. Her hand tightened on the hoe. "Last night you said you could accept me as Quinn."

"I was wrong." He took her elbow and started to guide her toward the swing.

She balked. "What happened after I left? Maybe if I knew…"

"I'll tell you what happened. I was up all night with Jason after Taylor told him about her stepdad."

"Stepdad?" Quinn opened her mouth to deny it, but let it fall shut. Taylor's father was Truman Regal III, but since the only father Taylor knew was Max, she might think of Winston in that way.

"Some guy named Daddy Win. Does that jog your memory?"

The blood drained from Quinn's face. "What did Taylor say?" Quinn had questioned Taylor about Winston, but she'd refused to tell her anything.

"Taylor told Jason a stepdad replaces your real dad. You have to call him Daddy and you have to follow his rules."

"Is Jason all right?"

"He was upset, but we spent the night talking. Now you and I are going to talk. I know you're not Quincy Matthews. I need you to trust me. I need you to tell me who you are."

She wanted to confide in him. But she couldn't drag him and Jason into her legal problems.

When she didn't say anything, Ace said, "I'm trying to understand. Taylor's first dad died, and then you remarried. Is that true?"

What could she say? Taylor's biological dad didn't die. Truman had left Quinn at the altar. Taylor's adopted father, Max, had died, but Taylor didn't know she was adopted.

Ace placed his hands on her shoulder, forcing her to look at him. "Quinn, say something. I want to help you—and Taylor."

The words stuck in her throat.

He let go of her and started pacing. "What I can't figure out is when you married this second guy? Before or after you went to Japan?"

He stopped and when she looked into his eyes, she didn't see anger, only confusion…and hurt.

He raked his fingers through his hair. "I thought I knew you. Not your name, but who you are and what kind of commitment it would take for you to trust a man enough to marry him—and have his child. But you've been married twice. You've cared and trusted two other men enough to marry them. Yet you can't trust me enough to tell me your name."

She reached out and put her hand on Ace's arm. "I'm trying to protect you."

"You don't need to protect me, Quinn. You need to be honest. How do you think I felt when Jason told me Taylor had a stepfather and I didn't even know? In a few months will I find out about some other guy in your life?"

"I'm not interested in anyone…but you."

"Then talk to me. Help me understand. Are you still married? Is that what you're hiding?"

"No, I'm not married."

"Okay, is it something about the divorce?"

Oh God, she couldn't do this. She couldn't lie to him anymore. But once she said it, she couldn't go back. She took a deep breath and told him the truth. "I've never been married."

Chapter Thirty-Four

Ace stared at Quinn in disbelief. He couldn't have heard right. "You've never been married?"

She nodded.

The idea that she'd been married, and more than once, had made him crazy with jealousy. To find out she'd never been married should have relieved him. Instead, it only confused him.

He tried to fit the pieces together with this new information. He reached for her left hand and stared down at the gold band. "Then you've never been a widow? And the husband I thought you were grieving for never existed?" He frowned. "Why did you let me think that?"

"It doesn't have anything to do with you, Ace."

"Of course it does." He dropped her hand. "Unless you're saying I don't matter?"

"That's not what I meant. Please, Ace, leave it alone."

He stepped back and stared at her. His tone changed. "How much of what I know about you is true?"

She flinched. "Not much."

"Is Taylor's dad alive? Are you hiding so her father won't find her?"

"Something like that."

He threw up his hands in frustration. "I don't want *not much* or *something like that*. Give me a *yes* or *no*."

"It's not that simple."

"I'll make it simple. Are you keeping Taylor away from her father? *Yes* or *no*?"

Her answer was barely audible. "Yes, but…"

"A child deserves to know both parents. Isn't that what you said?"

Quinn stepped forward, put her hand on his arm. "Not all men are like you, Ace."

Why did her touch make his heart ache? Why did he still want to believe her? Maybe she had legitimate reasons to run away. The thought of another man, one who might have hit or abused her, made his stomach knot. "Did he hurt you, Quinn? Is that it?"

"No, but some men are not meant to be fathers."

He jerked away. This time, he wasn't going to be swayed by her or the way she looked at him. She was keeping Taylor away from her father, the same way Stephanie had kept Jason away from him. "And who's the judge? You?"

"As long as I'm responsible for Taylor, yes. I have to protect her."

"Protect her? Did he hit Taylor?"

"No, he…"

"Well, at least you didn't lie. I asked Taylor if her stepfather had hurt her."

"You what?"

"You obviously weren't going to tell me the truth, so I asked Taylor."

"Is that why you whisked Taylor away? You wanted to question her behind my back?"

Ace had expected Quinn to be angry, but what he saw in her eyes was fear. "I didn't believe Jason when he told me Taylor had a stepfather, I needed to know the truth."

"This is between you and me, Ace." She stepped toward him and shoved her finger against his chest. "Leave my daughter out of this."

He grabbed her hand and pulled her into his arms. "I'm trying to help you and Taylor. Don't you get it? Talk to me, Quinn."

"You don't know what you're asking me to tell you. It's not just you and me. This will affect Taylor and Jason, too."

"It already affects them. You're blind if you can't see that." He squared her shoulders so she was facing him. "I know you're scared, but I can't go on waiting, hoping you'll trust me. If you don't respect me enough to tell the truth, then it ends…here."

She could see the finality in his eyes. The anger was gone, the coldness was gone. He was looking at her with regret.

She swallowed and fought against the tears. "Ace, don't leave…please."

"I can't take it anymore, Quinn. I can't be with you and pretend your problems don't matter." His hands slipped away from her. "If you don't have anything else to say, then this is good-bye."

She wanted to tell him, but she'd kept Taylor's birth a secret so long, she couldn't find the words.

He stared, waiting.

A clap of thunder broke the silence.

She shivered but remained silent.

Finally, he touched her cheek, his fingers lingering. Then he took once last pleading look and turned away.

His shoulders were hunched, and his steps slowed as he trudged toward his house.

She crossed her arms, hugging her body, trying to hold herself together. Tears welled in her eyes. She remembered the way Taylor's hand had slipped into Ace's. Taylor had trusted him so easily. If only Quinn could trust him, too.

At the edge of the woods, Ace turned. She blinked, waiting for him to deliver one final blow.

He stood there, looking at her with such pain in his eyes, the same pain she felt in her heart. Finally, he cleared his throat. "You have a beautiful daughter, Quinn. Just tell me one thing."

She took off her sunbonnet and nodded.

"What's her name?"

If he'd asked her anything else, she wouldn't have come unraveled, but something inside her broke loose. She struggled to answer. "Phoebe. Her name is Phoebe."

A boom of thunder and the heavens opened up. Quinn stood, numb to the rain pouring down on her. This was her last chance. She knew if Ace walked away this time, he would not come back.

She couldn't go through life alone. Everyone needed someone. If only she could trust him, believe he cared about her, believe that even if he knew the truth, he wouldn't walk. She choked back a sob and forced out the words, "And I'm Laney."

Chapter Thirty-Five

Ace stood at the edge of the hickory grove staring through the cloud burst. "Laney?" Had he heard right? Had Quinn really said she was Laney? Water dripped into his eyes, blurring his vision. He squinted at Quinn shivering like a frightened puppy left in the rain.

He took one step forward, then another, and another, until he was rushing across the wet grass. Without stopping, he snatched her hand. Together they dashed into the garden shed. Ace closed the door. The air was humid and dank. Only a dim light filtered in through the small, dust-covered window across the room.

His eyes adjusted, and he squinted around at the collection of lawn chairs, clay pots, and gardening supplies. Then Quinn came into focus. She was facing him, her big brown eyes unguarded. He studied her, searching for the spunky, sixteen-year-old girl he remembered. He touched her hair, slowly trailing his fingers through the wet strands. It curled just enough for him to imagine the way it once had looked—except now it was shorter and black, not honey-blonde. He traced each brow above her chocolate brown eyes. Not jade green.

"Contacts?"

She nodded.

He slid his finger down the curve of her nose—that seemed familiar—and stopped on her wide mouth. He brushed the pad of his thumb across her full lips. They quivered and parted. Her teeth were white and straight. No gap between the two upper.

"Braces?"

"Yes." She laughed nervously. "It's really me."

The voice. That was what was wrong. "Say my name?"

"Ace?"

Her voice was low and raspy, not lyrical the way he remembered. He shook his head. "No, say it in your real voice."

"My real voice?" Understanding glinted in her eyes. "I had surgery to remove the cysts on my vocal chords. This is my real voice."

He leaned in and caught her sweet, sweaty scent. It distracted him, making him want to taste her wet lips. He felt her breath on his face, warm and enticing. He forced himself to step back. He wanted to believe this was Laney, had fantasized about seeing her again. But as he stared at the woman in front of him, he still saw Quinn. Was she telling him the truth or was this another ruse? She'd lived with Laney in Japan. Did Quinn know Laney well enough to think she could fool him?

Her hand touched his arm and drew him back to her. She gazed at him with those big puppy-dog eyes. She seemed unaware of the effect she was having on him. He couldn't think when she looked at him like that.

Glancing away, he scanned the garden shed. Little had changed since their childhood, yet they were so different. How could that be? He remembered the hours they had shared here. "What did we call this place?"

"You mean the garden shed?"

"Yes. We gave it a special name."

"Oh, a test question—like Penelope posed to Odyssey when he returned after twenty years?" She straightened like a school girl being quizzed. "This was the ALE House. Your initials were first and last. Mine was in the middle."

Ace stared at her, and the two women seemed to merge into one—Quinn and Laney, Laney and Quinn. The cloud of doubt drifted away. This was Laney, his childhood friend, the girl he'd fallen in love with the summer he was eighteen—and the one he'd never forgotten.

He smiled, and teasingly tucked some wet strands of hair behind her ear. "Do you have any idea how many times I've thought about seeing you again? Of course, it was never in the ALE House." His smile waned. "Why, Laney? Why couldn't you tell me?"

She bit her lip in that nervous way he remembered. "That first day I bumped into you at the food pantry, I thought you were married, and you'd tell your wife. Then you broke into my house…"

"I was checking for vandals."

"Whatever. Anyway, you had a son—and your own problems."

He worked to leash his temper. "Don't you think that should have been my decision?"

"Maybe." Her eyes pleaded for understanding. "But I couldn't risk it. Oh Ace, I've made so many bad decisions."

"Finally, something we agree on." Gently, he took her hand and led her to the window. Kneeling, he pulled her down under the ledge. As children, they had come here on rainy days and huddled in the shed. This was where they'd told secrets too painful to be spoken in the light of a summer's day. Laney had told him her dad was killed in a truck accident, and a few days later, her mom had locked her out of the house because Laney looked so much like her dad it made her mom sad to see her.

Ace had confided about his parents, how they'd attended only one of his baseball games, but all of Craig's basketball games. Now Ace knew his brother had envied him for being able to play baseball without the pressure of his parents' critical eyes. But at the time…

Sighing, Ace leaned against the wall and slid his arm around her. "Tell me what happened after our last summer together."

She cleared her throat. "I called you the first time we moved. I wanted to give you my new address. We didn't have a phone so I saved up a coin purse full of quarters and found a pay phone. It was Saturday, and your mom answered. She said you were away at school. When I told her who I was, she said you had a new girlfriend, someone of your own kind."

Hurt, followed by anger, whipped through him. "I didn't even date that first year."

"Your mom was right. We are from different worlds. You've always lived in the same house on the same farm. You never worried about a bed at night or food on the table. You never came home from school and found the car packed and ready to go."

He put his hand under her chin and turned her face toward his. "The house and the farm…those are only things, Laney."

"You can say that because you've always had them. They gave you roots, a permanence I never knew—except for the few months in the summer when I came here."

"I always thought Hickory Hills must be boring for you after all those glitzy cities."

"Boring?" She chuckled wryly. "My life has never been boring— only empty." She lowered her head. "When you grow up without love, you question it, and begin to think you're not worthy."

The pain in her voice made him want to gather her in his arms and show her how much she deserved to be loved. "Quinn—no, Laney— whatever you're hiding, it's not going to change how I feel about you."

She clasped her hands on her lap. "I'm in trouble, Ace. Big trouble." She took a deep breath. "Do you remember Chrissy? She came to Hickory Hills the summer I was twelve."

"The girl with those cute little dimples."

"I told Chrissy you liked her."

He put his hand over hers. "Not as much as I liked you."

She gave him a weak smile. "Chrissy was always my friend. Whenever I was in trouble, she was there. When Mom was drinking, when I needed money, and even when I was pregnant, Chrissy helped me."

"She sounds like a good friend."

"She was. Oh Ace, I let her down. I should have been able to save her, but I couldn't." Laney fisted her hands and pressed them against her eyelids to keep from crying. A few tears leaked out and rolled down her cheeks.

With his finger, Ace gently wiped them away. "Take a deep breath and start at the beginning."

She swiped at her face. "In January, I received a letter from a lawyer telling me Grandma Elam was dead. That didn't make sense, because when I was sixteen, Mom told me Grandma had died from a stroke."

Ace leaned his head against the wall and closed his eyes. The injustice made him furious. His parents had been cold and indifferent, but the lie Laney's mother told had been cruel. Laney and Taylor would have brought Grandma Elam such joy. And Grandma Elam would have given Laney the love she deserved.

"In February, Chrissy e-mailed me. She sent the message we used when we needed help. *Friends forever, come together.* In Japan, the school year ends in March, so I returned to the States, to Detroit where Chrissy lived."

"Why did Chrissy need help?"

"She'd married her college sweetheart, but two years ago, Max died of a heart attack. Chrissy was grieving and not thinking clearly when she married Dr. Winston Prescott. Within months, Chrissy knew she'd made a mistake. She wanted a divorce, but he said he wouldn't let her go."

"So Chrissy wanted you to help her get away from her husband?"

"Yes. I stayed at Chrissy's house the night before we planned to leave. Chrissy had arranged everything—fake IDs, a car, clothes, cash, and the gun."

"The .38 you shot me with?"

She nodded. "I told Chrissy we didn't need a gun. I didn't realize the danger. To me, it was like a movie. We'd escape and have fun starting a new life together."

"What happened?"

"Her husband was supposed to be at a medical conference, but during the night, I was awakened by voices from Chrissy's bedroom. I was in the room down the hall and couldn't hear the words. One voice was a man...and he was angry. I wanted to call for help, but my cell was downstairs."

"What'd you do?"

Laney didn't answer. She crossed her arms and began rocking back and forth.

"It's okay." He wrapped his arm around her shoulders and tried to calm her. "It's okay."

His words seemed to agitate her more. "No. It's not okay." She wiggled free. "I-I didn't do anything. I should have done something to help her, and I didn't."

Her eyes appeared to be far away, focused on that night. "I crept down the hall and peeked into Chrissy's bedroom. She was sitting in the middle of the bed. Behind her was a Monet print of a Japanese bridge over a pond of water lilies. The picture was crooked. Why was I focusing on the picture, thinking someone should straighten it?

"Chrissy held the gun in her hand, pointed at the man standing at foot of the bed. His back was to the door, so all I could see was his shape. But I was still focused on that picture.

"Chrissy warned him to leave. Then it all slowed. Like a movie score, the song 'A Bridge Over Troubled Waters' began running through my head. While I watched, the man sidestepped to the corner of the bed. Chrissy told him to leave again and started counting.

"After that I'm not sure. I think the man dropped to his knees and rolled along the side of the bed toward the nightstand. My eyes darted to him. Maybe Chrissy's did too. He must have grabbed the cord on the bed-side lamp because it slid over the edge. The shade flew off, and the lamp crashed to the floor. The bulb popped, blinding me.

"The man was on his knees near the head of the bed. He had the gun. He pointed at Chrissy. I opened my mouth to warn her, but before I could say anything, I heard a pop. Chrissy jerked back. Her head thudded against the headboard, and then her eyes were blank."

Laney sucked in a hitching breath. "Oh, Ace. He killed her. I was standing in the doorway, watching, and he killed her. I—I didn't do anything."

Tears streamed down her cheeks. She was rocking harder now, and her words were faster. "I couldn't think. I ran into the nearest bedroom and hid in the closet. I was paralyzed. I stayed there, maybe an hour while he tore through the house. Finally, when I heard the front door slam, I raced into Chrissy's bedroom. I knew it was too late. I'd seen her blank eyes, but a part of me wouldn't accept she was gone. I touched her cheek—still warm; she didn't move. I turned away and almost tripped over the gun. I grabbed it instinctively. What if he came back? What if he tried to kill me? What if he hurt Phoebe?"

"Phoebe? Oh, Taylor." Ace's throat tightened. "Sweet Jesus, was she in the house? Did she see the murder?"

"No, she was staying with a friend."

Relief flooded through him. He put his hand on Laney's shoulder, hoping to comfort her. She flinched and twisted away. "I should have saved her."

"You saved yourself—and your daughter."

Her face was streaked with tears, and she stopped rocking and looked at him. "But I should have saved Chrissy."

"It's not your fault. You didn't kill her."

"The police think I did."

He frowned. "That's crazy. Why would they think you killed Chrissy?"

"Because, because..." Laney's face went white. She started breathing rapidly. She clutched her chest and gasped for air. Ace recognized the signs. She was hyperventilating.

He put his arm around her shoulders and tried to reassure her.

Her breathing came in shallow pants. "Winston. He knows."

Ace peered into her eyes. They weren't focused. "Take deep breaths." He placed a hand on her abdomen. "Slow, deep breaths." He touched her neck and gently pressed it forward, easing her head down. He spoke softly, trying to soothe her. "There's nothing to be afraid of. No one's going to hurt you."

"He knows. He knows," she gasped.

"Don't talk. Take slow, deep breaths."

"I have to tell you...P.R. said not to, but..."

"P.R.?" He moved his hands to her chin and lifted it. "What does P.R. have to do with this?"

"He's my lawyer. He told me..."

"Your lawyer?" His fingers tightened on her shoulders. "He knows you're Laney and didn't tell me?"

"Client...confidentiality..."

Ace's anger rose. He gritted his teeth. He needed to concentrate on Laney. She was white and clammy, her breathing shallow. "Slower, breathe slower. It's going to be all right. I'll call Ben. I'll go with you to the police. We'll straighten everything out."

She clutched his arm, became more distraught. "No. No police." Her whole body started shaking. "I was in the house. I have the gun. The police think I murdered Chrissy. "

"Why? She was your friend."

Laney lowered her head and took a deep breath. "Phoebe."

Ace frowned. "What does she have to do with this?"

She spoke slowly, her words barely audible. "At the hospital, I told you I left her with my mother when I went to Japan. You know what kind of woman my mother is. I could never do that. I—I left Phoebe with

Chrissy."

Ace leaned back against the wall and shut his eyes. When he'd imagined finding Laney, he fantasized they'd reconnect and continue with those carefree days of their youth. But they weren't teenagers, and she was right: her problems weren't simple. "What do you plan to do?"

She looked down. "I don't know."

But Ace knew. He saw it in her eyes. She'd do what she always did—run. She'd take Taylor—Phoebe—and leave. Her daughter would have the same unstable life Quinn'd had. Maybe Quinn wasn't even capable of staying in one place. Whenever life became difficult, she'd pack up and leave, just like her mother. Laney had left the country when she had difficulty, and she'd leave him.

The shed was stifling and musty. He felt closed in. He had to get some air. Standing, he looked through the brown-streaked window. The rain had stopped. He opened the door, letting the rain-soaked air wash over him.

Quinn felt a cool draft and lifted her head. As she watched, Ace stepped out of the shed. He was leaving. He'd said she could tell him anything, and his feelings wouldn't change. Why had she believed him? Why had she thought he was different? He was walking away, just like everyone else. Her whole body shook. She was cold, so cold—and alone.

She closed her eyes and lowered her head. A low guttural groan that she couldn't stop ripped out of her. She crossed her arms over her body trying to push the pain back inside.

She heard Ace call out. "Quinn?" He sounded so far away. "Laney?"

A warm hand was pulling her up. Ace. He'd come back. Of course, he wanted to tell her good-bye. Then he'd leave, and she'd be alone. She tried to pull herself together, but her voice was weak. "There's more. I haven't told you…"

He pulled her to him, his arms tightening around her. "It's okay. You've told me enough."

She felt safe and wanted to stay there forever, but she stepped back. She had to be strong to survive when he walked away. She waited until her heart slowed, and her breathing was even. "I need you to know all of it. Then when you leave…"

He gripped her shoulders. "I told you I'm not leaving."

190

She looked toward the open door. "But—but—"

"I needed some air. I'm not leaving."

She blinked up at him. Was it true?

"I told you I'd do anything for you. But first we have to figure out what to do."

Could she count on him? But she hadn't told him everything. "Ace, there's more."

"Laney, let's go inside."

He didn't wait for an answer, but nudged her forward. She tried to take a step. Her legs buckled. He caught her around the waist. "When was the last time you ate?"

She shrugged. "Ace, I have to tell you…"

"We'll talk later. You've said enough."

For weeks he'd insisted she tell him everything. Why didn't he want to hear it now? She gripped his arm. "You won't tell anyone. Promise me you won't tell."

He put his arms around her and pulled her up against him. She could feel the pounding of his heart "You shouldn't have to ask, but since you did, it shows how little you trust me."

She wanted to deny it, but couldn't.

His voice was low and angry. "I'm going to say this once more. I'm not leaving you, and we're going to figure this out—together. Now repeat it so I know you understand."

She leaned against him. He was solid and dependable. She wanted to believe it—believe in him. He made her feel as if she could do anything as long as he was next to her.

Ace's mouth moved to her ear. "I need to hear you say, you know I won't leave."

Her mouth formed the words, and she whispered, "You won't leave me."

Now all she had to do was make herself believe it.

Chapter Thirty-Six

Thunder rumbled, signaling the rain. Winston sat at his usual table and stared out the restaurant window at the impatient drivers honking their horns, caught in five o'clock traffic. On the sidewalk, people in brown brogues, wing-tipped oxfords, designer heels, ballet flats, Chuck Taylor high tops, and scuffed sneakers scurried by, heading home to their families.

Family. Winston had no one, except his sister.

The soft instrumental music floating through the restaurant wasn't soothing. The instruments sounded tinny and jangled his nerves. He checked his watch. Wendy was late. He reached up to loosen his tie and realized he hadn't bothered to put one on. He unbuttoned the collar of his white shirt, no longer crisp and starched, but stained and yellowed. Each day without Phoebe made it harder and harder for him to dress, leave the house, and go into the office. Oh, the patients shook their heads and wrung their hands. They tossed out trite phrases of sympathy. But when they left, they went home to their families, their children. He went home to silence.

In the beginning, he thought Phoebe would be gone a few days. That had morphed into weeks. Tomorrow would mark three months.

His initial euphoria over finding Bonnie Elam had ebbed. When he showed the engagement picture to Janeen, she'd confirmed Melana Elam was the woman who'd picked up Phoebe from her house. The newspaper had run the photograph, the police had dispatched the picture, but no one had seen Melana.

Winston hadn't told the detectives that Melana Elaim was Phoebe's biological mother or that she had ties to southern Illinois. Bonnie had found her husband's death certificate listing Franklin County as his place of birth and death.

Winston also hadn't shared the information that Truman Regal III might be Phoebe's biological father. Winston had hired a private investigator whose report described Truman as rich, thirty, and single. Last spring, he'd called off his engagement to a wealthy socialite, and his family had shipped him to Chicago to oversee the construction of three assisted-living homes. According to the file, Truman had never been married, paid child support, or listed himself as a father.

When the P.I. pulled out a picture of Truman, Winston gasped. Truman's hair was a rich cap of auburn. Not a carrot top like Lucille Ball or a common red like his own Ron-Howard hair, but a coppery ginger. The color looked so much like Phoebe's that Winston was convinced Truman was Phoebe's biological father. The pictures of Truman sporting a different woman on his arm each week led Winston to believe a daughter would cramp his playboy style.

That means Phoebe is all mine.

No one would ever love her as much as he did. When she was found, he would devote his life to her. She would happily throw her arms around him and tell him he was the bestest Daddy in the whole wide world.

"Winston."

His head swiveled toward his sister as she slid into the chair across the table. She had been caught in the rain and her hair curled into ringlets and her white blouse was wrinkled. "Sorry I'm late." She picked up the menu. "Have you ordered?"

He lifted his wine glass as if in a toast. "Just the Chardonnay."

Wendy rubbed her forehead. "I only want water tonight."

"Bad day?"

"One of the worst. A three-year-old girl died."

"Oh, Wendy." He laid a hand on hers. "Remember how many lives you've saved. You saved my Phoebe."

Wendy had been at his house and recognized Phoebe's distress after she'd taken a bite of a peanut butter and jelly sandwich Christine made. Wendy had given Phoebe a shot of epinephrine before taking her to the

ER. After that, Winston insisted on shopping for all the groceries, checking each label, and monitoring every ounce of Phoebe's food.

The waiter, attired in a white shirt, black vest, and bow tie approached the table. Winston ordered water and pecan chicken salad for Wendy and cedar-planked salmon for himself.

After the man spread the linen napkin on Wendy's lap and left, she asked. "How's the search coming?"

Winston unfolded his own napkin. "Nothing new."

"Something happened at the office today that might be important to you."

Nothing was as important as finding Phoebe, but he leaned closer, feigning interest.

"We received a call from a pharmaceutical company developing a vaccine for peanut hypersensitivity."

Now she had piqued his curiosity. "Is it close to being approved?"

"In a few years." She lowered her voice. "They were conducting a survey documenting the rise in the number of children with the peanut allergy."

He leaned back, no longer as interested. "And why is it increasing?"

"They're exploring eczema. A genetic defect of the skin allows bacteria to enter the body. The immune system overreacts. Eventually this leads to asthma, hay fever, and food allergies. Eczema is not a result of allergies, but the allergies are a result of eczema."

Winston frowned. "Why are you telling me this?"

"You might try calling the doctors' offices in that southern Illinois county. Tell them you're conducting a survey about the number of patients with peanut allergies."

"They won't give out patients' names."

"No, but they might give you some general information, such as whether or not they've treated a four-year-old girl recently."

Winston beamed as he leaned over and kissed Wendy on both cheeks. "Sis, you're the greatest."

"My other news isn't so great." She fidgeted in her chair. "Detective Beveridge has been snooping around. I'm afraid he might find something."

"Beveridge! That clumsy bulldog. He's nothing but a dumb mutt."

Wendy ran her hand over the linen tablecloth as if to smooth it out. "Remember when you warned me the police might check my alibi?"

"You said they never called." Winston tipped up his glass and sipped the last of wine.

"They never called me...they called Richard."

Winston coughed, almost choking on the wine. "Richard doesn't know anything, does he?"

"No, but he gave the detective access to our phone and credit card records."

"What?" Winston's voice boomed over the restaurant music. "How could Richard be so stupid?"

The waiter rushed to the table with a glass of water and set it in front of Wendy. "Is there anything I can get for you, sir?"

Winston lifted his empty glass, and the waiter scurried away to get more wine. Even the persnickety little prick, who Winston usually found so solicitous, put him on edge.

Wendy sipped her water and leaned forward. "Richard was only trying to help. He thought once the police ruled us out, they could concentrate on catching the real criminal."

Winston rubbed his temples. "I hope Richard doesn't try to help again."

"I'm worried about what the police might find. The first time I called you was from my office. The police don't have access to my records. But when you called me after...the accident, did you use your cell or your home phone?"

"My cell."

"Good. Then if they don't check the tower, we can say you called from Vegas when your flight arrived."

"And your credit cards are clear?"

She bit her fingernail. "I charged your airline ticket to Vegas."

"What? Why didn't you pay cash?"

"Winston, it was two a.m." She lowered her hand. "Where could I get that kind of cash in the middle of night? The ATM has a limit, and Richard would question a large withdrawal." She ran her finger around the edge of her water glass. "I think we should tell Richard the truth."

Winston grabbed her hand, almost tipping over the glass. "No. I forbid it!"

She pulled her hand away, moving it to rest on her stomach. "What if Detective Beveridge asks him why he flew to Vegas? What if Richard figures it out? He'll think you murdered Christine. If I talk to him, I can explain. Once he knows the gun was Christine's, and it accidentally went off when you were wrestling it away from her, he'll know you had no choice."

The waiter returned and refilled Winston's wine. Winston stared over at Wendy and noticed the way her hand was pressed protectively on her stomach. The past several times they'd dined, she'd drunk only water. He narrowed his eyes. "Are you pregnant?"

She flushed and nodded.

Winston gulped half of the wine and practically spit out his words. "Richard talked you into this, didn't he?"

"Don't blame Richard. I want a child, too."

Richard was a pharmaceutical rep, who Winston only tolerated for Wendy's sake. His brother-in-law was no more than a pill pusher and certainly not worthy of his sister. Once, he'd overheard Richard saying podiatrists shouldn't be considered physicians. That all they did was clip toenails.

Winston reached across the table and took his sister's hand. "I know you want a child, but I can't bear to see you suffer. After your last miscarriage, you were depressed for months."

"This time will be different."

He squeezed her hand. "I hope so."

"It will be." She slid her hand away from his. "I'm already four months along."

"Four months? Why didn't you tell me?"

"I know how you worry, so I waited until the critical stage was over."

"You carried the twins for five months." He hated reminding her, hated seeing the sparkle in her green eyes fade, but facing facts now would keep her from being devastated later. "Wendy, if this doesn't work out, promise me you'll look into adoption. Children don't have to be your blood for you to love them."

"That's true for you, Win." She turned away from him and stared out the window. "But it's not true for Richard. He won't discuss adoption."

The hurricane candle flickering in the window reflected the longing in his sister's face. The yellow flame leaped and danced, distorting her eyes until they became distended and mournful. Her sadness reminded him of the way she'd looked in seventh grade when the cheerleading roster was posted and she was an alternate. He'd solved that problem. The brakes on one of the cheerleader's bicycles failed and she broke her leg.

Well, Wendy was already pregnant, so he might as well support her. He lifted his glass, this time in a toast. "To parenthood."

She smiled and lifted her water glass. "To parenthood...for both of us." They clinked glasses and drank.

Then Wendy's face grew serious. "I'm worried about you, Winston."

"You don't need to worry about me."

"Someone needs to. Your hair hasn't been cut in weeks, I doubt if you shaved this morning, and your shirt is stained."

Winston glanced down at a small brown spot on the front of his shirt. He patted his hair, tufted around his head, and felt his bristly cheeks. "I'll stop by the barbershop on the way home."

"You can't go on like this."

With a flick of his wrist, he dismissed her concern. "It won't be much longer. Your idea about the survey is brilliant."

The waiter brought their order. Winston poked at his fish and thought of Richard. He was a problem. Winston closed his eyes and became lost in the darkness. For what seemed like hours, he swam in a black tunnel. Then he heard his sister's soft voice calling to him. The sound was far away. Then the soothing words tugged at him, pulling him out of the darkness. His eyelids fluttered. Once again he stared into the light.

Wendy let out an audible sigh of relief. "I thought your spells were over."

"Mostly." He didn't tell her they'd started again when Christine had asked for a divorce.

"Winston, I can't go on watching you fall apart. Promise me that if you don't find Phoebe soon, you'll give up the search."

He slammed his fist on the table. "How can you ask me to do that? She's my daughter."

Other diners turned and stared toward their table. He didn't care about them, but the worry in Wendy's eyes concerned him. He tried to placate her. "Give me until the Fourth of July. If I haven't found Phoebe by her birthday, I'll stop searching."

Her face brightened. "Really? You'd do that?"

"Of course. I would do anything for you."

She reached out and squeezed his hand. "Oh, Win, I knew you'd understand."

He didn't think she would be so understanding if she knew what he was about to do—even if it was for her own good.

Chapter Thirty-Seven

As soon as Ace tucked Jason into bed, he hurried to his home office and booted up the computer. For the last ten hours, all he'd thought about was Quinn. She'd asked him to call her Quinn, which wasn't a problem because that's how he thought of her. Laney had been a girl trapped by unfortunate circumstances. The death of her father, an alcoholic mother, and an unplanned pregnancy. Laney had fled to Japan. Quinn was the woman who'd returned.

Ace clicked on the search engine. Quinn had become so distraught when she'd told him about Chrissy's murder that he had backed off with his questions.

He ran over the facts that had been swirling in his head all day. One, Quinn had never been married. Two, she'd left her child with Chrissy and fled to Japan. Three, Chrissy's first husband died and she had married Winston Prescott. Four, Chrissy wanted out of the marriage and had asked Quinn to help her. Five, Quinn came back from Japan, but before Chrissy could escape, Winston shot her. Six, after Quinn witnessed the murder, she took Taylor and fled to Hickory Hills.

But Quinn had wanted to tell him something else—What more could she be hiding?

He needed to know the truth.

He typed in *Detroit News* and waited until the paper appeared. He checked the archives for murders in the city within the last six months. He touched the screen a few times, and he was staring at a front-page article about the murder of Christine Prescott. It confirmed the basic details that Quinn had told him. Then he read the last line.

The police are searching for the four-year-old daughter of Christine and Winston Prescott.

Ace couldn't breathe.

Taylor had said Daddy Win was her stepdad. Winston wouldn't legally be Taylor's father. Quinn had only said she'd left her with Chrissy when she was in Japan, and Summer had told him Quinn had been in Japan for two years.

But the paper listed Christine and Winston as parents of a four-year-old girl. He told himself it was a coincidence. Christine and Quinn could both have four-year-old daughters. The missing girl couldn't be Taylor.

Ace clicked on the next day's newspaper and found a picture of Chrissy. Her smiling face with its bow-shaped mouth and cute dimples was just the way he remembered it. Then he saw the picture at the bottom of the page. His stomach clenched. His mouth went dry. A little girl with long curly hair was clasping a small, stuffed black-and-white cow. The child didn't look much like Taylor, but Ace recognized the cow. Taylor had been clutching it the night Quinn had shot him.

Ace read the name under the picture, Phoebe Prescott. He bolted out of the chair. He paced back and forth, his heart pounding out the name. *Phoe-be Pres-scott.* Quinn hadn't said anything about letting Chrissy adopt Taylor. She said she had left her with Chrissy. Winston wouldn't be Taylor's legal father. Yet Taylor had said Daddy Win was her stepdad. If Chrissy had been responsible for Taylor for only two years, she wouldn't have had Taylor call her Mommy or say Winston was her stepdad.

His mind wouldn't accept it, didn't want to accept it. Taylor was Phoebe Prescott. Quinn hadn't left her daughter with Christine. Phoebe was Christine's daughter, just like the report said—not Quinn's.

Quinn had admitted Taylor's real name was Phoebe. There was no unplanned pregnancy. Quinn never had a child. Chrissy had. And Quinn had kidnapped her.

From the beginning, he'd known something was not right. He'd even asked P.R. to run a background check. Yesterday, Quinn had said that he needed to know all of it. Now he did.

He raked his fingers through his hair. Suppose the police thought Chrissy and Quinn had argued. Quinn even had the murder weapon.

Quinn was right. She could be charged with murder—and kidnapping. Is that what she'd wanted to tell him? To Ace, the world was black and white. Few gray areas existed.

But Chrissy had been murdered, and Taylor said her daddy was in heaven. He didn't think she'd lied. So who were Phoebe's parents? She had told Jason about Daddy Win, her stepdad. Did he have custody of Taylor?

Ace forced himself back to the computer and pulled up more articles about the murder.

Dr. Winston Prescott, husband of the murder victim, is no longer being investigated as a suspect. During the time of the murder, Prescott was attending a podiatrist convention in Las Vegas.

Winston. Daddy Win. Taylor had called him a bad man. Quinn said she'd seen him murder Chrissy. Who was this Winston Prescott?

Ace searched the podiatrists in Detroit and found Winston Prescott's website. If Winston was after Quinn, Ace needed to be prepared. At least he'd know what the guy looked like. Of course, he'd probably use a disguise, but his body type would be the same.

Dr. Winston Prescott's picture popped up on the screen. Pretty normal looking guy. Mid-thirties, medium build, short Opie-like red hair, no freckles. Ace clicked on a video clip. Winston, wearing a white coat and looking professional, sat at his desk and explained a surgical bunionectomy.

The only mannerism Ace noted was the way Winston steepled his hands together in front of him. He sounded like a competent doctor.

A doctor. Taylor had been afraid of doctors. Was Winston the reason?

Ace returned to Winston's homepage and was ready to close it when he noticed a link to his Facebook page. He clicked on it and stared in disbelief as picture after picture of Phoebe rolled across his screen.

Each one was dated. The first photos, taken in Florida in August, were labeled *honeymoon.* The next seven or eight pages seemed normal. Then in October, the pictures changed. Phoebe was dressed in ballet costumes and pageant gowns. She was still smiling, but she looked stiff and posed. The ones after Christmas showed a marked decline. Phoebe was thinner, and her smile—if she had one—had waned. Each one he clicked on showed her changing into the child he'd seen the day she walked into the food pantry. The last picture was dated March 13.

Ace leaned back in his chair and locked his fingers behind his head. Summer was a professional photographer and was always snapping photos of Kat and Levi. But the quality of Summer's pictures paled under the volume Winston had posted. Ace estimated he'd scrolled through more than a thousand pictures, all taken within six months.

He clicked on another link titled *photo albums*. These pictures were of a younger Winston. A short paragraph at the beginning explained that his first wife and child had died in a car crash. Ace scanned the album, and then paused on a photo of Winston's daughter when she was four years old. He noticed a resemblance to Taylor and frowned. He continued perusing the pictures. With each one, the resemblance between Taylor and Fiona became clearer. He stopped on a picture of Fiona dressed as a fairy. She was wearing a green-and-blue ballet costume that Ace was almost positive he'd seen on Taylor in another picture. A red-velvet Christmas dress and a white satin gown also looked familiar.

Ace returned to Phoebe's pictures and scrolled through them until he found the one of her dressed as a fairy. She was wearing the green-and-blue tutu over a satin leotard. The gossamer wings had been stiff when Fiona wore them, but on Taylor, they were slightly awry. He copied the two pictures and pasted them side by side. Wearing the same outfit and having the same color of dark, cherry-red hair made them look like twins.

A prickly fear inched up Ace's spine. One word pounded in his head. *Obsession.*

Winston was obsessed with Taylor. The gallery of pictures showed how he'd slowly transformed Taylor into a replica of his first daughter. Another realization hit Ace. Winston would never stop looking for Taylor.

Ace clenched his fist. At least he knew what he was up against. Quinn had witnessed her best friend being murdered and had kidnapped her daughter to protect her.

Now he understood why Quinn had not wanted him to become involved. Kidnapping was a federal offense.

For the time being, he was not going to tell Quinn he knew that

Taylor was not her daughter. He would pretend to believe just what she had told him. But he would also keep close guard on them because if Winston was obsessed with his stepdaughter, he would not stop looking for her.

Chapter Thirty-Eight

The next morning, Ace was groggy and blurry-eyed as he stood at the stove, scrambling eggs in an iron skillet. He swigged the last of his coffee and poured himself another cup. He hadn't gone to bed until after three a.m. and Jason had woken at seven.

Ace scraped the over-cooked eggs onto two plates and set them on the table where Jason was waiting. After Jason said a quick blessing for them, Ace automatically started eating.

Jason rose and walked to the refrigerator.

Ace glanced up. "Need something?"

"I can get it." Jason poured himself a glass of milk and sat back down.

"Sorry. Guess I'm not awake."

Jason shrugged. "It's okay."

Last night, Ace had pretended nothing was wrong, but Jason was too perceptive to be fooled for long. "I've got a little problem." That was certainly an understatement.

Jason blinked up at him. "What kind of problem?"

"Adult stuff."

"Girls?"

Ace put down his fork. "Why do you say that?"

"Aren't all problems about girls?"

Ace stared across the table at Jason. "Are all your problems about girls?"

"Pretty much."

That surprised Ace. "You and Mom having problems?"

"Naw. Just girls at school."

"You mean like girlfriends?"

His son nodded.

Ace propped his elbow on the table and rested his chin up on his hand. He thought he might be talking to his son about girls in a few years—not when he would be starting third grade. "So what do you do about your girl problems?"

"Talk to other guys."

Ace nodded. "That's good."

"Maybe you should talk to somebody."

Ace tried to keep from grinning. "Have someone in mind?"

"I could give you some pointers."

Jason's offer intrigued Ace. "Like what?"

"You can't just go up to a girl and ask her if she likes you."

"Why not?"

"They giggle and say they don't like you when they really do."

Ace picked up his coffee mug and took a drink. "If you can't ask the girl, what do you do?"

"Ask a friend to ask the girl. Like I'd ask Taylor for you." Ace practically spit out his coffee. "Ask Taylor what?"

"If her mom likes you."

Maybe having this conversation with Jason wasn't as absurd as he'd thought. "What do you think about Quinn?"

He shrugged. "She's okay. But not as pretty as Mom."

"Not many women are as pretty as your mother." The kid was loyal.

Ace saw Jason eyeing the rest of his eggs. "Want mine?"

Jason scooped the eggs onto his plate. Ace couldn't believe the amount of food a seven-year-old boy could pack away.

Jason finished the eggs, and then gave Ace a smug grin. "I kissed a girl once."

"You did? How was it?"

"Okay. Have you ever kissed Quinn?"

"Yeah."

"How was it?"

"Better than okay."

"So should I ask Taylor about her mom?"

"I don't want to get Taylor involved."

"You could write Quinn a note."

"A note? What would it say?"

"You'd ask if she likes you."

"Have you ever written a note asking a girl if she likes you?"

"Sure. At the bottom you make two boxes—*yes* and *no.*"

"Which one did your girl check?"

Jason rolled his eyes. "They always check *yes.*"

In the mind of a soon-to-be eight year old, it was as simple as that. *Check yes* or *no.*

Chapter Thirty-Nine

That evening, Ace sat on the deck drinking sweet tea and looking toward Quinn's place. He hadn't gone to the field today, not even to check on the crops. Instead, he'd spent the day in the shed, repairing machinery. He wanted to stay close. Quinn might need him. He didn't like her and Taylor being over there alone.

He'd phoned Quinn three times. "I want you to ride to Jason's game with me tonight."

"Is this a date or are you being my bodyguard?" Quinn asked.

"I don't care what you call it. I just want you with me."

The second call confirmed the time. The third one had been obsessive, and he knew it. Still, he couldn't stop from dialing her number. He had to make sure she was all right. He would have made a fourth call, but the battery on his phone died. In fact, it was currently plugged into the charger on his bedroom dresser.

Despite a shower and shave, Ace couldn't relax. All he could think about was Quinn and Taylor and whether they were in danger. He wished everything was as simple as Jason had said—*yes* or *no*. But Quinn had kidnapped Taylor and kidnapping wasn't simple.

He'd decided not to tell Quinn about the pictures on the Internet. She had enough to worry her. What troubled Ace was the long-range plan. Someone might eventually find out she was Laney. What would happen then? Taylor would be taken away. Quinn would be sent to jail, and he would be an accessory to kidnapping. Not a good mark on his record when he wanted to get custody of his son. But he meant what he'd said. He wasn't walking away from Quinn. He couldn't.

Jason's game didn't start for another hour, but he'd already left with Levi. Maybe Ace should mosey over and check on Quinn now. He could talk to her about his plan.

A dog barked. Ace looked up and saw Taylor and Gogo running across the lawn. He expected Quinn to follow. When she didn't, he turned his attention to Taylor.

She was wearing a glittery purple T-shirt and tennis shoes that lit up every time her feet hit the ground. Her face glowed as she skipped up the steps of the deck. She looked healthy, so different from the pitiful little creature he'd first seen at the food pantry. Then, he hadn't even been able to tell if she was a boy or a girl. Now he understood why Quinn had clipped her hair and dressed her in bib overalls.

"Where's your mom?" Ace asked.

"Getting ready. She tried to call you. Raven needs her, so we're going to town in a few minutes. I'm supposed to give these to Jason." She held up a brown sack.

"Jason's already at the ballpark. What's in the sack?"

"Cookies for after Jason's game."

Ace smacked the palm of his hand against his forehead. Some father he was. He'd forgotten he was in charge of snacks for the team. They'd bought juice boxes, but Jason had wanted homemade cookies.

"Tell your mom thanks."

Taylor straightened. "They're giggle cookies, and I helped."

"My favorite." Ace peeked into the sack and saw the individually wrapped snickerdoodles. "You won't tell if I eat one, will you?"

"I'm real good at keeping secrets." She made a big X over her chest. "Cross my heart."

"I bet you are." Ace reached into the sack and wondered how good she was at telling secrets. "You want one, Phoebe?"

"No, my tummy's full of cookie dough."

She hadn't even blinked at the name. Maybe he could get some answers without her knowing. "Do you have time to talk?"

"Mom said I have to be back in ten minutes."

Ace patted his knee. Taylor jumped into his lap and threw her arms around his neck. Delight shot through him. He held her close, wanting her to feel safe. She'd already charmed her way into his heart, but he needed to be sure that living here with Quinn was what was best for Taylor.

"I like having you next door. Do you like it here?"

"Uh-uh."

"I used to live in Chicago. Sometimes I miss it. Do you miss where you used to live?

Taylor shook her head so hard her auburn curls bounced.

"What if you could live any place in the whole wide world? Where would you live?"

"Disney World."

Ace burst out laughing. Not exactly what he had in mind, but maybe it would work.

"And who would you take to Disney World?"

"Gogo."

"What about people?"

"Kat and Jason and..."

"Any adults?"

"Mommy and Summer." She turned and looked at him. She put her finger up to her pursed lips and gave him a mischievous smile. "I'm not sure about you."

"What?" He frowned and pretended to be sad.

Taylor giggled, making his heart do little flip flops. Oh yeah, she was going to be some beauty when she grew up.

"What about Daddy Win?"

The smile faded, and she shook her head. She tried to slide off his lap, but he kept his arms wrapped around her, wanting her to feel safe.

"Mommy said I don't have to live with him. Not ever."

"Which Mommy?"

"Both. My real mommy and this mommy."

Real mommy. There it was. The truth as understood by the child who had lived it. Chrissy—not Quinn—was Taylor's mother.

"I miss my real mommy."

A lump stuck in his throat. "I know." He gently patted her back.

"She's in heaven with Daddy."

"Now you have two special angels watching over you."

"I can't remember Daddy, but Mommy was real pretty, like Jason's mom."

"Jason misses his mommy, too."

Taylor straightened. "No, he doesn't. He said, 'Boys should live with their dads 'cause they get to do guy stuff.' And I said, 'Girls should live with their mommies.'"

"So you like living here with this mommy?"

"Uh-huh. Jason thinks I'm lucky because I get to live with her all the time. He's going to ask if you'll let him stay. He's trying to be real good so you'll say yes."

Ace groaned. Jason hadn't complained this morning when Ace had forgotten the milk. In fact, Jason rarely complained about chores or bedtime or even eating his vegetables. Ace thought Jason had matured. Now he saw it differently. His son believed he had to be good so Ace would want him. His heart ached. Quinn was right. He should have told Jason he'd filed for custody.

Taylor slid off his lap. "Mommy said to tell you she'll be at the game later." Taylor patted her leg. "Come on, Gogo." Her shoes lit up as she and Gogo ran across the lawn.

Ace called after, "Don't tell your mom I ate a cookie, okay?"

She stopped and turned back to him. She put a hand up to her eyes to shade it from the sun. "I won't tell her you guessed my name either." Then she gave a quick wave and disappeared into the trees.

Chapter Forty

Quinn's hand shook as she pulled up to the ball diamond and parked along the first base line. She pried her fingers from the steering wheel and rolled down the window. The warm June breeze carried the familiar chant of *hey batta-batta* and the aroma of buttery popcorn and hot dogs. She scanned the spectators in the bleachers. When she spotted Taylor sitting near the third base line between Kat and Ace, Quinn relaxed.

She checked the scoreboard. Jason's team was losing 2-1 in the bottom of the fifth. She glanced toward first base. Jason stood with his back to her. In his white uniform and red cap, he looked so much like Ace as a boy. Her heart melted.

She'd missed most of the game because she'd guided another tour through the Old Slave House. Raven had looked so miserable that Quinn couldn't turn her down. Besides, this time, she was sure nothing would happen. Voices wouldn't scream at her; spirits wouldn't claw at her. Maybe she'd hear some creaky boards and feel a cold draft.

She was wrong.

The evil was real. The spirits had joined into one massive force, pulling her forward. Each step down the narrow hallway on the third floor felt as if she were being sucked in by a gigantic magnet. She reached the large cell under the eaves and gripped the latch. The door swung open. Voices flew out, shrieking like banshees. *Stay away. Don't come back, come back, come back.*

They were the mother voices, the ones who'd previously warned her. Quinn planned to heed their words. The tours helped Belle's bed and breakfast and were Quinn's only source of income other than interest on her savings, but she wouldn't go back to the Old Slave House.

Now, as she sat in the car, goose bumps covered her arms, and her insides quivered. She flipped down the visor and looked into the mirror. Raven had invited her to her home and given Quinn special treatment and a complete makeover. Her dark hair, caught up in a banana clip and pulled back from her face, highlighted her high cheek bones in a way her natural blonde hair never had. The humidity had curled wisps around her face, softening the effect.

After fixing the hair, Raven had pointed to her closet. "Try on that strawberry-printed dress. I bought it on sale last summer." Raven stretched out on the bed, propping up swollen ankles. "I'm never going to fit into that teeny spaghetti-strapped sundress again."

Quinn put it on and twirled in the mirror, loving the way the full skirt flitted around her legs. Raven had convinced her to wear the dress for the tour and Ace.

Quinn knew it wasn't a date. He was just being protective. Still, as she slid out of the car and strolled toward the bleachers, she felt self-conscious. She blamed the fluttering in her stomach on the Slave House—not Ace.

She stopped at end of the bleachers. When Ace looked down at her, the intensity of his gaze was disconcerting. She bit her lip nervously.

Taylor saw her and ran down the bleachers. "Mommy, you look so... so beau-ti-ful."

Quinn chuckled at the surprise in her daughter's voice. She followed Taylor up the bleachers and sat between her and Ace. "Sorry I missed most of the game."

She hoped he'd say she looked beautiful too, but his brows knitted together. "You okay?"

She folded her hands in her lap, trying to ignore the flutters. "Sure. Why?"

"You look a little...white."

White? Not beautiful, not even cute or pretty. Just white. She brushed her hands over her cheeks. "I guess the Old Slave House rattled me."

"What?" His brows lowered even more. "You went out there? Alone?"

"Not alone. Twelve were on the tour."

"Quinn, that was the stupidest…"

Taylor leaned over and pointed toward the diamond. "Jason's up."

Quinn felt relieved as they turned to watch Jason step into the batter's box. On the second pitch, he hit a line drive, sending the runner from third sprinting across home plate.

Taylor jumped up. "The game's tied."

Quinn clapped and cheered, but the next player struck out, leaving Jason stranded on first base.

Taylor crossed her arms and pouted. "Jason would have been the winning run."

Quinn slid her arm around Taylor's shoulders. "I know, but there's one more inning. Besides, it's only a game."

"What?" Taylor and Ace said together. They both stared at her as if she'd just said something ridiculous.

In the top of the seventh and final inning, Jason's team made two quick outs before the last batter in the lineup stepped into the box. The player was a girl and was walked to first. The next batter connected, sending the ball sailing over the fence—an automatic triple. The girl strolled across home plate, giving Jason's team the lead.

When the inning ended, the opposing team batted, but made three quick outs.

Taylor jumped up. "We won! We won!" She reached across Quinn and gave Ace a high five, then turned to Kat.

Ace put his hand on Quinn's arm. "We need to talk."

She glanced around at the crowded ballpark. "Here? Now?"

He shook his head and guided her down the bleachers. "Let's take a walk."

She balked. "I can't. Taylor."

"I asked Ben to watch Taylor. She'll be safe with him."

Quinn's eyes widened as Ben walked over to Kat and Taylor. "You didn't tell him, did you?"

"No, I didn't tell him." Her lack of trust rankled him. "I said I needed to talk to you and didn't want you to worry about Taylor because the concession stand sells peanuts."

Quinn walked over to tell Taylor where she was going. When she returned, Ace took her elbow and maneuvered her away from the crowded ball diamond. Once they were near the tennis courts, he stopped and faced her. "I don't want you going out to the Slave House alone."

"Okay."

"I mean it. If you need to go, I'll go with you."

"Okay."

Ace was skeptical. "You don't usually agree with me so readily."

"I happen to think you're right."

He hoped he could convince her to go along with his plan just as easily. He patted the pocket of his T-shirt. The note was additional insurance—in case his tongue thickened and he couldn't get out the words.

Slipping his arm around Quinn's waist, he led her across the park and past the lighted playground. His breathing came easier now. As long as he was touching her, had his hands securely on her, he knew she was safe.

They walked onto the arched footbridge connecting the playground to a small island surrounded by a lagoon. Lights from the empty playground cast dim shadows onto the concrete bridge. He turned and faced Quinn. He liked the way her hair was pulled back and the sassy little dress she was wearing. He liked the whole package and wanted to tell her how pretty she looked, but he knew she didn't handle compliments well. Maybe he should bypass her looks and show her how he felt.

He wanted her to be a permanent part of his life. But roots weren't something Quinn had experienced growing up. Nor was accepting help. He hoped he could change that.

He needed her to listen. He didn't want her to get huffy and stomp off. Placing his hands on her waist, he swung her around, lifting her onto the rail of the bridge.

Surprise registered in her eyes. "What are you doing?"

"Making sure you listen."

She glanced over her shoulder at the water below. "I could fall off."

He reached for her hands and laid them on his shoulders. "Not if you hold onto me."

She gripped his shoulders. He liked the feeling of her relying on him. A chorus of cicadas chirped, and the bright white moon cast its glow onto the water. In the background, the voice of the announcer read the line-up for the next baseball game. Down the block, a dog barked, and cars and trucks hummed along on the distant highway. But the soft summer breeze filled him with her sweet scent, making everything else fade.

He stretched out his arm and cupped his hand around the back of her neck. With her hair swept up, his fingers slid easily across her bare silky skin. He tightened his hold and leaned forward, finding her mouth. When his lips touched hers, he felt a quiver of hesitancy. He waited, keeping the kiss light, giving her time to adjust and accept him. Her lips warmed to his and he became lost in the taste. Her hands moved away from his shoulders and shoved against his chest. Surprised, he tottered and let go of her.

She tilted backward. He snatched her hand, pulling her forward, steadying her on the rail. "I told you to hold onto me."

"You also told me we needed to talk."

"We do."

"Well, you're not talking." She pulled her hand away. "Are you trying to…to throw me off balance?"

He grinned. "Is it working?"

She crossed her arms. "I don't know. It depends on what you have to say."

Why did women always have to have words that were never straight-forward? He wanted to tell her how brave he thought she was. How much he admired her. How he knew she was protecting Taylor from a murderer.

He had never broken the law. Never shoplifted a candy bar, ran a red light, or cheated on his taxes. He prided himself on being a law-abiding citizen. But if the law gave custody of Taylor to a murderer, the law was wrong. And he was willing to cross the line. But he couldn't tell her—or anyone—he knew about the kidnapping.

Right now, all he wanted to do was show her that he cared about her and Taylor. He would protect them because they were already a part of him. He wanted her to know that she wasn't alone, that she could lean on him. He was afraid to tell her how he felt, afraid to express how vulnerable he became when he thought about what could happen to her and Taylor without him. Love wasn't something he knew much about, and from what she'd said, Quinn hadn't experienced it much either. His first wife had closed his heart; Quinn had opened it. He hadn't been able to admit that he loved her—Quinn—Laney—until last night, when he realized he would do anything—even break the law—to keep her and Taylor safe.

Quinn uncrossed her arms and clutched the rail. "If you still have some questions…"

He pressed his fingers against her lips. "Sh-sh. I don't need you to tell me anything."

He moved his hand from her lips to stroke her cheek. "You don't know how difficult you're making this for me. I didn't expect you to look so…so…"

"White?"

He tilted his head and gazed at her flushed face. "No, so…kissable." He leaned forward. Quinn leaned back.

He straightened. "O—kay." This wasn't going the way he'd planned. She obviously wasn't feeling the currents he was lost in. "I'll start by thanking you."

Her brown eyes blinked, looking even more puzzled. "Oh, for baking the cookies."

Cookies weren't exactly what was on his mind, but if she wanted to talk cookies, he'd start with that. "You saved me from being voted worst dad of the year."

She arched her brows. "You could have thanked me at the ball diamond."

Why did women, particularly this woman, have such a hard time understanding what he was saying? "I wanted to thank you with a personal touch."

He reached behind her head and removed the clip. Her hair fell onto her neck, and he trailed his fingers through the silky strands.

She snatched her clip. "Are you trying to make me forget what we need to discuss?"

"I hope so." He leaned in. This time he didn't give her time to refuse. He pulled her against him and kissed her. Not slow and soft, but with all the passion and frustration that had built up inside him. He wanted her to know how he felt clear down to her curled-up toes.

Her lips responded. She slid off the rail and wrapped her arms around him. Her body moved into his, and she kissed him with her own passion. The taste of her, the feel of her as she melted against him, made his head spin. She was making it impossible to think. Tightening his hold, he pressed her back against the bridge.

The dog barking down the block cut through his thoughts, reminding him they were in a park. A very public park. Before he went a little wild and they both tumbled over the rail and into the lagoon, he inched back, giving himself and her a chance to recover.

Quinn blinked up at him. Her dark lashes fanned her beautiful, brown eyes. "That was...very personal. But I'm not exactly sure what it meant."

Was she kidding? She didn't sound like it. Ace frowned. Jason was right. Talking to girls never worked. He'd just put everything he felt into that kiss. The heat between them was enough to overload an electrical circuit, but she had no idea what it meant?

"Do you need another demonstration?"

She held up her hand to stop him. "No, I need you to tell me why you dragged me over here."

"I thought I was saying it."

"Your mouth seems to have a different agenda." She tapped her foot on the bridge.

"Okay." He took a deep breath and tried to clear his head. "I called P.R."

She let out a soft "oooh."

"I asked a few questions. Of course, he wouldn't tell me anything. He repeated what you've said all along. I don't need to get involved." He reached over and tucked a strand of hair behind her ear. "So I'm taking his advice."

He tried to pull her back into his arms, but her body went rigid. "What exactly are you saying?"

"I'm crazy about you, but..."

"But not crazy enough to get involved." She twisted away. Before he realized it, she was running down the bridge and disappeared into the darkness.

"Quinn!" He knew this would happen. "Quinn, wait!" He dashed after her.

Quinn heard Ace calling as she stumbled across the dimly lit playground. She had to get away. She didn't want him to see how much his leaving would hurt her. She had almost believed him, believed he wasn't like the rest, believed he wouldn't walk away.

When she was near the slide, he caught up with her and grasped her hand. "Why do you always do that? Run away. We weren't finished talking."

She jerked free. "It seemed pretty finished to me. You said you didn't want to get involved."

"What? Is that all you heard? If so, we have a big communication problem." He reached into his pocket. "Here." He put a small piece of paper in her hand. "I wrote you a note."

She stared at the paper. The memory of her wedding day came flooding back. She could see Truman's note, remembered opening it and reading his scribbled words. He didn't want her.

The blood rushed from her head. She felt faint and leaned over. The rejection thundered in her head. Truman didn't want her, didn't want their child. Only the notes were all mixed up. It was Ace. Ace didn't want her or Taylor. She couldn't breathe.

"Quinn?" He brushed his fingers over her bare shoulder.

The touch was gentle and caring, making something inside her shift.

"Are you okay?"

She straightened, stiffening her back. She wasn't going to let him do this. No one was ever going to dismiss her so carelessly again. She crumpled the note in her fist.

"Aren't you going to read it?"

"No." She lifted her chin. "Say it to my face."

"I thought I already did." He scooped his fingers through his hair and paced in front of her. "I said I was going to take P.R.'s advice. I don't need to know anything else. I said thank you because it seems to me you've been looking out for everybody—Taylor, Jason, me, but not yourself."

He stopped and fixed his midnight-blue eyes on her. He didn't step forward or try to touch her. "I get it. I know you can take care of yourself. I know you can take care of Taylor alone. You don't need me—or anyone. But you don't have to do everything alone. I can help you. I want to help you—if you'll let me."

Had she heard him right? Was he saying he wasn't going to walk away?

He took her hand. "Please. Read the note."

Her fingers shook as she unfolded the paper. *Do you want to be my girl?* At the bottom were two boxes—*yes* and *no*.

She sucked in a deep breath and slowly exhaled. She repeated it. Again Three times. The panic in her stomach eased. He wasn't leaving her. She relaxed, and her lips curved into a smile. "Was the note Jason's idea?"

Ace leaned against the slide and crossed his legs. "Guess you can tell. He said that's the way guys ask girls if they like them and, since I've been out of the dating scene for a while, I took his advice."

"So are you asking me out on a date?"

"A date?" He ran his hand across his forehead. "Something like that."

Ace was wrong when he'd said she didn't need him. Oh, she needed him. Her heart ached with how much she needed him, how much she wanted him to love her and Taylor and make them a part of his life.

"Are you going to give me an answer, or am I going to have to tell Jason I struck out?"

"I don't have a pencil."

He straightened. "I didn't think about that."

She tore off the bottom corner and tucked her answer into the pocket of his T-shirt. "Tell Jason you hit a home run."

"Good." He took a deep breath and pulled her into his arms. "Because I want you and Taylor to move in with me."

Chapter Forty-One

Quinn felt the warm afternoon sun filtering through the windshield of Ace's truck. She leaned back against the front seat, enjoying the blast of air-conditioning and the sound of Faith Hill singing *there's nowhere else I'd rather be.*

In total agreement, Quinn hummed along with the radio, even though she didn't know where Ace's black Dakota was headed. She turned away from the country road flanked with fields of knee-high corn. "Are we close?"

"Yep." Ace kept his eyes on the road and his large hands on the steering wheel.

Quinn hoped he wasn't dragging her out into the middle of nowhere to have another chat about moving in with him. For the past three days, he'd reasoned, cajoled, and even badgered her about moving in. He didn't seem angry when she'd refused, only determined to change her mind.

Quinn relaxed and enjoyed the summer day. She didn't want another discussion to spoil her good mood. "Ace, let's not talk about my moving in with you today, okay?"

He turned his head toward her. "Say yes and the discussion ends."

"What makes you think we could even live together?"

He pushed back his John Deere cap and grinned. "I think that answer is obvious."

Even though he smiled, she saw the lines in his forehead and the tension in his shoulders. Unbuckling her seatbelt, she leaned over and began massaging the tight muscles.

"M-m-m," Ace moaned with pleasure. "Don't stop." He reached out and ran the pad of his thumb down her cheek.

She started at the sensations quivering through her.

"See. We wouldn't have any problem living together."

Maybe their physical attraction wasn't a problem for him, but it was definitely a problem for her. The only man she'd ever been with was Truman. And she'd promised herself that the next time she slept with a man, it would be with her husband. Ace, however, hadn't mentioned marriage. He hadn't said he loved her or even suggested a permanent relationship. The whole discussion sounded like a business agreement. He'd asked her and Taylor to move in with him so they'd be safe. And he'd made it painfully clear that he intended to be a perfect gentleman, albeit one that was blatantly interested in her.

She closed her eyes and leaned her head against the seat as she remembered his words. "Don't worry about sleeping arrangements." He'd sounded almost cavalier. "You and Taylor can share the guest bedroom. Or, if you want separate rooms, Jason and I can bunk together. After all, you'll be our guests."

Guests. He'd repeated the word as if she hadn't heard it the first time. She'd have liked it better if he'd at least hinted that he wanted her to share his bed. Not that she would. No, of course she wouldn't, not with Taylor and Jason right down the hall.

"How long would we have to stay?"

"Until Chrissy's husband isn't a threat. After that..." He stopped, his blue eyes fixing her with such a smoldering look she could barely breathe. She waited, a long pregnant pause, for him to say she could stay as long as she wanted—or maybe forever. Instead, he cleared his throat. "Once I'm convinced you and Taylor are safe, you're free to leave. Go wherever you want."

Until they were safe. Physically at least. Emotionally, the situation was a minefield, for her and for Taylor. Quinn couldn't move Taylor in with Ace and let her become more attached to him, not after he'd so clearly said he expected them to leave. She couldn't let Taylor become invested in a family that may not stay with her, not after losing so much.

And what about Jason? She could see he needed a woman's attention and she already felt motherly toward him. Last night when they'd been sitting in the stands watching Levi's ball game, she'd said something to Taylor and then automatically kissed her cheek. When Quinn looked up, Jason was staring at her, his eyes filled with yearning. She hoped his own mother wasn't using him as a playing chip against Ace. Stephanie seemed to be devoting all her time to her new husband rather than her son who needed her, poor boy.

Instinctively, she'd leaned over and kissed Jason's cheek, too. His face turned fire-engine red, and she expected him to wipe it off with the back of his hand, especially when another baseball player ribbed him. "Yuck. Why'd you let her kiss you?"

Jason only shrugged, but that shrug spoke volumes.

No, she wouldn't—couldn't—move in and get used to the four of them as a family. Not when Ace wanted it to be only temporary.

"We're here."

Quinn felt the truck stop and opened her eyes. They were parked in a U-shaped clearing of purple flowering thistle, surrounded by a thicket of woods. Ahead was a clump of thorny briar that looked familiar. "Is this where we used to pick blackberries?"

He turned off the engine. "Yep, although you did more eating than picking."

She could almost taste the sweet wild berry juice trickling down her throat. Then she remembered all the prickly thorns. Her jean shorts and cotton tank top wouldn't be much protection. "I didn't dress for berry picking."

Ace turned. "Berries won't be ripe for another week or so." His eyes moved slowly over her bare arms and legs. "Nothing wrong with the way you're dressed."

"Oh, then..." She met his gaze, and his eyes focused themselves on her. She felt suddenly shy and blushed. This was the first time he'd ever asked her to go anywhere with him—alone. Maybe he'd planned something romantic, like a picnic in the woods—some wine, cheese, and plenty of privacy.

She watched as he reached under the seat and pulled out a shiny, silver box about the size of a briefcase. Setting it on the console between them, he removed the keys from the ignition and stuck one into the lock. The lid popped opened.

Quinn looked down and gasped. Cushioned inside on thick gray foam lay two guns. She stared at the smaller one on the left, a black, snub-nosed revolver with pearl handles. "That looks like my gun."

"It is your gun. Don't suppose you have a FOID card?"

"A FOID card?"

"Firearm Owner's Identification Card."

She shook her head. "Is that a problem?"

"Not for me."

Quinn stared at the gun. "When I left to go to Summer's, the gun was in the pantry, and I locked the doors."

"That's my point. Your locks are old. Anyone could break in."

Quinn's eyes widened. "You broke into my house?"

He lifted his key ring and dangled it in front of her face.

"You have a key to my house?"

"Had it for years."

Of course Grandma Elam would have given Ace a key. But that first night, he'd come through the trap door, so she'd assumed he didn't have one.

Ace slipped a large, silver key off the ring and held it out to her. "Since I have a key to your place, here's a key to mine."

She stared at the key lying in the palm of his hand and then up into his laser-blue eyes. Her breath hitched. The cab of the truck suddenly seemed small and stifling. "Ace, we've talked about this."

"And we'll keep talking about it until I get the answer I want."

"I appreciate your offer. You're very generous…"

His eyebrows shot up. "Generous? You think I'm being generous?"

She squirmed. "Yes, very generous…and thoughtful."

Ace banged against the steering wheel. "What's wrong with you, Quinn? Don't you get it? I'm trying to keep you and Taylor alive." His words reverberated through the cab.

When she didn't say anything, Ace put the key on the ring and jerked open the door. Before he climbed out, he said, "It's a good thing Grampa Elam taught me how to treat a girl because right now, I'd like to drag you out of here and shake some sense into you."

She gave him a wide-eyed, puppy dog look that hit him straight in the stomach. He slid out of the cab and marched to the front of the truck.

Leaning against the hood, he took several deep breaths. Ever since he learned about Winston, his insides had been knotted up like tangled fishing line. Just thinking about Winston finding Quinn and Taylor made him crazy. He couldn't let that happen.

He stared across at the wooded trees, mostly oaks and elms except for a lone white river birch. A movement to the left caught his eye. He tensed. Was someone watching? Waiting for him to let down his guard? Waiting to snatch Quinn and Taylor?

He squinted toward the massive oak, its top half bent to the ground and splintered by lightning. A gray squirrel scampered across the leafless branches and jumped to a neighboring tree. A flock of starlings squawked, flapping their wings and scattering. Ace chided himself for being paranoid, yet he couldn't keep from scanning the rest of the thicket.

He didn't want to frighten Quinn, but she needed to understand the danger. He'd never asked another woman to live with him, hadn't even considered it. Quinn's refusing wasn't a total surprise, but he thought she'd weaken after a few days. He knew she was afraid of commitment, so he offered her what he was sure would make her feel safe: a temporary situation, no strings, no pressure. Just what she wanted.

Once she moved in, however, he had no intention of letting her leave. He'd just let nature take its course, and she'd end up where he wanted her, in his bed with a wedding ring on her finger. Opening his eyes each day with her beside him, being able to touch her, stroke her thick dark hair, and bury himself in her scent…just the thought of it made him delirious with desire.

Removing his hat, he swiped the sweat off his forehead. Standing in the heat thinking about what he couldn't have wasn't helping. He might as well move on to Plan B.

He walked over to her side of the truck and opened the door. "Hand me the gun case and get the ammunition out of the glove compartment."

She glanced at him and then back at the gun case. She didn't move. He crossed his arms, and spread his feet, wide-legged. "Don't fight me on this, Quinn."

He breathed a sigh of relief as she slid out of the truck, carrying the gun case and two boxes of ammunition. He smiled. "Smart move."

He took the case from her and laid it on the hood of the truck. He picked up her snub-nosed revolver about half the size of his hand. "How many times have you shot this?"

"Just once. Well, twice—at you."

"Lucky me." He gave her a wry grin. "And since you won't move in with me—right now," he paused and shot her a sideways glance, waiting to see if she would correct him. When she didn't, he grinned widely and continued, "I'm going to teach you how to shoot."

"I know how to shoot. I hit you in the arm."

"That's my point. I'm still alive." He held out the gun.

She took the .38 and wrapped her fingers around the pearl handle. "*Arigatō.*"

Ace squinted at Quinn. "What?"

"Sorry. I think it's actually a good idea."

He uncrossed his arms and put one hand behind his ear. "Could you repeat that?"

"What? *Arigatō.* It means 'thank you' in Japanese?"

"No, the part about you agreeing with me."

She smiled sheepishly. "Showing me how to protect myself is...sweet."

"Sweet?" He gave her a cautious look. "I didn't buy you a box of chocolates."

"I don't need chocolates." She held up the ammunition. "You bought me a box of bullets. Most men would want to be macho and keep the little woman dependent on them. But a sweet man, one like you, would teach her how to protect herself."

He raised his eyebrows. How could a woman turn something like learning how to use a gun into something sweet? "You aren't trying to talk me out of this, are you?"

"No, sir." She saluted and laughed. The low, throaty sound worked its way inside him, loosening the knots.

Ace showed her how to load the shells into the cylinder, cock the trigger, aim, and shoot. She listened, asked questions, and did exactly as he instructed. When he thought she was ready, he led her across the field toward a clump of trees. He tacked the paper target onto a dead oak and walked back about twenty-five yards.

Standing behind her, he watched her fire off five shots. When she finished, she squinted back at him. "How did I do?"

"Where were you aiming?"

"At the target."

"You didn't even hit the tree."

When she reloaded, he moved beside her. He watched her fire and tried to stifle a chuckle. "Next time, don't close your eyes."

She opened her mouth as if to protest and then quickly shut it. In the second round, she hit the tree and the target twice.

Ace frowned. "How did you ever shoot me in the arm?"

"I was aiming for your head."

"Glad you weren't aiming for my arm."

When she finished, Ace practiced with the 9mm Luger he bought. He showed her the clip and how to load it. Moving back an additional twenty-five yards, he emptied four clips with eight bullets each. On the last round, each bullet hit inside the center ring, and two were bull's eyes.

"Pretty impressive."

Ace leaned over and picked up the casings from the ground. "Want to try?" He held out the Luger to her.

She shook her head. "Maybe next time."

"Next time?" He draped an arm around her shoulders and led her back to the truck. "I expected you to be reluctant, not ask to come back."

"It relieved some stress."

"I'll give you that box of chocolates for that."

She laughed. "A woman never turns down chocolates."

When they were in the cab, Quinn asked, "Jason has been hinting all week about a surprise for Taylor's birthday. Do you know what that's about?"

"I know Kat and Summer are involved, and it must be a big deal because Jason asked for my credit card."

Quinn thought about Taylor's other birthdays. Quinn's heart ached because she hadn't been with her daughter. July Fourth had always been the one day she couldn't push away the guilt. This year would be different. She would share it with Taylor.

Quinn remembered her own fifth birthday and the party. She and her mom had baked the cake the night before. Then they worked on the games. They'd taped the picture of the donkey to the refrigerator and had the tails ready to pin on. They found clothespins and an old mayonnaise jar to drop them in. She'd even rented her favorite movie, *Cinderella.*

Her stomach clenched as she remembered the day of the party. She'd brought three girlfriends home with her. When she opened the apartment door, she saw her mother all dressed up. She looked so pretty with her red lipstick and high-heeled shoes. Laney raced over to her, hugging her around the waist of her gauzy skirt.

Then the recliner squeaked, and she turned to see a man rise. "Let's go," he said, putting his arm around her mother and pulling her away.

Her mom wobbled toward the door, and Laney knew she'd been drinking. She didn't like it when her mom drank and went out with strangers while Daddy was gone trucking.

"Mrs. B's in the kitchen. She'll watch you and your little friends."

Laney willed back the tears. She knew her mother hated tears. She was five years old. She was a big girl now. But when the door closed, she wasn't strong enough to keep the tears inside. Of course, her daddy had made a big deal about her birthday when he came home. But why hadn't her mother wanted to be with her on her birthday? Why had she walked out the door without even wishing her happy birthday?

Quinn nibbled nervously on her bottom lip. Just because her fifth birthday had been bad, didn't mean Taylor's would be. So why did she have this feeling that she wasn't going to be happy about Taylor's birthday surprise.

Chapter Forty-Two

One hour.

Winston sat in the dark interior of the rented Cadillac parked in a thicket of pines. Steepling his fingers on the steering wheel, he watched the digital clock on the dash.

Fifty-nine minutes. *That's how long you have to live, Dickie boy. After that, you won't be making any wisecracks about podiatrists being toe-nail clippers, you won't be rejecting Wendy's idea to adopt, and you won't be able to give Bulldog any information to incriminate me.*

Winston had been parked near the edge of the country road since four a.m. Not a single vehicle had driven up or down the hills. If someone did spot him, Winston was confident he wouldn't be recognized. His orange Tigers' baseball cap was pulled low on his forehead, almost touching the over-sized, black-rimmed glasses. His T-shirt, jeans, and Nikes gave him the look of an average baseball fan, not a renowned podiatrist.

Fifty-five minutes.

Sweat pooled under his arms and soaked into his shirt. Removing his cap, Winston patted his clipped hair, now a dark, tobacco brown. He'd gotten his hair cut after Wendy had been so distraught over his unshaven face and disheveled appearance. He realized that if he couldn't take care of himself, how could any judge expects him to take care of Phoebe?

The next day, he joined the gym and began working out. He needed to be mentally and physically fit to outwit ole Dickie boy—and find Phoebe.

Forty minutes.

For over a week, Winston had plotted ways to get rid of Richard. A gun? Bulldog might become suspicious if two people close to Winston were shot in a span of four months. The cop might check his alibi again or find the airline ticket charged on Wendy's credit card. No, Winston wouldn't use his newly acquired gun on Richard. That gun was for Melana Elam.

Winston favored poison. A slow torture. But Richard refused to dine with him and Wendy. Planting poison at their house might endanger Wendy or her baby. No matter how foolish and besotted his sister was with Richard, Winston loved her. He would do anything—even murder her husband—for her own good. With ole Dickie boy out of the way, no one would object if Wendy adopted a child—and no one would discover that Wendy had helped him cover up Chrissy's death.

Winston had begun making daily phone calls to Wendy, pretending to check on her pregnancy. Even though Wendy protested, pleasure rippled through her voice. "Oh, Win, you don't have to call me every day. I'm fine."

"Balderdash. Of course I need to call. How else will I know you and your baby are healthy?"

The phone calls continued and, as he'd hoped, Wendy chatted about other things besides the baby. She talked about work, home, and Richard. He was a pharmaceutical rep for the Midwest. His job was to explain the product, drop off samples, and encourage doctors to write prescriptions for his company's drugs. Since Richard spent hours on the road, a fatal car accident wouldn't be suspicious.

The opportunity came when Winston learned Richard would be attending a three-day conference in Atlanta. During one of his calls to Wendy, Winston slipped in a seemingly innocuous question about the trip. "Does Richard expect you to drive him to the airport?"

"No, his flight is at seven a.m., so he'll have to leave home before five."

When Wendy was pregnant with the twins, she and Richard had moved out of the city to a rustic log cabin they referred to as "The Lodge." The rural road leading to The Lodge had a dangerous, half-mile section of three consecutive hills, called "Hades Hills" by the locals. The middle one was the shortest and most dangerous. Over the years, several cars had crashed through the guard rail and plunged into the rocky ravine below. Two years ago, a Mazda had flipped over the rail and lay undetected for months.

Winston picked up the night-vision binoculars and scanned the road. He rolled down the window, letting in the heavy night air filled with the scent of pine. The slivered moon made this stretch of highway dark—and deadly.

From his perch on top of the third hill, he could see the headlights of a car as it approached the first hill. He lowered the binoculars just as a flash of light rose above that hill, illuminating the night sky.

His heart slammed against his chest. It couldn't be Richard. He was thirty minutes early.

Winston steadied his hands and turned the key in the ignition. The engine roared to life, cutting through the silence. Would the sound alert Richard? Would he look toward the car?

Winston took a deep breath, shifted the car into gear, and inched forward. Without turning on the headlights, he pulled the car to the edge of the road and fixed his eyes on the first hill.

He waited for Richard's Jaguar. He held his breath and counted. When he reached five, a vehicle loped over the hill like a lumbering elephant. Winston collapsed against the seat. It wasn't Richard. The headlights were too high, the vehicle too big. Richard's Jaguar was a sporty convertible. The vehicle coasting down the first hill was a clunky SUV.

Winston ducked down in the front seat while the SUV passed. Then he sat up, rammed the car into reverse, and backed up into the thicket. Once he was parked in the pines, he reached into his pocket for a peppermint. The familiar minty taste coated his dry throat and helped him relax. Winston chided himself for panicking. He'd been so discombobulated, which almost made him forget to pick up the pre-paid cell phone lying on the passenger seat. The entire plan depended on precision.

Once he spotted Richard's car approaching the top of the first hill, Winston would drive down the last hill without turning on his headlights. He didn't have to guess how fast to drive. Richard had bragged often enough, "I always set the cruise two miles over the speed limit, and I've never gotten a ticket."

When Winston started up the middle hill, he'd speed dial Richard on the cell. Even if Richard didn't answer, the ringing would distract him. The few seconds he took his eyes off the road were critical.

When Richard glanced back, he would be staring directly into Winston's headlights. The only way Richard could avoid a head-on collision would be to swerve toward the guard rail. Hitting the rail at top speed would send the car crashing through the metal or flipping over the top. Either way, the results would be the same. The Jaguar—and Richard—would plummet over the side and smash into the rocks.

Of course, the possibility that Winston himself might be killed in the crash had occurred to him. But it was only a cruel twist of fate that he'd survived the first auto accident. Now all he had left to live for was Phoebe. If he didn't find her, he might as well be dead.

Winston hoped it would take days to discover Richard. The death couldn't interfere with Winston's weekend plans. At three o'clock tomorrow, he planned to meet with Truman in Chicago. Winston had chosen Wesley Peterson as his alias so he could wear his gold-monogrammed cuff links with his tailored Italian suit. He planned to discuss placing his father into one of Truman's assisted-living facilities. Of course, Winston's father had been dead for years.

During their chat, he'd mention his family had once lived in southern Illinois, specifically Mt. Vernon and Hickory Hills, the two towns in Franklin County that had confirmed recent cases of peanut hypersensitivity.

Hopefully, Truman would tell Winston he'd been engaged to a woman from one of those towns. Then Winston would be able to find his precious Phoebe.

On the phone, Truman had been very solicitous, even suggesting that if Winston stayed until Saturday, Truman could get him complimentary tickets to the Cubs/Cardinals game at Wrigley Field. Winston wasn't a sports fan, but yelling at the umpires might be just what he needed to release the tension that kept building inside him.

Ten minutes.

Winston went on alert. His heart pinged against his chest. His breathing increased. His eyes shifted from the hill to the clock. Hill…clock, hill…clock, hill.

Three minutes.

Like a hungry jackal waiting for its prey, Winston locked his eyes on the hill.

One minute.

The sky remained black.

The clock changed to five a.m.

Another minute clicked by. Two minutes. Three, four, five minutes. Richard was late. Soon commuters would begin their daily trek into the city. What if Richard had changed his plans? What if he wasn't coming?

Headlights low to the ground shined over the hill. Richard's Jaguar. Winston wiped his sweaty palms on his jeans. The theme song from the old Western *Rawhide* rambled through his mind. *Move them on, Winston, cut them out, Winston.*

He picked up the phone and rolled onto the highway. At the bottom of the hill, he steered into the wrong lane. Halfway up, he pressed Richard's number. As soon as he heard the phone dialing, he tossed it onto the seat and locked his hands on the steering wheel.

"Hello. Hello?"

Cackling, Winston ignored the string of *hellos*. In a few seconds, it would all be over for Dickie boy.

Beams of light shone over the hill. Winston flicked on his brights and diverted his gaze so the approaching headlights wouldn't shine into his eyes. Then, tightening his grip on the steering wheel, Winston stomped on the accelerator and plowed to the top of the hill.

A horn blasted. Tires squealed.

Through the windshield Winston saw the driver. For a blood-stopping second, he stared in disbelief. The driver was not Richard.

"Wendy!" Winston pumped the brake and swerved.

Metal on metal. Splintering glass.

His car plunged over the rail toward the gulley and disappeared into the darkness.

Chapter Forty-Three

Taylor's birthday on the Fourth of July was ten days away. But Summer and Jason insisted on giving Taylor her birthday surprise early. Everyone—she and Ace, Summer and Craig, Ben and Belle, and Raven—but not her husband—were gathered around the picnic table on Summer's patio.

When Jason whistled, the kids stopped playing tag and ran to the patio. Taylor didn't know about the surprise. "Mommy, what's going on?"

Quinn reached down and pushed a few curls off Taylor's forehead. "You'll see." Taylor was wearing the navy pinafore that Quinn had finished last night on Grandma's old Singer sewing machine. The sundress was scattered with white stars and had a red bow on each strap. The dress was supposed to be for Taylor's birthday, but she'd begged to wear it today.

Kat was dressed like a princess: silver high-heeled shoes, a pink crinoline gown, and a jeweled crown. She clomped over to Taylor and led her to the head of the picnic table. "We have a birthday surprise for you." She handed Taylor a manila envelope decorated with pink, glittery stickers.

Taylor beamed. "A surprise...for me?" With both hands she clutched the envelope to her chest. Then she glanced at Quinn. "Can I...I mean, may I open it?"

Quinn nodded, even though inside she'd gone cold. Surprises in her life were usually bad. A new place to live. New friends. New school.

Same problems. Nervously, she nibbled on her lip as she watched Taylor open the envelope.

Taylor pulled out a page from the *American Girl* catalog and held it up, confused.

Kat pointed to the picture. "You get to pick out your own American Girl doll."

Taylor jumped up and down. Her face gleamed with joy as she twirled around the patio like a ballerina. "An American Girl doll! Just what I wanted!"

Tears welled up in Quinn's eyes. Why had she been worried? The surprise was perfect. Taylor had asked for an American Girl doll, and Quinn had hoped to buy one for Christmas, since she wouldn't be able to afford one until then. She glanced around the table and saw all the smiling faces watching Taylor. Summer's family was giving Taylor more than a doll. They were showing her how much they loved her.

Summer picked up the envelope. "There's more." She shook out four tickets. "These are to the tea party at the American Girl Place. You and your mom are going to Chicago with Kat and me."

Kat and Taylor hugged each other and squealed excitedly.

Quinn sucked in her breath. Chicago! They couldn't go to Chicago. Someone might recognize them.

Ace slipped his arm around her waist and whispered, "I'll try to fix this." He looked at Jason. "Hey, son, I thought you said I'd like the surprise. The American Girl Place isn't exactly my cup of tea."

The others laughed at his pun.

"Don't worry, Dad." Jason held up a plain manila envelope. "I've got the guy-thing covered." He handed it to Taylor. "This is from me and Dad."

Taylor fumbled with the clasp. Impatient, Jason reached over and opened it, pulling out four tickets and waving them in the air. "We're taking you and your mom to a Cardinals/Cubs game at Wrigley."

Taylor's eyes widened. "A real baseball game? Like on TV?"

Jason puffed up with pride. "It was my idea."

"Mommy, Mommy." Taylor ran to Quinn and hugged her. "I'm going to get my doll and see a baseball game."

Quinn tried to smile, but the tightness in her chest made it almost impossible to breathe.

"Hey, Party Girl." Ace scooped Taylor up and swung her around. When he planted her back on the ground, he'd turned back just in time to see Quinn fleeing into the house.

Summer walked over to Ace. "Is Quinn all right? She looked pale."

Ace didn't know how to answer. He should have been expecting something like this from Summer. She'd surprised him and Craig with that fishing trip to Canada. Neither had wanted to go. But the trip had bonded them as brothers.

Summer's intentions were good, and Ace didn't want to hurt her, so he chose his words carefully. "Maybe you should have cleared the trip with Quinn—or at least me."

"I was afraid if Quinn knew, her pride wouldn't let her accept. I'll go talk to her."

Summer turned toward the house, but Ace put a hand on her arm. "Let's give her some time. I think she might be overwhelmed."

Summer frowned. "You don't look that happy either. Is it about the trip or about Quinn moving in with you?"

Ace couldn't hide his surprise. "She told you about that?"

"No. Craig mentioned it after you talked to him. I hinted to Quinn, but she didn't say anything." Summer looked around. The children were off playing, and the other adults had congregated around Raven. "Listen, Ace. I don't think asking Quinn to move in was such a hot idea."

He frowned. "Why not? You said we were good for each other."

"You are, but Craig didn't mention a wedding."

Ace jammed his hands in his pockets. "I don't think Quinn's ready to make a commitment."

"Are you?"

"I wouldn't be asking her to move in if I wasn't."

"I hope you made that clear to her."

"No, I told her she'd be free to leave."

"Ace!" Summer put her hands on her hips. "Why'd you do that?"

"Quinn's independent. I didn't want to scare her away."

Ace detected the disapproval in Summer's voice. "So you asked her to move in and basically said you didn't care when she left?"

"It wasn't like that. Quinn has some…issues, and I'm trying to help."

"Help? Living together will only cause more issues."

"Don't worry. She isn't moving in."

"Good, then you have time to do some romancing. Send her flowers, take her to a nice restaurant, or go out dancing."

"Quinn doesn't expect those things."

Summer slapped his shoulder. "That's exactly why you should give them to her."

Ace scratched his head. "That doesn't make sense. Why should I give her what she doesn't want?"

"*Expecting* is different than *enjoying* or *wanting*, Ace. Besides, have you thought about Taylor and Jason?"

"Sure. Quinn knows I love Taylor, and Jason likes Quinn, so that's not a problem."

"Isn't it? Have you seen the way that little girl looks at you or the way Jason looks at Quinn?"

Ace glanced over at Jason playing pitch and catch with Levi. "How does he look at Quinn?"

"The same way you do."

Ace wondered if he'd made a mistake. Maybe he should have clearly told Quinn how he felt rather than hoping she understood his intentions. "I can't think about this right now. Fill me in on the details about the trip."

Summer explained that they planned to ride the train to Chicago on Friday, go to the American Girl Place, and stay with Summer's mom. On Saturday, Ace and Jason would take Quinn and Taylor to the game, and on Sunday, they'd ride the train back to Hickory Hills.

Kat came running over to Summer. "Mommy, can Taylor spend the night?"

"You need to ask Quinn, but you know she usually doesn't let Taylor stay."

"Could you ask?" Kat put her hands together. "Please, please, please."

"Okay, I'll try."

Satisfied, Kat skipped off to tell Taylor.

Summer turned to Ace. "Do you think Quinn will let Taylor stay all night?"

"I'll try to convince her—especially if you let Jason spend the night with Levi."

Summer's blue eyes twinkled. "A perfect night for romance."

Chapter Forty-Four

Quinn sat alone in the front porch swing, her arms clutching her body as she moved back and forth. What was she going to do? How could she let Taylor go to Chicago? *Yokatta*—thank goodness—that Taylor was with Summer and she could think about the problem in private. The slap of the screen door made her look up. Ace. She swiped her damp cheeks with the back of her hand. At least she wouldn't have to pretend with him.

He walked over, sat down, and pulled her into his arms. She laid her head on his shoulder, relieved to have someone to lean on. "Oh, Ace, Taylor's so excited. I can't break her heart."

He gave her a gentle squeeze. "We'll figure something out."

Quinn pulled away. "What? We can't go to Chicago. What if someone recognizes me? What would happen to Taylor if I'm arrested for Chrissy's murder?"

Ace didn't know that Winston had legal custody of Taylor. Even though Quinn was her mother, she had signed away those rights. If Taylor was discovered, then she would be taken away from Quinn and handed back to a murderer. She couldn't risk that.

"If you go, we'll make sure no one recognizes you or Taylor."

Ace sounded so confident. She wanted to believe him. She didn't want him to walk away now. But how could they build anything together unless she was honest with him? She wanted to tell him everything. But telling him she'd kidnapped Taylor was huge. He was already so worried. He didn't need to take on more of her problems.

Ace cupped her face with his hands and steadied his eyes on her.

"I'll help you. Just tell me what you want."

"I want Taylor to be happy, to have a normal childhood."

"Like the one you didn't have?"

Quinn blinked back tears. "Yes. What's wrong with that?"

"Nothing, but we can't go back and fix the past. And I'm not sure I would."

She gazed up at him. "Why not?"

"It made me who I am. And it made you who you are, Quinn." He reached out and tucked a lock of hair behind her ear. "I like the way you've turned out—except for that little tiny stubborn streak."

Her lips curled into half a smile. If only he could fix it. If only she could take Taylor to Chicago and give her a perfect day of fun. But that was impossible. Quinn rose. "I need go home and think this through. Will you tell everyone I'm not feeling well and bring Taylor home with you?"

Quinn didn't wait for an answer, but turned and walked toward the steps.

Ace jumped out of the swing. "No, Laney. Wait!"

She turned back and frowned.

"You can't run away from this…and me."

"You called me Laney."

"What?"

"You said, 'Laney, wait.'"

"I'm sorry." He raked his fingers through his hair. "I've got so much on my mind, I guess it slipped. But in the last few days, I've realized that you're still the Laney I knew, only stronger and braver."

She moved back to him and wrapped her arms around his neck. "I'm not strong or brave, Ace, but you make me feel that way."

"Then don't shut me out." He put his hands on her hips and drew her to him. "It's not just your problem, Quinn." She could hear the frustration in his voice. "It's mine, too. Whatever happens, we do it together."

"I don't want to be afraid to go places."

"If you want to go to Chicago, we'll figure it out." His lips skimmed across her forehead. "Right now, you need to go back inside and pretend you're wild about Taylor's present."

She frowned. "I can't do that."

He placed his hands on her shoulders and stepped back. "Yes, you can. And there's something else."

"What?"

His eyes darkened. "When we go inside, Taylor's going to ask to spend the night with Kat. I want you to say *yes*."

She stiffened. "Why?"

"Because Jason is staying with Levi."

Before she could react, he lowered his head, and pressed his mouth against hers. His lips sent a hot flash of heat through her, igniting everything. The kiss deepened, became dangerous and seductive.

Reason slipped away. She understood what he was asking. She knew she should turn away. If she stayed the night with Ace, it would only hurt more when he decided to leave her.

She tried to draw back. He only tightened his hold. His lips opened, parting hers and promising unspoken desires. Her resolve broke. She answered his promises with those of her own.

Just for tonight, she told herself, she'd forget all the doubts. Just for tonight, she'd pretend he was madly in love with her. Just for tonight she'd believe in happily-ever-after.

Chapter Forty-Five

The familiar "Take Me Out to the Ball Game" signaled the seventh inning stretch at Wrigley Field. Quinn, Taylor, Jason, and Ace, dressed in Cardinals caps, T-shirts, and sunglasses, stood and linked arms. Along with the other Cardinals fans, they swayed and sang, "...root, root, root for the Cardinals..."

They'd arrived at the stadium two hours before the game to devour hot dogs and watch batting practice. To Quinn, the fans were as fascinating as the practice. Some dyed their hair or wore wigs. Others smeared their faces or bodies with red or blue. The garb was as varied as the people. The constant din of cheering left no doubt which were Cubs fans and which were Cardinals. Over the chatter of the crowd, the vendors worked the stands, *Get your ice-cold drinks here, hotdogs, peanuts, popcorn.*

Quinn basked in the sun, soaking in the delicious smells and sounds. A cool breeze was blowing in from Lake Michigan, and the game was tied, 2-2. The Saturday summer afternoon was perfect. Their seats behind the dugout were perfect. In fact, Quinn thought the whole trip was perfect.

Taylor had been awestruck at the American Girl Place, agog with the choices of doll clothes and accessories. She stared at the beauty salon with its tiny chairs filled with American Girls having their hair styled by beauticians. And her mouth dropped open when she saw the doll hospital.

Without grumbling, Ace and Jason had followed them through the store packed with mothers and giggling girls. The tea party was another matter. They escorted the girls to the door and met up with them afterwards.

They'd even gone to the Hershey Place on Magnificent Mile and had their photos taken and sayings put on their own personalized chocolate bars. Ace had grinned when she showed him what hers said. "Chocolate—almost as sweet as target shooting."

They hadn't taken the train. Too dangerous. Ace had driven the six of them to Chicago in Summer's van. Craig was working there, so Summer and Kat would ride back with him, and Ace would drive them back in the van after the game. They spent the night with Summer's mom, Irene, a petite widow in her late 50's. Her light blond hair, twinkling blue eyes, and gracious welcome reminded Quinn of Summer. Irene winked at Ace and pointed to Quinn with the wooden spoon she'd been using to stir the pot of spaghetti on the stove. "It's about time you found yourself a good woman."

Quinn blushed as Ace slid his arm possessively around her waist. She didn't know how to control the jumble of emotions his touch stirred. She'd been as nervous as a teenager the night she'd stayed with him. No, more nervous, because she'd dreamed about being with Ace since she was sixteen.

But those earlier dreams had faded as soon as Ace's fingers glided over her bare skin. His touch, so feather-light, and his gentleness, so unexpected, revealed a tenderness she'd never known a man could have.

She'd lost her virginity in the backseat of Truman's red vintage 1968 Camaro. Truman had been all bravado, pawing and poking, satisfying himself. Afterwards, he'd whooped and hollered as if he'd won the lottery. She'd been mystified about why a few minutes of groping and pain was such a big deal.

With Ace, it began as a slow dance. He led, she followed. The natural rhythms of their bodies were so in tune, they made their own music. What started as a leisurely Tennessee Waltz ended in an explosive Texas Two-Step that left her reeling.

Afterwards, she lay next to Ace, heart racing, head spinning. Every part of her body tingled. She was almost giddy with this strange, new sensation. She waited for him to turn to her, give her a slow, satisfied grin, take her in his arms, and tell her how much he loved her, how long he'd dreamed about being with her.

When he didn't reach for her or say anything, she turned to face him. Resting her elbow on the bed, she propped her head up and blinked down at him. A shaft of moonlight shone in through the window and fell on his face. He looked peaceful—eyes closed, jaw slack, and lips parted in a slight smile. She leaned closer, inhaling his masculine scent, and reveling in the warmth of his breath on her flushed cheek. She thought he was teasing, pretending to be asleep.

She touched his lips, started to trace her finger over the curves of his very kissable mouth. *Zzz-zzz-zzz.*

She jerked back. Ace was snoring. Each *zzz* ripped through her heart. Ace wasn't pretending to be asleep. He *was* asleep. He'd rocked her world, but obviously, she hadn't rocked his.

Lying back and staring up at the ceiling, she understood that love made all the difference. Being with Ace had lived up to the romantic movies and songs. Each touch had been a new revelation, yet his silence confused her. She thought once she'd given herself to him, he'd tell her he loved her—had always loved her.

But she was the one with the love and needs and wants. Emotion squeezed her heart. She'd dreamed of a life with Ace. She and Taylor, Ace and Jason, and maybe even another child they could have together. She cupped her hands around her belly and imagined Ace's baby growing inside her. Did he want more children? She didn't even know. Well, it didn't matter. What had seemed earth-shattering to her must have been boring to Ace. She'd been foolish to believe in dreams. Foolish to believe in love.

She slid to the edge of the bed and sat up, ready to flee before she made a complete idiot of herself. As her bare feet hit the floor, Ace's hand brushed across her bare shoulder. His touch ignited a tiny spark of hope. She glanced back at him, waiting for some tender words of love.

"Well, this kind of changes things."

She tried not to sound disappointed. "Do you only have one line? I've heard that one before."

"I remember. You were sixteen, and I thought you were a cute tomboy—until I kissed you."

She closed her eyes. "And now?"

He toyed with her hair, sending a new wave of shivers down her spine. "You're definitely not a tomboy, and this was way better than a kiss."

Confused, she opened her eyes. When he didn't say anything else, she swallowed her disappointment and decided to match his blasé manner. She turned away and stretched like a lazy cat, feigning the same ennui he seemed to feel. "You know, this doesn't change anything." To her own ears, her voice sounded hollow, the words completely unbelievable.

"You're kidding, right?" His hand found the sensitive skin at nape of her neck and began to massage it. "Nothing?"

She bit back a moan. Crossing her arms over her bare breasts, she hunched forward. "I'm not moving in with you, Ace." Her words were barely a whisper. She waited for a reply.

The room was heavy with silence. Maybe he hadn't heard her. She cleared her throat and spoke louder. "I said I'm not moving in with you."

He removed his hand from her neck. "Okay, Quinn. I get it. I won't ask you again."

She was hurt and confused. Surely he knew she would not be here in his bed unless she loved him. She had given him everything, held nothing back. But he hadn't said anything about love.

She started to stand, flee, before he saw the hurt, but his hand caught hers. "Don't go."

She didn't want to leave, but if she stayed the night, she'd want to stay forever.

He tugged lightly, pulling her back to him. "Please. I need you—just for tonight. I won't rest if you leave."

He needed her. She wanted love, but she'd accept need, because she didn't want to leave and couldn't deny him—or her heart.

The roar of the crowd brought her back to the baseball game and to her feet. With the other cheering Cardinals fans, she watched the ball sail over the ivy-covered brick wall in centerfield. A home run. The Cardinals were leading, 3-2.

Jason and Taylor jumped up and down and clapped. Quinn reached around them to give Ace a high five. When her hand hit his, he caught it and linked his fingers through hers, tugging her toward him.

She smiled. "Thanks for the trip."

He pulled her closer, until his breath was warm on her face. "You can thank me later."

She flushed, powerless to stop the love she felt for him. He'd taken them to Chicago and kept her and Taylor safe.

Suddenly, black billowy rain clouds covered the sun, and the sky darkened. Quinn glanced around the ballpark. Before, the wigs and painted faces had seemed whimsical. Now, they looked motley and sinister.

She pulled away from Ace and rubbed her hands over the goose bumps on arms. Winston could be watching. Right now, he could be disguised in a blue wig or red face, and she wouldn't even recognize him.

When the others dropped back into their seats, Quinn remained standing. She shouldn't have drunk so much soda. Wiggling passed Taylor and Jason, she stopped in front of Ace. "I have to go to the restroom. I'll be back before the end of the game."

His large hand closed over hers, and he rose. "Come on, kids."

Jason stood, but Taylor groaned. "Aw, Mom, we want to see the last inning."

"It's okay, Ace. I'll be fine. You stay here with the kids."

He didn't let go of her hand. "We talked about this, Quinn. Remember? Everyone stays together—the Four Musketeers."

Quinn nodded, and the four of them walked up the steps and out to the corridor. The men's restroom was closest, the women's a little farther. Ace pointed to the entrance of their section. "We'll meet back there."

* * * *

Ace and Jason waited at the designated entrance. Overhead, thunder rumbled. Ace glanced up at the dark sky. "Only three more outs. Even if it rains, the Cards win." He patted Jason on the back. "The game was a good idea, son."

Jason's shoulders straightened. "Do you think Quinn liked it?"

"Quinn?" Ace thought Jason would ask about Taylor. "Yes, Quinn and Taylor both liked the game—and you."

Jason's smile stretched wider, and then disappeared. "Will Mom be mad if I don't go to her dumb wedding?"

Ace knew she'd be furious, but he'd learned negative comments about Stephanie only hurt Jason. "Think of it this way. What if you were playing in the Little League World Series and you gave someone you loved a ticket, but that person didn't show up?"

Jason twisted his mouth and considered the question. "But the World Series is way more important than a wedding."

"Not to your mother."

Jason's serious blue eyes looked up at him. "I guess that means I gotta go."

Ace tugged on the bill of Jason's cap. "Smart boy."

"Dad, have you ever thought about getting married?"

"Married?" Ace cleared his throat. "It's crossed my mind. Have you thought about me getting married?"

Jason nodded. "I think Quinn's perfect for us."

"Quinn? Perfect?" Ace's eyebrows shot up. He would have laughed out loud, but Jason seemed serious. "How do you figure?"

"Well, she's not married."

"True."

"So she probably needs a couple of guys to chop wood or kill spiders and snakes."

"I suppose." Ace stroked his chin. "How do you feel about Taylor?"

"She's all right...for a girl. But she can be stubborn when she's scared."

Was that what made Quinn so stubborn, too?

"I know baseball's only a game to Quinn, but she's a way better cook than you."

"Ouch."

"And she's pretty, isn't she?"

Ace grinned. "Very pretty."

"I think she could be as pretty as Mom. She just doesn't bother with all that stuff on her face."

"Do you think she should?"

"Nah. I like her the way she is." Jason stared down at his sneakers, dragging his toe across the concrete. "She doesn't even care when I kiss her."

So even his son had fallen for Quinn. Couldn't blame the kid. Ace checked his watch. Quinn and Taylor should have finished.

"Don't worry, Dad. Girls always take longer."

Maybe asking Quinn to move in had been a colossal mistake. Maybe he should have started the old-fashion way. He realized he should have been more romantic when she'd spent the night. He should have chilled a bottle of wine or put on some soft music. But the minute she'd responded to his kiss on Summer's porch, all he could think about was getting her into his bed. The sight of her, naked with the moonlight glowing around her, had completely undone him.

As soon as he'd touched her soft skin and ran his fingers down her back, he felt the heat. She'd been so much more than he expected. He'd hoped for the passion, and she was definitely passionate. What he hadn't expected was a shy sweetness mixed with an almost pure innocence. She had been so trusting, so open—completely without guile.

Afterward, for the first time in days, he'd been able to shut his eyes and not see Winston. As long as she was beside him, he didn't have to worry about her safety. He'd finally relaxed and drifted off to sleep. When he awoke, the pillow beside him was empty.

But she was just on the edge of the bed with her back to him. Only after he reached out and put his hand on her shoulder was he able to breathe again. He finally verbalized what he's been feeling. "Well, this changes things."

But her words had stung. "For me, this doesn't change anything."

For him, everything had changed. Ace knew when a woman responded—and she'd responded. With each touch, she opened, again and again, giving herself completely. A woman like Quinn didn't surrender to a man—unless it mattered.

He needed honesty. Stephanie had lied to him from the beginning. First about birth control and later about the men. Several times, Ace had found her in the arms of another man. Stephanie always had a ready answer—an old friend, her daddy's client…He wouldn't marry a woman he didn't trust.

He'd wait for Quinn to tell him about Taylor—to admit she wasn't her daughter, that she'd kidnapped Taylor to protect her. He understood why Quinn would be concerned about involving him in kidnapping, but she had to realize he was already involved.

"There they are." Jason pointed toward Taylor and Quinn walking out of the restroom.

As Ace watched, a man bumped into Quinn. The man was a few inches shorter than Quinn and was wearing sunglasses and a Cubs cap with the bill turned backwards. He reached for Quinn's arm and held onto it.

Ace's heart stopped. Winston. He'd found them. Ace grabbed Jason's hand and pulled him across the hallway.

Chapter Forty-Six

"Laney, is that you?"

Quinn recognized the voice. Fear ripped through her. She had to protect Taylor. Tightening her grip on Taylor's hand, Quinn stepped in front of her.

The man repeated her name. "Laney?"

"I-I think you have me confused with someone else."

He didn't let go of her arm. "Your voice is different...but you look like Melana Elam."

Quinn tried to twist free. Her hair was tucked under her ball cap, and she was wearing sunglasses, so he couldn't see the change in her hair color and eyes.

"Guess I thought you were Laney. Must be because a man was in my office yesterday asking about her."

Quinn gasped. "A man? Who?"

Truman's thick lips curved into a smug grin. "I knew it was you." He pointed behind her. "Your kid?"

Quinn shook her head and nudged Taylor farther behind. She didn't want him to see Taylor. He might figure out Taylor was his daughter.

A familiar hand gripped her shoulder. Ace. He pulled her toward him, releasing Truman's hold. "You okay?"

Her throat was closed with fear. All she could do was nod.

Ace reached for her hand. As soon as her hand slid into his, she felt safe. More importantly she knew Ace would keep Taylor safe.

Ace jerked his head toward Truman. "Who's this?"

Quinn had to stay calm. She couldn't fall apart in front of Truman.

"A college friend." She introduced them. "Truman Regal...Ace Edleston. Ace...Truman."

The air between the two men bristled; neither offered a hand.

Ace nudged her. "Let's go."

Truman reached out and grabbed Quinn's arm again.

Ace's voice was feral. "Get your hands off her."

"Let the lady speak for herself. Am I bothering you?"

Ace raised his fist. "You're bothering me."

Before Quinn could stop him, Ace shifted around her and threw a punch. Truman dodged Ace's fist, but it clipped the side of his mouth and knocked him against the wall.

Quinn gasped.

Truman wiped the back of his hand across his bloody lip. He glared at Ace, but didn't fight back.

Quinn turned to Ace and pleaded with her eyes, hoping he'd understand. "I need to talk to Truman." She pointed to a souvenir stand across the corridor. "Take the kids over there and buy them something."

"I'm not leaving you here with him."

"I'll be fine."

Truman reached into his pocket and pulled out a gold money clip. He whipped off a fifty. Before Quinn realized what he was doing, Truman reached around her and gave the money to Taylor. "Just so you know there's no hard feeling between your daddy and me."

Quinn put her hand on Ace's arm. "Please. Take the kids and go."

"Are you saying you want to stay here with this joker?"

"I need to talk to him. I'll be all right."

Truman chuckled. "Seems like the ace isn't the high card today, pal. Guess you weren't counting on a joker." Truman laughed again.

Ace clenched his fist. Why was Truman taunting him? Why was he holding onto Quinn as if he owned her? He looked at Quinn. She waved him away, shooing him toward the souvenir stand. He either stayed and pulverized Truman in front of Jason and Taylor or listened to Quinn. How many times had he jumped to the wrong conclusion? If Ace wanted Quinn to trust him, he needed to trust her.

Using every ounce of restraint Ace stepped back. "I can buy my kids their own souvenirs." He turned to Taylor. "Give the man his money."

Truman held out his hand, palm up.

Before Ace could stop her, Taylor wadded up the fifty and threw it at Truman, striking him in the chest.

Truman snarled. "Get that brat outta here."

Ace took Taylor's hand and gave it squeeze of approval. "We'll be right over there." He lifted his chin toward the souvenir stand. "Five minutes."

Quinn nodded and watched Ace lead Taylor and Jason away. With each step, the pounding in her heart slowed. Her secret was safe. Truman wouldn't know Taylor was his daughter.

But at the souvenir stand, Taylor picked up a new cap and removed the old one. Dark auburn curls, the same shade as Truman's, sprang into view.

Quinn's heart knocked in her chest. She stepped in front of Truman. Had he seen Taylor's hair? Would he know she hadn't gone through with the abortion?

She touched his shoulder and turned him around so he couldn't see Taylor. He smiled. She backed up. Too late she realized she was up against a concrete wall. Truman placed his hands on each side, pinning her there.

His breath reeked of beer and cigars. He lifted one hand and ran a finger down her cheek.

She shivered in revulsion. "You've had too much to drink."

He laughed. "I can still make you tremble. I knew you hadn't gotten over me."

Bile rose in her stomach. She'd find out what she needed to know and get away. "Who was asking about me yesterday?"

Truman reached up and took off her hat. He ran his fingers through her hair. "I'd rather talk about you and me."

She slapped his hand away. "There is no you and me. You made that clear when you left me at the altar."

"Maybe I made a mistake."

Quinn glanced over Truman's shoulder. The corridor was filling with fans leaving the game. She put her hands on Truman's chest and pushed.

He didn't budge. "You still have fire. I like that."

251

She cringed. How could she have loved this man? Memories flooded back. Truman showing off in public—kissing her, tossing around money, and bragging. For the first time, Quinn was glad he'd left her at the altar.

Quinn recoiled at his foul breath. "What was the man's name?"

"Wesley Peterson."

Quinn nibbled on her bottom lip, trying to remember someone with that name.

"Stop it."

She jerked. "What?"

He traced a finger over her lips. "You know I don't like you biting your lip."

Quinn felt herself slipping into the familiar role of trying to please him. He didn't like the gap in her front teeth, so she'd worn braces. He didn't like her wearing high heels, so she'd worn flats. He didn't like her curly hair, so she'd spent hours straightening it. The list went on and on.

She'd changed to please him. She thought if she could be the way he wanted, he'd love her—really, really love her.

Instead, he'd stripped away her self-esteem. Truman's manipulation had started on their very first date. He 'suggested' how to dress, where to shop, and who to see. It was Truman's way of controlling her, molding her into his own little Stepford girlfriend.

Quinn would never do that again. Not for him or anyone. "Let me give you my phone number." She shifted, angling her body so she could shove him away.

He relaxed his hold enough for her to slip her purse off her shoulder. Reaching inside, she dug out an old envelope and wrote down a bogus number. As she tore off the corner, the final cheer erupted from the stadium. The game was over. Now was her chance. She held out the phone number. "Here. If anyone's looking for me again, call."

He reached for the number, and she shoved her shoulder against his chest.

Surprised, he wobbled back, and she broke free. She sprinted through the fans and across the corridor to where Ace stood with Taylor and Jason.

"Let's go." She grabbed Taylor's hand and pulled her into the crowd. She maneuvered through people, making sure Ace was never more than a few steps behind.

The van was parked a block away. By the time they reached it, the rain had begun, a gentle cooling mist. Quinn wished for a cloud burst to wash away the vile feel of Truman.

She buckled Taylor into the car seat, walked to the passenger side, and opened the door.

As Quinn started to climb inside, Ace placed his hand on the door and shut it. "We're not going anywhere until you do some explaining."

Chapter Forty-Seven

Ace gritted his teeth as the wipers squeaked against the dry windshield of the van. He hadn't noticed when the rain had stopped. Turning off the wipers, he glanced over at Quinn huddled against the passenger door. Her head was down, and her arms were wrapped around her hunched body. He'd tried to talk to her after the game, tried to find out what was going on, but she'd become hysterical, screaming they had to leave.

They were an hour out of Chicago, and he couldn't wait any longer. He needed to know who Truman was and why Quinn was so scared. Spotting a McDonald's sign, he exited the highway and pulled into the parking lot.

Quinn's head jerked up. "Why are we stopping?"

He pointed to the two yellow arches.

She tightened her arms around herself. "I'm not hungry."

Ace turned to the back seat. "How about it, kids? Anyone for Happy Meals and play time?"

Jason and Taylor cheered and unbuckled their seat belts. Ace released the side doors of the van, and the kids scrambled out. He walked to Quinn's door and opened it. "Coming?"

She didn't look happy, but she followed them inside.

As soon as Jason and Taylor spotted the maze of overhead purple tunnels, they raced to the play area. Ace helped Taylor untie her sneakers and stored them in the cubicle with Jason's.

After they climbed into the tunnel, he turned his attention to Quinn. He stepped closer and slid his arm around her waist. She was trembling.

"You okay?"

She didn't answer, only leaned into him and laid her head on his chest. Overwhelmed with a fierce protectiveness, he wrapped his arms around her and held her close. The scent of rain mixed with the sweet fragrance of her hair made the smell of French fries disappear. All he was aware of was Quinn safely wrapped in his arms.

Seeing Truman with his hands on her had made him insanely jealous. But as Quinn leaned against him, the tightness eased. She was here in his arms, and she didn't act as if she wanted to be anywhere else. He waited until she stopped trembling, before he tilted her head back and gazed into her eyes. "We need to talk."

"Could—could I have some coffee first?"

He didn't want to leave her, but she looked as if she could use some coffee. He walked to the counter and returned a few minutes later carrying two cups. Quinn was sitting in a booth near the play area where she could keep an eye on the kids, so Ace placed the coffees on the table and slid in across from her.

He waited until she took a drink before he reached across the table and laced his fingers through hers. "I need to know about Truman. You introduced him as an old friend. Does that mean old *boy*friend?"

"Not exactly." She didn't look up from her coffee. "Former fiancé."

"Fiancé!" Ace held onto her hand, forcing her to look him in the eye.

Of course, he knew she'd had boyfriends. But a fiancé meant Quinn had been engaged, had been—at one point—ready to make a lifetime commitment.

She'd always moved around, even lived overseas, so he thought she'd be reluctant to settle down. Maybe Summer was right. Maybe Quinn wanted stability. Inwardly, he groaned. He'd made sure she thought he wasn't interested in anything permanent. He'd told her he'd stand by her, help fight the murder charge, protect her and Taylor, but she was free to leave at any time.

Quinn had a history of leaving. Had she walked away from the engagement or had Truman? Would she pack up and leave now if someone discovered who she was or if she knew how serious he was?

He breathed deeply and removed his hands, wrapping them around the warm coffee cup. "You said you'd never been married. You didn't mention being engaged."

Quinn glanced up at him. "It was a bad time in my life."

"What happened?"

She ran a finger around the rim of her cup. Ace needed to know, deserved to know, but telling him wouldn't be easy. She lowered her head. No matter how much time had passed, and no matter how much she loathed Truman, she couldn't get over the humiliation. Truman had rejected her in front of her friends and his family. He'd just walked away. She'd sent back the wedding gifts, written the apology notes, and paid the bills.

Even now, she couldn't bring herself to look at Ace. Telling him felt like living through the rejection all over again.

He reached over and squeezed her hand. "Why didn't you get married?"

She took a deep breath. "Truman changed his mind." She fought back the tears, and her voice quivered. "He decided he didn't want to get—to get married...at least not to me."

"So you still care about this guy?"

Her head jerked up. "No, of course not!" She leaned forward, eyes flashing. She had to make sure Ace understood Truman meant nothing to her. "I'm glad we didn't get married."

"Then why did you stay with him today and send me away?"

She glanced toward the play area. Taylor and Jason were still crawling through the tunnels. Gripping Ace's hand, she pulled him closer and whispered, "Someone came to Truman's office asking about me."

Ace stiffened. "When?"

"Yesterday."

"Who was it?"

"Some guy who used to live in Hickory Hills. When Truman told him he'd been engaged to a girl from there, the man became very interested. According to Truman, he asked all about me. I thought maybe it was Winston, but Truman gave me a different name."

Ace's hand tightened on hers. "Winston probably wouldn't use his real name. Did you ask what he looked like?"

"No." She'd been so worried about Taylor she hadn't thought

clearly. "The man's name was Wesley something. Oh, Ace! What if it *was* Winston?"

Ace gave her hand a reassuring squeeze. "I told you I'll protect you and Taylor." He took a drink of coffee and then leveled his eyes on hers. "Unless you plan on leaving."

The intensity of those blue eyes made her squirm. From the beginning, she'd been prepared to run. Two suitcases were packed and stashed under her bed. But her life had changed. Ace had changed it. He was reliable. He was willing to stand by her, protect her. He was *the* one. She loved him. She thought about all the times she should have been honest with him and knew if she wasn't honest now, she'd regret it.

She met his gaze. "That was my original plan."

His mouth hardened almost undiscernibly. "And now?"

"I can't leave." She glanced over at the play area. "It wouldn't be good for Taylor."

"Is that the only reason?"

She looked at him. Couldn't he see how she felt about him? Saying she loved him was too risky. "I'd have a hard time replacing my bodyguard."

"Is that all I am to you, a bodyguard?"

She heard the hurt in his voice. "No. You're much more than that." She took a deep breath. "That's why I need to tell you about Taylor."

Ace kept his hand locked on hers. This was what he'd been waiting for. She finally trusted him enough to admit that Taylor was Chrissy's daughter, not hers. He reassured her, "You know I'd do anything for you, don't you?"

She nodded, but he saw doubt in her eyes. She took another drink of coffee, while he patiently waited. When she put her cup down, she said, "I asked you to take the kids with you because I didn't want Truman near Taylor."

Ace frowned. "What does Truman have to do with Taylor?"

"He's—he's her father."

Ace jerked back "Father?" He'd expected Quinn to say she wasn't Taylor's mother. Instead, Quinn was telling him Truman was Taylor's father. "Whoa. Back up." Ace let go of her hand. "Truman barely glanced at Taylor, and Taylor said she didn't know him."

"Truman doesn't know he has a daughter."

"Let's see if I understand this. You and Truman had a child together, but you never told him?"

"I told him I was pregnant, but he wasn't ready to be a father."

"But you were engaged, right? He should have manned up."

"Truman didn't see it that way. He paid for an abortion."

Ace couldn't keep the scorn out of his voice. "A real stand-up guy."

"I couldn't go through with it."

Ace listened as Quinn explained that she'd been pregnant with Truman's child, but didn't have enough money to raise the baby alone, so she'd given the baby up for adoption. He supposed he might have believed it, except he knew Taylor was not Quinn's daughter. He was actually impressed with how elaborate and detailed she'd made the lie so he would believe it.

He reached for the cup, wrapping his hands around it. "Where does Chrissy come into this?"

"Chrissy was married to Max, but he was sterile. They'd applied for adoption, but to get a healthy white infant takes years. So Chrissy suggested they adopt my baby. At the time, it seemed like the perfect solution."

"So Taylor is your daughter?"

Quinn frowned. "Of course she's my daughter. Why would you even question that?"

"After you told me about Chrissy's murder, I wanted to find out what kind of problems we were up against, so I searched the Internet and read the newspaper accounts. That's when I learned Chrissy's four-year-old daughter was missing. I saw a picture of Chrissy's daughter holding a stuffed cow. I know Taylor is Phoebe Prescott. Chrissy's daughter—not yours."

"Haven't you been listening? I gave Taylor up for adoption. She's my daughter, but not legally, because I signed away my rights."

"Do you have a birth certificate with your name listed as the mother?"

"My God, Ace, don't you believe me?" She could see the doubt in his face. "I don't have a birth certificate, and the adoption records are sealed until she's eighteen."

Ace rose. "I can find out another way."

"What are you doing?"

"I'm going to ask Taylor."

"No!" Quinn jumped up. She couldn't let him talk to Taylor. How would Taylor feel if she found out Chrissy wasn't her real mother? And how would Taylor feel about Quinn giving her away? Yes, she'd done it out of necessity and love, but Taylor might not understand.

"Please, Ace." Quinn grabbed his arm and pulled him back down. "You can't talk to Taylor about this."

"I already have."

The words shattered her world. "You told Taylor I was her mother?"

"Of course not. I was talking to her and asked about her parents. She said you weren't her *real* mother."

Quinn collapsed against the booth. Relief flooded through her. "Taylor doesn't know I'm her mother. I don't want her to know—until she's ready. I hadn't seen Taylor for almost five years. I can't just spring that on her until she gets to know me."

With those words, Ace could see her story begin to fall apart. "Five years? I thought you were in Japan for only two, when you said you left her with Chrissy."

"Two years?" Then Quinn remembered the story she'd told Summer. "Actually, I left the States three weeks after Taylor was born and didn't return until a few months ago. I told Summer that I'd been gone for only two years because I was afraid of being found out."

Ace rubbed his hand over his forehead. "I'm having a hard time keeping up with what's true."

"It's not that complicated. When I first moved here, I needed to explain why I didn't know Taylor's likes or dislikes. So I told Summer that Taylor hadn't lived with me for two years. Chrissy didn't tell Taylor she was adopted. I haven't told anyone either because Taylor should be the first to know."

"So why are you telling me?"

"Because I don't want any more lies between us." She stood. "I'm tired, Ace. My head hurts. Can we just go home?"

He didn't move. "I can't get back in the van and drive for three more hours with all these unanswered questions."

"I wouldn't lie to you about giving up my baby or about Truman being her father."

He crossed his arms over his chest. "You lied before."

Quinn sank into the booth. Yes, she'd lied to him, but it was to protect Taylor. She thought the night they'd shared had brought them closer. For a short time, all her defenses had slipped away.

Was that the problem? Tendrils of fear fisted in her stomach. She felt sick. She tried to push the thought away, but couldn't. "Is this about the other night? It wasn't what you expected, so you want an excuse to walk away."

He scowled. "What are you talking about?"

"I think you heard me."

"Quinn, I have no idea how your mind works." He picked up the cup of coffee and chugged the last swallow.

"Ok, if you want me to say it. The night we had sex, and you were bored."

He choked. "Bored. How did you come up with such an idiotic idea?"

"Because you were snoring."

"I was sleeping."

"So you admit it."

Ace slapped the palm of his hand against his forehead. "Sometimes I wonder if we even speak the same language." He stood and moved over to her. Gripping her shoulders, he pulled her out of the booth and drew her against him. The contact was electrifying.

He lifted her chin with his finger and stared directly into her eyes. "I could lie and tell you how bored I was, but you matter to me." He took a breath, and she could see he was fighting for control. "I'm going to say this as clearly and plainly as I can. There wasn't one inch of you that was boring. And you might describe what happened as sex, but for me, there was a lot more than that going on."

She caught her breath. The way his blue eyes were smoldering said even more than his words. They were filled with desire and something that looked like...love? For a moment all she could do was stare at him in confusion. "But...but you dozed off."

His hands slid away from her, and he sank into the booth. "I was…relaxed. After I found out about Winston on the Internet, I couldn't eat, I couldn't sleep. But then you agreed to come home with me. When you were lying beside me, I knew you were safe."

She sat down, reached across the table, and took his hand. "Why didn't you tell me?"

His words were slow and deliberate. "I thought I showed you." He held her gaze until she blushed. "I'm not looking for a way to walk away, Quinn. But you have to level with me. I was lied to by Stephanie, and I won't be lied to again. Do you understand that?"

"I lied to protect Taylor…and you."

"I don't need you to protect me. I need the facts so I can make my own decisions."

She could hear the quiet demand in his voice. "All right. What do you want to know?"

He cleared his throat. "It's hard for me to believe you gave your child away. I think you would have loved her too much."

"I loved her too much to keep her."

He groaned. "What's that supposed to mean? And don't give me some story about how you couldn't buy the things she needed. Single mothers do it all the time."

"You're right. There is more." Superficial answers weren't going to appease him. He'd claw and scratch until he uncovered the truth. "When I was young, I never played with dolls. To me, feeding and dressing a doll wasn't much fun. I had to worry about feeding and dressing myself."

"That explains why you never made me play house with you." He gave her a wry grin. "But tomboys grow up."

"Yes, but even as an adult I never thought babies were very cute. To me they were squirmy little mysteries. What I'm trying to say is, I wasn't cut out to be a mother."

"That's the most ridiculous thing I've ever heard. Where did you come up with that idea?"

"My mother said…"

"Quinn." He put his fingers on her lips. "You're not your mother."

She sighed. "I know. I've tried my whole life not to be like her."

"And you're not. You're an amazing mother." He brushed a stray lock off her forehead. "You must be able to see how much Taylor loves you."

"I tell myself she does. Then she has one of her temper tantrums."

"When was the last time she had a tantrum?"

"She had one..." Quinn frowned. "I can't remember."

"See. You listen to her. You've helped her more than you know. But it's not just Taylor. Jason's crazy about you, and so is Kat. Children can't be fooled."

"But they're easy to love."

"That's my point. They're easy for *you* to love. And the child doesn't have to be biologically yours."

"But Taylor is biologically my daughter." She covered her face with her hands. She felt so much regret. If she lost Ace because of the lies, it was her own fault, and she'd have to live with that. "I know I've made mistakes. Big ones. I'm not perfect."

"I'm not asking you to be perfect, just honest. I need to know we can have that kind of relationship."

"I'm trying to be honest. How can I make you believe me?"

"Lay everything out. No more secrets. If there's anything that's not true or you're holding back, tell me now."

He was asking her to move out of her comfort zone. He wanted to know things that were not easy for her to say. But now was the time to take the risk, or this might be another regret.

"Okay." She swallowed. "That night at your house changed things for me, too. I said I'd never move in with you because..." She could barely force out the words. "Because it would be too painful to leave."

"Why would you have to leave?"

"Because...that's what always happens. I always lose the people who are important to me. My dad, my grandparents, Chrissy, the baby, Truman...even you."

"Oh, Quinn." He felt a lump in his throat. He rose, moved to her side of the booth, and put his arm around her. "You know your dad, your grandparents, and Chrissy didn't have a choice."

"I know." She leaned her head on his shoulder. "Still...it hurts."

"And, for the record, I never left you. Circumstances kept us apart."

She shrugged. "Do you ever wonder what would've happened if we hadn't lost track of each other?"

"I'd like to think we'd still be together."

She reached up and ran her hand over the prickly whiskers on his cheek. "It worked out better this way."

"Why? Because we're older and wiser?"

She smiled. "No. Because I have Taylor, and you have Jason."

His heart swelled. "Only a mother would say something like that." He looked over at Taylor. She had the same curly hair, the same gap in her front teeth coming in, and that same stubborn streak as Quinn. When she'd thrown that money at Truman, it had reminded him of Laney. Relief flooded through him. How could he have doubted that she was Quinn's daughter. "Taylor really is your daughter."

Quinn nodded. "If you didn't think Taylor was my daughter, that means you thought I'd kidnapped her. And you were still willing to help me keep her?"

"I said I'd do anything for you. All anyone has to do is look at you and Taylor to know you belong together."

"Oh, Ace, I feel so guilty for giving her up."

He put his hands on her shoulders and turned her to face him. "Let it go, Quinn."

She searched his eyes. "How?"

"After the divorce, Stephanie made me feel guilty every time I wanted to see Jason. She said she didn't think it was good to disrupt his life because of what I wanted. And I bought into that. I let her decide when I could see my son. But you made me realize Jason needs me."

"That's different, Ace."

"Did you have an abortion? Did you abandon Taylor?"

"Of course not. I love Taylor."

"Then you only did what most mothers do—what you thought was best for your child."

Jason walked up to the booth. "Dad."

Quinn smiled and looked over at Jason.

"Have you asked Quinn yet?"

She looked back at Ace. "Asked me what?"

"Sh-sh." Ace pressed his lips together and put his finger over them. "Guys can have secrets, too."

Jason gave her a sideways glance. "Can we eat now?"

"Okay, but we need to hit the road." Ace rose and put his hand on Jason's shoulder. "I'll order Happy Meals to go." He turned to Quinn. "Do you want anything?"

Oh yeah, she wanted everything. "The full meal deal."

Ace's eyebrows shot up. "I thought you weren't hungry."

She didn't mean a sandwich, fries, and drink. She wanted the full meal deal with him. Marriage, kids, and a house with a white picket fence. She'd told him everything, and he hadn't walked away. What would he say if he knew she loved him?

"Hamburger or chicken?" asked Ace.

"Chicken. Definitely chicken."

Chapter Forty-Eight

Winston lay in the bed-and-breakfast's four-poster bed, his eyes closed. He willed his mind to stay in numbing darkness, to delay the force of the pain that would hit when he awakened. Images from the crash reeled through his head. A faint light from the moon lit the highway as he pressed his foot on the accelerator and raced up Hades Hills. One thought was pulsing through his mind, *kill Richard.*

His sweaty hands, inside surgical gloves, gripped the steering wheel tighter. When he crested the hill, he switched on the headlights. They beamed onto the Jaguar, flooding the interior. Two people were inside. Richard was not behind the wheel. Wendy was driving.

Winston swerved, avoiding the car, and headed straight for the guardrail. His car careened through the rail. Metal against metal. The Caddy shot into space. Defying gravity, the car floated, suspended above the ground. Then it nosed down, plummeting toward the pine trees and boulders.

He didn't remember the impact. When he gained consciousness, he was trapped inside the car. Trying not to panic, he unbuckled his seatbelt, found his cell phone on the floor, and retrieved the gun from the glove compartment. He used the butt of the gun to break out the side window.

Shards of sharp glass scraped his hands and arms as he crawled through. His left arm hung limp and unnatural. Probably broken, but he couldn't worry about that. Using his good arm, he scooted away from the wreck so he would be safe if the gas tank exploded.

He leaned against the trunk of a pine and stared at the path of the car. If it had hit a few feet one way or the other, it would have crashed into the forest. Instead, the Cadillac topped a line of white pines, which slowed its speed and softened the crash.

Winston pushed away from the tree and stood wobbly. He didn't have the strength to climb up the gulley, so he climbed down. The descent was agonizing, especially in the muggy summer morning. His baseball cap had been left behind in the car. Sweat dripped from his head. One slip of his white Nikes on the jagged rocks and he'd tumble end over end, breaking bones and possibly his skull. His carcass would lie with the empty cicada shells until some turkey buzzards smelled his bloated body baking in the sun. Then they'd circle overhead, mewing, before swooping down and pecking at his raw flesh. His eyes, a delicacy, would go first.

That gruesome image kept him sure-footed and slow. After more than an hour, Winston spotted a rural road lined with clumps of serviceberry and buckthorn bushes. He stumbled to the bushes and collapsed. Hidden from the road, he devised a plan to stop the next vehicle and have the driver take him to the hospital. The first vehicle rambling toward him was a farm truck loaded with grain. *Too noticeable driving into the city.* The second was a rusted-out car with a roaring muffler. *Too noisy.* The third was an SUV. *Perfect.*

Winston staggered onto the highway, praying the driver wouldn't plow into him. The brakes squealed and the hood of a maroon SUV stopped inches in front of him. The driver's door flew open, and a short, plump woman with a long, brown ponytail rushed toward him. He asked the woman to drive him to the Henry Ford Hospital. She agreed and had him lean on her as she helped him into the passenger side. Strapped in the back of the SUV was a sleepy-eyed toddler caressing a fuzzy pink blanket and sucking on a binky.

On the drive to the hospital the woman shifted her eyes from the highway to him. She seemed nervous. Maybe she spotted the gun under his shirt, tucked into the waistband of his jeans. Or maybe she thought he was some kind of serial killer. When she pulled up to the entry, her curly-haired little girl was asleep, so Winston had little trouble convincing the motherly Mary Ann to drop him off at the emergency room door. When he shut the door, she looked relieved.

As soon as the SUV swung out of the parking lot, he hurried around the corner and sat on a wooden bench near the main entrance. He waited until a group of people walked toward the door. Slipping in behind, he followed them through the main entrance to the bank of elevators.

Henry Ford was where Winston performed most of his podiatric operations, so he knew the layout. He rode the elevator down to surgery, showered in the men's locker room, bagged his clothes, and donned green surgical scrubs. Next he tended to his bruises and lacerations. The shock of the wreck had begun to wear off, and the pain from his arm increased.

He bungled his ID number twice before he logged onto the computer in the doctor's lounge and sent two prescriptions for Wesley Peterson to the hospital pharmacy. Then he checked the patient registration. Neither Richard nor Wendy had been admitted.

Before he left the hospital, he stopped at the pharmacy and picked up the Oxycontin and a sling that he had requested for Wesley Peterson. After taking the pain pill, he left the hospital and boarded a city bus that dropped him a few blocks from his house. He was unsteady and had to stop twice to keep his balance as walked the rest of the way. At home, he worked on setting the humerus bone in his left arm. He found nothing humorous about the break, and even after it was in place and supported with the sling, the pain continued.

He hadn't wanted to cancel his appointment with Truman for the following day, so he flew to Chicago, had a driver pick him up at Midway and was, as scheduled, sitting in Truman's high-rise office overlooking Lake Michigan right on time.

Truman liked to talk, as long as it was about himself. He pontificated on all kinds of subjects: his women, his wealth, and his accomplishments.

When Truman finally asked Winston about himself, he said, "I live in southern Illinois. Right now in Mt. Vernon, but I used to live in Hickory Hills. Do you know anyone from there?"

"I was engaged to a girl who had a grandmother in Hickory Hills."

Bingo. "What's her name? Maybe I know her."

"Melana Elam."

A clash of cymbals jerked Winston out of his reverie. The sound was followed by a tuba and a trumpet. Was a band playing, or was he still dreaming?

He threw his right arm over his face, blocking the needles of sunlight shooting from the curtain-less windows across the room. He squinted and scanned the bedroom, trying to orient himself. On the wall across from the four-poster bed hung a pair of crossed javelins, and on each side of the massive oak door flickered bronze sconces. Winston wondered if the nightmare had transported him to medieval times. But the rush of the air-conditioning and the cell phone plugged into the charger on the nightstand assured him he was in the twenty-first century and in the same guest room he'd checked into yesterday.

His wristwatch said 8:00 a.m. He reached for the bottle of pills and popped two into his mouth. Closing his eyes, he waited for the drug to ease the pain in his arm. But the pills couldn't take away the agony of seeing his sister behind the wheel of the Jaguar.

Thank God, Wendy and her unborn child hadn't been killed. She'd called him in Chicago. "Richard's in critical condition. I need you."

Of course, he'd flown back to Detroit immediately and stayed by his sister's side. He had explained away his own injuries by fabricating a story about wrecking the car he'd rented in Chicago. But his injuries and pain were for naught because Richard was expected to have a complete recovery.

Well, at least nothing could be traced back to Winston. When the police found the wrecked Caddy, they'd know the name of the hit-and-run driver—Wesley Peterson. But no fingerprints would point to him, and his DNA was not on record. So no one would know he caused the accident. After reassuring Wendy about himself and playing the caring brother-in-law to Richard, he begged off, saying he had an urgent meeting back in Chicago that he needed to get to, but that he'd check in with Wendy every day, same as before. He left Detroit on a ticket back to Chicago and then had driven himself down to this pathetic small town.

Outside, the sound of discordant instruments continued to scrape against his raw nerves. Easing himself out of bed, Winston inhaled against the sharp pain in his arm as he padded to the window overlooking the street. A high school band, dressed in black pants and white shirts, was warming up for the parade.

Yesterday, when he checked in, the receptionist told him about the Fourth of July parade. Today, America would be celebrating with him as he was reunited with his daughter on her birthday.

Winston was wobbly as he walked into the adjoining bathroom. He leaned against the sink and stared at the unfamiliar face in the mirror of the medicine cabinet. He hadn't shaved since the accident more than a week ago. His facial hair was no longer scraggy, but had grown into a neat beard. He applied Grecian formula to the new growth to make it match his tobacco-brown hair.

He reached for the black-framed glasses on the counter and slipped them on. Seeing the overall effect, Winston was satisfied that the beard, hair color, and glasses would keep Melana from recognizing him.

A gentle rap on the bedroom door startled him. Winston, still dressed in his green-striped pajamas, crossed the room, opened the door, and peeked out. Standing in the hallway was the woman who had checked him into the bed and breakfast. She was pregnant, and her motherly glow made him think of her as a dark-haired siren.

"Good morning, Mr. Jenkins."

The pills were making it difficult for his mind to focus. Then Winston remembered that Stanley Jenkins was the name he'd used to register.

"You asked about tickets to today's twilight tour. We've had a cancellation." Her soft, melodious voice fit into his image of her as a siren. "Are you still interested?"

Winston searched his memory for the woman's name—something associated with that black, silky hair that tumbled down her back. Remembering, he quoted some lines of poetry: "While I nodded, nearly napping, suddenly there came a tapping/As of someone gently rapping, rapping at my chamber door."

Her smile widened. "A fan of Poe?"

"It seemed appropriate. What time does the tour of the Old Slave House begin, Raven?"

Chapter Forty-Nine

Quinn stood on the sidewalk near the bed and breakfast. A warm summer breeze ruffled the skirt of her strawberry sundress. A few feet away, Taylor stood in line, waiting to register Gogo for the parade. The puppy was dressed like a firecracker, her body wrapped in a knitted blue huggie and her tail decorated in red to resemble a flickering flame.

Most of the children were dressed in patriotic costumes representing historical, book, or film characters. Taylor had refused to dress up, but had put on the navy blue pinafore with white stars that Quinn had made.

The traditional children's parade was led by the high school band and kicked off the Fourth of July Festival. The band, like a group of Pied Pipers, marched around the town square and the children followed them. The parade ended in the park where the judging was held.

Quinn remembered the year she and Ace entered the parade as Raggedy Ann and Andy. They'd worn orange mop wigs, red-checked shirts, and denim bibs. Hers had a skirt with a ruffled, white apron. She'd participated in the parade every summer she stayed at Hickory Hills. But the only time she or Ace had won a blue ribbon was when they entered together. Even back then, there was something special about them when they were together.

She and Ace had seen each other every day since they returned from Chicago. They'd stolen kisses when Taylor and Jason weren't watching and talked on the phone after the children were tucked into bed. She looked forward to Ace's nightly call and loved to hear about his day and tell him about hers.

On Tuesday, she'd asked Ace for advice. "Taylor refuses to wear a costume for the children's parade. I wanted her to be Lady Liberty and made a sunburst crown for her head, but she wouldn't try it on."

Ace cleared his throat. "Did she tell you why?"

"Only that she doesn't want to be someone else." Quinn let out an exasperated sigh. "What should I do?"

"Listen to your daughter, Quinn. Maybe Taylor could make a costume for Gogo and enter the pet category."

The next night on the phone Quinn told Ace how excited Taylor had been about a costume for Gogo. "How did you know?"

Ace was silent for a long time before he said, "A few weeks ago, I saw some pictures of Taylor on the Internet. They were pretty unsettling."

"Pictures of Taylor on the Internet? And you didn't tell me? Were they...oh God, were they porn?"

"Nothing like that, but I didn't tell you because I knew you'd be upset."

Her hand gripped the phone. She was upset, especially because he hadn't told her about the pictures, but she bit back an angry retort. Now she understood how her omissions must have hurt him. "I want to see them."

"I'm not sure that's a good idea, Quinn."

"The more I know about Taylor, the more I'll be able to help her."

Another hesitation. "If that's what you want."

The next afternoon Summer took the kids swimming, and Quinn walked over to Ace's. They went to his office and pulled up Winston's Facebook page. Each time a new set of pictures appeared on the monitor, Quinn felt ill. Finally, when she stared at Taylor looking malnourished, Quinn ran to the bathroom and heaved until her insides felt raw. When she came out, Ace pulled her into his arms. He hadn't said anything, just held her until she quit shaking.

Now, as she stood on the sidewalk, she no longer felt warm. The sun was still shining, but goose bumps rippled up her arms, and an icy chill ran through her. Quinn had expected to be brimming with joy. For the first time, she would spend the day with her daughter on her birthday. But an uneasiness lodged behind her breast bone.

She'd wanted to walk with Taylor in the parade, but Taylor had been belligerent. "I'm five and can walk by myself."

Their compromise was for Taylor to walk in the parade, alone, while Quinn followed close by on the sidewalk. As Taylor led Gogo to her place in line, a slight breeze lifted the hairs on the back of Quinn's neck. She looked around at the crowded street lined with unfamiliar faces, and her skin prickled. One of those unfamiliar faces could be Winston.

Chapter Fifty

Ace parked the car down the block from where the children were lined up for the parade. He wasn't happy about Quinn's decision to come separately, but it made sense for him to drive the car to pick up Miss May while Quinn used his truck to take Jason, his bike, Taylor, and Gogo. The fear he'd felt in Chicago when Truman had grabbed Quinn hadn't gone away. What if the man who'd come to Truman's office was Winston? Truman could have told him something that would lead him straight to Quinn.

He scanned the unfamiliar faces lined up and down the parade route. Then he spotted Jason, straddling the bike and waiting for the parade to begin. Jason was dressed as Abe Lincoln with a full beard and a stove-top hat. Rolled up in the pocket of his long-tailed coat was a copy of the Emancipation Proclamation. According to local legend, while campaigning, Lincoln had visited Hickory Hills and had attended a party at the Old Slave House. Maybe Lincoln had seen the slaves and been influenced to draft the document.

As Ace watched, Quinn walked up to Jason. She was wearing that perky little sundress he liked, along with a straw bonnet and sunglasses. She leaned over and said something that made Jason laugh. Ace had begun to notice the little ways Quinn showed Jason he mattered and was cared for. He doubted if Quinn was aware of what she was doing, but somehow she sensed how much Jason needed a motherly touch.

Seeing Quinn and his son laughing together put an extra spring in his stride as he walked around the car and opened the door for Miss May. She looked patriotic in her blue polyester pants suit with a red-and-white

273

polka dotted scarf. He held out his arm, and together they strolled to their usual spot under the maple on the boulevard of the Methodist Church.

"You're a dear boy." She patted his hand as he helped her settle into a lawn chair. "Not like my nephew, who didn't have time to come down for the holiday."

Ace let the remark pass. Nothing could dampen his spirits today. At breakfast, he'd confided in Jason. "I've decided you're right. Quinn is perfect for us, and today I'm going to ask her to marry me."

"All right!" Jason gave his dad a high five. "Do you have a ring? You have to have a ring. Girls love things like that."

"I think I have that covered."

When Laney was sixteen, they'd gone to a local pizza parlor, and while they'd waited for their food, they plugged quarters into the arcade games. One of the prizes was a round, plastic egg with a rhinestone ring inside. Ace had widened the adjustable band and slipped the ring onto her finger. "Someday maybe I'll give you a real diamond."

Reaching into the pocket of his khaki shorts now, he pulled out a similar egg and handed it to Jason.

His son opened it, and his eyes widened as he stared at the gold band with a small diamond, not quite half a carat. "Wow! She'll really like this."

Ace knew Quinn would recognize Grandma Elam's ring. When she had offered it to him, she'd said, "Give it to a girl you fancy enough to make your wife."

Ace rubbed his hand over the pocket of his khakis and felt the egg. He had never given the ring to Stephanie. She would have sneered at the small diamond. He should have known then she wasn't right for him. But if all went well, today he'd slip the ring onto Quinn's finger.

Hearing the band, he looked down the street at the American flag. Miss May rose and Ace kept his arm near so she could hold onto him.

Ace spotted Jason's stove-top hat, just before he rode into view. He honked his horn—*ugha, ugha*—and waved. Behind the bicycles were the children in patriotic costumes, followed by the pets.

He caught a glimpse of Quinn walking down the sidewalk toward him, the skirt of strawberry dress swaying from side to side, accentuating her figure. His throat caught. She glanced up, and their eyes met. Her

274

face lit up with a smile that shot straight into his heart.

She strolled over and kissed Miss May on her rouged cheek. Then she turned to him and planted one on his cheek. The pleasure of her kissing him with all the world to see made his heart beat as loudly as the band.

Miss May pointed toward the street. "Here comes Taylor. She reminds me of Grandma Elam's little granddaughter. I can't think of her name." She turned to Ace. "You know who I mean. That cute little tomboy you liked so much."

Ace looked toward Taylor. "You mean Laney?"

Quinn elbowed him. "So she was cute, and you liked her?"

He winked at her. "Yeah, I liked her, and she was cute, but not as cute as Taylor."

Quinn laughed. "Finally, we agree on something."

Chapter Fifty-One

Winston's stomach rumbled as he stood near the entrance of the park and watched the children in the parade stream by him. He felt dizzy and should have eaten breakfast. He was wearing a cap and sunglasses, but the sun was hot and sweat dripped from his forehead. The pain in his arm had not let up, even after he'd swallowed two more pills.

Why hadn't he spotted Phoebe? If she was in this town, she would be in the parade, decked out as a beautiful storybook princess. But each time a girl he thought might be Phoebe approached, he was disappointed.

A puppy dressed as a firecracker turned in front of Winston. The puppy lifted her leg and peed, inches from where Winston stood. Winston stared down at the puddle near his feet. The acrid smell of urine was nauseating. He turned to snap at the little girl being led into the park by the puppy on a leash.

The girl's back was to him, and she wasn't wearing a costume, just a navy blue dress printed with white stars and a red satin ribbon tied at the waist. Something about the way she moved caught his attention. She was taller than Phoebe, and her hair was short and curly, but the color was a perfect burnished red.

Winston followed her into the park and watched as she climbed the steps to the bandstand and paraded in front of a row of judges. Before she descended the stairs, she stopped and turned toward the audience.

Winston gasped. The girl had black-rimmed glasses and two missing front teeth. How could he have thought this homely-looking urchin with that disgusting mutt was his precious Phoebe?

He should have known the girl couldn't possibly be his daughter.

Phoebe loved fancy clothes and would have dressed up in a gown and worn fashionable shoes—not canvas sneakers. The last few times they'd played dress up, Phoebe had been petulant, but that was Chrissy's fault. She'd turned the child against him. Now that Chrissy was gone, Phoebe would be delighted to pose in Fee's gowns. Maybe he'd even enter her in a pageant. He smiled, imagining Phoebe with a trophy and saying it was all because of her Daddy Win.

* * * *

The sun warmed Ace's bare back as he perched on the stool of the dunk tank above a pool of icy water. Quinn stood outside the fence, collecting tickets and distributing baseballs. Jason and Taylor were inside, retrieving the used balls on the ground. So far, Ace hadn't enjoyed the festival as much as he hoped. They'd eaten Coney dogs and drank lemon shake-ups, ridden the tilt-a-whirl until they were so dizzy no one could stand up straight, and he'd kissed Quinn at the top of the Ferris Wheel while Jason and Taylor made loud smooching noises. But he hadn't been able to relax. Too many strangers made him uneasy.

From his perch, he scanned the crowd. If Winston were here, Ace wasn't sure he'd recognize him. Winston could be anyone—even the man with his arm in the sling ambling toward the dunk tank. He was the same height and build, but the baseball cap and sunglasses hid his face. The man was looking in their direction, but with the sunglasses, Ace couldn't tell if he was watching Quinn or Taylor.

"Having a good time?" Ace asked Taylor, who was standing near the side of the dunk tank.

She grinned, then reached up and smacked the target. Ace plunged into the pool of frigid water. When he came up sputtering, Taylor was rolling on the ground, laughing. Ace glanced toward the man with the sling. He was gone.

After Ace finished his shift at the dunk tank, they walked to the picnic area to set up the tables for Taylor's birthday, a family potluck before the fireworks. Raven was first to arrive. She looked tired, and her ankles were swollen. Ace led her to a table and told her to relax while he carried the sacks of paper plates, chips, and the birthday cake from her car.

While Quinn and Taylor checked out the cake decorated with a princess crown, Ace whispered to Raven. "After we eat, can you watch the kids while Quinn and I take a short walk?"

Raven nodded. "Be back before six-thirty. I have to lead a tour of the Slave House at seven."

"No problem."

Ace had considered popping the question during the fireworks, but it would be dark, and he wanted to see Quinn's face. The perfect place to propose would be on the bridge.

During supper, he managed only a few bites of the chicken leg and a couple spoonfuls of potato salad.

"Where's your appetite?" asked Quinn. "I thought after that workout in the dunk tank, you'd be famished."

"I guess I'm queasy from the rides." But he knew the rumbling in his gut had less to do with the rides and more to do with his impending proposal.

Most of the family had come to the picnic, except Raven's husband, who couldn't get a flight back from his business trip, and Ben, who was on duty.

"Come on, brother," Craig said after everyone finished eating. "Let's show these kids how to play baseball."

Ace begged off, saying he was tired. Craig arched his eyebrows in surprise.

Quinn rose to follow the others, but Ace took her hand. "Aren't you going to keep me company?"

Quinn sat back down and glanced across the table at Raven. "You didn't eat much either. Are you feeling all right?"

"The twins have been crazy today." She looked around. "I hope Ben stops by. I want him to check out this guy staying at the Castle. He gave me a phony license plate number. I thought maybe he was having a *tete-a-tete*, but no one showed up."

Quinn sat up straighter. "What state was the license from?"

"It was..." Raven bent over. "Oh God, something's wrong." She grabbed her stomach. "The babies."

Raven's eyes rolled back, and her body went slack. Ace shot up and around the table in time to catch Raven before she slid to the ground. As he glanced at the picnic table, he saw spots of blood where Raven had been sitting.

"Quinn, we have to get Raven to the hospital."

"I'll call an ambulance."

"The hospital is only four blocks away. It'll be faster to take her." He reached into his pocket and tossed her the keys. "Drive my truck over here. I'll call Doc Morgan and have him meet us there."

As Quinn sprinted across the park toward the truck, Ace pulled out his cell phone and called the hospital. When he hung up, he yelled for Craig. His tone alerted everyone, and they stopped playing ball and rushed over. Summer saw Raven lying on the ground and poured ice water from a thermos onto a rag and bent down. When Summer placed the cold rag on Raven's forehead, her eyes fluttered opened.

"Don't try to get up," Summer said. "We're taking you to the hospital."

Ace rose and paced back and forth, watching for the truck. "Where's Quinn? She should have been here by now."

"She's probably caught in traffic," said Belle. "Everyone's coming into the park for the fireworks. I'll call Ben so he can escort us to the hospital." After Belle made the call, she continued to worry aloud. "The bakery girl called in sick and Raven did the extra work. I told her not to push herself. I wanted her to go home and rest, but she wouldn't listen. Let me go to the hospital with her. Maybe I can do something."

"Craig and I'll stay here with the kids," said Summer. "Ace, do you want to leave Jason and Taylor with us?"

"Jason can stay, but you'll have to check with Quinn about Taylor."

Taylor crossed her arms. "If Jason gets to stay, I do, too. It's my birthday."

Ace pulled Taylor aside. "This is serious, Taylor. Raven needs to go to the hospital, and your mommy isn't going to have time to worry about you."

Taylor's eyes widened. "Is Raven having her babies?"

"Let's hope not. If you want to help Raven, do what your mommy says." He leveled a stern look at her. "Understand?"

Ace heard the truck and glanced up as Quinn careened across the grass. She stopped a few feet from the picnic table and flung open the door. "Put Raven in the back with me." Quinn motioned to Taylor and Jason. "You kids get in the front."

"Jason's staying with Summer and Craig," said Ace. "Taylor wants to stay, too."

"Taylor, get in the back with me."

Taylor crossed her arms. "I want to ride in front."

"Taylor!" screamed Quinn.

Belle hurried over and grabbed Taylor's hand. "She can ride in the front with me."

Craig and Ace hoisted Raven up under the arms and helped her into the back of the cab.

As Ace started to shut the door, Raven clutched her stomach and groaned. "Oh no! I was supposed to lead the tour to the slave house. It starts in thirty minutes."

Belle turned and looked at Quinn. "I hate to ask, Quinn. I know it's Taylor's birthday, but would you lead the tour?"

Chapter Fifty-Two

"I hate to ask you, Quinn. I know it's Taylor's birthday, but would you lead the tour?"

Winston leaned against the large oak, listening to the conversation near the picnic area. He'd seen Raven and had started to walk over to tell her he'd be staying another night. When he was a few yards away, she'd swooned. The man across the table rushed to her side, catching her as she collapsed.

Winston's hands itched to touch Raven's feet. Ever since he'd spotted her plump pink toes beneath the check-in counter, he'd fantasized about them, imagined manipulating them and relieving the swollen discomfort. If he applied pressure to the right points, her beautiful brown eyes would darken and her lush lashes would flutter up at him. Pain shot through his useless arm. His fantasy faded. Then he'd heard the word *birthday*.

He focused his attention on the woman named Quinn and the girl called Taylor—the same girl he'd twice mistaken for Phoebe. Was it possible for a child to change that much in four months? Her front teeth were missing, her hair was shorter, and she wore glasses. But what bothered him the most was her body. She was no longer petite. If she added a few more pounds, she would actually be plump.

A police siren shrieked through the park. Winston inched away, pressing back against the tree. The high-pitch filled the air. His heart pounded like the *rat-a-tat-tat* of a machine gun. A few feet from him, a black-and-white cruiser with red-and-blue lights pulsing screeched to a halt. The truck roared across the grass and pulled behind the police car, which cleared the way for them to exit the park.

Winston sagged against the tree. The police weren't looking for him. Pain radiated from his arm. He took several deep breaths and tried to concentrate.

Peeking around the tree, he checked to see if the girl called Taylor had left in the truck. She was still here and had resumed playing baseball with the others. If he could get a closer look, maybe he'd spot something to convince him she was Phoebe.

He waited for her to bat. When it was her turn, she stepped up to the crumpled pizza box being used for home plate. She looked ridiculous playing baseball in a dress and wearing a cap with the bill turned to the side. If this was Phoebe, she should be competing for Miss Firecracker, not chasing grubby balls.

On the first pitch, the girl swung and missed. On the second, she smacked the ball, sending it down the third base line. Lowering her head, she fisted her hands and raced toward first. Safe. Jumping up and down, her dress billowed around her legs. His Phoebe was way too prim and proper for such childish behavior.

The next player swung three straight times and was out. The inning was over. The girl stomped over to a pile of gloves behind home plate, picked one up, and loped out to right field.

Maybe he could talk to the girl. He strolled by the picnic tables where the woman with the blonde ponytail was packing away leftover food. She glanced his way. He lowered his head, continuing across the grass toward the girl. Maybe if he called to Phoebe, she'd hear the name, turn, and recognize him. Then he remembered his beard and brown hair.

Two teenagers holding hands walked around him and started across the grassy outfield. Winston followed. If he veered a few feet left and kept walking, he'd be able to reach out and touch the girl. He took one step in her direction, then another and another. She was less than ten feet away, almost in reach.

Whack. The batter hit the ball. It sailed straight toward the girl. The third baseman and centerfielder charged after it. With outstretched gloves, they headed toward him. All three missed. The ball plunked onto the ground next to him and rolled toward the outfield. The trio scrambled after it, dashing by Winston. He hurried to the opposite side, stopping near the edge of the makeshift field.

The next batter approached the plate. The girl was alone in right field. Winston lowered his head. His eyes darted from side to side. No one seemed to be watching. Quietly, he called out, "Phoe-be." The name floated in the air. "Phoe-be."

The girl turned. Winston crooked his bony finger, beckoning to her. She moved, but not toward him. Furious, he snapped his fingers the way he did whenever she became stubborn and refused to obey

The girl froze.

Winston hurried toward her.

A boy playing second base called out. "Taylor, turn around. You can't catch a ball with your back to the plate."

The girl didn't move.

The boy yelled again. "Taylor. Quit playing like a girl."

Winston was within two arms' lengths, but the boy reached her first. "What's wrong with you? Don't you want to win?"

The girl raised her arm and pointed at Winston. The boy stared in his direction, as the girl choked out his name. "Daddy Win."

A surge of joy shot through him, and he stretched out his arms. "Phoebe. Come to Daddy."

The boy grabbed Phoebe's hand and dragged her behind as he ran toward the picnic tables. The woman with the ponytail was staring at the two children—and him.

Winston turned and fished in his pocket for a peppermint. He'd been so close. A few more feet and he would have touched his Phoebe. But that obstreperous little twerp had whisked her away. He popped the peppermint into his mouth.

He'd found his daughter. Phoebe had recognized him. These people could change her looks, but they couldn't sever the bond between them. Inside, she was still his little girl, and he would always be her Daddy Win.

Sucking on the peppermint, he turned and shuffled away. The soothing mint cleared his mind. He'd snatch Phoebe, but not in the park. Too many people. The woman who'd been with Phoebe was the key.

Who was this Quinn? Had she kidnapped Phoebe? The police had found Melana Elam's fingerprints at his house, but the woman didn't look like Melana. Had she picked up Phoebe from the sleepover? Had she been at the house the night Chrissy had pulled the gun on him?

Winston needed answers. The Old Slave House seemed like the perfect place to get them.

Chapter Fifty-Three

Quinn had stayed away from the Old Slave House after the mother voices had warned her. *Don't come back, come back, come back.* All her instincts told her not to go, but Quinn ignored them as she led a caravan of cars toward the house. She'd convinced herself the fear was irrational. Nothing bad had happened on her two previous tours. She'd been unnerved, but wasn't that to be expected when the voices of dead spirits filled your head?

As she steered the car up the winding lane, the three-story, red-clapboard house came into view. Quinn wanted to believe the impressive house on top of the hill was nothing more than an opulent mansion. But when she parked her car and set foot on the soil, something shifted. The earth seemed to shake. Unbalanced, she grabbed her sunhat and braced herself against the car. The white freedom bell on the front lawn rang. No one was near it, yet the bronze clapper swung back and forth. *Clang. Clang. Clang.* A metallic taste of fear welled up in her throat. This was no ordinary house. This place was evil.

Steadying herself, she glanced at the others climbing from their vehicles. Some pointed to the bell, now silent; others stared at the attic window on the third floor. No one appeared ready to flee.

Quinn righted the sunglasses on the bridge of her nose and removed her hat. Belle and Raven were counting on her. She was finished running. She would face whatever lurked inside.

Placing her hat on the passenger seat, she picked up her cell and the clipboard with the names of the people on the tour. She marched to the white picket fence and opened the gate. As the people walked past, she forced herself to smile and follow them up the sidewalk. Her sandals slapped against the concrete, echoing the words clambering in her head. *Go back, go back, go back.* The hair on the nape of her neck rose. Not daring to glance up at the dusty window, she kept her eyes fixed straight ahead. But she felt the spirits. They were watching her.

Quinn stepped onto the porch and worked on a welcoming smile before she turned and faced the twenty-five people on the tour. She checked the clipboard and called out the four names of people who hadn't been at The Castle. Three were teenagers, a girl and two boys. The girl—pale with spiked hair and black pants and shirt—stood between the boys. One had a shaved head; the other had a shaggy mullet and the beginnings of a goatee. The fourth person, Stanley Jenkins, stood near the whipping post. His arm was in a sling, and his black Chicago cap was pulled down obscuring his face.

Quinn checked off the names and began. "Welcome to Hickory Hills Plantation, sometimes called the Crenshaw Place, or, as the tour is named, the Old Slave House. I'm Quincy Matthews, and I promise, today you will not leave without being affected. I don't usually conduct this tour; too many spirits and ghosts still lurk inside."

Tittering from the teenagers made her glance at them. The boys were elbowing the girl and grinning. Quinn wondered if they'd be so jocular after the tour.

She led them around the exterior of the house and read its history. The group was attentive but asked few questions: they were anxious to go inside.

Back on the porch, she slid the key into the lock. *Click.* The front door swung open.

A cacophony of voices slammed into her. Stumbling, she fell against the door. *Go back, go back, go back.*

Wild-eyed, she spun toward the group. Their faces remained unchanged as they trooped by her and into the house.

Stiffening her shoulders, she clamped down on her fear. The voices couldn't physically hurt her. All they could do was scream. Still, once the group was inside and the door shut, her chest tightened. She felt trapped like one of the slave girls, trussed up in chains to be dragged upstairs.

Quinn pushed her sunglasses to the top of her head and moved into the first room. She described the lavish décor with the red-velvet drapes and lush velour chairs. She pointed to the gilded-framed picture above the mantel and gasped. The glass covering the picture of the Slave House was cracked. The dark, jagged line looked as if lightning were striking the house.

Quinn swallowed. "Remember this floor. Imagine the people who lived here. Compare their surroundings to the slave quarters."

She led the tour up the stairs to the second floor. In the middle, wooden cases displayed period artifacts. The people milled around the cases, peering through the glass tops. They read the newspaper clippings tacked onto the cracked walls. But their eyes continually strayed to the unpainted steps leading to the third floor.

Their restless murmurings became louder, and Quinn moved to the scarred staircase. A cold draft swooped down, surrounding her with an icy chill. She shivered. She glanced over her shoulder. Everyone was staring at her, impatient to see the attic.

Fighting back her fear, she gripped the banister and slowly climbed upward. With each step, the voices grew louder. *Go back, go back, go back.*

When she reached the top, she stopped. Muted color from the sun bleeding into the horizon filtered through the dusty dormer window. The light cast an eerie red glow onto the plaster-less walls, making the entire attic appear to be stained in blood.

The unexpected sight cast a pall on the group. Their voices changed to whispers as they skirted around her. Quinn steadied herself, placing her palm against the door of the large cell under the eaves where the women had been housed. She almost expected to feel wet, sticky blood. She pulled the door open. Wails of women and their babies rushed out. She stepped back, afraid of what might happen if she entered.

Staying in the hallway, she explained the size of the cell and the number of women who might have been restrained there. With a trembling hand, she motioned the others to enter. The teens were the first to go in and the last to come out. When they exited, their bantering had disappeared. The girl with the spiked black hair and goth makeup looked even paler, and she clutched the arm of the boy with the goatee.

Quinn hurried down the narrow hall, opening slatted cell doors for the people to enter. The cell at the end of the hallway had a row of iron bars across the front. Here was where Uncle Bob had been caged. She glanced at her notes. "Supposedly this slave was used as a stud..."

When she turned to gesture toward the cell, her hand moved, like it was caught in a magnetic field that pulled it forward and locked it onto a cold iron bar. As if someone flipped a switch, a man appeared inside the cell. He was sitting on the floor, grinning, naked but for a loin cloth. His huge black body glistened with sweat. Muscular legs, large as logs, stretched spread eagle in front of him. Iron shackles secured his ankles to the floor, and overhead metal chains restrained his wrists. Blood-shot eyes stared at her as he chanted in a melodious African dialect that beckoned her forward.

Her fingers gripped the metal bar. She watched herself opening the cage and entering. The chains above Uncle Bob rattled as he stretched out his shackled arms to welcome her. Like a maiden trussed up for sacrifice, she walked stiff-legged toward him. The chains snapped. His arms broke free.

She tried to flee, but he grabbed her neck. His arm squeezed her like a vice and shut off her oxygen. She couldn't breathe. He held onto her until her body slumped. Then he flung her across the room. Her head thudded against the wall. Her neck snapped, and her lifeless body slumped to the floor.

Quinn closed her eyes and tried to drive the image away. Her fingers were still fused onto the bar. She jerked free and fled into the next cell.

She collapsed against the door, pushing it shut. Her heart pounded in her ears. The cell was pitch-black. A strange scent, something like peppermint, permeated the room. The hair on her arms prickled. Labored breathing filled the air. She was not alone. Through the mine-shaft darkness two white eyeballs stared at her. The clipboard and cell phone slipped from her fingers, clattering to the floor.

She screamed and turned to the door. Clawing at the wood, she tried to pry it open. A hand clamped onto her arm. This was no apparition. She was trapped in this tiny cell, pinned against the door by evil.

Moist, hot breath slithered across her neck and curled into her ear. "Quincy, isn't it?" The hand relaxed its hold. One finger slid up her arm.

"I didn't mean to frighten you."

She shuddered, shaken by a violent welter of emotions—panic, fear, revulsion, and a vague unsettling memory. The voice sounded familiar. As she struggled to identify it, the door creaked open, pushing her back against the man's chest.

Light splintered into the room as the teenage boy with the bald head peeked inside. "You okay?"

Before she could answer, he spoke to someone behind him. "I told you the scream wasn't a ghost."

Quinn grabbed the door, practically ripping it out of his hands, and rushed out. The man followed. The light filtering through the window spotlighted him in red. It was the man with his arm in the sling. His lips curved into a satanic grin. She peered under the bill of his cap, trying to see his face, but it was obscured by a beard and pair of black-framed glasses.

The teenage boy moved next to her. "What's wrong?"

Before Quinn could answer, the man stepped forward. "I must have frightened her." He held out her cell phone and clipboard.

Fighting back revulsion, Quinn took the phone, but he held onto the clipboard and tugged her toward him. Hot breath whispered into her ear. "I hear it's your daughter's birthday today. How old is she?"

Terror pulsed through her. Where had he seen Taylor? Was she still at the park with Jason? Why hadn't Quinn insisted that Taylor go to the hospital with Ace? He would make sure she was safe.

Bile rose in her throat. She yanked the clipboard away and struggled to speak. "This concludes our tour." Her voice quivered. "You're free to spend the last ten minutes looking around. Make sure your name is checked off the list when you leave. You wouldn't want to accidentally spend the night."

The group laughed nervously as she wove through them. She raced down the hall and fled to the second floor. Gasping, she bent over and gulped in mouthfuls of air.

Footsteps clomped down the stairs. Quinn whirled around. The man was across the room, staring at her. *Get away, away, away,* pounded in her head. Quinn stumbled to the opposite wall, putting the glass cases between them.

The man's lips, not quite hidden by his beard, curled into a sneer. "Be seeing you."

She swallowed. "I-I need to check off your name."

"You're a smart lady. I'm sure you'll figure it out." He swaggered across the room and down the stairs.

She listened for the front door to slam and then moved to the curtain-less window. From above, she watched him walk to his car. As he opened the door, he looked up and spotted her. His hand moved to his cap, saluting her with two fingers. Quinn shuddered and stepped away, pressing her back against the wall so he couldn't see her. Holding her breath, she stayed there until she heard the car's engine and the tires spin out on the graveled road.

Then she tiptoed to the window and watched the trail of dust swirling behind the silver Lexus. That's when she noticed the license was not an Illinois plate. Squinting, she tried to identify it, but the car swerved into a bend near the middle of the lane and disappeared. As soon as it vanished, she let out a relieved breath.

Fifteen minutes later, Quinn watched the last couple drive away from the house. She felt like skipping down the sidewalk. She was free. But the voices still filled her head. *Go back, go back, go back.* The cell phone rang. Her body jerked. Then Ace's name popped up on the screen, and she smiled.

"Hey, Quinn."

Hearing his voice steadied her nerves. "How's Raven?"

She must have still sounded shaken because Ace asked, "What's wrong?"

She laughed nervously. "The tour always rattles me, but it's over. What about Raven?"

"The contractions have stopped, and Doc Morgan said if she's stable for another hour, they won't have to transfer her to a hospital with a neonatal unit."

"And the babies?"

"Two strong heart beats."

She said a silent prayer of thanks. "That's wonderful."

"I'll be at the park in about thirty minutes. I want to ask you something."

"About Taylor..."

"No, about you and me. Meet me at the bridge?"

She agreed and hung up. As she walked toward the gate, the voices screamed louder. *Go back, go back, go back.* She scowled. Why hadn't their words changed? Why should she go back? Over her shoulder, she stared at the house. A red haze glowed around it. Shrugging, she latched the gate and hurried to the car.

She slipped the key into the ignition. As she stretched the seatbelt across her, she relaxed and thought about the rest of the evening with Ace, Jason, and Taylor. She started the car and shifted it into reverse. Something brushed against her hair. She reached back and felt cold metal. Her eyes darted to the rearview mirror. Her heart jumped. The man in the black cap was staring back at her. In his hand was a gun, aimed at the side of her head.

She opened her mouth.

"Don't scream."

That voice. Her chest tightened.

"Be a good girl, Quincy, and you won't get hurt."

She'd heard that voice before. Almost the exact words—except he had been saying them to Chrissy.

Winston. Oh my God. The man is Winston.

Chapter Fifty-Four

A barn. Phoebe was living in a barn!

Winston stood behind Quincy, pointing the Glock at her back. He tapped his foot as he waited for her to relock the barn doors. Her car was hidden in the woods near the Old Slave House, and his car, which they'd driven here, was now parked inside the barn.

Click. The padlock snapped shut. Winston brandished the gun and shoved Quincy up the outside stairs. When they reached the landing, she fumbled with the key.

"Hurry up," he said in a low growl.

Click. The key turned, and the front door swung open. He poked the pistol into her back, pushing her inside. When he crossed the threshold, his mouth fell open. The hayloft wasn't even finished. Overhead, in what he supposed was the great room, were exposed barn rafters, and on the wall adjacent to the wood stove were weathered barn planks. Some might call the decor rustic. To him, it was still a barn, a place to house animals—not his precious Phoebe.

Through a wide expanse of windows, the fading sunset cast dim shadows into the room. Soon it would be dark and the moon would rise. Blood moon. The killing time.

He needed to remain calm and wait until he had Phoebe back before killing Quincy. What if Phoebe intended to sleep over at a friend's? What if another little girl returned with Phoebe? What if...?

The questions were endless. He would stick to his original plan. When it was dark, Quincy would make a call, say she was ill, and ask someone to bring Phoebe here. Once Phoebe and he were reunited,

Quincy would be superfluous.

"Where's Phoebe's room?

She pointed to the hallway at the far end of the kitchen.

"Lead the way."

Winston followed Quincy as she walked toward the kitchen. With each step, her sundress swished against her shapely legs. His eyes slid to her feet. For some reason, she had slipped her sandals off at the door, and her feet were now bare. Long, tanned, naked feet, at least a size 10. He had to get a full view.

"Stop."

Quincy halted in the middle of the kitchen. Winston checked to make sure she couldn't reach anything from the counters. Reassured, he moved forward until her full foot came into view. He stared at the second toe protruding past the first. Morton's toe, just like Phoebe's and her grandmother's.

She might be calling herself Quincy Matthews, but Winston knew who she was. She was Melana Elam, Phoebe's biological mother. His gaze lingered on her painted toenails, a delicious-looking cotton candy pink.

What would it feel like to touch her feet? Would they be as soft as Phoebe's or as erotic as Bonnie's? What would it be like to massage Quincy's feet, to stroke the sensuous bottoms or suck on those long, luscious toes? Thinking about the fantasy aroused him.

Pain throbbed through his arm. He grabbed the back of a chair and bent over. The bottle of Oxycontin was in his front pocket. He should have taken another dose over an hour ago. But he couldn't hold a gun and take a pill at the same time—and he couldn't massage any feet.

He straightened up. "Move."

She led him through the kitchen, down the hallway, and to the first bedroom. As soon as he stepped across the threshold, the odor hit him. Not the sweet scent of Phoebe, but the stench of an animal. He zeroed in on the far corner with a small bed and a rubber ball.

Poor Phoebe. Living in a barn was bad enough, but sharing a room with a disgusting dog was appalling. His stomach soured. A dog had been hopping on Phoebe's bed, slobbering in her face, and nipping at her precious feet. He shivered with revulsion.

Keeping his gun pointed at Quincy, he sank onto the bottom bunk. Phoebe's bed. Even the smell of the dog couldn't keep him from coveting the pillow with the scent of Phoebe's beautiful hair.

He glanced up at Quincy. The need to touch Phoebe's things overwhelmed him. But he couldn't satisfy himself and worry about Quincy. An open door with a skeleton key in the lock led to an adjoining bathroom. If Quincy was locked away, he'd be free to explore Phoebe's room.

He rose and motioned Quincy through the door and into the closet-sized, window-less bathroom, barely large enough for a pedestal sink with a medicine chest above, a commode, and a claw-footed bathtub. He waved the gun at the mirror. "Take everything out of the cabinet."

Quincy opened the door. Methodically she started to remove the supplies, lining them up on the stool. A box of band-aids, a bottle of baby aspirin, disinfectant, cough syrup, a thermometer.

Winston's patience snapped. Pulling his arm from the sling, he swung it across the shelf. Bottles and pills spilled into the sink and onto the floor. He swiped across another shelf, emptying it. He checked for razor blades, scissors, or other dangerous items. Next, he yanked back the shower curtain and inspected the caddy with Miss Kitty shampoo and soap.

Satisfied that Quincy wouldn't find anything to use as a weapon, he shoved the gun into her back and pushed her against the wall. "I'm going to pack Phoebe's things for our trip. If you want to come with us, stay put and don't try anything."

"I can pack for Phoebe. I know what she..."

"I'm her father. I know what she wants."

Backing out of the bathroom, he closed the door and locked it. Excitement pulsed through him. Forcing himself to breathe normally, he pulled the Oxycontin from his pocket and swallowed two pills. Then, unable to control his desire, he rushed across the room and opened the closet.

Chapter Fifty-Five

Quinn waited behind the bathroom door, gripping the handle of the plunger. For the last ten minutes, she'd heard sounds from Phoebe's room—drawers opening and closing, the closet door creaking. What was Winston doing? Why had he locked her in the bathroom? He could have killed her. But he was keeping her alive. Why?

She hadn't wanted to bring him here. She'd tried to think of another place. Ace's? Winston might kill Jason or Ace. Besides, Ace's guns were locked in the basement. At least her gun was in the pantry—if she could get to it.

Creak. The closet door closed. Footsteps coming toward the bathroom. The skeleton key in the lock rattled. Her heart pounded. She eased away from the bathroom wall and raised the wooden handle over her head.

Squeak. The door swung open. She smelled him—cloying peppermint mixed with sweat. His shoes slapped against the black-and-white linoleum. One, two, three steps. The Glock came into view. The barrel was inching past the door.

Wait. Wait. She had one chance.

She saw his finger on the trigger, then his wrist.

Now.

With one powerful whack, she smashed the wooden handle against his arm.

He screamed, "*Argh!*" His grip loosened.

She grabbed for the gun, trying to wrench it away.

He squeezed the trigger. *Bang.*

The explosion echoed through the tiny bathroom. The bullet struck the medicine chest, shattering the mirror, sending shards of glass splattering the room. The smell of gunpowder filled the air. She lurched for the open door.

Winston grabbed her around the waist, dragging her back. He tightened his hold, crushing her ribs, cutting off her oxygen. She kicked his legs, and clawed his arms. He held on, lifting her off the ground and shaking her like a rag doll.

She felt as if she were trapped in Uncle Bob's cage, only this time it was real. And it was Winston. He wound his other arm around her neck, closing her windpipe. She couldn't breathe. Her fingernails dug into his hand, piercing the skin. "Need...air."

He squeezed tighter. Her head throbbed. Color began to recede. In the distance, she heard laughter. A high-pitched maniacal laugh.

Was this what it felt like to die?

She thought of Taylor and found one last surge of energy. Her fingernails tore at his arm, ripping his skin and drawing blood. Like a python playing with its prey, Winston squeezed tighter.

Her head drooped, lolling to one side. Her body went slack. His grip loosened, allowing her lungs to expand. She struggled for air. She was no longer on her feet, but flying through the air, head first toward the bathtub. The image at the Old Slave House of her hitting the wall and snapping her neck flashed in her mind. She lowered her head, covering it with her arms. She crashed into the bathtub, thumping against the solid porcelain and crumpling onto the floor.

Everything faded.

Chapter Fifty-Six

Ace paced back and forth, across the white concrete footbridge to the small island, and back to the park. After he left the hospital, he hadn't checked on Jason and Taylor. He was too impatient to propose to Quinn, to see her face when he gave her Gramma Elam's ring. He checked his watch again. She was late. When he'd call her at the Old Slave House, he'd said thirty minutes. He shouldn't have let her go there alone. He should have asked her to marry him this morning. Then he could have relaxed and enjoyed the day with his fiancée—that is, if she said yes.

She might refuse. The death of her father and being raised by an alcoholic mother had forced Quinn to depend on herself. Trusting anyone else was almost impossible. But she had trusted him, hadn't she? She'd told him about Taylor.

He'd tried to comfort her, convince her to let go of the past and the guilt. But it was difficult for her to accept help. She'd endured childbirth, adoption, and four years in Japan—alone. He did not want her to face the murder charge and the custody battle alone. He would support her. They'd fight for Taylor—together. Then the four of them would become a family.

Ace stopped pacing and glanced toward the entrance to the park. He searched for Quinn's car. The traffic flowing through the bricked archway had thinned, but the congestion could have delayed her. Or she could have had car trouble. A stalled engine? A flat tire?

He pulled out his cell. If she wasn't here in five minutes, he'd call. He didn't want to sound desperate, although he was beginning to feel that way.

He blinked at the phone. It was turned off. After talking to Quinn, he'd returned to the hospital, and because of the "no cell phone" signs, he'd shut it off.

He turned it on again. One missed call from Summer. He didn't need to call his sister-in-law. Belle said she would phone Summer and update her on Raven. Then he saw a text from Summer. *Jason needs to talk to you.* Ace knew what that was about. Jason had pestered him all day about the proposal. He'd phone Jason afterwards.

Ace hit Quinn's number on speed dial and the listened to it ringing.

Chapter Fifty-Seven

Winston stared down at Quincy's body lying on the bathroom floor. Was she dead? Had he killed her?

Tiptoeing around the broken glass, he sidled to the sink. Cautiously, he laid the gun on the edge. He splashed cold water onto his flushed face. He dug into the pocket of his jeans, pulled out a peppermint, and popped it into his mouth. Closing his eyes, he sucked on the soothing sweetness, waiting for the candy to calm him.

He'd kill Quincy—after she phoned for Phoebe to come home. He needed to see Phoebe, hold her in his arms. Then everything would be all right.

He glanced down at Quincy's still body. What if she was dead? If she was, it was her fault. She'd made him do it. But he'd have to wait until after the fireworks to get his Phoebe.

His gaze slid over Quincy, past her head, down her back, to her feet. Oh, those large, luscious feet and titillating toes. They teased him, begging to be touched. Her feet were so much like Phoebe's—except over-sized. They tormented him, making his hands twitch. Swaying, he leaned against the sink and groaned.

If he was going to be stuck waiting for Phoebe, why not indulge in some provocative pleasure? He'd never feasted on a cadaver. His mouth turned warm and wet. He drooled. His tongue slithered across his bottom lip, lapping up the sweet minty saliva. O-o-h, what he could do with those feet.

The floor was littered with pill bottles and broken glass. He'd have to drag Quincy out of the bathroom. He wasn't sure he had the strength—especially if she was dead weight. He laughed aloud. Dead weight. Maybe she was unconscious—or trying to deceive him. He didn't bend down to check her pulse. What if she attacked him again?

Retrieving the gun from the sink, he stepped toward her body. Cautiously, he stuck out his foot. With the front of his brown leather loafers, he nudged her leg. She didn't move. He kicked harder. No response.

She didn't seem to be pretending. She might actually be dead. Sliding the gun into the waistband of his jeans, he dropped to his knees and grabbed the hem of her strawberry dress. Pulling, he inched her body away from the tub. Then he turned her onto her back. Her body thudded against the floor.

He placed a bath mat under her and seized the skirt of the sundress. Sweating and straining, he began the battle, inching her body toward the door.

Heave...strain...pull. Heave...strain...pull.

He dragged Quincy over the threshold and into Phoebe's room. Collapsing onto Phoebe's bed, he grabbed Phoebe's pillow, caressing it against his cheek. His scraggy beard kept him from feeling its softness, and the scent was foreign—not his Phoebe's. He dropped the pillow onto the floor and propped it under Quincy's legs. He pulled the gun from his waistband and lowered himself to her elevated feet. Bowing his head, he began licking his way down the thick, meaty flesh.

He pressed the gun against her instep, gliding the barrel up and down, skimming the bottom of her foot. He moaned and lowered his mouth over her little toe. He began to nibble, taking small bites of the dainty delicacy. The toe tasted sweet and erotic. He slid his tongue over the pink pedicured toenail and sucked on the wet flesh.

Finishing with the little digit, he moved on, licking and sucking each delicious toe. Eventually his mouth reached the big toe, the hallux. He smacked his lips. Oh yeah, Quincy Matthew's feet were definitely worth the trouble.

In the distance he heard the muted ringing of a cell phone again. The monotonous music continued, pricking his fantasy.

Chapter Fifty-Eight

Quinn heard her phone in the distance, but her eyelids wouldn't open. Her body was stiff as she lay stretched out on the hardwood floor.

Scenes from the Slave House flashed through her head. Being trapped with Uncle Bob. Hitting the wall. Her neck snapping. But she wasn't dead.

Had the voices sent the vision? She'd been too frightened to cross the threshold into their room. She remembered their words *go back, go back, go back.* She hadn't understood what the mother voices had meant.

Mother voices, that's the way she always thought of them. Other mothers warning her. Their children had been taken from them and sold into slavery. They'd been powerless, voiceless. But their spirits had risen up to protect her. The voices of mothers trying to safeguard another mother and her child.

Quinn had never thought she'd want to be a mother. But the moment she felt the stirring in her womb, she'd become protective. Oh how she'd wanted to keep her child, watch her take that first step and hear her say that first word. But she had so little to give. Her daughter deserved everything—a carefree childhood with a mother and a father. But most of all, she deserved the security Quinn had yearned for and never found.

She'd given up her daughter and flown half-way around the world. The guilt had followed her. Every day she wondered if she'd made the right decision. Good mothers don't give away their babies.

But the voices validated her as a mother. They had accepted her. She felt the burden lift. No more doubts. She'd made the right decision. Taylor had been loved and cherished. Chrissy and Max had given her

301

child a firm foundation and more stability than Quinn could have provided. But with those loving parents gone, Quinn had to protect her from Winston, who was dangerous.

The slave women had warned Quinn, but that was all they could do. She would have to save Taylor. It was up to her.

She heard a moan. Her breath caught. Something was touching her foot. Her eyelids fluttered open. Winston. He was kneeling over her feet, licking her big toe.

Panic rushed through her. What would he lick next? Her ankle? Her calf? Beyond? She shuddered.

Winston jerked back. "So, you're alive. Well, it's time to make yourself useful. You're going to call Phoebe." He ran his tongue around the corners of his mouth. "Tell her you're sick, and she has to come home."

Quinn made no effort to move. She would rather die than have Winston anywhere near Taylor.

He stood and gestured with his gun. "Get up. Your phone is in the other room."

She tried to sound assertive. "I won't call Phoebe."

Winston shrugged. "Your choice. I don't mind shooting you, but then I'd have to go to the park. Other children are there, like that obnoxious little boy. Too bad if he or others get in the way."

Oh God. Quinn could envision the massacre. In an effort to grab Taylor, Winston might randomly shoot his way out of the park. She wanted to protect her daughter, but not by endangering the lives of other children. She had to think of another way.

"Okay." Quinn struggled to sit up. "I'll call."

"I guess you're not such a feeble-minded wench after all."

He gestured with the gun toward the kitchen. She rose, and her legs wobbled as she staggered forward. Winston followed, a few steps behind. When they reached the table, he picked up her phone. "Two missed calls from someone called Ace."

"He's my neighbor. He's the one I should call to bring Phoebe home."

"All right. Say you want him to drop Phoebe off, but you're too sick to see him."

Quinn's heart pounded. This was her chance. If she could talk to Ace, he would understand. He would come for Winston.

She reached for the phone. Winston held onto it. "Repeat what you're going to say."

"Please, bring Phoebe home. But don't come in, I'm too sick."

He nodded, and she took the phone. She dialed Ace. She waited for it to ring.

Suddenly Winston jerked the phone out of her hand. "Not Phoebe." His face pulsated red. "Not Phoebe. Taylor. At the park, they called her Taylor."

Chapter Fifty-Nine

Ace stood on the bridge and raked his fingers through his hair. The park lights had already come on. The night air was heavy, filled with the smell of smoke bombs and popping firecrackers. He stared down at his cell. He'd left Quinn two messages. Why hadn't she called? He checked the signal. All the bars were lit, but his battery was low.

Another five minutes passed. Then the phone rang. He saw Quinn's number and blurted out, "Where are you? Are you all right?"

"I-I'm home."

Her voice sounded strange. "What's wrong?"

"I don't feel well."

He leaned against the bridge. "How long before you get here?"

"I'm not coming."

His spirits plummeted. "Are you feeling that bad?"

"I must have picked up a bug. Could you bring Taylor home now?"

"Why don't you let her spend the night with Jason and me? That way she won't miss out on the fireworks, and you can take care of yourself."

"No, no. I need her to come home." Ace frowned. Quinn sounded more than sick. She sounded desperate.

"O—kay, if that's what you want. I'll bring her home now. We can sit on the dock. Sometimes you can see the fireworks from town."

"Just send Taylor up. I don't want you to catch whatever I have."

"Quinn, I really want to see you tonight."

"I can't, Ace. We'll talk tomorrow."

His eyebrows drew together and his frown deepened. Quinn

sounded as if she needed him. Of course, she'd never admit to needing anyone. She was too independent. "Can I do something for you? Get anything to make you feel better?"

"A box of chocolates."

"Chocolates?"

Click.

"Quinn? Quinn? Are you there?" He stared at the screen. *Call ended.* Frustrated, he clenched the phone.

Women. He tapped his forehead with his palm. He certainly didn't understand them. Why did women want chocolate when they weren't feeling well?

He walked off the bridge toward the picnic area where Taylor, Jason, and the family were waiting for the fireworks to begin. Taylor would be disappointed when he told her she had to go home. He felt the same way.

Maybe the night didn't have to be a complete wash. It might be romantic if he put the ring and a note in a box of chocolates. But where could he buy chocolates at this time of night? Almost everything was closed. Maybe the convenience store at the edge of town.

He'd find chocolates somewhere. After all he'd promised her a box of chocolates when... He stopped. His whole body froze. Quinn had talked about chocolates the day he'd taken her to the woods and shown her how to use her gun. What was it she'd said? Something like, "Shooting was better than a box of chocolates."

He punched in Summer's number. The battery light blinked. His phone went dead.

Chapter Sixty

"Chocolate!" Winston slapped the phone away. It landed on the floor, and he smashed his heel into the case, pounding on it until the phone splintered apart. "Why did you tell him to bring you chocolates?"

"I always want chocolate when I'm not feeling well."

Winston felt his anger escalating. If he didn't see his daughter soon, he'd crack like the phone scattered on the floor. "It'll take longer for Phoebe to get here."

"Can I pack my things now?"

Winston wagged the gun at her. "I said I'd take you with us—if you were a good girl." He shook his head. "You were not a good girl, Melana Elam. You were very, very bad."

He saw her flinch as he said her real name.

"Thought you'd fooled me, didn't you? I know who you are. I also know you're Phoebe's biological mother."

Her eyes widened. "If you know I'm her mother, then you understand. I was only trying to protect my—our daughter."

"Protect her? From me?" He was outraged. "I would never hurt Phoebe. I love her."

"I know you do, Winston. I can hear it in your voice, and I saw those pictures on the Internet. You bought her all those beautiful clothes."

"Chrissy never understood about dressing up Phoebe."

"I do." Quincy's voice changed to an alluring purr. "She's special. She's Daddy's little girl."

"Yes, yes." What a relief. Someone understood. Why hadn't Chrissy understood? Just thinking about dressing Phoebe in elegant gowns sent heat pulsing through his body. "How long before Phoebe gets here from town?"

"Usually about fifteen minutes, but tonight the traffic is heavy because of the fireworks, and Ace will have to stop for chocolates, so it'll be a little over half an hour." Her voice changed, became low and sultry. "Give me a second chance, Winston. Tell me what I can do to make up for being a bad girl."

Winston knew she was faking, pretending to care about his needs, but why not go along with it? "I might be persuaded to take you with Phoebe and me—if you did something to please me."

She lowered her long lashes and blinked up at him. "What do you want me to do?"

He saw her tremble. He liked that, liked that she understood he had the power. "Go lie on the sofa."

She hesitated, then turned and swayed across the room. Sitting on the edge of the sofa, she looked back at him. Her face flushed. "What-what are you going to do?"

He didn't answer. He was too indignant. What kind of animal did she think he was? He would never force himself on a woman. He pointed his gun at the end of the couch. "Put your feet there."

She stretched out on the couch, extending her long legs over the end. "Are you going to do that wonderful thing that made my toes tingle?"

"So you liked it?"

"Oh yes." She wiggled her toes. "No one's ever done that to me before."

"Georgeanna loved it—but Chrissy said it was perverse."

"She didn't understand, did she?"

What a shame he had to kill Quincy. Well, at least he'd make the last few minutes of her life pleasurable. He crossed the room and knelt at the end of the couch.

She gave him a hooded look. "Afterwards I could make you coffee. It will keep us awake on the drive."

"Coffee? Us?" His mind barely heard the words. He was already salivating.

Chapter Sixty-One

Ace bent down as he weaved through the dark thicket of hickories toward the loft. In his hand was the 9mm Luger. The trees cleared. He hunched over and moved into the open toward the warm glow of light from the windows.

Snap. A twig broke under his foot. He crouched lower, waiting. The lights remained on. No one appeared at the window. He eased forward, willing Quinn to walk by the windows. *Show me you're all right. Show me you're alive.*

As far as he could see into the loft, nothing looked amiss. But the feeling that Quinn was in danger wouldn't go away.

He'd tried to remember her exact words that day in the woods. Something about shooting being better than chocolate. He hoped his instincts were wrong. He hoped his biggest problem would be explaining to Quinn why he hadn't brought Taylor. Quinn might be mad. She might think he was being overly protective or maybe a little crazy. Well, if she did, he'd deal with it. He'd promised to protect her and Taylor, and he would—no matter how foolish it might seem.

The night air was still. He crept to the corner of the barn. Each step made his stomach clench. He reached the barn doors and slipped the key into the padlock. *Click.* He opened it and inched the door toward him.

Creak. Holding his breath, Ace wedged his body inside. A beam of moonlight shot through the crack, illuminating the trunk of a car.

Ace's heart slammed against his chest. It was not Quinn's Ford. The car was a Lexus. Winston—or someone Winston had sent—was here.

Ace had never felt this kind of terror. Lifting the Luger, he looked up. The floorboards, had they groaned? A soft padding of footsteps overhead.

Thump. Thump. Thump. Definitely footsteps, heavier ones than Quinn could make.

Sweat broke out on his brow, but inside Ace turned steely cold. He forced himself to wait. Plan. A reckless attack might work with someone like Winston, but what if he'd hired a professional?

A shiver cut through him. Not from the cool night air, but from fear that he might be too late. Flattening his hand on the side of the car, he inched forward, feeling the metal. The back door. The driver's door. The hood. The metal was cold—the engine was cool.

Whoever was in the loft had been here long enough to kill Quinn. But he'd heard two sets of footsteps. Quinn was alive, had to be alive. His own heart was still beating.

He pushed away from the car. One step, two, three. His hand tightened on the railing. He lifted the gun and began to climb the steps. A muffled sound drifted from above. Voices, he was almost sure he heard voices.

* * * *

Quinn's legs wobbled as she walked toward the kitchen to fix coffee. Winston followed, his Glock pressed against her back. She'd convinced him to let her pack food for Phoebe by reminding him how many snacks contained peanuts or peanut products.

Bile rose in her throat as she suppressed the repulsive memory of Winston's mouth on her feet. She couldn't think about that now. She needed to focus. Her life and Taylor's depended on it.

Winston acted as if he would take her with him, but she wasn't fooled. Once Taylor arrived, he'd kill her. Winston knew she was Melana Elam—Phoebe's biological mother. He also must suspect she'd been in the house the night Chrissy had been killed. With Quinn dead, there would be no witness. Winston would have sole custody of Taylor.

That idea terrified her. Winston said he would never hurt Taylor, and in his mind he believed that. But lying on the couch, enduring his touch, had been worse than any physical pain. Quincy would die before she'd let him touch Taylor.

Where was Ace? He'd promised to protect them. Why wasn't he here? Had he even understood her message? Twenty minutes had passed since she'd called. She'd exaggerated by ten or fifteen minutes when she'd told Winston the trip from town would take at least half an hour.

If Ace hadn't understood, he and Phoebe would be here soon. What if Ace came in? Winston would shoot him. Oh God, why had she even involved Ace? Well, he wasn't here. She needed him, had counted on him, but he hadn't come.

Quinn had to rely on herself. She'd watched a TV show on abduction. The advice was never to get into a car. Once you do, the odds of survival declined. If Taylor was going to stay unharmed, it was up to Quinn. She'd have to protect her daughter—alone.

Quinn cleared her mind. By the time she reached the pantry, her legs had stopped shaking, and her hands were steadier. Winston entered first and did a cursory inspection before slipping out and motioning her forward. Straight ahead on the top shelf sat the red coffee can with the .38 inside. A small box of ammo that Ace had bought her was hidden behind it. She reached for the can. One hand steadied it; the other slid to the back and reached into the box. One, two, three bullets.

"Hurry up," Winston growled.

She needed five bullets to fill the cylinder, but she'd have to make do with the three. She fisted the bullets and lowered the can. Through the clear lid, she saw the gun still lying on the cloth Ace had given her for cleaning. She balanced the can to keep the Smith and Wesson from shifting to the side. To cover any suspicious noise, she continued to talk, suggesting possible snacks for Phoebe. "Cookies? Ding Dongs? Crackers?"

Winston dismissed most of them, and Quinn realized why Taylor had been so thin. Daddy Win had not allowed her to eat anything he thought was unhealthy.

"Parents shovel in sugar and wonder why their kids are fat brats." Winston ranted about food while Quinn set the can on the counter next to the coffee pot. With her back to him, she reached inside. Thank goodness Ace had told her to leave the cylinder open.

She slid in the first bullet.

"There's only one scoopful of coffee. In the cabinet on your right are the filters and more coffee. Should I get them, or will you?"

She slid in the second bullet.

"Use what you have."

She ignored his answer and placed the lid on the can. When she crossed to the cupboard, he didn't protest, but stepped back, keeping the gun on her. After finding the filters and coffee, she put them next to the three-pound can. "I need water."

Winston mumbled something, but didn't object when she walked to the sink, filled the carafe, and returned to pour the water into the pot. She wanted to load the last bullet. She hoped she'd have more than a fifty percent chance of the gun firing on the first try. She might not get a second chance.

While she put in the filter, she lifted one foot and pressed it against her opposite leg. She slid it slowly up and down her calf, hoping to distract him. Behind her, she heard a sharp intake of breath. She removed the can's lid.

She slid in the third bullet.

Then without bothering to measure, she dumped coffee into the filter. If her plan worked, Winston wouldn't ever drink coffee again.

"How much longer?"

Quinn pressed the switch to *brew*. "About five minutes."

She turned her foot, angling it so Winston would have a full view. Her toes began to wiggle as her hand reached into the can and gripped the gun. She closed the cylinder. Holding her breath, she pulled out the revolver, turned, and aimed it at Winston.

* * * *

Winston's eyes moved from Quincy's leg to her feet. Her bare toes dancing across the floor lured him back into his fantasy. Her foot turned. He saw a flash of metal. He didn't realize it was a gun until he heard the click.

Instinctively, he jerked back, waiting for the pain. Nothing happened. He laughed, almost nervously. "Stupid woman."

She aimed and pulled the trigger again. Nothing.

His lips twisted into a sneer. "Forget to load it?"

Her big brown eyes filled with fear. He would enjoy this kill—one bullet at a time.

Winston lifted the gun, aimed, and squeezed the trigger.

Chapter Sixty-Two

Ace stood on the ladder and slowly lifted the trap door leading into the loft.

Crack.

The sound of the gunshot shattered his control. He threw open the door and pushed the top part his body through the opening. Quinn was at the other end of the kitchen. Between them was a man with his back to Ace.

The trap door banged against the floor, and the man whirled toward him.

Ace lifted his Luger and yelled, "Get down, Quinn!" Then he pulled the trigger.

Quinn's shot hit first, striking the man from behind. His eyes bulged, and his glasses slid down the bridge of his nose. Ace had aimed at the heart, but the man had tumbled forward and the bullet struck his forehead. His knees buckled. His fingers opened, letting the gun clatter to the floor. Then he thudded next to it.

"Quinn, get down!" Ace shouted again as he pushed off the ladder and into the room.

The man lay sprawled on the floor, motionless. Ace glanced at Quinn. Her gun was still in both hands, pointed at the man. Ace gasped as he saw a large red circle of blood on the front of her dress.

Oh God, she's been shot.

He wanted to go to her, but he had to make sure the man was dead. He lunged forward and knocked the gun away. Cautiously, he touched the man's wrist, feeling for a pulse. Nothing. Ace inched closer and checked the neck. He looked up at Quinn. "He's dead."

Her eyes were blank. Where was she hit? She must be in shock, like the night she'd shot him. He kept his voice soft. "Quinn. It's Ace. Put your gun down. It's over."

She didn't move.

He stood, resisting the urge to run to her. He didn't want her to shoot him again. "Quinn, look at me. It's Ace. I'm here. You're safe now."

The gun remained pointed forward, but her eyes, dilated and full of fear, shifted to him. "Taylor?" Her voice was raspy and soft. "Where's Taylor?"

He moved a step closer. "Taylor's safe. She's at the park, and she's safe."

Quinn lowered the gun. Her body slumped against the cabinet. In two long strides, Ace crossed the room. He pried the gun out of her fingers. "Where are you hit?"

She looked down at her bloody dress. "Hit?"

Ace laid the guns on the counter and jerked open drawers until he found a dishtowel. He placed it in Quinn's hand and pressed it against the stain in her dress. "Push down and hold it tight." He gathered her to him and lifted her into his arms. The back of her dress was sticky with blood. The exit wound. At least the bullet wasn't lodged in her body, but he couldn't tell how badly she'd been injured.

For the first time, Quinn seemed to realize he was there. "Ace, thank God you came." Her body trembled and then sank against his. "I needed you, and you came."

Outside, footsteps clattered up the stairs. Ace tensed. An accomplice? The guns were across the room, lying on the counter.

A fist pounded on the door. "Quinn, it's Ben. Open up. Jason sent me. Are you all right?"

Relief washed over Ace. "Ben, it's Ace. Quinn's been shot. Call for help. Then come in through the barn doors and up the ladder. There's another man in here. He's dead."

Ace heard Ben radio for the EMTs and then run down the stairs.

How had Jason known Quinn was in danger? Ace wondered as he carried Quinn to the couch and gently laid her on a pillow to staunch the exit wound. Her face was white, and her eyes unfocused. He covered her hand, forcing the towel firmly against the front of her dress where she'd been wounded. Silently he swore. If he'd only arrived sooner.

"Tell me again, Ace. Is Winston dead? Is he really dead? Did you shoot him?"

"Yes. It's over. Winston's never going to hurt you or Taylor again."

Ace started to rise to get another towel.

Quinn reached up and took his hand, pulling him back to her. "You saved my life."

He looked down at her. "It was more like you saved mine. Winston had his gun aimed at me. You shot him. You didn't need my help, Quinn."

She squeezed his hand. "Yes, I did. I still do." Her voice quivered. "I-I don't think I can handle this alone."

She closed her eyes. It was comforting to have Ace here, to know he'd protected Taylor and her. She'd trusted him, and he'd come.

She felt light-headed. Ace was staring down at her with a strange expression on his face. She could hear him calling her name, telling her to hold on, but the sound grew fainter and fainter, and she faded into darkness.

Chapter Sixty-Three

Ace paced outside the curtained cubicle of the emergency room. Doc Morgan had forced him to leave Quinn's side, but Ace couldn't sit in the waiting room. He was too tense. He rubbed a hand across his eyes, but the image of Quinn's pale face and all that blood wouldn't go away.

In the ambulance, the EMTs said she had a shoulder wound, but they hadn't been able to stop the bleeding. People didn't die from shoulder wounds, did they?

He couldn't lose her. He needed her. Jason needed her. He checked the clock on the wall again. 11:30. Twelve hours ago he'd been at the park, laughing with Quinn, holding her hand, and thinking about their future. Now he wondered if they had a future.

If she was all right—and she had to be all right—he would ask her to marry him tonight. But what if he was too late?

He stopped pacing and leaned against the wall. He closed his eyes, not wanting to think he might have lost Quinn.

A hand tapped him on the shoulder. He jerked up and saw Doc Morgan. "How is she?"

"Looks better than you."

Ace rubbed his hands over his stubbly whiskers. "Is she going to be all right?"

"She's weak. She's lost a lot of blood. But yeah, she'll be all right."

His body went limp with relief. "Can I see her?"

"She's asking for Taylor—and you."

* * * *

Quinn's eyelids felt heavy, and they kept closing by themselves. She wanted to see Taylor and Ace. Where were they? She needed to see them. Needed to make sure they were all right. She heard the familiar clomp of cowboy boots coming down the hall. Ace. She thought he'd been in the ambulance with her, holding her hand and whispering he loved her. Had that been real? Had he said *love?*

She felt Ace's warm lips brush across her forehead. She forced her eyes open and started at his bloody shirt. "Were you shot, too?"

He shook his head. "No, it's your blood." His arms remained stiffly at his side. "I'm sorry, Quinn, I failed. I should never have let you go to the Slave House alone. I should never have let Winston get near you."

Her injured shoulder was in a sling strapped to her body, but her right hand reached up and took his. She brought his hand to her lips and kissed it. "Sh-sh. Doc Morgan says I'm lucky. Nothing major was hit."

He ran his hand over the purple knot on her forehead. "What about your head?"

She slipped her hand from his and gingerly felt the bump where she'd hit the bathtub. "I have a hard head."

Ace grinned. "Yeah, I know that. I just want to make sure you can think clearly when I propose."

Her eyes opened wide. "Propose...what?"

He didn't answer, only stared at her with those blue eyes in a way that made her think he meant propose—as in marriage. But when he reached into his pocket, he pulled out a plastic egg. "I brought you something."

She stared at the green egg in the palm of his hand and was puzzled. "Chocolates?"

She couldn't open it one-handed, so he opened it. When she saw it, her breath caught. "Grandma Elam's ring." Tears trickled down her cheeks. "Oh, Ace. It's beautiful."

He picked up the ring and slipped it onto her finger. "How does it feel?"

She spread her fingers and stared at the twinkling diamond. Emotions bubbled in her chest. It felt good, so good.

"There's a note."

He handed her the slip of paper. Awkwardly, Quinn unfolded it and read the words. *Will you marry me?*

Below the question were two boxes. Each with the same answer.

Quinn grinned as she laced her fingers through his and pulled him down to her. She brushed her lips against his. "Yes...and yes."

Chapter Sixty-Four

Quinn wiped the sweat from her forehead as she stood at the stove putting ears of corn into a big pot of boiling water. The August humidity curled wisps of hair that framed her face. Now that the town knew she was really little Laney Elam, she no longer straightened or dyed her hair. The roots were a natural honey blonde while the ends remained dark brown. The color was similar to the corn silks she'd scrubbed from the roasting ears she was boiling for dinner.

The locals had closed ranks around her, accepting her as one of their own and protecting her from the press. No one uttered a single word against her. To them, she was a hero for protecting her friend's daughter and killing that murderer.

But she couldn't go back to being Laney. That life had been too hard. She was Quinn now, and as Quinn, she was strong enough to agree to marry Ace and try to reclaim her daughter. She ran her hand over her shoulder where she'd been shot. The pain was gone and, according to Doc Morgan, in a few weeks the wound would be completely healed. But time had not healed the pain of losing Taylor.

Quinn hadn't seen her daughter since the Fourth of July at the hospital. That night, Ben had informed everyone that Taylor couldn't stay with Quinn until the legalities were cleared up.

When Ace discovered Ben planned to put Taylor in the protective custody of the Illinois Department of Children and Family Services, he and Ben had almost come to blows. Quinn didn't want Taylor to be taken care of by DCFS either. She suggested Taylor could stay with Chrissy's mom. Taylor like the idea of seeing her Nana, and Ben said he'd try to make it happen.

Quinn thought the separation would be for a few days, maybe a week, but a month had passed. She wasn't allowed to have any contact with Taylor, except for a weekly letter sent through the court.

Quinn moved to the table and sat down to finish this week's letter before Ace and Jason arrived for supper. Gogo trotted over and rubbed her wet nose against Quinn's leg. Quinn reached down and petted her. "You miss her, too, don't you, girl?"

Gogo whined in agreement. The puppy had become a scavenger, hunting for items of Taylor's to drag around the house. Last week, she'd found a fuzzy pink sock under the bed. Today, the puppy was dragging around Taylor's black-and-white cow. Quinn had taken Lovey down from the closet, and Gogo had found it.

She filled Taylor's letter with cheery news about Jason winning his ball game, Ace catching a basket of fish, and Gogo's playful antics. She closed with a promise they'd all be together soon. But Quinn wasn't as optimistic as she sounded. The hearing wasn't until October. What if Quinn wasn't granted custody?

No charges had been filed against Quinn in Chrissy's death. Quinn had given the gun and additional information to the Detroit police. When they interrogated Winston's sister, Wendy confirmed that Winston had confessed he'd accidentally shot his wife. The police didn't think there was anything accidental about Chrissy's death, but since Winston was dead, no further investigation was conducted.

Quinn had been cleared in Winston's death, but she had been charged with kidnapping Phoebe Prescott. Since Quinn was guilty, according to P.R., the best she could hope for was probation or a suspended sentence. A felony conviction meant Quinn would never teach again, but she didn't regret her actions. She had kept Taylor safe and away from Winston.

Legal fees had already used up most of her savings, but it didn't matter how much it cost, she would never stop until she got her daughter back. This was Taylor's home, and she belonged here with her and Ace and Jason.

"Don't worry about the cost," Ace told her one night, when she was feeling depressed. "If we need more money, I can sell off a few acres."

Yes, Ace would do that, and Quinn would let him. But Jason was already saying he wanted to be a farmer. She would feel guilty if any of the family land had to be sold.

Gogo barked, and Quinn sealed the letter just as Ace and Jason walked through the screen door. Scampering close behind was Jason's dog, Babe.

Jason grinned at her. "Hey, Mom."

Quinn smiled back. "Hey, Son."

Jason had asked if he had to wait until the wedding to call her 'mom.' Each time Quinn heard it, a new feeling of awe rippled through her. *Mom.* This wonderful little boy wanted her as his mother.

Ace walked over, took her hands, and pulled her up to him. He brushed his lips across her flushed cheek. "Something smells good." His playful tone said he wasn't just referring to supper.

Quinn wrapped her arms around his neck and leaned against him. She closed her eyes, breathed in his woodsy scent, and felt the strength of his love. She'd finally found the place she belonged—here in Hickory Hills and in Ace's arms. "I'm going to miss you."

Tomorrow, Ace and Jason were flying to London for Stephanie's wedding. They would be gone for two weeks. Ace had asked Quinn to go with them, but she wasn't allowed to leave the country.

Ace lifted her chin and gazed at her. "Tell me you want me to stay, and I will."

Quinn's breath caught. The blueness of his eyes surrounded her, warming her with love.

She was honest with him as she always tried to be now. "I want you to stay...but Jason needs to be at the wedding, and he can't fly alone."

"I'm old enough to fly by myself," said Jason, who was on the floor playing with the dogs.

Quinn turned toward him. "The airlines might think you're old enough, but I'm not trusting my son with strangers."

Her words seemed to appease him. "Okay. But can I leave Babe here? Gogo's lonely without Taylor."

The dogs started yipping.

"I think they like the idea. You might as well bring Nugget, too."

"I was hoping you'd say that."

Quinn walked over and tousled his hair. She had a feeling Jason was more worried about her being lonely than Gogo and was touched.

She moved to the cupboard, pulled out plates, and began to set the table. "Summer was here today. She said we need to discuss wedding plans before you leave."

Ace reached into the silverware drawer and followed her to the table. "I thought women made all the wedding plans."

Quinn stared across the table at him. "It's an important day for both of us, and you said we should make the big decisions together."

"If it was up to me, we'd already be married. But you want Taylor here, so I'm willing to wait—just not too long."

Quinn reached over and touched his arm. "Thanks for understanding."

Ace was surprised by how much Quinn had changed. She was opening up, trusting him, and asking for advice—although she didn't always take it.

"Summer thinks we should have a church wedding instead of a ceremony in front of a judge," said Quinn. "She even said she'd be the photographer, Raven would make the cake, and Belle would host the reception at The Castle. All three are offering their services free as a wedding present to us."

Ace looked surprised. "Don't you want a church wedding?"

"I want something simple."

"Okay. Tell Summer you want a simple church wedding."

"But guys don't like all that formal stuff, and besides, you've already been married."

He stepped toward her and caught her around the waist. "Not to the right woman." He drew her closer. "I wouldn't mind seeing you in a fancy dress and having a few witnesses when you promise to love, honor, and obey."

Quinn grinned up at him. "I might have a little trouble with that last one."

Ace raised an eyebrow. "Only a little? That's progress."

"Geez," said Jason. "Cut out all the gushy stuff. I'm hungry."

Quinn laughed. "Wash your hands and we'll eat."

Jason went to the sink and then slid into his place at the table. "Will

I get to be in the wedding?"

"You boys sound like you really want a wedding."

Ace sat next to Jason and continued, "You've always said you wanted a family. Well, you seem to have one, and they want to celebrate with you. Do you want to shut them out on one of the most important days of your life?"

"I hadn't thought about it like that." Quinn put the platter of corn on the table before she sat down. "But weddings are expensive. Right now I need money to get Taylor back."

Ace knew Quinn had too much pride to allow him to pay for more than half of the expenses, so he didn't offer. He suspected Summer's sudden interest in wedding plans was her way of helping Quinn cope with Taylor's absence. The dark circles under Quinn's eyes and the weight she'd lost were visible signs of how worried she was.

The dogs in the corner started to growl. Ace turned to see what the commotion was. Gogo's teeth were clamped onto a front leg of the Taylor's stuffed cow and Babe's on a back leg. They were tugging in opposite directions.

Jason rose to rescue the stuffed animal, but before he could reach it, the cow's belly ripped open. Out of the cow exploded money. Lots of money. All three stared at the green bills fluttering around the kitchen.

Quinn's mouth dropped open. Jason's eyes widened. Ace threw back his head and laughed. "Well, I'll be. It's a cash cow."

Jason jumped up and began gathering the money. "We're rich! We're rich!"

The dogs barked, adding to the excitement.

Leaning over, Ace picked up several bills. "They're all C-notes."

Jason's smile faded. "You mean they're counterfeit?"

Ace chuckled. "No, a C-note is a one-hundred dollar bill."

"Wow! They're all hundreds."

Quinn sank to the floor. "It's the money Chrissy hid, and I couldn't find." Tears filled her eyes and spilled down her cheeks. "She said Max had a sizeable life insurance policy and the rest was half of her joint account with Winston."

Quinn picked up the cow and reached inside to scoop out the remaining bills. Her fingers felt something soft. "There's more." She pulled out a small blue velvet bag and opened the drawstrings. As she looked inside, her heart raced.

Ace knelt beside her. "What did you find?"

She tipped the bag and poured a few gems into the palm of her hand. "These look like diamonds."

Ace reached for the bag and pulled a slip of paper out. "Holy cow!"

"What is it?" asked Quinn.

"Real diamonds. This is a receipt for a quarter of a million dollars' worth." He pulled her up, twirled her around, and let out a whoop. "Looks we're going to have a church wedding and get our daughter back."

Chapter Sixty-Five

Quinn sat on the bench outside the courtroom, staring at the massive double doors. A blast of cold air spewed from the overhead register. A woman dressed in a black suit juggled a stack of legal folders as she walked down the hall. The click of her high-heeled shoes against the marble floor reminded Quinn that for other people, today was just an ordinary work day.

But for Quinn, nothing was ordinary about this day. Right now Mrs. June Carlson, Chrissy's mom, was on the other side of those closed wooden doors telling the judge about Taylor.

Taylor? Was her daughter even called that name? To Chrissy's mom, her granddaughter had always been Phoebe.

P.R. had prepped her for the hearing. "Your daughter's legal name is Phoebe Prescott. When you're on the stand, refer to her as Phoebe."

Goosebumps rose on Quinn's arm. How confusing this must be for Taylor—Phoebe. And the judge who was hearing the case...what must she think? Would she see Quinn as a responsible parent, or an immature, flighty woman incapable of caring for a child?

That was the question Quinn had asked herself ever since last week, when P.R. had phoned to tell her the court date had been moved up.

She'd been overjoyed. "When?"

"In ten days."

The phone almost slipped from her hand. Had she heard P.R. right? Not October, but the end of August. "Ten days? That's good, isn't it?"

P.R. sounded matter of fact. "Court dates routinely get changed. But my guess is, since you're getting a lot of press, they want this over before other adoptive mothers and natural mothers use the case to further their own agendas."

Quinn didn't want to be a spokesperson for natural mothers or adoptive mothers. She just wanted her daughter back.

P.R. didn't even sound excited when he said, "We also drew a woman judge."

"Isn't that a plus?"

"Maybe. But women judges also don't want to appear soft or biased. In any case, we need to be prepared. Have you been approved as a foster parent?"

Legally, Taylor was not Quinn's daughter, so Quinn had to go through the normal adoption procedure, starting with becoming a foster parent. She'd completed the paper work, and the social worker had come and inspected her home—and Quinn. The last hurdle was the test for the well water. After three tries, the sample was approved.

When she'd learned the hearing had been moved up, she decided not to tell Ace, who was still in Great Britain. That night, when he'd called, she'd tried to sound normal. "The connection's so clear, Ace. You sound like you're next door."

"Nope. I'm in London. And you were right about bringing Jason. Stephanie's been different, not so—hostile. We've reached an understanding, to do what's best for Jason. I have some pretty big news. Stephanie will be traveling with her husband for business, so she's agreed to let Jason stay in Hickory Hills for the school year."

"Oh, Ace. That's wonderful." Then she'd choked up.

"Quinn? Quinn are you crying?"

She wiped the back of her hands across her cheeks. "Yes, but they're happy tears." She'd missed Ace—had expected that—but she hadn't expected how much she'd missed Jason. She wanted to see one of his shy smiles, hear him call her *Mom*, but most of all, she wanted to wrap her arms around him and love him forever.

"I couldn't wait to tell you." Then the joy in his voice had turned wistful. "I wish you were here, Quinn."

She'd answered in a low, breathy whisper, "Me, too." But the thrill of knowing Jason would be living in Hickory Hills had rippled through her, filling some of her emptiness. At least she would have one child if...if... No, she couldn't think like that. Ace's news was wonderful, and she wanted to hold onto that happiness. Yet even to her own ears, her words had sounded strained. "What do you think about Stephanie's fiancé?"

"I like him. He has a son from a previous marriage, so he understands. Came right out and said he doesn't want to replace me."

"Oh, Ace, he couldn't replace you."

"I told Jason I was okay with whatever he wanted to call his new stepdad. For now, Jason decided on Steven. But I think the guy will be a solid husband for Stephanie and positive role model for Jason."

Quinn could hear the relief in Ace's voice, and she'd felt relieved too. "That's good."

"So how was your day?"

That day had been a roller coast of highs—thinking about seeing Taylor—and lows—worrying about the court's decision. But Ace had sounded so happy and was too far away to burden with the change of the court date. "Well, I missed you." At least that was honest.

"Stephanie's wedding celebrations will be over tomorrow. Jason's excited about sight-seeing. He wants to visit the Tower of London and tour some castles."

Hearing Ace's voice calmed her, reminded her that he would be gone only a short time. She didn't need him to fly back early just to hold her hand, not even for a hearing a week-and-a-half away.

"Quinn, I'm doing all the talking here."

She'd cleared her throat uneasily. "Well, I took the dogs for a walk, drove into town to check on Miss May, stopped by the library. You know, the usual stuff."

"Are you sure? There's something more. You sound...distracted."

She'd tried to laugh it off. "Must be the connection."

"No, like you said, the connection's clear." Ace had paused. "Quinn, don't make me worry. I'm too far away."

"Really, I'm fine."

Ace was quiet for so long Quinn wondered if they'd been cut off. "Ace? Are you there?"

"Yeah."

Silence.

"Ace?"

"Still here."

More silence. "So why aren't you talking?"

"I'm waiting on you."

"Well, I told you about my day, maybe you want to hear—"

"The truth. I want to hear the truth. No more secrets, Quinn, remember?"

He was right. She couldn't keep secrets and expect to have a solid marriage. "Okay. Something did happen today." She struggled to keep her voice steady. "The custody hearing has been moved up."

"That's great. So why don't you sound happy?"

"I am happy—but also nervous."

"When is it?"

Quinn took a deep breath. "Next Friday."

"But-but that's before we're back. I want to be there."

"I know, but you and Jason have all those plans—"

"Quinn, let me make my own decisions."

But the next night, he'd told her that he hadn't been able to change the tickets.

And now Quinn sat on the bench alone, waiting. She wished Ace were here, sitting beside her, reassuring her in that easy way of his. Through the window a beam of sunlight caught the facets of the diamond engagement ring. Since Ace had slipped the ring on her finger, she'd felt a renewal of her Grandma's love. But right now, even the ring didn't help the ache in her heart.

The courtroom door swung open. Quinn looked up. This was it. Whatever happened once she walked through those doors would determine the course of her life—and Taylor's.

Quinn took a last calming breath, squared her shoulders, and rose. As she walked into the courtroom and down the aisle toward the bench, she reminded herself to be strong.

After she had taken the oath and P.R. had gone through the preliminary questions, he asked about her finances. "Are you currently working?"

"No. I thought it was more important to spend time with Taylor." *Oh God, Taylor's legal name was Phoebe Prescott.* P.R. had drilled her to call her Phoebe. What would the judge think? That she didn't even know her daughter's name?

Panicking, her eyes flitted to P. R. for help. But when she looked toward the courtroom her eyes slid past P.R. and she was lost in that familiar ocean of blue. Ace. He was sitting in the first row, smiling. And then he winked at her.

She blushed and smiled back. All her nervousness disappeared. He was here. She would never have to be alone again. Good or bad, Ace would always be there to support her.

She returned her attention to P.R. "I called Phoebe 'Taylor' to protect her from the man who murdered her mother. And I stayed home to take care of Phoebe, to help her adjust to the loss of her mother and her new life."

"And you are currently capable of supporting yourself and your daughter?"

She thought about the diamonds she'd found in the stuffed cow and about the large balance in her bank account even after the college trust fund she'd set up for Taylor. "Yes. Very capable."

Then P.R. held up a white envelope with Laney written on the front. "Is this letter addressed to you from Christine Prescott?"

Quinn took the envelope and steadied her hands as she pulled out the letter. Chrissy's flowery handwriting stared up at her. The letter had been in the suitcase with the one addressed to Phoebe. When Quinn opened it a few weeks ago, she'd discovered this additional letter, addressed to her.

"Yes. This is from Chrissy."

"Would you read the letter for the court?"

Quinn's voice quavered. "Dear Forever Friend." She paused and smiled up at the judge in her stately black robe. "That's what we called each other."

The judge didn't return her smile, but her brown eyes were warm. Quinn wondered if she was a mother, if she had a child and knew about wanting to be with that child so much that the pain reached into the very marrow of your bones.

Chrissy and she had come through everything together. Now she hoped one last time, Chrissy's words would give her what she needed.

She lowered her eyes and continued to read. "That day under the hardwood tree when we became sisters was the luckiest day of my life. I always thought I was the one helping you, but in the end, you helped me.

"What a rare gift to have your friendship and to be chosen to take care of your beautiful baby. I know that day in the hospital, you had doubts. I saw the longing and sadness in your eyes. Phoebe was in my arms. Your arms were empty.

"I told myself you'd be okay. That this child was meant for Max and me. That you could have another baby.

"We adored her. Our three years as a family were magical. We experienced more happiness than others share in a lifetime.

"Then Max died, and everything changed. You wanted to be there for me. You wrote asking if I needed your help. You offered to fly back from Japan and help Phoebe and me. I'd lost Max, and I was afraid I'd lose Phoebe, too. So I wasn't honest. I told you I didn't need you. But I did...and so did Phoebe.

"In my grief, I made a horrible mistake. I let Winston into our lives. He seemed to love Phoebe, and I thought he would be like Max. But his love was obsessive—and sick.

"If you are reading this letter, then Winston followed through on his threats to kill me. I only pray that Phoebe is with you. Please, protect our daughter. She belongs with you.

"I hope Phoebe remembers me and knows she has two mothers who love her and will continue to love her. You on earth—me in heaven.

"I was blessed to watch Phoebe take her first step, but you will watch her walk out into the world and make a difference—just as you walked into my life and made a difference.

"Friends forever, come together—Love, Chrissy."

Quinn's hands shook and tears rolled down her cheeks. She folded the letter. Chrissy had said it all. She prayed the judge was listening and understood how much they had loved each other—and their daughter.

When she finished her testimony, she was allowed to rise. Time seemed to slow as she walked toward Ace and slipped into the bench beside him. He reached out and took her hand, squeezing it encouragingly.

Then the judge began. "The law is clear about what legally

constitutes a mother, and the court upholds those actions when a mother voluntarily signs away those rights. Melana Elam admitted that she freely did so. I have talked to Christine Prescott's mother and I have met with Phoebe. It's clear that Phoebe is a bright child and has a strong mind.

"She doesn't know Miss Elam is her biological mother, but she has already bonded with her, and she made it clear that she wants to live with Miss Elam and..."

Quinn didn't hear the rest. All she heard was that her daughter had told the judge she wanted to be with her. She wanted Quinn to be her mother.

"So in view of the unusual circumstances, the court is granting Miss Elam temporary custody of Phoebe Prescott with allowance as a foster mother and visitation rights for Mrs. June Carlson."

At the sound of judge's gavel, Ace pulled her up and into his arms. He gave her a squeeze. "We have our daughter, Quinn. Our daughter—and our son."

P.R. tapped her on one shoulder. "Someone's waiting to see you."

Quinn linked her fingers with Ace and followed P.R. out of the courtroom. And there she was. Taylor. Standing in the hallway near the elevator. She looked so grown up. Her hair was longer, and she was taller. Beside her, with his stubborn cowlick and his loopy grin, was Jason.

Quinn stepped forward, but Taylor and Jason were already running toward her. Quinn opened her arms, ready to embrace her new life as a wife—and mother.

About the Author

Sue Stewart Ade lives in her hometown of Pana, Illinois with her husband, Larry. They have two children, Missy and Nelson, and four grandchildren. Sue has taught creative writing in high school and college. Her short stories have been published in anthologies and have won awards at Indiana University, Midwest Writers, and Central Indiana Writers. *Friends Forever* was a finalist in the Pacific Northwest Literary Contest.

Sue wrote her first novel in fifth grade to share with her girlfriends at slumber parties. She enjoys sharing her writing with friends and family.

Author Contacts

Website: http://sueade.com/
Facebook: https://www.facebook.com/SueStewartAde/
Twitter: Sue Ade @sueade890